FORESTTON

THE HOVAN NARRATIVES

CHRISTOPHER IOLAIRE

C IOLAIRE PUBLISHING, LLC

Published by C Iolaire Publishing, LLC.

Copyright © 2026 by Christopher Iolaire

Published by C Iolaire Publishing, LLC.

Website: ciolairepublishing.com

ISBN979-8-9943853-0-2

Trade paperback first edition May 2026

Forestton

The Hovan Narratives

By

Christopher Iolaire

For updates, subscribe to The Hovan Narratives newsletter at Christopheriolai re.com

Next in the series:

Shetteca

The Hovan Narratives

Dedication

To my family,
Both nuclear and extended,
For all their support, patience, and critiques.

"No man is an island. At least, I'm not."

Contents

Portions of this story were translated from accounts of the recent past both written and oral. Specific events spurred by the actions detailed in this narrative continue to unfold. Effort was taken to make the translations as literal as possible. When this was not possible, storytelling and reader comprehension were the priorities.

"Knowledge is power, but only if used wisely."

Northern Part of Arre'ielle

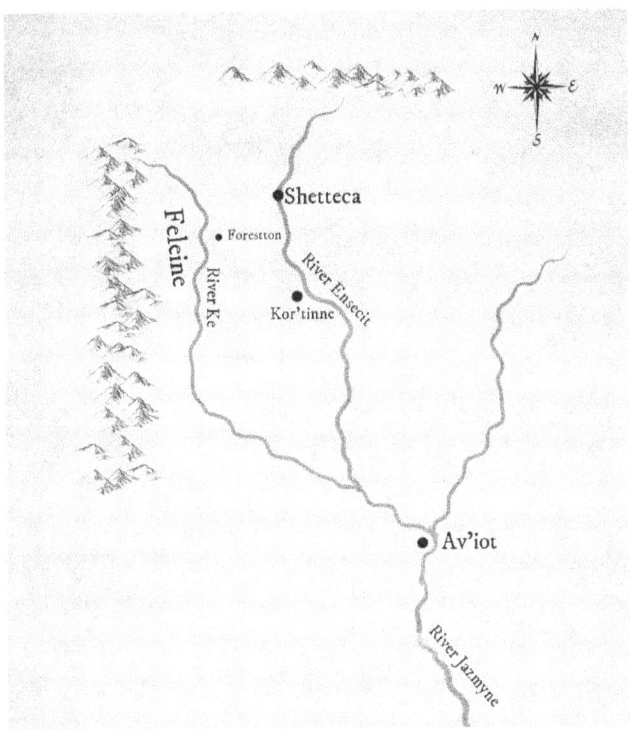

Scale: Forestton to River Ke is almost a one day ride by orvbac.

CHAPTER 1

BOSTON

Julian watched the beautiful young woman with a smile on her face walk toward him across Boston's South Station. That she was his friend's younger sister did not detract from the serenity of the moment, from seeing Melissa with a backpack slung over one shoulder, her long dark brown hair partly obscuring the backpack. Neither did the thought that she would not believe a word of his life story beyond 'he was born'. The contentment he felt played tag with other feelings, sadness and lonely pain, as it spurred the memory of another smile, one that he would never see again, which floated uncontrolled through his consciousness.

"Welcome to Boston, Melissa. How was the trip?"

"Easy enough. I got some schoolwork done on the train. Now I'm ready to see penguins."

"Want some food first?"

"Nope. Penguins!"

Her smile and laugh nearly triggered a smile in Julian. The enjoyment of being in the friendly company of Melissa was something he looked forward to, but it always stirred the memories of what he had lost. He chose not to dwell on the similarities between Melissa and Suzhanee. Her beauty made her desirable in other ways, but Julian did not feel comfortable going there. At least not yet.

He reached for the backpack. "Penguins it is."

"Penguins sound so eloquent when you say it with your accent."

They got out of the taxi near the aquarium. As they walked toward the entrance, the wind off Boston Harbor played with Melissa's long hair before she caught it and secured it to her neck with her scarf.

Julian opened the mobile ticket app on his phone. "I bought the tickets online. It is cheaper and easier."

"How much do I owe you?"

Julian squinted his deep blue eyes as he looked at Melissa. "Nothing. Consider this and dinner an early college graduation present."

Her brown eyes met his gaze as she continued to smile. "Hmm, my brother may not like you taking his pretty sister out for a romantic dinner in the North End."

"Who said you were pretty?"

Melissa laughed. "Every boy I've ever spoken to."

"Probably true. Did those boys mention your intelligence and charm as well?"

"Ah, penguins, dinner, and flattery. Tom will not like this."

"Your mother likes me. She would like that I am feeding you."

"Feeding me, yes. A romantic dinner in the North End? Maybe not so much. And it's not my mother you have to worry about."

"I think your dad would appreciate a great Italian meal. Who said anything about a romantic dinner?"

"Table for two. Glass of Chianti. Call it what you will."

"I call it an excuse for me to get another wonderful Italian dinner in Boston."

"So, I'm just a means to an end?"

"At least I am not just trying to get you into bed."

Melissa slipped her arm around Julian's arm. "That's why I like you. That, and you take me to see penguins!"

———◆———

Julian held the door for Melissa as she entered the small restaurant, leaving the chill of the Boston evening outside. Warm air carrying delicious scents welcomed them in.

"Two, please," Julian said to the hostess.

She picked up two menus and walked them to a table by the window.

Julian held the chair for Melissa as she seated herself. He brought both coats to the coat check before joining her at the table.

"Always a man with manners."

"My father would have nothing else from his son."

"Suggestions?" asked Melissa, looking at the menu.

"I think everything is excellent. At least it used to be. It has been two years since I came. For me, the spaghetti and meatballs. I do not have an Italian grandmother to make it for me. Chianti?"

"Yes please. I think a seafood pasta dish."

The two glasses of red wine came just after the bread and olive oil. Julian raised his glass to toast. "To a successful interview tomorrow."

"Yes. I'm nervous." After the first sip of wine, Melissa continued. "The internship went well. If I can turn it into a job, that would be great."

Julian leaned forward on his elbows, hands surrounding his wine glass. "The internship and the job you hope to get are doing the same thing? Same company?"

He watched Melissa wrap her hair around her right hand and throw it across her back. She took another taste of her wine and put her glass down.

"I interned in New York with a different division of the same company."

Julian continued to lean forward on his elbows as she spoke.

With her hair pulled back off her face, she appeared ready for the office. He imagined she would secure her hair with a clip or a tie for the interview to keep it behind her shoulders. Not the sexy look she had a moment before, with her dark hair adding a perfect border to her beautiful face, drawing out the lighter shade of her brown eyes.

His blue eyes held her brown eyes until his gaze wandered to her cheekbones and down to her lips, watching them move as they formed words. He then noted the small gestures of her hands, gently emphasizing parts of the story in tune with the sparkle of her eyes.

When she paused, they each sipped Chianti. Julian said, "And you could live here in Boston, near Tom and Cathy."

"True, and they could help me find a place to live. If I get the job offer." Melissa relaxed back in her chair. She explained her mother's concern that she would move so far away and the benefit of having her brother Tom nearby to lower her mother's apprehension. The upturn of her lips gave evidence of her excitement about life in a new city and the hope of getting the job she wanted.

"Many of my friends had trouble finding a good internship and are now struggling to get any job. I was lucky my dad had a connection from his military days."

Julian drank more wine, basking in the presence of the beautiful, vibrant, intelligent woman. She was happy. For Julian, that was an enjoyment to be near, even if she incited memories of his deceased wife, Suzhanee, both by her looks and outgoing confidence. But Melissa knew none of that. She did not know that her similarities to Suzhanee were an attraction, but also not. Bittersweet.

He noticed that Melissa had stopped talking and was watching him.

When he refocused on her eyes, she smiled. "You sit there and let me go on and on." She paused. "There are things going on behind those charming, blue eyes. They are distracted, but not vacant."

"I was simply watching your enthusiasm. It is nice to hear you so excited and happy and have a plan for success."

"Deflecting again. I don't think you and simple go together. You are a hard one to get to talk about yourself. Maybe we need more wine."

"Not too much wine. I have to drive you to Tom's apartment later."

"You dropped two clues tonight. Your grandmother is not Italian, and your father is well mannered."

"Was. He passed away."

"I'm sorry. But another clue. Your mother?"

"Passed away also."

"Any siblings?" asked Melissa.

"No brothers or sisters."

"All alone. No family?"

"I have my close friends. My past has some painful parts. We all do, I guess, if you live long enough. Escaping the country of my birth allows me to escape the memories for a time. I do not see you that often, but I enjoy being with you. I can just be."

Julian tasted the red wine as he considered how much to say. "When I go back home, there are expectations and formalities and reminders. Even with Tom, he expects me to show up with thousands of words written. And he knows my story. You know nothing about my life, and that comforts me. You are outgoing, fun, smart. I can enjoy your presence. And your beauty. With you, I can just be." Julian raised his glass. "To you."

Julian finished his wine. Melissa emptied her glass. She then signaled to the server for another round.

"That's the best story I've ever heard for telling me absolutely nothing. Maybe with more wine, you will at least tell me where you are from. Just telling you, I'm not sleeping with you without knowing where you are from."

"See! You can make that joke because you know it will not happen. No expectations or pressure with us. We can simply enjoy good wine and good food and good company. And watching penguins. Now, pick your meal so we can order and enjoy another glass of wine."

"Okay for now. But only because I don't want you to feel uncomfortable around me."

The waitress delivered the two glasses of red wine and took their order.

"It translates to Forestton."

"What does?"

"The village I go back to. Forestton. Town from the forest. Forest-ton."

Julian followed Melissa down the hallway toward her brother's apartment. She was texting, no doubt letting Tom know they were here. He stood next to her, holding her backpack as she knocked on the door. As the door opened, Melissa threw her arms around Julian's neck and slumped against his chest. Instinctively, Julian grabbed her around the waist to steady her.

"No, Julian," Melissa whined. "I am not going back to your hotel room. Stop asking. I'm not sleeping with you. And no more wine. No, no, no."

Julian braced Melissa against his body and looked at Tom standing in the doorway.

"No more wine." Melissa rolled her head back and forth across Julian's chest.

Tom stood straight, equal in height to the man holding up his sister.

Julian saw Tom's lips press thin, and his eyes begin to squint. Julian hoped Tom realized Melissa's act was a joke before Tom hit him.

Laughter exploded from Tom's wife, sliding past her husband.

Melissa stood up and grinned at her brother. "Got you!"

Cathy continued to laugh next to Tom.

"May we come in?" Melissa asked, still smiling.

Cathy moved her husband out of the way. "Yes. Come in."

Melissa stepped inside and hugged Cathy.

Julian followed. "I swear only two glasses of wine. It was a joke."

Tom nodded, his lips finally slipping into a smile. "Thanks for getting her from the train station."

Melissa opened her backpack. "Look. He bought me a stuffed penguin from the gift shop."

"He's cute," said Cathy. "Now that you've delivered her, can I get you something to drink?"

"No more wine," complained Melissa in whiny exaggeration.

"I will pass," Julian said. "I have to drive to the hotel."

"You're welcome to crash on the couch," said Cathy. "Save you a few bucks."

"Too late to cancel. I need to finish up some writing. You guys should have space for family time and rest. You both have work tomorrow." Turning to Melissa, he added, "You have to get ready for an important interview."

"Are you sure?" asked Tom.

Julian nodded. "See you Saturday."

Melissa gave Julian a hug. "Thank you, Julian." She took her backpack from him.

"Text me tomorrow to let me know how it went."

"Of course."

Julian exited the building into the cold Boston night and pulled his scarf tight against his neck. He walked toward his car on the quiet street alone, but satisfied that he had held himself to his decision not to intrude on the mini family reunion. He began to estimate how long it had been since he had last seen his mother; how long since she had crossed over. His father had been even longer.

⸺◆⸺

On Friday afternoon, Melissa had texted Julian that she thought the interview went well, adding that she expected him for breakfast Saturday morning.

As instructed, Julian knocked on the apartment door shortly before nine.

Tom answered, poking his head out and checking the hallway. "No woman falling all over you this time?"

"She is inside."

Tom chuckled. "So is breakfast."

Julian sat at the table, not interrupting Cathy and Melissa, who were busy making plans for their Saturday trip around Boston.

"Morning, handsome," said Melissa. "Want to come tour Boston with us today? Oh wait, you have to spend the day stuck in the apartment working with my brother. Bummer."

Julian saw her smile and accepted her gentle teasing. "I have to earn money somehow."

"Dinner later?"

"Yes," said Julian.

⸺⟡⸺

When the door closed behind Cathy and Melissa, Julian pulled his laptop from his backpack and set it up in the space vacated by the breakfast dishes.

Julian handed Tom a flash drive. "Another fifteen thousand words. I have written through the fourteenth chapter. Here."

"Awesome! I've revised and expanded the first twenty eight thousand words. Got a few ideas to run past you and a cover idea. Read through the changes and let me know what you think."

"They are all good. My English is not good enough to correct your corrections."

"Too bad you can't write with your accent. It makes everything sound more interesting."

"Melissa liked the way I said penguins. Not sure if I was pronouncing it wrong or just ... interesting."

"She likes a lot more about you than just your accent."

"Being with her is fun and," Julian rolled his hands in front of himself, trying to come up with a better word, "healing." He waved for Tom to give him words.

"Therapeutic, restorative, curative."

"I guess. Those sound better."

"You're a good friend, Julian, but I don't want you dating Melissa."

The blunt statement took Julian by surprise. He was not looking to further the relationship with Melissa, but hearing such a straightforward assertion upset him.

"Melissa knows nothing about you and wouldn't believe a word of it if you told her. She doesn't even know how old you are. She thinks you're only a little older than me."

"I know that. I am not looking to get romantic with her. But being around her outgoing, positive, smiling personality is ... restorative. She is a tonic for my soul, without knowing it."

"I don't want her to get hurt."

Julian nodded. "I will keep her priorities above mine."

"I would appreciate that." Tom plugged the flash drive into his computer. "Any updates on the trouble in Forestton?"

"Prince Ti'ek does not think it is serious. His father is getting more concerned. I may have to go back early." Julian paused. "Hope to avoid that. I walk into the house, and memories of Suzhanee smack me in the face. I know it has been a few years, but I cannot shake the pain."

"You should go back to work."

"My work got her killed. Not exactly a safe haven from memories."

Tom rested his elbows on the table and stared at Julian. "It will give you something positive to do. Charge a reduced fee if it makes you feel philanthropic. Helping people will make you feel better and give you a purpose again. Few can do what you do." Tom laughed. "No one here."

"It is time for us to focus on the writing."

"Go back to work at home! Get out among people. Stop moping around. I know that sounds cruel. Do what made you *you*! Be around people. Help them. Do good things! But don't drag Melissa into it!"

Julian returned Tom's stare, torn between being irritated at being told what to do and the recognition that Tom was a friend trying to help.

"You have never seen me be me."

"Resilience is a skill," said Tom. "You must practice it. Now, let's focus on this novel so you have time to get back to your calling."

———◦———

Julian followed Tom into the noisy restaurant. The tables were filling up. They probably would not get a table without a wait if they came much later on a Saturday night.

Melissa and Cathy were sitting at a table with something pale green and probably alcoholic in a wide brimmed glass in front of each of them. Tom leaned in and kissed his wife. Melissa looked at them and then up at Julian. She spread her palms as if asking, 'Where is my kiss?'

Julian sat next to her. "And risk the wrath of your brother?"

"He's a puppy."

"Only to you and Cathy."

"Scared of Tom?"

"No," said Julian. "But not stupid. Besides, no expectations between us. Keep that perfect smile on your face and enjoy your drink. Whatever that is."

"You have the most positive rejections I have ever heard."

"Not a rejection. An acceptance of what we are."

"I may need this drink to figure out what you just said."

"Shut up and drink."

Melissa smiled. "Sounds like *you* need a drink." She waved to the waiter. "Red wine?"

Julian surveyed the restaurant. "This looks more like a cold beer type of place."

When the pint glass of Samuel Adams arrived, Julian asked, "Did you get to the Old North Church?"

"Of course! Close to where we had dinner." She smiled. "The Constitution, though, was too far to walk on a cold day, so we skipped it. Seeing the grand old ship is still on my list of things to see in Boston."

Julian drank his beer and watched Melissa tell the story of her day. Her smile never left, and again Julian felt at peace as he listened. They leaned close to each other so Julian could hear her over the noisy backdrop of the tavern. Her scent had a hint of perfume.

Julian looked down at an empty pint glass. Melissa was now quiet and watching him.

"You have that lost in thought look again."

"Sorry. Problems at home may require me to go back. Thinking about it. Trying to avoid it until I have to return."

"Why do you just let me talk? I must sound like a self-absorbed airhead."

"I like listening to you. Seeing your smile, happy, enjoying life."

"And you are not happy, enjoying life? You rarely smile."

"That reflects my past, that I hope not to discuss," said Julian.

"Maybe I want to know."

"Need another drink?" asked Julian.

Melissa started laughing. "Another deflection. Alright. For now."

They walked down the street a few steps behind Tom and Cathy. Melissa wrapped her arm around Julian's arm.

"I think Cathy is stopping Tom from turning around. He told me he didn't think it was a good idea for us to date."

"Protective older brother. Not a bad thing. I understand his concerns."

Melissa looked up at Julian. "You understand his concerns, but neither of you is going to tell me, are you?"

"My past has some painful parts, as I said. I am still coming to terms with my most recent loss. So, I am not a good candidate for a relationship just yet. I really enjoy being with you, though. Your joyful positivity soaks into me. Helps me. Also, if I told you the story of my life, it would give you pause. I am a good man! Still, you would have things to consider. And you may not choose to continue. So, no expectations. We can walk down the street with you on my arm and enjoy the chilly Boston night."

"Safely kept in my ignorance."

"No offense intended to your intelligence or maturity."

"The most pleasant of rejections."

"Not a rejection. An understanding that I am not ready for you. And our homes are worlds apart."

"You could stay. You don't want to go home anyway."

"But I have to. And I should. You could come."

Julian walked next to Melissa with his arm still holding hers, noting the break in the conversation.

"Boston is far enough. I don't even know what language they speak there."

"It is not English. Hence, my accent you like so much."

"It seems my protective, older brother has a point."

Julian's silence was his answer.

Melissa continued. "So for now, we will remain the best of friends. I still would like to hear about you. Let you talk for a change."

"When I am ready."

Julian felt a tug on his arm and turned to look at Melissa. A smile did not accompany her brown eyes.

"What hurt you so bad?"

They took a few more steps as Julian thought about what to say. "Thank you for your concern. The reason is simple. My story, though, is not. Another time might be better."

Julian watched Melissa nod, accepting the answer. "My man of mystery."

Julian followed Melissa into Tom's apartment, keeping his coat on while others shed theirs, and picked up his laptop.

"You're really leaving tonight?" asked Melissa. "I'll sleep on the couch if that makes it easier."

"Never!" joked Julian. "I slept in worse places than a couch. You have the early Amtrak back to New York. The Berkshires are only a couple of hours drive."

"Okay, tall, blond, and handsome. When am I going to see you again?"

"Not sure. Text and call."

"Please let me know if you leave the country, so I know you're not just leaving me unread. Tom says there's no cell service in Forestton."

Julian noticed Tom's reaction to the mention of the town's name. "I told her the name. She asked nicely."

CHAPTER 2

THE LODGE

Just after midnight, Julian saw the turnoff that led to the one lane bridge crossing a swift, narrow stream. He got out, opened the gate, drove his SUV over the bridge, and then closed the gate behind him. He knew that opening the gate would send a signal, though he was not sure if anyone was awake at this hour to hear it. The long driveway up to the lodge in the Berkshire Mountains of western Massachusetts ended in a gravel lot. The gravel crunched under the tires, though a thin layer of fresh snow hid the small, blue gray pebbles. Grabbing his backpack and small suitcase from the back of his SUV, he breathed in the crisp, cold air, and headed toward the main entrance of the old two story building.

The front door opened before he reached the two steps leading up onto the porch. The bright light from the recessed fixtures in the porch ceiling lit a smiling Caucasian man waiting in the doorway.

Julian looked at the man, shorter than himself, taking in details such as the wavy brown hair, lighter than the man's eyes, that shifted in the breeze. Julian noted that the man could use a shave.

Nice touch.

"Hello, Racine."

"Good to see you, Julian. It has been a while. Come in out of the cold. The wine is breathing."

"You did not need to wait up."

"No worries. Sanlar watched the Bruins. Gladiators on ice, he calls them. They beat some team on the west coast called the Ducks. Warriors fighting ducks?" Racine chuckled. "Welcome."

Julian pushed his suitcase into a corner as Racine locked the heavy wooden door.

The two faced each other.

"I find it unsettling to watch this in a mirror," said Racine, "though I know it is harmless."

Racine's hair darkened to black and straightened. His skin seemed to develop an instant tan but continued to deepen in color. His eyes switched to jade and shone from a face now more oval with a narrow nose. The need for a shave was gone. His face to Julian did not suggest youth, but Julian would have had trouble guessing his age if he did not already know.

"There it is," said Julian. "The ageless face of a middle aged elf. I would not like looking into a mirror and not seeing myself."

"The hardest part was getting the magic to move the hair with the breeze. Come. The wine and Sanlar are in the Fireplace Room. Lily said to say hello, but she has gone to bed."

Julian hung his coat on a coat tree. He walked with Racine across the lobby toward a hallway. Julian noticed Racine's ever present limp.

No. I am not the only one with a painful past.

Two black Labs came running down the hall, tails wagging. They bypassed Racine.

Julian dropped to one knee to greet the energetic dogs. "Berk! Shire! How are you?"

He hugged each dog and scratched their heads. When he stood up, they sprinted back down the hall and turned into the Fireplace Room. Julian followed them in. True to its name, the room glowed in the calming, flickering colors of a wood fire. The large, rounded stones used to build the huge hearth and chimney that dominated the east wall seemed appropriate to this sitting room in the old rod and gun club.

Sanlar met them and handed each a glass of red wine. "Here, my friends. I heard you coming."

Sanlar had the same deep tan skin color as Racine. He matched Racine in height, the same height that all adult elves seemed to be, though he was more muscular. The fluidity and grace of his movements spoke of supreme athletic talent and dexterity. His eyes were piercing dark brown. His straight black hair, common among elves, was loose and shoulder length. He spoke with an accent that was much stronger than either Julian's or Racine's.

"Thank you." Julian accepted the glass with a small bow.

"Chianti Riserva," added Racine. "In honor of your trip to the North End for dinner. Though Tom did not seem too happy that you were out with Melissa."

"So he told me. And her. We are just friends."

"Yes," said a smirking Sanlar. "Until you are not."

Julian ignored Sanlar's comment and his smirk. "The fire smells wonderful!"

Racine waved toward the couch. "Sit and relax."

Julian sank into the couch along the wall opposite the fireplace and closed his eyes. He rolled wine around his mouth, savoring the soft tannins. The scent of the fire filled his nose.

"Tom taught me a new word. Restorative. Enjoying excellent wine, breathing in the calming scent of a wood fire, and relaxing on a comfortable couch in the company of friends is restorative." He opened his eyes. "Thank you for receiving me so late and allowing me to stay a few nights."

Racine accepted his thanks with a nod and a salute with his wine glass. "You are always welcome and need not ask to come. The room upstairs is ready for you. Besides, you will earn your keep tomorrow."

Sanlar added. "We will train together when he is done with you. Maybe some cross country skiing too."

Julian took a big sip of wine. Then he placed his glass on the end table and sat back. A dog jumped onto the couch and lay across his lap. He closed his eyes again as he petted the dog.

"Look forward to it."

⎯⎯⎯◦⎯⎯⎯

Julian startled awake. Unsure where he was, blankets twisted around his legs, his shirt drenched with sweat, he swung his head left and right, searching for a landmark. A deep breath calmed him as he recognized his room on the second floor of the lodge. His head hurt from the tension created by the nightmare that had interrupted his sleep yet again. Untangling himself, he stood and pulled off his damp shirt. He threw it onto the floor. Taking a dry long sleeve tee shirt from his dresser, he slipped it on and layered with a sweatshirt to warm up.

The aging staircase of the wooden lodge was difficult to descend quietly. While most of the guest rooms were on the second floor, Julian knew Racine slept in a room at the back of the first floor. Next to it was the suite that Sanlar and Lily shared. Julian walked slowly down the stairs, hoping to limit the creaking.

He reached the first floor and turned into the dining room. On the server behind a set of tumblers, rectangular bottles of whiskey sat side by side like books on a shelf. Picking up a glass, he slid out the bourbon and poured two fingers of the whiskey. He drank half before adding another splash. With a nod of sarcastic appreciation, he read the label: Estate Distillery.

Leave it to an elf to find a local farm that makes excellent bourbon.

Taking the glass and the bottle with him, he walked into the kitchen.

Looking out the window, Julian saw trees and hills silhouetted against the pale pink dawn sky. He sat at the table, leaning on his elbows, slowly swirling his drink, head bowed.

Suzhanee, losing you still hurts. I am so sorry I could not protect you.

Footsteps behind him prompted Julian to look up.

Racine stood in the entryway to the kitchen. "The stairs are not quiet. It is early for bourbon." Racine spoke in his native language.

"It has been some time since I spoke Dahican. Sorry I woke you. I will use magic next time. I was hoping the drink would put me back to sleep."

"Nightmares?"

Julian nodded yes. "I hope you do not mind me drinking some of your bourbon. Wine did not seem enough."

Racine disappeared for a moment. He returned with an empty glass and handed it to Julian. "I do not mind."

Julian poured some of the amber liquid in and gave the tumbler back to Racine.

Racine tasted the whiskey. "It has been forty nine years. Things still trigger those memories."

"It has only been five for me. I think Melissa was the trigger this time. Not that much is ever needed."

"I know your pain," Racine said.

"I know you do. The same nightmare. The same ending. The same pain."

Julian looked at the green eyes of his host. They seemed sad in the dim light.

Racine sat down in the chair across the table. "I know."

They dropped their gazes to stare at the bourbon in front of them.

Julian stayed quiet, having no more words to add.

"I was so confident." Racine began his quiet, staccato account. "When the attack began, I was in disbelief. I do not know how long they watched us, but they took out the two magicians in the first surge. They knew."

Racine took a larger sip. "We fought! We fought hard! Volleys of flaming arrows hit the carriages. If I had known then the magic that I know now, I could have saved them. We put out all the fires we could. But it was not enough. Smoke and flames forced my wife and mother from their carriage. Elf after elf threw themselves in front of them, shielding them from the arrows with their bodies. And we fought! We fought well! They could not break our lines."

Racine paused. Julian heard the elf take a slow breath in and then out before continuing. "Then I heard a scream that was not from a soldier. I saw my bride had grabbed a shield, trying to protect my mother from the arrows. So brave of her! The shield was not enough. She cried when she fell. Then my mother fell, pierced. My rage exploded! With nothing left to defend, not caring if we lived, we attacked. We were ruthless! Brutal! Finally, they broke and ran. I would have pursued, but Sanlar stopped me. We had too many hurt, he said."

Racine drank more. "We turned for home. Walking, those unable to walk riding the few mounts left or being dragged on litters. I limped, refusing a mount. My penance. Still feeling he had to protect the duke's son, Sanlar sent a rider to my father. The snow elves reached us first and escorted us through the pass. The duke rode out to protect us and met us as we descended into the foothills. It is the greatest shame of my life having to make that report to my father."

Julian added another finger of bourbon to each glass.

Racine drained his glass. He stood.

Julian felt a hand grip his shoulder. He wished he knew what to say to comfort the elf. But in five years, he had found no words to comfort himself. He did not look up, but he heard Racine.

"Sadly, you are not alone. My only advice is to continue to live. Do not isolate yourself. There is good in the universe, too. Choose to be part of the good. It can be restorative."

⸺◆⸺

Julian came down the main stairs, less worried this time about making noise since it was midmorning. He entered the kitchen and poured himself a glass of water. He nodded hello to Racine.

"Bourbon?" said Racine.

"Water. Hydrate to help with the headache."

"Sanlar cooked breakfast. He left you some wrapped on the counter. I am ready for you in the back workroom when you finish."

"I will eat quick. Then join you."

Julian entered the workroom to find two tables with numerous pieces of jewelry, large coins, small knives, and keys laid out on them.

"I labeled each with the magic it needs," explained Racine. "Disguise magic on the silver chains, invisibility on the rings, protection on the coins ... If we can get all these done, this batch should last us through the spring, at least."

"Do you want your lesson before or after?" asked Julian.

"After, thank you. When we finish with these, you can spar with Sanlar or cross country ski with him and Lily before it gets dark. My lesson can wait until tonight and another tomorrow. Anything you want before we get started?"

"Coffee."

<hr>

Julian exchanged thrusts and parries with Sanlar in a stylized sparring drill. They each held dull practice knives. Julian recognized that Sanlar, the master, was going at a speed that Julian could handle, but still challenged him. Practicing in the large basement, Sanlar had turned off his disguise magic. Julian preferred seeing the elf without the magic. The Hispanic man persona that Sanlar adopted when visible to others never seemed right to Julian. Perhaps because he was comfortable with elves and knew Sanlar for what he was.

Sanlar's knife grazed Julian's forearm. "Too slow," instructed Sanlar.

Julian thought that Sanlar's accent did not sound so strong when he spoke in Dahican. His momentary loss of focus caused him to get touched by the knife again.

"Move off line."

Julian focused and moved through the rest of the exercise.

"You seem out of practice. Your protector should challenge you more."

Julian answered in Dahican. "The next time I see her, I will not tell her that." Julian hoped his touch of humor would end Sanlar's train of thought.

"Her place is by your side. She should keep your training intense if she allows you to travel without her."

"I am in no danger here." Julian spoke without humor, but stated what seemed to be an obvious fact, wanting to end the elf's criticism of his absent protector. "No need for her to follow me to a place where she does not know the language or customs."

"None of us knew the language or customs when we came. If she is your protector, she should learn and be with you. And not let your training lapse. That is her job!"

"Sanlar, please do not speak ill of my protector. She would come if I asked. There is nothing for her to defend me from here. She better serves me and Forestton by helping to deal with the cret'len annoyance in western Forestton."

Julian noted Sanlar raising his hand in a truce. "Miserable little creatures. Cret'len are an annoyance by just existing. But hopefully, nothing more."

Sanlar handed Julian a curved wooden sword. "Mind your footwork."

He drove Julian off the practice mat several times. "At least your sword work is no worse."

Noting the sarcasm in Sanlar's comment, Julian responded in kind. "Thank you, Master."

"I suppose if your protector is in western Forestton and you were in Boston, you did not train with her this week."

"No," admitted Julian.

Sanlar collected the swords and hung them on holders on the wall. He took down two short staffs and tossed one to Julian. "You train with her regularly, do you not?"

Julian hesitated to answer, not wanting to continue this conversation or to lie. "I practice what I need."

Sanlar twirled the staff in one hand, warming up his wrists. He switched hands. "I do not approve of your practice schedule. From your tone, I assume she does not either. If you avoid your home because of the memories of your wife, then bring your protector here. We can all train together."

Sanlar moved his staff into the ready position.

Julian mirrored him, but did not respond to the elf's suggestion.

Sanlar pointed his staff at Julian. "Your protector is not here because you do not want her here. You are avoiding her too. Instead, you have her chasing cret'len in the snow."

Sanlar's conclusions upset Julian, mainly because they were too accurate.

Sanlar circled Julian on the mat. "Staff is your weapon of choice. Impress me."

Irritated, Julian answered, "My weapon of choice only when I choose a weapon."

"Sometimes, that choice is made for you."

And Sanlar attacked.

Julian met Sanlar's attack and countered. After five rounds, each had won once and sparred to a draw three times.

"Very good. At least you practice staff."

Sanlar hung both staffs back on the wall. "You cannot hide from your memories, my friend. Stop trying. Work hard to make new ones."

Sanlar headed for the stairs. "I will send Racine down. Give him his magic lesson while I shower and cook dinner."

Julian laid out two floor pillows a few body lengths apart. He sat on one cross legged with his arms resting on his knees. He closed his eyes.

Now we enter my realm. My expertise. I am the master here.

He opened his eyes when he heard footsteps coming down the stairs. Julian nodded to Racine, who sat on the other floor pillow.

Julian made a slight hand gesture, nothing more than a roll of his hand. Reaching out with his mind, he addressed the elf sitting across from him.

"Welcome, Lord Racine. Am I being clearly received?"

"Yes, Lord Wizard. Am I?"

"Yes. Excellent. It has been some time since we attempted mental contact. I am glad that we have maintained our link. With your permission, I would like to contact you after I return to Forestton. To test if we can contact over that great distance."

"I would think that we can. It would be a gift to have you assess my magic more frequently, even though nothing replaces one on one training with a wizard."

"My plan is to train offensive magic tomorrow, defense today. 'Defense prepared before opponent engaged' to quote my teacher. Does my agenda meet with your approval, Lord Racine?"

"Yes. And please, just Racine. I have long since given up the title."

"You are, and will remain, the firstborn child of a duke. Still, I will honor your request."

"I would like to start with you evaluating my ability to move three plus myself by magic."

"Allow me to stay in your mind as you weave the spell to move by magic. I will assess your strength."

With his left hand, Julian made a quick, almost imperceptible motion. He watched Racine begin hand motions, actions to focus the mind. He observed the outline of the magic that Racine was building.

The elf held his left hand as a vertical blade as he built a sphere of magic around it. The soft glow expanded on three sides like a barely visible, inflating, but lopsided balloon.

Satisfied with the structure of the magic, Julian closed his eyes and moved his focus inside Racine's mind to judge its power. He then left the elf's mind, opened his eyes, and spoke aloud.

"Excellent, Racine. The structure and the power are more than enough to transport three plus yourself. Just be ready for the extra strain when you execute the magic."

Julian stood. "Time to practice defensive magic."

An hour later, with Racine's lesson concluded, Julian returned to his room to wash up. After a quick shower, Julian found Sanlar and Lily in the kitchen, finishing up dinner.

"Can I help?"

"Feed the dogs, please," said Lily. "Then let them out."

Though his own eyes were blue, Lily's blue eyes seemed unusual to Julian when framed by the black hair and brown skin of the elf. Maybe they struck him as different because blue eyes were rare among elves. Then again, blue eyes were uncommon in humans back home as well. Often enough, children had teased him when he was young for his unusual eyes and blond hair.

Julian picked up the two dogs' bowls. Immediately the dogs ran to him, dancing around, tails wagging, nearly tripping him, as he poured kibble into the bowls.

"There are the happy puppies," said Julian as he placed the bowls on the floor. He retreated toward the backdoor as Berk and Shire ate.

"Okay. Now, outside, you two."

Tails still wagging, the two black Labs rushed out the open door into the snow. Berk pushed snow into the air and tried to catch it with his mouth. Shire sprinted in circles around Julian before stopping in front of him, paws stretching out in front, tail held high and wagging.

"Oh, you want to play, do you?" Julian rushed at Shire. The nimble black Lab darted to the side, out of Julian's reach. Berk ran behind Julian.

"And you too." Julian chased the two dogs around in the snow, never coming close to catching them.

"All right, all right. You win. Go take care of your business, you merry Labs."

The two dogs wandered over to the trees on the right side of the backyard. Julian walked away from the lodge to the foot of the hill rising from the backyard. The Sun had dipped behind the forested ridge, though the sky was still blue. Shadows under the trees had not darkened yet to black. Julian noticed three deer looking down from the edge of the woods, motionless.

Shire appeared at Julian's side, soon followed by Berk. The dogs stared at the deer. Julian looked at the Labs, who began creeping forward.

"Berk. Shire. Home." Julian took a step back toward the house, showing the dogs which way he wanted them to move. "Come. You had your dinner. Let them find theirs. Come, my friends. Back to your nice, warm house. Let them be."

⸺⸻◦⸻⸺

The fire was lit, filling the Fireplace Room with its aromatic scent. Julian relaxed in a cushioned chair to the side of the hearth with a glass of wine in his hand. Racine sat in one on the opposite side. Sanlar was relaxing on the couch with his arm around Lily. The dogs were curled up next to each other, eyes closed, on a big dog bed. The dinner dishes were cleaned and stacked in the drying rack.

"We leave for Boston tomorrow night," said Sanlar. "Come with us. We will put you to work. I have heard that you have some skills."

Julian chuckled at Sanlar's comment, but sipped on his red wine to delay his answer. He was unsure what he wanted to do.

"Enough," chided Sanlar. "You have mourned, but now you must take control and move on. You did all that you could. Be content with that. You could do no more!"

"Easy, Sanlar," said Racine. "He may take solace because he did all that he could to save his wife, but not find peace. It does not stop the nightmares. Such a painful loss. We are both on this planet for a reason."

Lily put Sanlar's hand to her lips and kissed it. "I know you are spurring him into action out of compassion, but emotions are not rational."

She turned to look at Julian.

"I agree with Sanlar though, that you need to stop hiding in your house. You are welcome to join us in Boston, if for nothing more than to have dinner with us. But the schedule for this week is full. We will not have much time for sit down meals."

"If you are not coming to Boston, then stay here and take care of the dogs," offered Sanlar. "Bring your protector over and train. No more mourning by yourself. You must be in motion. And not alone. Let your protector do her job. Does she speak Dahican? My Rel'ellon is out of practice, like your sword work."

Julian took another taste of wine and ignored Sanlar's question and comment. He did not want to bring his protector, Laexa, to the lodge, nor did he want to go back to his house and be alone. If he brought Laexa here, he might as well go home to Forestton. Going to Boston did not appeal to him either. Maybe staying with the dogs would be a suitable compromise. Their only expectation was playing and running in the snow in the woods. He wanted to be alone, but not. Anonymous, but with people. That was part of the attraction of Melissa.

"You are welcome to stay here if you wish," offered Racine. "Shire and Berk would be happy to have you. You have a few weeks until you must go, I think. If all goes well, we will be back late Friday. We would be happy to meet Captain Laexa."

"Bring your protector over," urged Sanlar. "To practice with me, if not both of us. I also would like to meet her."

"I may stay," said Julian. "And will think about bringing Captain Laexa here."

That defeats the point of escaping Forestton.

"It may be time to move on," Julian added, not voicing his thoughts.

CHAPTER 3

THE ROCKLAND HOUSE

Julian parked his SUV in the detached garage that was at the end of the long driveway to his house in Rockland County, an hour north of New York City. He had bought this post Civil War era, two story farm house three years ago. The house rested on a tree rimmed, three acre plot; the last remnant of a dairy farm. Modern houses surrounded it in a newly designed neighborhood on what had been pastures. His neighbors assumed that whoever bought this largest plot with the lengthy driveway would tear down the old house and replace it with a mansion. Julian did not want that attention. Not here. Besides, he liked the aging rural building. It reminded him of the home he had grown up in. And the repairs kept him busy.

The snow crunched under his boots as he walked across the yard. The porch stairs creaked as they always did when he climbed the three steps to the back door. He unlocked the door and stomped the snow off his boots before stepping into the kitchen.

Job one tomorrow is to shovel the snow. Then, tackle the rest of the to do list. Tonight, finish up the writing I promised Tom. Cannot delay going to Forestton for too much longer.

⊹

Julian sat at the small desk in his living room, reading what he had typed on his laptop.

Chapter 15

On Your Own

Verian came into the laboratory and sat down on a bench next to his master's worktable. His master worked for a few moments more, surely just to irritate him, thought Verian. Then, she raised her head from the vials in which she was mixing ingredients.

"Now you must again show me that you have learned some of what I have taught."

"What is it you wish me to do, Master?" said Verian.

"Bring me the body of a goblin chief. That will prove to me you have some of the skill and wits needed to survive. When you have done that, I will show you what we can learn from a dead goblin and of what use the body is. Do not delay returning it to me. A rotting body is of no use. Use your magic. Keep it fresh."

When his master finished speaking, Verian did not leave. He sat and thought. A goblin chief alone should not be difficult to handle, but what about his tribe? They are small, but how big is a tribe? What marks distinguish a chief from other goblins? Where are they normally found during this part of the year? He must plan.

Finally, Verian stood up and walked toward the door.

"Where are you going, Verian?"

"To the library. If there is a use for dead goblins, surely you must have learned it there because you never leave this house."

"I have dared not leave since I took you on as a student. You might kill yourself with all you think you know. Bring me the goblin chief and I will show what can be done with him."

"Dare not leave? You need not leave since you send me off on every errand of yours. I am still off to the library. You are always so cryptic. I must learn more about them if I wish to cull a chief. He would be well protected, I fear. Knowledge is power. I am off to learn and grow strong."

The master smiled at her student as he left the laboratory. She even liked the sarcasm. Lowering her head, she brushed the strands of gray hair out of her eyes and resumed the work on the materials in the vials and flasks in front of her. It would soon become a healing potion. One day she would teach this skill to Verian as well, if he survived long enough.

Julian hit the save icon on his computer and stretched as the computer clicked.

A solid day's work. Next, introduce Verian to the redhead with the quick wit and fast hands. This should satisfy Tom. Get this to him, *and he can fix my English and connect the scenes.*

When the computer finished, Julian turned it off and stood up. He stretched again. Feeling hungry, he walked into the kitchen and made himself a sandwich. Grabbing a beer out of the refrigerator, he sat down and ate. Halfway through his sandwich, he glanced at the kitchen clock.

Damn, seven o'clock.

After finishing the sandwich, he washed the plate and knife and leaned against the kitchen counter.

Too late to drive down and visit Melissa. Give Cova another lesson?

Julian did a quick time calculation in his head.

Ahhh, it's not yet dawn there.

He slowly worked on his beer for a few more minutes and then chugged the rest. Taking a jacket out of the closet and his keys from his desk, he tucked his shoulder length blond hair under a Boston Bruins cap. He walked out the kitchen door onto his back porch and locked the door behind him. Descending the steps and crossing the yard to the detached garage, he pulled open the garage door. He backed his car out.

Julian strolled around the mall, watching people go by; in and out of stores and into another. Hundreds of people walking and shopping, all in relative safety and a state of unconcern. Julian found the mall captivating.

Older couples shopped in indoor havens. Mothers rushed for sales and children's' birthday presents. Teenagers spent their parents' money and met up with friends. Young adults seemed to live at the mall. They worked here, ate here, shopped here, and hung out here.

Suzhanee, by the time I was their age...

Still, Julian found the teenagers the most interesting to watch: girls trying to meet someone special, boys hoping to get a date, exchanging gossip about sports, complaints about parents and school.

I wonder how I would have fared if I had grown up here, Suzhanee. Far different from the rural home of my parents. It's as foreign as their language. I can handle the language now, but I will never lose my accent. I will never completely fit in here.

He ordered food at the food court and took his vegetable lo mein to a table near the edge of the sitting area. People walked by as he ate, not noticing him. Julian could spend hours watching people move around. People who seemed oblivious to others right next to them. The anonymity of being one of the crowd created a feeling of safety, but also loneliness.

When Julian finished eating, he walked across the mall into the bookstore. A solid day of writing put him in the mood for a well earned night of reading.

Julian enjoyed novels. Reading had helped him learn English, beginning when he first arrived in Scotland four years ago. Over the past few years, he had explored several genres.

Selfish pride drew him to the fantasy section of the bookstore. He found the novel he had helped write, though the only author listed was Bill Tolle. A pen name Tom had created, combining his love of Shakespeare and Tolkien. Julian wanted a share of the little money the book made and enjoyed the creative process, so different from his other career. But he also avoided the publicity and the commitments of an author.

Several fantasy books caught his interest. He flipped through a couple, looking to be captured by one. Perhaps he could read *The Lord of the Rings* again. But no, he would get enchanted by the story yet again and would not stop reading until they reached Lothlorien. That would keep him up all night.

He prowled through the store, searching for a tasty morsel. Julian settled on one of the seemingly endless supply of *Dragonrider of Pern* novels. Men and women riding friendly dragons. What a ridiculous concept! Yet the story and characters enthralled him. He hoped this new book was no different. He bought it and went home.

Settling into his favorite place to read, a dark wood rocking chair, he opened his latest purchase. His last thought before becoming engrossed in the novel was how much this new life contrasted with his old life. His mind needed rest more than his body. For a while at least, it would have a distraction.

CHAPTER 4

A COLD MORNING

Hiding in the shadows, the young watcher tried to escape the chilling breeze and complete his watch of the wizard's house in the small town of Forestton. The approaching Blessed Beginning Festival brought the expectation that the wizard would return to his home. Or at least, so the novice watcher had been told by the man paying him. Return from where, the young man did not know. However, the wizard had not always done the expected since the death of his wife.

The watcher, barely old enough to not be called a boy, pulled a heavy cloak tight across his shoulders and cursed the freezing morning air. The biting cold nipped at his ears. He hid his ears under his hat. He rubbed his wrapped hands together to warm them before slipping them beneath his stained, gray cloak. Seeking shelter in the shadows that the growing light spread across the ground, he squatted at the base of a building, not wanting to sit in the thin layer of snow covering the frozen ground. Swirling around buildings, the shifting breeze found a gap in his cloth layers, and he shivered. It had been a long, cold trip north from the capital city of Avi'ot, but the fee offered was more than an inexperienced man could ask for. Perhaps the rare job of spying on a wizard's house in the freezing cold paid better than most. To regain his concentration, he again focused on the large house, seeking a sign of the wizard's return.

Showing an elegant display of strength, the wizard's two-story stone residence stood apart from the village's wooden structures. It bore the same mix of darker old granite pieces and lighter new blocks, though smaller, as Forestton's rebuilt curtain wall. The only decorations visible were the polished finish to the speckled, off white stones, the ornamental bars on the windows, and a stone statue of a mountain talon bird above the front entrance, which faced the courtyard. Light green, translucent curtains framed by auburn drapes visible through the barred windows hinted that the inside was more comfortable than the bare stone exterior appeared.

Besides Prince Ti'ek and Captain Laexa, who both seemed to live in the house, the watcher had seen no one cross the large rectangular flagstones leading to the front entrance. From listening to the locals, the watcher had learned that the unusual alliance of the young elf prince and the seasoned female captain shared the governing of Forestton in the wizard's absence.

The fledgling spy felt uneasy watching the wizard's home and wondered if the favor was being returned. Ego and money held him to his task. Still, he had no ambition to steal from it.

The watcher's eyes squinted. In the eastern room on the second floor, a yellowish light flickered to life. It glowed for only a short time, long enough for someone to wash and dress. Soon after it went out, a steady white light shone from a ground floor window.

The watcher had learned that this progression of lights marked the start of the morning routine of the elf Ti'ek. For the handful of mornings that the watcher had observed the house, the elven prince had left with the First Captain of Forestton, Captain Laexa. The watcher had seen the light from Captain Laexa's bedroom much earlier this morning. She had left alone.

In the western room on the second floor, the auburn drapes opened, letting in the morning light. The three moons overhead had passed through several cycles since anyone had last seen activity in this room. The Lord Wizard Hovan had returned home to Forestton.

With his mission done, the watcher grinned with pleasure. He stood and walked toward the Forest Inn, seeking warmth and food. He decided to rest until tomorrow morning before starting on the cold road south back to the capital city of Avi'ot to deliver his report and collect the rest of his money.

CHAPTER 5

RETURN TO FORESTTON

The Wizard Hovan looked out the window at the star that held the planet in orbit. The star, called the Giver, teased the stone walls protecting the town of Forestton with dreams of warmth.

You are not giving much warmth, Giver. At least you are providing light as we start this visit of yours.

The Giver's rays flowed into the second floor bedroom. Hovan, wrapped in a warm blanket, crossed a rug to a stone washstand. He washed his face and hair in the night chilled water. He resisted the temptation to use magic to warm the water. Instead, he let the cold water chase away the last remnants of sleep and remind him where he was. He rubbed his blond hair with a towel, which, when dried, would fall past his shoulders. He chose not to shave the stubble on his youthful looking face. Dressed in a warm cloth shirt and light brown pants pulled over leggings, he slipped his arms into a comfortable cloak, but did not pull it tight, instead letting the morning chill invigorate his body. With his dark wood short staff in hand, he walked into the hallway.

Hovan stopped and stared at the closed door at the end of the hallway, letting out a slow breath. Loneliness and sadness prevented a smile and threatened a tear.

Suzhanee, I still miss you. Will I ever not?

He lowered his chin to his chest, crossed the hallway, and descended to the main floor.

The Wizard Hovan entered the kitchen and breathed in the pleasant aroma of hot tea mixed with the scents of meats, bread, and cheese. Ti'ek was ferrying warm plates of food from the counter next to the large stove to the decorative tiles protecting the wooden kitchen table. He wore a thick shirt, dyed auburn, with a high collar to keep his neck warm. It fell below his waist, except on his left side. The short side of the shirt was tucked behind the pommel of his curved sword belted to his waist. A rustle of metal made Hovan think Ti'ek wore the metal ring and turquoise leather jerkin underneath his shirt that he favored. The elf wore warm pants similar to those that Hovan had on, but in a smaller size.

Hovan nodded good morning to the prince. "Thank you for making breakfast, Prince Ti'ek."

"You are welcome, Lord Wizard Hovan," responded the prince in a formal tone following the use of his title. In a casual manner, he added, "You seemed very tired when you arrived last night."

Hovan nodded. "Adjusting to the time change. And the season. It is colder here. The Giver is not giving heat."

"We are the northernmost district, and the growing season has not yet begun. She will bring warmth here last."

"Thank you for the geography lesson."

Prince Ti'ek smirked as he pulled his straight, black hair into a tie behind his neck and sat to eat. He undid his belt and placed his sheathed sword on the seat next to him. "You look as pale as ever."

"At least no one will mistake me for a relative of yours."

"Certainly not with those blue eyes," said Ti'ek.

The wizard looked over at Ti'ek.

The elf's jade eyes sparkled with amusement at his own joke. "Not even ruby or gold," Ti'ek added.

Hovan stayed quiet as he began to eat. The food was tasty enough, though it was late in the cold season. The fruits from the last harvest were most likely gone. He missed the fruits and vegetables he often ate when he was at his other home in Rockland.

"Hungry?" asked the prince when the wizard filled his plate a second time. "But then, a growing boy needs a good breakfast."

The wizard looked at the shorter elf, acknowledging the joke with a slight chuckle between bites. "Same jokes? I guess Laexa is not here because she is tired of hearing them."

"She is not known for her sense of humor."

"I ate only a little yesterday. I was busy preparing my other house since I will be away from it for a time. How have Forestton's shops been doing?"

"Business talk at the morning meal, Hovan?" Ti'ek groaned.

"Each moment of life is an experience that can teach the observant."

"Religious excerpts and business questions before we are done eating? Humans have no patience. The farmers celebrated the last growing season's harvest, as you know. Our storerooms were full before the cold season set in. Business in the shops has been slow but steady. The farmers have been coming into town since they have money from the excellent harvest. Your percentage seems appropriate. For more precise information, check with your money manager."

A click and thud signaled the opening and closing of the front door. The tapping of footsteps, sounding like boots on the tile floor, paused the conversation.

A woman, wearing a brown leather armor shirt visible under a dark green cloak with insignias on each shoulder, walked into the kitchen. Her reddish brown hair, twisted into a pragmatic tail, fell between her shoulders. With her hair pulled back, her chestnut eyes, beautiful and focused, captured Hovan's attention. The First Captain of Forestton, almost as tall as the human wizard, was taller than Ti'ek. In her middle thirties, she looked older than both.

"Good morning, Captain Laexa," said the wizard. "Welcome to the new growing season. Care for breakfast?"

"No, thank you. Welcome home, Lord Wizard Hovan. I wish you a Blessed Beginning. I have checked the reports from the night watch. This visit of the Giver has dawned bright with no trouble to be seen. I directed the patrol to stay in town on alert."

"The patrol is in town?" asked Hovan. "Are you worried about the patrol or Forestton?"

"You have returned to your home. Your arrival is expected. You are the Lord of Forestton, and I am your protector. I had the patrol stay since you and the prince may not be available early should something happen. You two are the only ones in town trained in magic."

"Should something happen?" Hovan put his food down and sat back in his chair. "Here? During the cold season?"

"Yes. The cret'len made frequent raids through the western Forestton region... during this cold season. They are not a danger to us behind the walls, even the ones riding wolves, though they are a danger to the farmers. What if they are not alone? What if they are just waiting for your return?"

"You are that worried?" Hovan raised his eyebrows in question and surprise.

Laexa nodded. "Even with the prince joining the patrols."

Hovan picked up his mug of warm tea as he turned to Ti'ek. "Thank you for riding patrols in the snow and cold."

"With the troubles occurring in the western ranches and you not here, I tried to be reliable. Lead by example, as my teacher says. I joined the rotation of patrols riding to the River Ke."

"Ti'ek accepted responsibility as a caretaker of Forestton," added Laexa.

"Can you imagine that? Me, responsible!" Ti'ek pointed at the wizard. "It is your fault too, Hovan!"

"Mine? I have not been here since the start of the cold season. How is it my fault?"

"My father and you have instilled in me the need to act, when action is required."

"One needs a safe place to live." The wizard lowered his voice. "Ti'ek, I do not ask that you stay here."

"I prefer it to the formality expected of me in Shetteca. Plus, Laexa and Vay are good training partners. Do not worry about me, my friend. I am a young elf. I make my own choices."

"Yes, unless Mother insists he come home," said Laexa.

Hovan watched the smile leave Ti'ek's lips at Laexa's unexpected counter, but quickly return.

"Obligations of family and rank," said Ti'ek. "I need to return to the city of Shetteca when called."

"Join us, Laexa." The wizard waved toward a chair. "Tell me of the patrols."

"More business at mealtime! Will you honor no elven customs in the presence of an elven prince?"

Hovan noticed the playful glint shining in Ti'ek's jade eyes. This was at odds with the stiff posture of the captain. Ti'ek's glances in her direction indicated that he noticed her stance as well.

"Knowledge is power," said Hovan. "The patrols?"

Ti'ek refilled Hovan's mug. "Have some Westgate morning tea. Private blend! Warm tea, a blessing on a cold morning! Drink. Warm your heart. We will enjoy our morning meal." He filled another mug and handed it to Laexa.

"How noble of you, Prince Ti'ek, to fight so to preserve the sanctity of the meal." She accepted the mug and took a seat at the table.

Ti'ek raised his mug to her, acknowledging her compliment. "A Blessed Beginning to you, Captain Laexa."

"About the patrols," persisted Hovan.

Ti'ek dropped his head in joking despair. "Defeated."

"The cret'len are a problem this cold season," said Laexa. "They crossed the river repeatedly."

"Lord Keen and Ti'ek told me. The river froze."

"It froze enough for creatures of their small size and their wolves to make it across. The ice also stops us from crossing because it would not support the weight of a mounted patrol. Captain Vay objects to stopping at the river and urges us to cross on foot. I resisted the temptation. There are many cret'len. Many ride wolves. Despite the complaints made to us and to Lord Ke'en in Shetteca, I have not asked for permission to cross the river. Prince Ti'ek here does not see the need. I am worried!"

Hovan sat watching his first captain deliver her report. Her tone was tense, like smoldering embers. He knew his captain well enough to know that she was angry.

I think I know why she is upset. But I am back now. This could not wait until I finished breakfast?

"Yes, she was worried!" said Ti'ek. "She pestered me until I thought of returning to Shetteca, but I rode the patrols instead. She had some crazy notion of a forthcoming attack on the western ranches. Cret'len do not do that! They are short, fur covered, round faced annoyances! They make an elf look tall!"

The elf tasted his Westgate tea. "There was no loss of life. Only livestock and some damage. I thought that crossing the river would endanger lives. I suggested strengthening our presence along the river."

The prince's lips turned up in amusement. "To do just that, I rode the patrols! Provide some magic and elven insight."

"You speak in the past," noted the wizard. "She speaks in the present. Why did you not report this to me sooner?" Hovan realized his mistake too late. His words fanned the embers into a flame.

"Report it to you sooner?" challenged Laexa. "You have not spoken to me since the first snow. You stayed away the entire cold season! If you want to know what is going on, come visit the town that you are lord of! I am not a magician or an elf who can speak in your mind. The people closer to the river need to be protected. You want to know what I think? Ask me!"

The wizard leaned back in his chair with his two hands wrapped around his warm mug of tea. He looked at the first captain and began to speak, but stopped short of words. She was tense, eyes fixed on him, back rigid.

Two reasons she is mad with me. Not simply because I went to the other planet without her.

Laexa continued. "I am your protector and the protector of Forestton. I cannot protect you if you are away and do not take me with you. To the best of my ability, I protect Forestton, but I am not a wizard. The cret'len have crossed the river! Why would they do that? Something has changed. The prince does not think there is a problem. His father and you rely on his judgment, but neither of you consults me!"

Three reasons. By the Ones, she is right. Her judgment is too valuable to be ignored. I did not think the cret'len were this big of a problem. Yes, of course, because I did not ask her. And she is the first captain. Take a breath and apologize.

Hovan breathed in and out. "Points taken, Captain."

He took slow breaths, trying to suppress the visions of a dark haired woman that again floated through his thoughts. "It still hurts. I know it has been seasons. So much here holds a memory of Suzhanee. I go there and, for a brief time, I can forget."

"Allow me to pack up her things and give them to her sister," Laexa said.

"I have not spoken to her family since she died. They never forgave me for her death."

"Something you have in common with them."

As if waving a flag of truce, the wizard put his mug on the table and sat at attention. "Please, Captain, tell me about the raids. I am asking now."

"I am the First Captain of Forestton. I should not be the last person asked."

"Acknowledged. My mistake. Drama is not your way. Give me the reports about the cret'len activity in western Forestton region. Please."

Laexa nodded, seeming to accept Hovan's admittance of a mistake and offer of a truce.

"I think they are mapping the area from the river to the road. I would fear a campaign against Forestton itself if we saw more than cret'len and wolves."

Hovan turned to look at the prince to gather the prince's thoughts.

"It does not seem that serious to me," stated Ti'ek. "I left it to my father to convince you to come back, if he thought it warranted that. We knew you would be here for the Blessed Beginning festivities."

"He did say he was growing more worried," admitted Hovan. "Cret'len? Could they have grown so foolish as to forget the lesson taught them a mere ten growing seasons ago?"

"Grown foolish?" objected Ti'ek. "Were they ever anything else?"

"They cannot match wits with your father, but they are smarter than you give them credit for," said the wizard. "Though small, they are agile and fast! They know there is safety in numbers. The wolves and the cret'len work well together."

Hovan turned back to Laexa. "Maps, Captain?"

Ti'ek interrupted, shaking his head. "A few drawings found on some of the cret'len we killed. Nothing capable of directing an army. Basic landforms mostly. We are talking about cret'len."

"What if they combined all the drawings into one map?"

"I do not think so," said Ti'ek.

"Many details were missing," Laexa admitted, "but we did not see all the sketches."

"When did the cret'len stop?"

"They may not have stopped," said Laexa. "Though, the cret'len have not crossed the river for almost two hands of visits of the Giver. Perhaps with the cold season nearing its end and the ice on the river breaking, they are moving back into the foothills."

"That is not that long ago!" stated Hovan.

"Far too recent for the farmers to forget!" said Laexa. "The agricultural guild made several requests for aid from us, Shetteca, and the king."

The wizard nodded understanding. "They speak for the farmers. I expect the merchant's guild supported their requests for aid. Mercenaries offer their services to help patrol the river?"

"Of course," said Laexa. "Yes, the mercenary guild offered their paid help. Lord Ke'en is reluctant to hire any. Followers of Protection supported our patrols. I am happy for their aid. This will be easier to handle, Wizard, now that you are here."

"My father did not want the southern lords voicing that we could not handle our own problems," added Ti'ek. "We have."

The wizard turned quiet as he chewed on some cheese, thinking through the ramifications, ignoring Laexa's additional comment about his absence. Ti'ek's support of his father was expected. The farmers and ranchers of the Shetteca district still harbored fears born from the War for Arre'ielle, which had begun twelve circles of the Giver past, and the Battle of Shetteca, which ended the siege of that city. Living in open fields, often far from the safety of towering walls, they had suffered the most. Though apprehensive and with horrible memories, that did not mean that they were not accurate indicators of future problems. Indeed, the most sensitive elements of any system often are the most reliable indicators of change.

Hovan also understood the motivation behind the mercenary guild voicing its concern over the problem. For paid warriors and magicians, trouble meant income. Such work had proved profitable for the wizard. As his talents and abilities had grown in fame and strength, so had the difficulty of the problems he was hired to solve. And the fee he could charge. His interests now lay in ensuring the continued safety of Forestton and the growth of the local economy. Attention to detail was ever important. Anticipation of a problem was the best way to prevent one.

Knowledge is power.

"Were the cret'len chased off or killed?" asked Hovan.

"Most were content to scatter and run before we could engage them, especially the wolf riders," replied Ti'ek. "We killed some."

"Then you did not see the final versions of these maps."

As if outnumbered, Ti'ek deferred to Laexa with a wave of his hand.

"No," she said. "If they had a map, then fleeing from us to get it across the river makes sense. A rotation of Shettecan and Forestton patrols secures the camp at the north ford, keeping a constant watch. But they can cross in many places when the river is ice. Constructing a permanent base along the road near the ford is being considered when the weather warms. I would not commit more of the garrison until we can predict their movements."

"No ranchers or farmers were killed, you said, but were any injured?"

"A few sustained injuries chasing off the cret'len and wolves," answered the captain. "More often, livestock was taken or killed. I expect for food. Minor damage to barns and other structures. The cret'len avoided most houses. They did not seem interested in them."

The wizard's blue eyes met the jade green eyes of the elf, then the chestnut eyes of the woman. "I do not like potential enemies having a map of this land. Even if they do not plan on using it, they may sell it to someone who may...or perhaps someone paid them to make it."

Hovan leaned on the table and looked at Laexa in silent question.

"Why would the cret'len make a map for themselves?" Laexa voiced the question that had just occurred to Hovan.

"That is why you are so concerned," said the wizard. "I understand now. The cret'len have been fine living in abandoned Feleine. Perhaps too well. Either someone else is pushing them or they are getting over confident. My guess is that they are not acting alone. Thoughts, Laexa?"

"Their actions seemed too organized for ones of their ability to have planned. Cret'len cannot plan campaigns months in advance."

"I protest the use of the word 'campaign'," argued Ti'ek. "A few scratchings do not signify an imminent battle! Since the raids began, she has been having flashbacks of the war and the battle. The cret'len have backed off."

"Have they?" challenged Laexa.

Hovan took a sip of tea. "Are they quiet because they left or because, like water receding before a larger wave comes, they are planning something bigger? In either case, I think a trip west before the growing season is in order to find out."

"You wish to cross the River Ke?" asked Ti'ek.

"You do not approve?" asked Hovan.

"No force from Arre'ielle has crossed that river in ten growing seasons. Not since the king needed to evacuate Feleine, pulling Arre'ielle's forces back across the river. My father, though, thinks as you do, once the patrols can ford the river. What will the king say?"

"I think the king will voice support for your father, the crown prince, and a favored wizard. And you, Laexa?" Hovan asked, though he knew her answer before she said it.

"I am the one who thinks there is a problem. Besides, you are not going without me. Captain Vay will want to come."

Hovan acknowledged her with a nod. "I will also inform him that I will travel to Shetteca with more than just my protector. We will take a patrol for safety. We can plan in Shetteca with Lord Ke'en after we welcome the new growing season."

Laexa turned to look at Ti'ek.

"Yes, I am going too," said the elf. "I will stay in Shetteca until all three moons have come and gone. Mother insists."

Hovan leaned back in his chair and continued eating and drinking while rolling thoughts around in his mind. He finished his tea. "Westgate tea is my favorite. I have missed it. Prince Ti'ek, care to ride the patrol with me tomorrow?"

"See with your own eyes? Knowledge is power." Ti'ek nodded, accepting the offer. "We will start slow while you learn to ride again."

"Your jokes used to be better." The wizard grinned before turning to Laexa. "A double patrol. Captain Vay is with us. Captain Wod Dein stays with the garrison. Meet with your approval?"

"Yes. Hovan, there are things that need to be attended to. If you ride tomorrow, then we should address the management of Forestton now."

"Yes, I know." Hovan knew he could no longer avoid the administrative tasks that had to be addressed with the start of the growing season approaching. Even though he wanted to.

Boring is too weak a word.

"Last piece of business," interrupted Ti'ek. "A young man has been watching the house. News courtesy of Taz'niet. She added she hopes it merits her an invitation to your Blessed Beginning party. What would you like done?"

"She always receives an invitation!"

"I think she asked for an invitation to remind you to host the party. You have not yet started planning. You have ordered nothing."

The wizard nodded and then changed tone. "Collect and question this man. Be careful. It is a poor technique to be spotted. He may want to be seen." Hovan stood up. "So much for a slow homecoming. Time for me to check on Forestton."

CHAPTER 6

FORESTTON

Dressed in his warm, dark green cloak with two stylized trees on each shoulder, one tree smaller than the other forming Forestton's symbol, the wizard Hovan, short staff in hand, left his house with the prince and his first captain.

"He hides here," said Ti'ek. "Watching for your return, I suspect. Taz'niet says he is staying at her inn when not watching the house."

"Where else but the Forest Inn when in Forestton?"

The prince smiled. "She charges him extra. She does not like that he spies on you."

"Remind me to leave a big tip next time we dine there. Which will be tonight. My treat."

"If you insist," joked Ti'ek.

Snow crunched under their feet as they headed toward the gates. Few people walked the streets in the cold.

When they neared the town's entrance, Hovan's eyes took in the beauty of the three flags playing with the wind above the gates. The large, rectangular standard of Arre'ielle caught the breeze above the colorful flag of Shetteca. In the lowest position, the green square flag of Forestton flew, showing the two tree symbol with a flying red hawk added.

Hovan lowered his eyes and noticed the muscular, dark skinned Captain Wod Dein standing in conversation with the light skinned Captain Vay. Creases spreading out from the corners of Captain Vay's red eyes hinted that, though the two shared the same rank, Vay was the senior, more experienced soldier. They both turned at the wizard's approach and bowed.

"Welcome to the new growing season, Captains," said Hovan.

"I wish you a Blessed Beginning, Lord Wizard," both men responded.

"Prince Ti'ek, head to the Forest Inn and detain the watcher," instructed the wizard. "Make sure he pays for the room before putting him in the barracks prison. Captain Wod Dein, close the gate until Prince Ti'ek has captured the man. Choose a handful of men from the garrison and have them accompany the prince."

"Yes, Lord Wizard." Captain Wod Dein pointed at five soldiers who left with the prince.

"Captain Vay, have the patrol stand down, but prepare a double patrol for tomorrow to ride to the River Ke. I ride with you."

"Yes, Lord Hovan. We are due to relieve the Shettecan patrol at the ford. We should leave early."

"Lord Wizard Hovan?" prodded Captain Laexa.

The three captains of Forestton stood waiting: the First Captain Laexa, the Garrison Captain Wod Dein, and the Patrol Captain Vay. The wizard did not disappoint.

"Yes. Yes. Captain's Meeting. My house. Let us get this over with."

The three captains smiled at his annoyance.

❖

The Giver had long passed her zenith when Hovan closed the last of a series of portfolios. Each folder addressed a separate division that kept the town of Forestton operating, protected, and growing. It had taken him longer than expected to administer to all the Forestton business that needed attention as the new growing season approached. He had been away longer than usual. The remaining details could wait. He was hungry, but wanted to stretch his legs first.

Hovan walked with Laexa toward the gates and climbed the stairs to the top of the curtain wall. Standing on the bastion south of the gates, he enjoyed the sights of the town. His home! He had not seen the village since before the snows. Returning, though, was bittersweet. The flags of Arre'ielle, Shetteca, and Forestton waved in the chilly breeze. Soldiers watched from their stations on the wall. Lit by the rays of the Giver, the brown grasses beyond the wall lay dormant, anticipating the warmer weather to come. Ready to burst into bloom when the visits of the Giver lengthened, the leafless trees waited past the grassy field and swayed in the breeze.

The wizard began a circuit around the wall, enjoying the short hike, inspecting it for any damage from the cold season. His captains had reported none, so that was what he expected to find. The parapet was clear of snow, as it should be. Whether the prince had helped with magic or his soldiers had used more mundane means did not matter. He completed his circuit and stood above the gates with Captain Laexa standing next to him.

"Welcome home, Hovan."

"Thank you. Will you join me later for dinner?"

"Yes. The Forest Inn?"

"Where else but the Forest Inn when in Forestton? And to pay my compliments to Taz'niet for her watchfulness."

CHAPTER 7

WE RIDE

The scent of burning wood mixing with the aroma of warm food greeted Hovan, Ti'ek, and Laexa when they entered the Forest Inn, creating an atmosphere of unspoken welcome. The crackling fire and soft conversations from the patrons helped create a soothing ambiance. Hovan anticipated a wonderful meal at the inn, known for its excellent food and drink.

The wizard looked up at the lights in the main room of the Forest Inn. They glowed by magic, the only magic that the owner, a tall woman named Taz'niet, could perform. When she had asked, he had taught her the simple spell. It helped her keep some of the unsavory visitors that came in off the road civil by proclaiming herself a magician, with control of the lights serving as her proof.

Hovan chose a table near the large fireplace, which added additional light and, more importantly, heat. Dark green woven clothes, the color of Forestton, covered the wooden tables. He noted that only half as many tables that the room could hold were in the main room. The wizard knew Taz'niet would add more tables during the busy season, but for now, the extra space allowed her customers to talk in near private conversation.

When his hunger had been satisfied, Hovan sat back, enjoying a second glass of wine as he listened to the elf prince tell humorous stories of events that had happened while he had been away. The wizard had long since learned that the elven custom of not discussing business at meals did not preclude the telling of stories.

The swirl of cold air when the main door opened and the march of boots across the wood floor chilled the demeanor of the room. Hovan sat up and put down his wine glass. A soldier dressed in the dark green uniform of Forestton, decorated with a lieutenant's insignia, strode over to their table.

"My apologies, Lords and Captain. A man wearing a Shettecan uniform waits at the gates. He claims to have ridden in from their Shettecan patrol at the ford, sent by the patrol officer to request our aid. He reports that wolf riders are attempting to cross and that they outnumber the patrol."

"Where is Captain Wod Dein?" asked Captain Laexa.

"On the wall above the gates. He will not open the gates after dark without permission."

Laexa nodded approval. "Return to the captain and tell him we are on our way. Send for Captain Vay."

The soldier bowed and left.

The wizard picked up his staff. "I will meet you at the gates."

Captain Laexa and Prince Ti'ek headed for the door.

The wizard joined Taz'niet at the bar. "My compliments yet again for the wonderful climate, food, and wine of your inn. I regret I cannot finish the bottle."

He deposited ten large coins on the counter.

"Lord Wizard?" questioned the innkeeper. "Since when do you pay for dinner?"

"My thanks for keeping an eye on my home while I was away. I also expect that a scout from Shetteca will come through those doors soon, requesting a meal. Feed him, please."

"As you wish. I will cork the bottle until your return."

Hovan leaned in. "You always have an invitation to my Blessed Beginning gathering! I have not forgotten!"

"No, of course not, Lord Hovan." Taz'niet wore a mischievous smile. "I wish you a Blessed Beginning."

Her hands covered the coins.

⸻◦⸻

Hovan climbed the stairs to the top of the wall. He met Prince Ti'ek, who stood with the hood of his cloak guarding his face from both the light and the cold.

"Protector Laexa requested I wait here," said Ti'ek. "I expect no trouble, but she exudes that air of command. How dangerous can one man be?"

"Depends on the one man," responded Hovan. "You are third to the throne of Arre'ielle. Your parents would agree with the captain that it is prudent for you to wait here."

"She asks that you remain with me."

Hovan nodded.

Do not be where you are expected.

One of the many lessons he learned from his teacher wandered into the wizard's thoughts. He expected no trouble, but Laexa was cautious when opportunity allowed.

Hovan waited with the prince and watched his three captains, who stood on the wall above the closed gates. The wizard peered over the crenelations. He saw the man whom Laexa was questioning sitting on a saddled riding animal with large, straight horns. When Laexa seemed satisfied, she called for the gates to be opened and let him walk his horned mount into town. Hovan returned down the stairs with Ti'ek.

The wizard let Laexa continue to question the man, but waved for Captain Vay to join him. "Captain, do you know him?"

"I have seen him in the Shettecan patrols before, but I did not know his name. He correctly identified the Shettecan patrol officer and their schedule. His uniform is as it should be."

"Are you convinced?"

"Yes, Lord."

"Good enough for me." The wizard moved forward to join the conversation.

Captain Laexa met him halfway. "A large group of cret'len riding wolves is threatening to cross the River Ke. The rider estimates six hands of wolf riders! The current has prevented the river from freezing again. They have thrown branches in at two locations to dam the water. The Shettecan patrol leader fears the current has slowed enough and will freeze overnight, allowing them to cross in the morning."

"That is a lot of wolves," said Hovan. "Recommendations?"

Ti'ek's answer was brief. "We ride."

"Yes," both Captain Laexa and Captain Vay agreed.

Laexa continued. "I am concerned though by the timing of this crossing and your arrival."

"Understood," answered the wizard.

"If the first captain is concerned, perhaps you should stay, Lord Hovan," said Captain Vay. "Our patrols can handle this."

"I have confidence in your patrols, Captain Vay." Hovan turned to Ti'ek, his student and friend. "Prince, what is the question here?"

"Why are so many wolf riders gathered there? Why do they want to cross the river?"

"Very good," said the wizard. "Yes, two questions. I want to know what is enticing them to cross or what is pushing them."

"Complete their mapping?" offered Laexa. "It would be faster on wolves. No runners to slow them down."

"Could be," said the wizard. "Could be searching for food. This is a large group to feed. If so, they may present a greater threat to those living near the river than past crossings. We have a responsibility to protect the farms and ranches. Yes, Protector Laexa?"

"Yes," confirmed Laexa.

"Both thoughts may be correct," continued Hovan. "If they are being controlled, then by whom? If there are more than just cret'len riding wolves, I should be there."

"Agreed," said Laexa. "Still, the timing concerns me. Now we travel in the dark."

"Then they will not see us coming. A group of cret'len, even on wolves, is not a genuine threat to us. I will convince them that crossing the river again is a bad idea. Captain Vay, plan for a double patrol. Captain Laexa, send the Shettecan soldier to get a meal at the Forest Inn. Taz'niet knows he is coming."

Both captains bowed and left. The wizard and the prince walked back to the wizard's house.

"We ride?" joked the wizard. "No elven proverb. No mission statement. Just a simple 'We ride'?"

"Did more need to be said?"

"No, but you and concise seldom go together."

The prince laughed. "Remember, I am responsible now."

CHAPTER 8

THE RIVER KE

In his kitchen, the wizard packed provisions, filling the second of two saddle bags that were laid across the table. He expected the Giver would rise and set several times before he returned to Forestton, but he did not plan on eating only soldier's rations while away.

The wizard slung the bags over his shoulder as he exited the kitchen. They came to rest against the leather quiver which held his short staff diagonally across his back. Captain Laexa waited for him by the main door, dressed for a cold ride.

Before reaching her, he slowed to a stop, took a deep breath, and turned into the large gathering room near the front of his house. Taking slow, measured breaths, he gazed into the room.

Breathe in - count to three. Breathe out - count to three. Repeat.

Laexa appeared at his side and put a comforting hand on his shoulder.

"I both love and hate that painting," said Hovan.

"Take it down. You may find your smile sooner."

Hovan touched her hand in thanks. "This is my last connection to her. You speak with logic, but all I feel is emotion."

Hovan squeezed Laexa's hand, still resting on his shoulder. "Come. We have work to do." Turning, he walked with her to the front door.

They walked out the front door and found Ti'ek waiting with three saddled orvbacs, two of them packed and ready. Hovan's mount recognized him. It wagged its fur covered tail and shook its head as if saying hello. Hovan walked over to his orvbac, breathed in its musky smell, and petted the long, furry face before scratching it between the straight horns.

"Thank you for taking care of Forestton while I was away. It will be good to ride with you, my friends. Your company on the road is welcome. Time to go."

As Hovan strapped his supplies to his orvbac, Ti'ek held the reins.

"Your prisoner requests to speak to you. He made his plea when I arrested him and again when Captain Wod Dein questioned him. He says he has words for your ears only. My title of prince was not enough to loosen his tongue."

"That will earn him extra time behind bars. He is in no position to demand or choose to whom he speaks."

Hovan climbed into the saddle and pointed toward the gates. "We ride."

——◆——

The Forestton patrol rode through the snowy night with few stops for rest. When the Giver peeked over the trees and offered her angled, yellow morning light, the patrol was moving cautiously upstream along the ridgeline above the River Ke. The road descended the hillside in two switchbacks before reaching the ford in the river. They rode their mounts north away from the road through ankle deep snow, passing among scattered groups of trees.

When Forestton met Shetteca, the patrols merged. As Captain Vay spoke with his counterpart, the wizard dismounted, secured his mount, and stretched. Wolves with riders walked among the trees along the far bank, darker motion against the white snow.

Captain Laexa and Prince Ti'ek joined the wizard to hear Captain Vay's report.

"The Shettecan officer reports the wolf riders have not crossed. The river did not freeze enough overnight. He thinks it will by tomorrow morning. There are two sites where they have tried to create logjams. A single patrol cannot guard both spots plus the ford. He has offered to stay and reinforce our patrol."

"Understood," said Hovan. "Anything other than wolf riders to report?"

"Nothing they have seen or heard."

"Anyone in the Shetteca patrol capable of magic?"

"No, Lord."

Everyone stayed quiet as Hovan completed his visual survey.

"Too many wolves to let be. Time for them to understand that these lands are under my protection. Captain Laexa and Captain Vay with me. Prince Ti'ek, prepare your defensive spells. I think it is best, Prince, if you watch from here. Support us, if need be, with magic."

The leader of the Shettecan patrol approached Captain Vay. "Captain, how many soldiers should we send with you? There are many wolves across the river!"

"You have never seen a wizard work, have you?" asked Vay.

"No."

"Watch."

The wizard chuckled at the exchange between the captains. He cupped his hands together as if he were making a snowball. He then drew them apart. A faint glimmer of red appeared between his hands. Hovan spread his hands apart until the glow surrounded him. He pushed it further, extending it and then separating the shield into three. He provided a personal barrier for himself and each captain. When the glows protected all three, Hovan let them fade from view. With one captain on each side, he walked down the hillside through the light cover of snow.

Hovan stood on the river bank, counting the wolves. "Five straight across. Four more up the hill."

"Five or six in the trees north," added Laexa.

"A few among the trees downstream," Vay said. "More at the logjam upstream, most likely."

Hovan continued to scan the riverbank. "I see nothing other than wolves and cret'len."

The wolves staring at them from across the river began to growl and test the ice. Not confident in its strength, they did not venture far from shore. The cret'len riders fired arrows. A few deflected off the red glow that flashed, protecting the wizard and the captains.

"Growling at me and shooting arrows?" asked Hovan. "Not very nice."

Hovan spread the fingers of one hand and thrust it forward. Small spheres of orange fire shots from each finger. They sped across the river faster than an arrow and struck the wolves. They yelped in pain before stumbling and falling, spilling their riders. Another volley of fire darts from the opposite hand ended their cret'len riders' attempt to rise. More fire darts streaked through the trees, finding other wolves. The cret'len that the wizard let live ran off.

"Not killing all the cret'len, Lord?" asked Vay.

"Leaving some to tell others to stay away. They are less dangerous without their wolves."

Hovan rotated his right hand around an unseen sphere. A ball of fire materialized in the space he had encircled. Grabbing it, he thrust his arm forward. The fireball sped away. It exploded above the logjam, freeing the river. The current grabbed hold of the broken branches and dragged them away.

Hovan walked upstream and cleared the second logjam.

The wizard and his captains stood on the riverbank, looking across into the abandoned district of Feleine. Motionless bodies of the cret'len and wolves killed by the wizard stained the snow. The slanted rays of the Giver angled through the bare branches, highlighting the grays and browns of the dormant woods and the white ground.

"Eager to return to Feleine, Captain Vay?"

"Yes, Lord Wizard."

"I want to know what these cret'len are doing there," stated Hovan. "Learn why they are not leaving us alone. Something is not right. Well done, Captains, for recognizing a problem and protecting Forestton and this part of the Shetteca district."

"I recommend we cross now, Lord Hovan," said Laexa. "Check the bodies for maps."

Captain Vay nodded in agreement, but said nothing.

"I am the Lord of Forestton. Forestton ends at the river, as does the district of Shetteca. I should get permission before crossing."

"If I may be so bold, Lord," said Vay. "We could cross and ask for forgiveness later, if needed, instead of permission now."

"You may always be so bold with me, Captain Vay. I value your judgement. But, like Captain Laexa, I need permission. Lord Ke'en is the Lord of Shetteca and my friend. He would be held responsible if we crossed and something went wrong."

"We could ask Prince Ti'ek," continued Vay.

"He knows better than to say yes without asking his father. I will contact Lord Ke'en. He will probably have to make the request to the king. A moment, please."

The wizard flipped his hand and reached out with his mind.

"Lord Ke'en? I have a request."

"Good morning, Hovan. Ti'ek tells me you are at the river. Is the problem solved?"

"We dealt with the cret'len and wolves. We wish to cross the River Ke and inspect the bodies."

"You are asking for permission?" Ke'en laughed. "The Shettecan patrol must be there."

"Yes. If I were alone, no one would know."

"You have my permission, but I will contact Lady Velina to request permission from the king."

Hovan waited quietly on the riverbank.

A waste of time. Contact Lord Ke'en in Shetteca, who then asks Lady Velina in Avi'ot, who can then ask King Dargladre simply to fly over a river. Formalities and responsibilities.

But he would not expose his friend to criticism by breaking the chain of command. Although Hovan had rarely seen the young king since Suzhanee died, he considered him a friend and would no more expose him to ridicule than he would Ke'en by leading a force across without permission.

"It is cold," was Hovan's only comment to express his annoyance at standing by the River Ke waiting for permission that he expected to be granted.

"Hovan, the king grants permission. However, Prince Ti'ek may not enter Feleine. He must stay with the patrols. I told him."

"Thank you. If we find anything of interest, we will let you know."

"Captains, we have permission. I will put flying spells on each of you. We stay together."

The Wizard and his two Captains floated across the river and landed softly on the flat space just past the riverbank. Laexa and Vay began examining bodies while Hovan stood, scanning their surroundings.

The bodies of the cret'len were half the height of the humans. Short fur, in shades of brown, covered their bodies except for their round faces. Poorly made leather sacks and packs were slung over shoulders or tied around waists. Inferior quality long knives and short bows lay nearby or still in holders. The trio moved from body to body, sifting through the bags and packs.

"Here," said Laexa, offering Hovan a folded piece of paper. Hovan unfolded it and examined the sketches. The map marked hills, streams, and larger farms between the main caravan road that ran past Forestton and the river, forming the opposite border.

"And a knife is worth keeping. He did not make this." Laexa showed it to Hovan.

"Maps like that one are what you have been finding?" Hovan handed the paper back to Laexa.

"No. This is a more complete version."

"They are not just here to find food. If this big cret'len has these, what does the chief have?"

"It is early in the morning," said Captain Vay. "If I were chief, I would not be here in the cold without reason."

"No," agreed the wizard. "I would be in one of the abandoned buildings by the ford with a fire burning."

"Maybe this one was the chief," suggested Laexa. "This is a large group of cret'len and wolves for there to be more."

"I agree with Captain Laexa," said Vay.

"There are only three of us," said Laexa. "We would find it difficult to fight off another group of this size without the river as a buffer. We found what we came for. I suggest we withdraw."

Hovan nodded agreement.

They floated back across the river and climbed up the hillside toward Prince Ti'ek.

"That seemed easy," said Ti'ek.

"They could not attack us because the river was between us. They did not run away fast enough."

"That is not normal behavior for them," noted the prince. "Usually, they run away immediately."

"Perhaps they thought the river would keep them safe, Lord," offered Captain Vay.

"Or they did not know a wizard was here, and we did not scare them," said Captain Laexa.

"Or something scares them more," said Hovan. He handed the map to Ti'ek. "Why would they have this?"

Ti'ek studied it.

"This could be called a map," he admitted. "I sent an image to my father."

"I offer that they are not planning to stay on their side of the river in Feleine," said Laexa.

"If so, then we should take the battle to them," said Vay. "Keep the fighting on the Feleine side. Protect our farmers and ranchers."

"You both make excellent points. However, we cannot cross in force until the river is clear of ice."

Hovan looked at each of the three standing in a circle of four. The captains and the prince he considered his inner circle of advisors, along with Lord Ke'en and Lady Shar in Shetteca.

"I do not believe that cret'len made this for themselves," said the wizard. "But then, for whom?"

Laexa spoke. "Whoever it is, they are across the river and do not plan to stay there."

"I want to go across now," growled Captain Vay. "They should not be there! This is not their home!"

Hovan put his hand on Vay's shoulder. "I know, Captain. An expedition into Feleine must wait until the river thaws. However, we will make that trip. I will need your expertise with us. We rode through the night. We should sleep and then decide what to do."

Hovan woke up when the Giver was at her highest. He joined Laexa near a fire. "Anything to report?"

"No. It is quiet."

"We will stay until the morning. Then I want to tour the western ranches."

The Giver finished its daily travel and set. Then rose again with no more cret'len or wolves being seen or heard.

"I leave the river under your watchful eyes, Captain Vay. The prince has told the Shettecan patrol to remain."

—◆—

At a comfortable pace, Hovan, Laexa, and Ti'ek rode their orvbacs through the picturesque landscape of low rolling hills during several bright, though cold, visits of the Giver. They rode among the homesteads in the western area of the Foreston region in the Shetteca district. The trio stopped and talked with many of the people, renewing acquaintances with some, reassuring others, and collecting information at each stop. Frequent conversations added to the wizard's enjoyment of the trip. The discussions and changing vistas and riding alongside Laexa and Ti'ek kept Hovan's mind from wandering too often to memories of Suzhanee. The farmers and ranchers of western Forestton greeted them with respect, most glad to see the prince, the wizard, and the captain. Many though expressed displeasure at the raids, which had become too common during this cold season.

The Giver rose and set almost a handful of times before they returned through the gates of Forestton. Hovan avoided the painting and averted his eyes from the doorway down the hall from his room. Hovan reached his bed, tired and not at all concerned about leaving the prisoner in jail for another night.

CHAPTER 9

THE WATCHER

Hovan rose soon after the Giver. He returned the favor and prepared the morning meal for Laexa and Ti'ek. After they finished eating, Hovan picked up a cloth bag and led Ti'ek outside the walls for instruction. The wizard had not given Ti'ek a lesson since the cold season began. Laexa joined them.

"Speed and accuracy practice using fire darts," said Hovan. He emptied eight stone spheres, each the size of a small melon, onto the ground. "One hand only. Ready?" Hovan threw two stones across the frozen field without waiting for an answer.

Thrusting his left hand forward, Ti'ek launched two red fire darts and hit both stones before they stopped rolling. "I never said I was ready."

"Neither will an opponent."

Ti'ek laughed.

The wizard closed his hand. Both stones rolled back to him. Hovan sent them rolling further down the practice field and spread wider apart. Ti'ek hit both again before they stopped.

"Very good."

Hovan added a third stone. Ti'ek hit all three. Hovan spread them wider on the next throw. The prince succeeded. Hovan added more distance. Ti'ek was successful again.

"Excellent. You have been practicing. Maybe you can still beat your sister."

Laexa laughed at the tease.

"Cova is my equal only in height," said Ti'ek.

Hovan separated the stones into pairs. "Pick up the pace. Use only one hand." Hovan sent a pair of stones rolling across the field, followed by the second pair, requiring Ti'ek to use two spells.

The wizard added a third stone to each group. Then, he varied the number of stones. "Switch hands."

After Ti'ek missed a stone, Hovan said, "Alternate hands."

Ti'ek's speed increased when he could use both hands.

Hovan kept Ti'ek at practice, varying the number of stones, the spread, and the distance down range. He pushed Ti'ek by repeatedly throwing the stones out, forcing the elf to perform spell upon spell. These were simple spells, but as with all magic, repetition was tiring.

When Ti'ek missed two of four close stones, Hovan called for a break.

"Well done! Your accuracy and endurance are excellent. Still, you are relying on your hands too much. Magic is in the mind. The hands only focus it."

"Yes, yes, I know." The elf stretched his arms over his head and took deep breaths.

"The hands only guide. There were magicians who specialized in this game. Some of them I could not beat in competition. However, I would not want them by my side if there were real trouble. I would rather have you."

"He is trying to make you feel better after your misses," Laexa teased Ti'ek.

Ti'ek smiled. "I am still faster than Cova."

"You are, but she is gaining," said Hovan. "Well done, Ti'ek. I am cold. Practice is over."

The wizard returned to his house and changed his clothes. He decided it was time to visit his prisoner.

Hovan and Laexa approached the jail cell. Standing tall, the wizard studied the prisoner, scanning him from the worn boots up to the messy brown hair, being thorough and slow.

Satisfied that he had shaken his guest's confidence, he spoke. "You have insulted Prince Ti'ek and broken the laws of my town. The only reason I have not yet killed you is that I have not deemed you important enough. Now, however, I have the time."

Hovan raised his arm and pointed a single finger at the prisoner.

"Wait, wait. Did the elf not tell you?"

A dart of orange flame shot from the wizard's finger and shattered on the wall behind the prisoner's head. "You will use our proper titles when addressing us."

The prisoner swallowed. "Yes, Lord Wizard. The prince, the prince. I told him I have information for you."

"Better. Whatever information you might have, you deemed not worthy of the prince's attention. Why should I bother waiting to hear it?"

"Leu'mey sent me to watch your house. He told me to tell you, and only you, if you found me."

"Do you think it wise to insult the Crown Prince's son?"

"He is an elf. Can he be trusted?"

"Careful," cautioned the wizard.

"Leu'mey said to tell only you, I swear!" pleaded the watcher.

"Each man makes his own decisions. What did he instruct you to say?"

The watcher recited, "He will not complete the job without renegotiating the fee."

"Leu'mey told you to tell me that?" asked Hovan in feigned disbelief.

"Yes! Those were his exact words!"

Hovan shot fire darts at the prisoner's feet, backing him up against the wall. "Why should I believe you?"

"That is what he said! I swear it by the One I serve."

"Do not invoke the Ones! You are a thief. You do not serve anyone but yourself."

Three fire darts floated around the prisoner's head, pulsing in and out.

The prisoner fell to his knees and raised his hands as if he could bat the burning spheres away. "That is what Leu'mey said!"

Hovan closed his hand. The fire darts popped and vanished. "How much did he pay you to spy on me?"

"Sixteen silver pieces."

"He did not pay you that much! The only thing about Leu'mey that is not cheap is the fees he charges. The most he paid you was twelve pieces. How much?"

"Ten, but he said he would give me more for expenses if I succeeded."

Looking at Laexa, Hovan gestured toward the door.

As they walked back to the wizard's house, Laexa congratulated Hovan. "You handled that well. What just happened?"

"An old trick: send a person who you know will get caught. Deliver a message without seeming to deliver a message. Leu'mey just sent me a message."

"What is the message?"

"Since I did not hire him, someone else must have. It is someone whom Leu'mey thinks is worthy of note. He expects me to pay more than them. We will travel to Avi'ot in the morning."

Laexa grumbled.

⸺◆⸺

After the morning meal, Hovan, Laexa, and Ti'ek stood in the main hallway of the wizard's house, arguing. Hovan and Laexa wore cloaks, ready for travel. Hovan's cloak was auburn, the color of a Follower of Knowledge. Laexa's was dark green, the color of Forestton.

"I still say that you need more support," said Ti'ek.

"Laexa will have to be enough," said Hovan. "She is my protector. Leu'mey will not only accept her presence, but expect it. Any more would compromise Leu'mey or cause him to avoid us. I certainly cannot bring the son of Shetteca, third to the throne!"

"You are going to meet a man whose morals are determined by the price offered. Meeting at a site of his choosing. Because someone else with questionable motives wants information about you."

"If I do not come back, you have my permission to find and kill Leu'mey. I want to know who got his attention. Cret'len and wolves are crossing the river. Now this?"

"Send someone else."

"I doubt he would talk to anyone else." Hovan pointed at Laexa and himself. "Who has a better chance of escaping than us?"

He raised his hand, signifying he would argue no further. "I appreciate your concern. I have not spoken to Leu'mey since I moved to Forestton. Now he has sent word. I want the rest of the message! Take the patrol and bring the bags to Shetteca. If we can join you here, we will. If not, we will meet you in Shetteca. Ke'en already knows we are going. I do not know how long it will take. Let the prisoner go in the morning. Make sure he leaves town."

"Let him go?"

"It will not help my dealings with Leu'mey if I kill his messenger. The boy was just doing his job. Ready, Laexa?"

"I hate traveling like this."

"Avi'ot is a long ride in the cold. I have contacted Lady Velina. She knows we are coming."

Laexa put her hand on Hovan's shoulder. Hovan positioned his left hand vertically before him like a blade. As he whispered, his right hand drew magic from his left hand as if he were stretching dough. Hovan and Laexa vanished, leaving Prince Ti'ek standing alone in the wizard's house.

CHAPTER 10

KING DARGLADRE

Hovan became cognizant of his surroundings sooner than Laexa. His head hurt and he felt nauseous, both common symptoms of traveling by magic. He knew the effects passed quick enough once the traveler had regained consciousness. Arriving in this stunned, nonresponsive condition, vulnerable, Hovan knew to be one reason Laexa did not like to travel by magic. The feeling of sickness was another. Hovan agreed with her on both counts, but the ability to move great distances in moments made the effects worth dealing with.

Hovan recovered faster than Laexa did. He thought it was because he was the weaver of the magic and more accustomed to this type of travel. She remained next to him with her hand on his shoulder as if she were a statue dressed in the dark green of Forestton. They stood in the center of the room on a vibrant mosaic tile inlay. Hovan recognized the design of stylized yellow eyes spread across the floor as the motif of the Royal Secret Room in the king's palace. The wizard and the first had arrived in Avi'ot, the capital city of Arre'ielle.

As Laexa began to move, Hovan directed her toward the one way door out of the secret room. Hovan pushed it open with his hip and maneuvered Laexa to one of the cushioned armchairs in the receiving room. He closed the door, resetting the room for someone else to use.

Hovan rang the bell that hung on the magic imbued, floor to ceiling steel gate that prevented passage down the hallway. Two guards descended the staircase at the end of the short hallway.

"Lord Wizard Hovan," he announced himself. "And the first captain of Forest-ton, Captain Laexa."

"Lady Wizard Velina informed us you would be arriving." They bowed in greeting.

One guard unlocked the gate, allowing entrance into Avi'ot. Laexa, mostly recovered, followed Hovan through. The gate clanged closed behind them. The guards escorted them upstairs to the main hall.

"This close to celebration, etiquette requires that I announce myself to King Dargladre and to Lady Wizard Velina," said Hovan. "I must wait until they have time to receive me or until I am told that they do not. Time that you can spend making our presence known. It will be quicker to let Leu'mey find us."

"He must be expecting us."

"Yes. I am safe enough here in the palace. Head to the market. Make some purchases, get noticed, and be careful."

The wizard changed tone. "If you find that Sojourn Mountain red wine I like so much, purchase a case or three! No merchant in Shetteca would question such a purchase."

"True, Shetteca white is a step down."

"Well, do not tell them that. Be careful, Laexa. Watch your back."

Captain Laexa nodded and left.

The king sent word that he would enjoy meeting with Hovan, but obligations would keep him busy for a time. Hovan sat waiting.

After lunch, an aide escorted the wizard into one of the king's receiving rooms. King Dargladre approached from the other side of the room, dressed as if he had just left a royal engagement. He still wore the king's golden yellow robe, the color of his family, over a tan shirt buttoned up to the neck. A dark brown vest closed with silver buttons matched the handle of the dagger on his belt.

Lady Wizard Velina, the royal wizard and the king's protector, moved to the side of the room, allowing space for King Dargladre to greet Hovan in private. The smile gracing her face softened the stare of her dark eyes, darker even than her skin. She wore brown robes, the color of a protector, emblazoned with both the yellow symbol of the king and her rank of captain of the Wizard's Corp.

Velina wears a smile. A stress free moment for the royal wizard.

Should I tell her that her skin is the color of milk chocolate? I would need to bring some from Earth for her to understand.

Suddenly, the king halted and made a quick gesture with his hands. As he raised his left hand to point, Hovan struck the floor with his staff without thinking, and a pale red glow surrounded him. Two darts of yellow flame shot from the king's fingers. Hovan tilted his head as if asking a question. He angled himself and dropped to one knee. With his staff held horizontal in front of himself, Hovan deflected the two flames toward Velina. A soft tan glow sprang into existence around the dark skinned wizard. The two yellow flames flew into the glow and dissipated.

Hovan got to his feet.

The king exclaimed, "I am improving!"

"Yes, you are, King."

"Still, I am not fast enough. You did two spells to my one."

"Why did you send the fire darts at me?" asked Lady Velina in a playful cadence.

"It would be treason to endanger the king's life. I wish you a Blessed Beginning, King Dargladre, Lady Wizard Velina." Hovan bowed to both.

"Welcome, Lord Wizard Hovan," returned the king. "Welcome! It is good to see you again! It has been longer than I would wish. I am sorry you needed to wait."

The king walked toward Hovan with a smile on his face and his eyes meeting the wizard's. His wavy brown hair hung loose, accentuating his oval face. His complexion was darker than Hovan's light skin, but not as tanned as the elves. Hovan noted the maturity in his eyes and demeanor despite his young age. Six circles of the Giver spent sitting on the throne must have fueled a growing confidence in his yellow eyes. Lessons learned from Lord Ke'en for the three growing seasons before had helped. Lord Ke'en's time as king regent, though short, allowed time for the king's son to mature and learn.

"Come, Lord Wizard, sit and talk. I promise the wine is excellent! I have missed our conversations."

When the king had topped off the wine in both wizards' glasses, he asked, "How big a problem are the raids west of Forestton?"

"Shetteca and I can handle it."

"Do you need help?"

"That is very generous. I do not think we need any."

"What are you planning?"

"I have not discussed the details with Ke'en and Shar yet. I will celebrate the new growing season in Shetteca. We will talk then. Once the snows retreat up the mountains, the basic plan is to cross the River Ke into Feleine and chase off or, if needed, remove the cret'len."

"You and Lord Ke'en are very close." The king smiled. "You do not always call him by title."

"We have a long history together, King Dargladre. Long, at least, by human standards."

"A long history," repeated the king. "You look barely older than I do, Lord Hovan." The king refocused. "My advisors think there may be more than cret'len. What do you think?"

"I do not know."

"You need more information to form a conclusion. I understand. Tell me your working hypothesis. Do not let philosophical methodology stop you."

Hovan sipped his wine as he studied the king. And then smiled. "Very good, King Dargladre. No report suggested anything more than cret'len and wolves, but I think we will encounter more. We will certainly prepare for more. The cret'len clearly made a map, but that is not their way. Does the king object to a force from Arre'ielle crossing the River Ke?"

"Object? Not at all! In fact, I plan on joining this expedition. I am sure Lady Wizard Velina will now voice her objections again."

"An unnecessary risk!" stated Lady Velina. The creases at the corners of her light brown eyes hinted at both her age and concern. Her emotions were often difficult to decipher. Not this time, however. "Lord Wizard Hovan, please talk him out of this!"

King Dargladre countered Lady Velina's objection in a tone which suggested to Hovan that they had discussed this before. "You will use your magic to return me to Avi'ot at the first sign of danger, Lady Velina. A moment after the hint of danger to my life, we will be gone. This is a rare opportunity that I am taking advantage of!"

Hovan sat silent for a moment. "We would be honored."

Velina glared at Hovan.

"Honored, but not sure why," said the king.

"No, I am not."

"My kingdom is being threatened. A response is required, I think. I am inexperienced in combat. This is an opportunity to learn from you and Lord Ke'en."

As he spoke, the king tallied the reasons with his fingers. "The war forced my father to abandon Feleine. Joining you will provide me with a rare chance to travel in that lost district! The trip would also allow a visit to the district and city of Shetteca. I can show support for and solidarity with a powerful district leader and the elf next in line to the throne. I can spend time with Lord Ke'en and Lady Shar as well as yourself. Finally, for six circles of the Giver, I have been king, but seldom ventured out of Avi'ot."

"All excellent reasons," agreed Hovan. To placate the royal wizard, he continued. "Lady Velina is properly concerned about your safety. You are safer here in the palace than on an expedition into Feleine."

The king smiled. "I trust Lady Velina, the royal wizard and my protector, and the king's guard that will surround me. Send word of what you would like us to bring: archers, magicians, infantry. Deliver it yourself if you can. I do not wish to lead this campaign, but observe... at a safe distance. I hope that my forcing my presence upon you does not upset you."

"The king's will. You are making your father proud."

"Hovan, that is not helping!" said Velina.

"I think it is true, and the king seems decided," said Hovan. "The king needs to be a king."

"He can be king without putting himself in danger, Lord Wizard," said Velina, using Hovan's title as evidence that he should know better.

Velina mentally contacted Hovan.

Hovan opened his mind to receive what he knew was going to be the mental equivalent of a scolding. He sometimes regretted that being a wizard meant he had to accept mental communiques from the royal wizard, captain of the wizard's corp.

"He respects your judgment! Impress upon him how dangerous this is!"

"We are going, Lady Velina," stated the king, unable to hear the mental communication between the two wizards. "I want to see Feleine and Shetteca. I cannot govern well what I do not know well!"

The king turned to Hovan. "Thank you for the compliment. I have one more question for you. Why are you here?"

Hovan stalled by taking another sip of his wine. "Seeking information."

"About me?"

"No, King Dargladre."

"Then?"

"Word reached me that someone is seeking information about me and doing so through channels that suggest they do not bear me good wishes. If true, I want to know who."

"What?!" said Velina. "Why are you out in public with only Captain Laexa as guard?"

"I think the team of Captain Laexa and myself is the most effective."

Turning to the king, Velina renewed her objections. "Your Majesty, you must reconsider your decision to go to Feleine! The troubles in Feleine and this news cannot be unrelated."

To Hovan, she demanded, *"Help me protect the king!"*

"Though I do not know for sure, King Dargladre, I had the same thought," said Hovan.

"I had expected more than that!" Velina complained.

"I am joining the expedition into Feleine, pending new information. For too long, I have been in Avi'ot! I can gain both experience and firsthand knowledge of the kingdom."

To Hovan, King Dargladre asked, "How will you find out?".

"A man who does not always live by the king's laws sent me a message; a seller of information."

"Sounds expensive."

"Yes. I will need to pay for the message and the cost of the messenger."

"Dangerous?"

"Perhaps, but that is the game I must play. And why Laexa will be suitable as my companion."

"Stay in the palace tonight," said the king. "At least you can sleep without fear of attack."

"Most kind," said Hovan. "Thank you."

"You are not helping," was Velina's final thought.

CHAPTER 11

LEU'MEY

Captain Laexa, wearing her Forestton green cloak with the first captain rank displayed just below the shoulder, walked to the guard's station of the palace and requested entrance. The officer on duty directed her to the third floor tavern.

She stopped at the entrance and scanned the room, more out of habit than any genuine concern. Inside the king's palace, this eating area should be safe and, in addition, required a certain rank to gain admission. Her first captain's rank may be enough, but the lord wizard's title certainly was. Her arrival was evidently expected. One of the soldiers guarding the door waved her in and motioned to a man sitting across the room.

Hovan sat near a wide door filled with windows that opened onto a balcony. When the weather was warmer, the doors would be folded against the wall, allowing a breeze to flow through and meals to be taken outside. Now, the windows of the sealed door allowed in only the glowing light of the Giver. The wizard sat with a half empty glass of ale resting on the table, rays of the Giver splashing across the table. He evidently looked for the captain's return, noticing her arrival as soon as she passed the guard.

As she walked across the room, Laexa considered the contrast of the wizard sitting alone by a window with her memories of him sitting in the Forest Inn laughing with Suzhanee.

Yes, he is changed. Loved and lost. And lost his smile. Few people see past his wizard demeanor. I am one, but Suzhanee knew him in a way that I never will.

Laexa folded her cloak across the back of the chair and sat.

"Anything of note in the market?" asked Hovan.

Laexa shook her head no. "I found your wine, though. How do we find Leu'mey?"

"I think we need to let him find us. Join me for dinner in the city? The East Wall Restaurant?"

"Expensive."

"If you want to attract attention, be noticeable."

"If someone is looking for you, that may not be the safest move."

"The restaurant has its own security. And I can handle anyone I see coming."

"Leaving me with all the ones you do not see," said Laexa.

"My protector." Hovan nodded in agreement.

"Request a guard detail."

"Excellent idea! Be even more noticeable."

Laexa chuckled. "Not what I was thinking."

"We return here tonight. The king has offered us rooms."

"Very kind. I may actually sleep."

"Care for a drink?"

"Not until we have safely returned."

The wizard pushed the chair back. "Please have the defensive magic of your hawk pendant turned on until we are inside the restaurant."

Laexa walked through the city next to Hovan, surrounded by an escort of four soldiers. In Avi'ot, most would recognize the Lord Wizard Hovan, for he had served as the royal wizard to King Regent Ke'en. Laexa knew that many would recognize all seven wizards, six active and one retired, at least in name if not in person. Their procession through the city would turn heads. She hoped the attention they received would be the good kind and not what she feared.

When Hovan and Laexa had finished dinner, the four man guard detail returned them to the palace.

"Give me your hawk pendant, please," said Hovan. "I will recharge the magic."

"Yes. If we are going to walk through the market tomorrow, I want it at full strength."

Though further south than Forestton, the weather in Avi'ot was still cold. As Hovan and Laexa prepared to head to the market, Laexa debated the need for a cloak as she watched Hovan weave his defensive shell around himself. The charged hawk pendant would protect her from projectiles when she turned it on. Decided,

Laexa attached the clasp of the cloak at her neck. She threw the wings of the cloak over her shoulders, keeping her arms free and her sword and daggers visible and accessible. Once past the guards at the palace entrance, she mentally activated the defensive magic stored in the pendent.

Captain Laexa followed the wizard through the streets toward the large open market close to the western gate of the city. Her eyes scanned the crowd, cross streets, and overhanging balconies. Judging by the head movements of the wizard, he was doing the same. She had his back. That was her job. She hoped his reputation preceded him because there were too many positions to account for safely.

Hovan and Laexa entered the Avi'ot market after noon. Laexa had already arranged for the purchase and delivery of the three cases of the red wine minus four bottles. The first caravan north would take them to Forestton. With nothing more to buy, the wizard and his first wandered through the market square. The captain's hand rested on the hilt of her sword, studying anyone who passed close. Hovan wore his auburn travel cloak and walked with his short staff in use as a walking stick. His quiver, positioned on his back, awaited to receive the staff should he require both hands for magic.

The quickest of the three moons above had barely moved when a boy approached the wizard. He stopped when Laexa grasped her sword hilt and held out a note. Hovan nodded to Laexa. Laexa scanned the crowd, assessing if this were a distraction providing an opportunity for an attack. The captain then took the paper from the child, handed it to the wizard, and continued scanning the market. The boy ran and disappeared into the crowd.

Hovan read the brief message. "Attack no one unless I am hit. Play the game, my friend."

They entered a tavern called Zoveh and surveyed the inside. The name meant 'from where?' implying that, once inside, no one cared where you came from.

Of course, they care. We will be noticed as soon as we enter.

Wooden tables spread out across the main floor of the well lit room. A bar stretched along the far wall. A staircase climbed the left wall and led to the balconied second floor. Two men relaxed at tables on the balcony. An older man sitting alone at a table looked up as Hovan approached. His gray hair, gathered into a ponytail, grew only from the sides of his head. Hovan seated himself across from Leu'mey. Captain Laexa stood back, keeping a watchful eye.

Hovan laid a cloth bag of coins on the table. "I would like some information."

Leu'mey untied the clasp and looked in. "The harvest in the south was particularly good last growing season. Politically, though, the South is uneasy with the king being unmarried and childless and an elf heir to the throne. They need to be careful because their nearest neighbors outside the kingdom are the Dahica Elves. There is a fair amount of merchant traffic between the two areas. Plus, the king is related to Lord Ke'en through his mother."

"My sources tell me that someone is seeking information about me. I want to know who."

"That is a small bag of coins asking a man to condemn himself."

"I need to know!" stated Hovan.

Matching Hovan's intensity, Leu'mey answered in a slow tempo, emphasizing each word. "Death in the flesh would soon find me if I told you, even if I knew. Do you understand me? You should prepare... to leave." Leu'mey put his hand on the bag of coins.

"I understand you. Those coins are not yours until you answer my question."

"You paid and asked. I answered. They are mine. Your not liking my answer changes nothing."

As the intensity of the voices increased, Laexa grabbed the hilt of her sword.

Hovan stood and stepped back from the table, his auburn cloak flaring out around him. His staff attracted the bag of coins as if it were a magnet. Leu'mey grabbed the bag. The magical attraction pulled the bag across the table and Leu'mey with it.

Laexa saw the two men on the balcony raise crossbows, aiming them at the wizard and his first. She started to unsheathe her sword, but Hovan lowered his staff. Leu'mey sat back down with the bag of coins in his hand. A red glow glimmered around the wizard.

"Be careful what you do, Leu'mey. Some enemies are not worth having."

"That is why I will tell you nothing."

"You will hear from me again."

"Bring more coins," said a smiling Leu'mey.

Hovan and Laexa backed out of the tavern.

"Talk later," said Hovan. "Move now."

The tone of the wizard's voice silenced any words of protest from Laexa. They walked through the streets, taking the shortest way back to the palace. Laexa quickened her pace to keep up with the wizard, alert to his heightened state of awareness. The wizard used his short staff as a walking stick, keeping it available as a weapon. His right hand was steady, not swinging as he walked, ready to craft magic. His eyes watchful.

A sealed message waited for them in their room in the palace, bearing the king's yellow seal. Hovan broke it open and read the lone sentence. "The king wishes to know what we learned."

"So do I," inquired Laexa.

"We played the game. I got the message. I am to be prepared."

Laexa sat in a chair and stared at Hovan. "Preparers are looking for you?"

"Did you notice his careful use of language? Leu'mey would not openly cross them."

"May the One you serve protect you! Cret'len crossing the river! And this. These cannot be unrelated."

"I agree. The Preparers will use any means possible to bring death and despair. The cret'len may be a convenient tool for them."

"Why you?"

"Besides fighting for the king during the war and not dying? My miraculous escape from them and death was an affront to their belief that death is a requisite step to the next life. A step one should welcome and they seek to hasten. Our subsequent victory at Shetteca, with me playing a significant part when they thought me dead, must have enraged them. Furthermore, I accepted a commission to close one of their strongholds."

"Many people were involved in that," argued Laexa.

"Not the one after the war," corrected Hovan. "This other one was before. And before we met." Hovan held his forehead in his fingers as if he had a headache. "I accepted a solo job. Lord Ke'en was unavailable, but Suzhanee was with me. Before she and I married. I did not handle it well." With a tilt of his head, Hovan added, "It was profitable, though."

"Why now?"

"They have wanted me dead for many cycles of the Giver. Finding me is not hard. Finding me in a vulnerable position is the tricky part. I am a wizard, and I have you. Why now, I do not know. Perhaps they have gathered enough numbers to be active in Arre'ielle again. If they want more than just to annoy Forestton, then they need to get rid of me." The wizard sat down next to his protector. "Cret'len are one thing. Cret'len being driven by Preparers are another."

"This suggests a bigger problem than we thought."

"It may just be rumors."

"Then you paid a lot of coin for rumors. Leu'mey took a risk and spent a great deal of effort to get those coins. Makes me think this may be more than just rumors. If Preparers want you, perhaps you should not go to Feleine."

Hovan nodded in partial agreement. "Trying to draw me out of Forestton? Send others to Feleine? If it is not safe for a wizard, then it is too dangerous to send others. Solving large problems is how I made my fame and fortune."

"I doubt cret'len are the only problem in Feleine."

"Then we may need a wizard. My safety, Forestton's safety, may require that we deal with this." Hovan thought for a moment. "We need more information. Give me a moment while I contact Lady Velina and Lord Ke'en."

Laexa sat quietly. Her job had just become more difficult.

If protecting him were easy, then he would not need me. I knew the risks when I took the job.

She heard the wizard exhale in frustration.

"The Royal Wizard Velina is demanding that I convince the king to abandon his plans to go to Feleine. I respect the king's move. Bold and decisive! Though I acknowledge the danger. I do not know what to do."

Hovan began writing a response to the king.

"Avoiding the king?" asked Laexa.

He nodded. When he finished, he delivered the sealed message and two bottles of the red wine to an aide of the king.

"We need to get back to Forestton," rationalized Hovan. "It is a shame that King Dargladre is not capable of mental communication."

"Evading Lady Velina's directive by not seeing the king before you leave," concluded Laexa. "Interesting solution. Are you prepared for a reprimand?"

"No, but it saves me from facing the king and arguing against a move I think is right. Time to go."

CHAPTER 12

SHETTECA

The wizard could not travel to Shetteca with the same ease with which he had traveled to Avi'ot. He had too much to bring with him. Magic had its limits. Only in Forestton long enough to see the stars pass overhead twice, the Wizard Hovan, wearing his thick auburn travel cloak, was again leaving his town, but this time on orvbac. With Prince Ti'ek, Captain Laexa, and a lightly supplied mounted patrol, the wizard rode out of the gates soon after the first meal. Extra saddlebags lay across the backs of the mounts of the wizard, the prince, and the first captain. The trip from Forestton to Shetteca, the city of Lord Ke'en, took three visits of the Giver by merchant wagon. They would certainly move quicker than that, provided they met no trouble along the way.

The wizard and the patrol started north toward the small range of hills separating the farming region of Forestton from that of Shetteca. They rode in their customary positions. Hovan and Ti'ek led two lines of soldiers riding orvbacs with Laexa directly behind Hovan. Hovan kept a quiet watch for tracks in the drifting snow along the roadside and listened for noises other than hoofbeats and sighing branches. The wind hid much, though.

After lunch, the road took a slight bend to the east, following a wide path running northeast through the dormant, skeletal trees of the cold season. They traveled northeast over forested hills for the rest of the day. Little conversation interrupted the chilled silence of the forest. Nothing more than wind and cold disturbed them.

Just short of nightfall, they moved off the road into one of the large resting areas that were common along the king's roads traveled by caravans.

"Standing travel orders, Lieutenant."

"Yes, Lord Wizard."

Men collected what wood was available, tended to the orvbacs, and cleared an area of snow and debris. Other soldiers stood watch, bows in hand, near the campsite and hidden along the roadside among the trees. Laexa and the lieutenant led small groups, searching the forest near the road. Both returned with nothing to report.

With the camp secure, the prince asked, "How many ki'vas? Five?"

"If you wish," answered the wizard. "Someone must stand watch, though. You make two. I will construct three."

Ti'ek moved away to find space to erect his ki'vas.

Hovan wove a spell with choreographic hand motions. A dome like structure shimmered into existence. It reflected the surrounding snow and branches, blending in so well that it was near invisible. He created a second one beside the first, followed by another. A man could stand inside and there was room for five or six people to sleep. A fire cracked to life in the cold wood positioned in the center of each ki'vas. The rising smoke melted into the walls and disappeared.

Ti'ek made a visual comparison of the ones he had built and the ones the wizard had constructed. In a proud voice loud enough to be overheard, he said, "They look identical."

Hovan continued to unsaddle his orvbac and did not turn to face the elf. He asked in an equally loud voice, "Do yours have a fire burning inside?"

The silence of the prince raised a round of laughter from the soldiers.

The wizard constructed a larger ki'vas to house the orvbacs. While their fur and layer of fat could protect them from the cold, their scent may attract unwanted visitors. The ki'vas would lessen the smell and hide them from sight.

Hovan, Laexa, and Ti'ek claimed one ki'vas for themselves and did not take part in the night watch schedule. They went to sleep close to the fire, wrapped in warm blankets. Hovan slept in fits, often waking, too uneasy to sleep well far from the safety of manned walls. He noticed Laexa leaving to join the dawn watch, the time of most trouble.

Hovan woke up early the next morning feeling sick, his throat sore, body aching from more than just sleeping on the ground. They packed and got moving. By early morning, the small rolling hills had leveled out to the farmlands of northern Arre'ielle. Knee high grasses dominated the land not farmed, replacing the trees and shrubs which grew in the hills. Ranches and farms became visible in the patterns rising from the frozen landscape. The sight of farmhouses or the scent of burning wood encouraged them forward. From the hills, the caravan road ran almost straight north to Shetteca.

On the plains, snow survived in patches. However, the brown, crushed stalks of crops from the previous growing season poked above the white ground cover of snow. Twisted, matted down in sections, and dead, they provided little to entertain the eyes. Even the orvbacs seemed to find the sight unappetizing as they shook and shivered. With trees no longer shielding them from the north wind and the road wide and straight, the company moved fast. Rests were short and infrequent. No one wished to stand in the gusts that grew stronger as the day progressed. Snowflakes fell.

Finally, their destination came into view. Shetteca, the principal city of the District of Shetteca, looked to Hovan to be a place that might be warm. They hurried on through the snow.

Hovan rode, feeling worse. He watched the gray walls of Shetteca grow larger as they neared. They seemed to rise straight out of the brown northern plains and straddled both sides of the quick flowing but narrow River Ensecit, derived from the elven word for turquoise. The aqua blue color of the water came from its glacial beginnings in the mountains to the northwest. Hovan pulled his cloak tight and continued on.

The company rode through the arched entryway of the city as the Giver neared the tops of the distant mountains. Hovan issued orders to his men, supplied each with a bonus, and granted them leave to celebrate in the city.

Hovan, Laexa, and Ti'ek rode at a walk through the snow toward the eastern side of the city. The saddlebags, temptingly stuffed, lay over the backs of the orvbacs. The wizard had no fear, however, that someone might try to liberate them. Not with the wizard, the prince, and the first guarding them.

As they traversed the busy city, the wizard watched the reactions of the citizens. Few approached the wizard or the crown prince's son riding at his side. Their eyes, which looked away as they drew near, seemed to follow them when they rode past. Soldiers saluted and landowners bowed, but few people offered more than greetings.

A lesson from his teacher drifted through the wizard's mind.

A reputation can be a useful tool. Respect and fear dictate influence. The more people respect or fear you, the less you need to do to get them to do what you want.

The trio reached the Temple of Knowledge, attached to one of the central libraries. To Hovan, the Temple of Knowledge, and the central library attached to it, with its curving dome and many round windows, seemed out of place amongst the sharper rectangular peaks and pointed towers typical of human architecture. Faint maroon swirls mixed in a sea of dark gray rectangular blocks gave the stone walls an illusionary spirit as snow drifted past. The clear elven influence in its design was common to all the central libraries in this quarter of the world.

Hovan led the way into the courtyard and dismounted. He tied his orvbac to a stone rail, thumping it on its shoulder, thanking it for the trip. He slung one of the heavy saddlebags over his shoulder. "Please hand me the other."

"I will carry one," offered Ti'ek. "You are not feeling well."

The wizard shook his head no. "I am required to deliver these two myself. Bring the other set."

He settled the saddlebags on his shoulders and walked in through the wide doors, in their customary open position.

The three moved across the vestibule toward the double door entrance to the library. Two men stood guard at the inner entrance. Hovan, glad to be in from the cold, looked up at the painted ceiling. A large mural of a red talon bird soaring across the sky blue arched ceiling dominated the spacious entrance way. With its eyes directed below, the talon bird seemed to scrutinize those entering or leaving.

Several rows of benches filled the second half of the room, dotted with pairs of white slippers. White wraps to cover the shoulders for warmth hung on wooden hooks on the wall. The three took off their dirty travel boots and cloaks. They slid the boots under their spot on the bench and put on clean library slippers. They exchanged their travel cloaks for shoulder wraps.

Hovan, Laexa, and Ti'ek presented themselves to the men standing guard. A guard nodded acceptance and escorted them to the high priest's private chambers.

Hovan, between sneezes, stoked the fire as Ti'ek uncorked a bottle of aromatic red wine. Laexa cut up a cheese wedge. With the fire burning bright and the cups filled, the three sat back, warming up inside and out. The conversation drifted to a discussion of the geography of the land to the west of Forestton and Shetteca.

High Priest Thesian arrived and, without so much as a 'Sorry for keeping you waiting', went over to the saddlebags and opened them. He wore auburn robes of a similar color to Hovan's cloak. He was clean shaven. His hair, a mix of brown and gray, fell to his shoulder. A pair of piercing gold eyes shone from a face developing creases from age.

"I wish you a Blessed Beginning, Priest Thesian," said Hovan. "Four hundred thirty one gold. I have paid for another circle of the Giver. Count them if you wish."

Thesian looked at Hovan and smiled. He then turned to the bound stacks of rectangular coins glittering at him. "There is no need. Welcome to the new growing season, Prince, Wizard, First."

"The other bag contains maps of a large area called North America and the texts on religions you requested."

"Monotheism. Different from our way, or perhaps not." The high priest briefly looked over the materials the wizard had brought him. "Thank you, Hovan. How are you?"

"Outside of a nasty cold and a growing fever," Hovan sniffled, "well enough." In a reflective voice, he added, "I have paid again. How about you?"

"If I were not high priest, I would enjoy life a little more. Managing this place can be a pain in my ass. As you know, the library doors rarely close."

"Quit," suggested Ti'ek, handing Thesian a glass of red wine.

"Get rid of my four hundred thirty one gold piece lease on life," said Hovan, "and I will show you some enjoyment that you will not want reported anywhere, much less in this library."

"Never," joked Thesian as he sat. "You are the steadiest source of income we have."

"I want to live," came Hovan's flippant response.

Thesian studied the wizard's face. "Good. I am glad."

"I know I made a deal with the One I serve, but I am retired now. Can we re-negotiate my annual fee?"

"The fee you pay each new growing season honors not only the deal you agreed to but also the work you are called to do."

"This is not the life I hoped for." A waterfall of memories rushed over him, starting with the siege of Shetteca, when he had made his deal, and Suzhanee's death, yet again making him question why he continued.

"But it is life."

The priest turned to Laexa. "How are you, Captain Laexa?"

"Well, thank you, Priest. I wish you a Blessed Beginning."

"And how are you, Prince Ti'ek?"

"Still enjoying youth, Priest Thesian."

The priest looked at all three and asked, "What are your plans for the cret'len?"

Ti'ek answered for the group. "Once the river has thawed, Shetteca, with Forestton support, will cross the River Ke."

"It has been some time since a military contingent from Arre'ielle crossed that river. Any new information?"

"Preparers are collecting information about Hovan," answered Ti'ek.

The priest's audible intake of air preceded his saying, "You think there is a connection between this Preparer and cret'len activity?"

"We do."

Hovan let his two friends answer the priest's questions as he swam through memories, drew heat in from the fire, and drank wine.

"Cret'len would not threaten Forestton, surely?" The high priest looked for agreement in the expressions of the three facing him.

"No," answered Laexa. "Why are they leaving Feleine? Preparers may be the answer. Still, I think it is too easy for them to cross the river. The river is not Lordic's Wall, which defended Feleine for generations. We must defend the ford and western Forestton better. Also, the Preparers may have recruited more than cret'len."

"Who would be with them?" asked Thesian.

"We can guess," continued Laexa. "I do not understand why the cret'len would risk the wrath of Shetteca unless someone was pushing them and they had help. The reports suggest they were more organized than you would expect. Raiding parties ran arranged sweeps through the area as if surveying quadrants."

"History tells us that whenever the cret'len become a problem, someone is controlling them," said Hovan, having dammed the flow of his memories for the moment. "The news from Avi'ot raises this to a different level."

"You always seem to be in the thick of it, Hovan, even retired," said Thesian. "Send me a report when you return."

"As always, Thesian, as always," replied Hovan.

With the brief interview over and the deliveries made, they took their leave of the high priest. Hovan detoured through the cherished library section. He strolled through the main section, gazing at the stacks of books, maps, and reference manuals that composed the main floor of this central library. The sight filled his eyes and mind. These wooden bookcases contained the material concerning the mundane world.

Looking up, Hovan saw the central white stone balconies telescoping up to the wide central dome above him. The openings to the rooms off the balconies held books on less referenced subjects, including magic. Each central library, though similar, had differences as well. Of all the libraries, Hovan found this one the most beautiful. He stood near the center of the white tile floor, visually feasting on the beauty of the architecture.

People passed by as he turned around.

Hovan reflected on one of the guiding tenets of the One he served.

Regardless of which One they serve, the library welcomes anyone seeking information. The advancement of society only occurs when knowledge reaches everyone.

A smile graced his lips. He thought of Suzhanee, her smile, and her flowing, dark brown hair. That memory evoked pain, but also fondness, for he had met Suzhanee here. Visiting this library was bittersweet. He could not come here and not think of his wife, both meeting her and losing her.

When Hovan had finished savoring the sight and gained some control of his thoughts and emotions, the three travelers left. After putting their own boots and cloaks on, they mounted the orvbacs and rode slowly toward the district leaders' residence. They stabled their mounts behind the walls of the inner gate.

"Laexa, I am safe here and do not need a bodyguard," said Hovan. "Enjoy the festivities as you would like. You are welcome to join us at the district leaders' celebration. Or celebrate in the city, if you wish."

"We have already decided that the lady will be the guest of the prince, my somber friend," Ti'ek said.

"It will be my pleasure!" Laexa said with a smile.

A fit of coughing from Hovan encouraged them to move inside.

"Come, you need warm food and hot tea," said Laexa.

"Have it sent to my room. I want to lie down. Please extend my apologies to Ke'en and Shar for not greeting them upon my arrival." Nodding to Ti'ek, Hovan left with Laexa and headed toward their normal set of rooms.

The wizard went to his bedroom and crawled under the heavy blankets. When the meal arrived, he forced himself to eat some of the hot food and sip some tea. He then slept.

CHAPTER 13

THE BLESSED BEGINNING FESTIVAL

Ti'ek walked through the palace, the current home of his family, greeting all he met and speaking with many. Landowners, most from the Shetteca district, had come into the city to celebrate the Festival of the Blessed Beginning hosted by the district leaders. Most of the conversations began the same way.

"Welcome, Prince Ti'ek, to the new growing season. We are delighted that the Crown Prince has extended us an invitation and provided rooms for us. Ahh, the festival will be as excellent as last season's harvest!"

Ti'ek would agree and then thank them for honoring his parents by making the trip. Questions about health and family would follow, interspersed with a joke if the prince knew the family well enough.

Their excitement and optimism were contagious. The smile left his face only to emphasize surprise at a shared secret. His wandering through the palace was uplifting.

Ti'ek weaved his way through the citadel to his rooms high on the west side. He had chosen these rooms for the view of the distant mountains and the proximity to his parents and younger siblings. A large tapestry hung on the wall, presenting the flag of Shetteca. Saffron colored rays from the Giver reached out from behind a white cloud in the upper corner. Its soft rays sparkled off a wide turquoise river which meandered through a sage background. The tapestry captured the attention of anyone who entered the room. Ti'ek nodded to the flag as if acknowledging that it had accomplished its mission of being the first item noticed.

Display cases on the east and west walls each bore tributes to Prince Ti'ek's other allegiances. Ti'ek briefly scanned these as he ambled past. A wooden plaque with his lineage engraved on it stood on the top shelf. The next shelf held the standards of the elven King of Dahica and of Ti'ek's uncle, the Duke of Westgate, his father's older brother.

Opposite this stood an array of items identifying him as someone in the service of the One of Knowledge and as an associate of the Wizard Hovan. A mahogany talon bird in flight, with eyes searching the entrance room, stretched out over the top of the dark wood case. A light colored wood plague with Forestton's flag engraved on it rested on the top shelf. Various books occupied the two bottom shelves.

The elf warmed some water with magic, washed, and changed into fresh clothes. Refreshed and relieved of his travel clothes, he walked to his parents' chambers.

Ti'ek stopped in the wide entrance hall and waited. His father, Crown Prince Ke'en, sat reading a document. Swiftly casting aside the papers, Ke'en rose to greet his son. The proud elf's body flexed with strength and grace as he strode toward his firstborn. His casual dress was neat and spoke of a warrior. The two pairs of green eyes met in a gaze that was as intense as the smile on their lips was joyful. Their right hands clasped the wrist of the other.

"Welcome, eldest son!"

"Welcome to the new growing season, Father."

"And to you!" Ke'en put his arm around Ti'ek. Together they walked into the study. "Your mother will be ready for dinner in a moment. A long moment, I fear." The district leader smiled and resumed his position at the end of the couch. Ti'ek found a comfortable chair to appreciate.

"Anything new in the reports?" asked Ti'ek.

"Not yet. Scouts are moving along the river."

"It will be some time before the river is clear of ice, allowing our orvbacs to cross safely."

"Then, Shetteca with Forestton move into Feleine!" stated Ke'en.

"Yes. And the king joins us!"

"The king. Yes, Hovan already contacted me." A broad smile spread across Ke'en's face. "The king comes north!" After a pause and a change in tone, he continued. "I wonder if that is wise, though. There may be more to this western business than cret'len stirring up trouble."

"That thought has occurred to several people."

"Lady Velina strongly opposes the king going to Feleine. I understand the king's wish to see more of his country, but also Velina's concern."

The smile returned to Ke'en's face after a pause. "Ahhh, it will be like old times: the wizard and the elf united again. I will enjoy casting off the cloak of office and wearing the simple robe of a warrior. Responsibility makes me restless. What about you, my never-at-home son? Certainly, you will not miss this reunion?"

"Of course not. Responsibility is indeed a heavy cloak."

The father laughed aloud at the copied phrase. "If Hovan has taught you responsibility, I will proclaim his teaching prowess in the royal court!"

"Alas, for my youth and innocence, I fear he has. Already my heart has slowed a beat."

"Wisdom compensates for any loss of youth's strength. You have lost none of youth's strength!"

In his best rapscallion voice, Ti'ek insisted, "Yeah, but Dad, the girls like youth!"

A voice from the doorway interrupted their indecent laughter. "His father's son! At least he has the courtesy to take it out of court." The Lady Shar looked from her husband to her son, obviously caught between happiness at seeing her son and disapproval of the topic of conversation. A light red tunic, lighter than her deep ruby eyes, extended down below her waist. Leather pants kept her legs warm. A light green tie held her straight black hair, common to almost all elves, in place behind her neck and down her back.

"Good evening, Lady," said the young elf.

"Do not 'lady' me. Stand up and give me a proper hug, or I will not leave your side through all the festival." In a pleasantly threatening voice, she purred, "Having a beautiful lady, such as your mother, by your side endlessly will do more to ruin your chances with the young ladies of Shetteca than any loss of youth."

Ti'ek sprang to his feet and squeezed his mother in a tight embrace.

"Will that get rid of you?"

"Not likely," she said and smiled.

"Not likely, indeed," moaned Ke'en. "She attached herself to me so tightly that I had no choice but to marry her."

"My hand on a knife at his throat had nothing to do with the proposal," explained Shar to her son, her smile still shining.

Perplexed, Ti'ek looked at his mother, his equal in height, and said, "I thought he married you for your intelligence and beauty."

Shar kissed her son on the cheek. "I will leave you alone." The mother hugged her son again. "Where is Hovan? Certainly, he did not fear intruding on a family reunion."

"Sick. The mighty Wizard Hovan has a fever and will not be joining us for dinner tonight."

"Unfortunate," said Shar. "His presence at court this evening would help."

"What is wrong?" asked Ti'ek, looking from one parent to another. "If it is important, I will go wake him. Send a healer if need be."

"It is not important," Ke'en said. "Lord Gerritt is upset because of the attempted murder of one of his favorite landowners. He says to all who will listen that the attempt came from the north. Hovan's presence would have been a show of northern unity and power. The king's counsel think it was personal but promised support."

The district leader raised his hand and stopped his son before he could start. "Let him recover. I know my friend well enough to know that he will not miss tomorrow's celebration. He will be there to support us. Besides, our combined efforts against the cret'len will better serve the situation. Gerritt will hear of our victory!"

"The news from Avi'ot that Preparers look for our friend may make him question the north's involvement," suggested Ti'ek.

"Few will hear that news," said Ke'en. "How is our friend?"

"Much the same. I have not seen him smile, even after wine and one of my stories. It pains me to see his pain. Particularly knowing that I was part of the failure."

"Not every battle is won," quoted Shar. "Hovan has never once leveled a finger of blame in your direction."

"No, he keeps all the blame for himself."

"As knowledgeable as he is," said Ke'en, "he does not know how to stop the hurt and let go."

"Laexa and I shoulder the burden of Forestton to give him time to find his cure. But his sadness is a burden, too. It is a relief to be home, see the faces of these excited festival goers, and leave Forestton to someone else." Ti'ek took a deep breath and smiled. "Worries can wait until after the festival."

Ke'en repeated. "Worries can wait. Yes. I like that thought."

"Will you accompany your father on the campaign into Feleine?" asked Shar.

Ti'ek nodded.

"I feel safer knowing you will be with us," said Ke'en. "Do you ride with Forestton or with Shetteca?"

"Forestton. I have spent more time riding with them and know my role with them better."

The crown prince smiled at his wife. "His parents' son. Wisdom is being acquired in youth." The proud smile on his face matched Shar's smile.

On the last visit of the Giver before the equinox, Ti'ek split his time between resting, greeting those arriving, talking with his family, and playing with his young brother. In the late afternoon, he withdrew to his rooms to get ready for the celebration.

Ti'ek dressed in a turquoise shirt and pants of a darker shade. A cloak, which could be closed by buttons just above his waist in elven fashion, hung from his shoulders and matched the darker turquoise of his pants. Brown boots flowed halfway up his calves. A dagger with a green jewel set in the end of its pommel hung on his belt. When he was ready, he joined his parents in their suite.

Ti'ek watched his father drape a light aqua blue cloak, the color of Shetteca and her flowing gown and a match to his own attire, around his wife's shoulders. Ke'en offered his arm to her. Celebrating in his own palace, Lord Ke'en wore no weapon, though Ti'ek knew he always had his magic. Escorting his wife, the three left the suite to collect the younger children.

The first collected was the youngest, Donnan. Ti'ek threw him into the air and caught the giggling younger brother. The youngest sister, Givette, joined her parents and wished both of them and her brothers a Blessed Beginning.

"Welcome to the new growing season, sister." Ti'ek performed a deep bow, turning Donnan upside down in his arms. His cloak fell across the laughing youngster's face.

Givette smiled at the antics.

Ti'ek moved ahead down the hallway, whispering in Donnan's ear. When they reached the door to their sister Cada's rooms, Ti'ek released his younger brother. Donnan slipped behind the door and ran inside.

Ti'ek leaned against the wall, waiting as the others caught up. Casually, he informed the others, "I sent Donnan in to get the ladies."

"Ti'ek," warned Shar.

A scream erupted from inside. The soft running footsteps of a child ended abruptly. Chuckling exploded into laughter.

Cova fully opened the door, carrying Donnan in her arms. "Whose monster is this?"

"Mother, control your child," reprimanded the eldest son.

"Return the conjuration to the wizard's student," replied the Lady Shar, pointing at Ti'ek.

"We will join you in a moment. After we fix the damage." She withdrew inside while Ti'ek congratulated Donnan.

"He is hard enough to handle without you spurring him on, Ti'ek," scolded Givette.

The father put his arm around his youngest daughter while looking at his two sons. "Do not confuse control with teaching, Givette. I trust Ti'ek will not stretch fun to the point of irritation."

"If you like, I will send Donnan in to apologize," offered Ti'ek.

Shar rolled her eyes and shook her head no. "Once is funny. Twice is annoying."

The door opened, revealing Cova and Cada.

"Welcome to the new growing season, Ti'ek," said Cada.

"And to you both." Ti'ek straightened up and gazed at his younger sisters. "You both look stunning!"

"I have seen the Giver for over five hands of orbits, scarcely elder brother," said Cova. "It is time I developed serious suitors. When better than at the Blessed Beginning?"

"Indeed. I see Cada had the same thought. If neither of you receives an offer tonight, put it down to indecision. This new resolution would have nothing to do with the visit of Duke Tober from Dahica and his sons, would it?"

"The pickings are slim for an elven princess in this part of the world." Cada smiled.

"Kindly make sure that I am the quickly notified third party of any developing interests," said Ke'en.

"Yes, Father," replied Cova and Cada almost in unison.

Together, the family descended to the crowded, noisy banquet hall.

A small gong rang, quieting the hall. A clear voice called out, "The district leaders of Shetteca, Crown Prince Ke'en and Princess Shar."

Ti'ek felt pride as his parents walked through the large entryway and took their positions on the dais. Together, they turned and looked out at the colorfully dressed crowd, most in shades of green, blue, or turquoise, with some reds and browns.

"Princess Givette and Prince Donnan." The two youngest children held hands as they walked to join their parents on the dais.

"Princess Cada."

"Princess Cova."

"Prince Ti'ek."

Ti'ek stood with his family, honored to be at his parents' side. He spotted Hovan and Laexa seated at a table close by. Perhaps seeking news from outside the country, the wizard dined with Duke Tober and his sons.

Lord Ke'en spoke. "Welcome to the new growing season, my friends! With another cold season passed, we look forward with promise. The promise of peace and the prosperity that comes with it. I wish to make two toasts." He raised his wine goblet. "First, to King Dargladre. We wish him health and wisdom and thank him for the benefits we receive from living in his kingdom!"

The room cheered, "To the king."

The room grew silent for a moment as they drank.

"Second, to us! We who have forged a stable north and take pride in our work and in our district."

The room cheered and drank.

"No one is entirely without worries. The worries of harvest, of transportation, of skirmishes, of rule. The best worry of all: children. Tonight, I ask something of you! Save your worries for the new season, where I am sure they wait to meet you!" Lord Ke'en looked at Ti'ek and smiled before continuing. "We begin with the ceremonial planting."

Again, the room cheered as the guests began finding their seats. One man remained standing.

"I want to make a toast," yelled the elderly Baron of Chelle in a slow cadence.

The room quieted down to a low buzz at the unexpected request.

Lord Ke'en nodded permission.

"I am old and wish to enjoy the remaining time awarded me. This new growing season, my daughter takes over the rule of Chelle." He paused and looked around the hall.

Few applauded. Ti'ek knew this already and wondered if applause was appropriate.

"I have lived in the north all my life. Through wars, good harvests and bad. Never did I think I would have an elven leader over me. With little cheer did I greet the prospect: darker skin and strange eyes, not born here, different customs, seem to live forever. However, I am an honest man! I know another when I see him, be he a man or an elf. Tonight, I want to toast Shetteca."

He raised his wine glass and held it up while he met the district leader's eyes.

"As I near my life's end, I look forward for my children. Do you know what I see? I see them facing a bright future! My life has been worth the trouble! I owe that partly to you, Lord Ke'en and Lady Shar. My struggles and pain have been rewarded! I toast Prince Ke'en and Princess Shar."

The baron drained his glass as many others in the room stood and drank to the district leaders' health.

Prince Ti'ek stood with the guests and toasted his parents. He surveyed the room of assembled nobles and landowners, thanking them for their work.

Fear may motivate. Love does as well.

Lord Ke'en began speaking again. "Thank you for your kind words, Baron. Now for the first planting of the new growing season."

Before each member of the district leaders' family was a small pot of dirt, a metal spoon, and a seed. They each dug a small hole in the dirt with the spoon and planted the seed. Using water from their own glass, they each watered their seed. They placed the pots before them to display them throughout the evening.

"Our northern tradition continues. Ask which ever One you serve to bless us with a good harvest. Tonight, enjoy yourselves! Dinner first, then dancing, and then welcome the equinox as you wish. Dinner first! Let us eat."

Servers brought the food to the many tables. When all was ready, Princess Givette began the meal with the first bite, continuing another tradition. The youngest daughter begins the new growing season. The prospect of maturing youth and new life to come. Once started, the gathered guests freely ate and drank. Low music drifted across the hall, mixing with the conversations and inspiring a few bits of singing.

As dinner passed, the music grew louder, and couples made their way to the dance floor. Ti'ek watched his father swirl his smiling mother around the floor. The elven couple danced and then talked with everyone as they strolled through the room. Then danced some more. His parents exchanged warm embraces with Hovan and talked with Duke Tober. Ti'ek watched them as they again made their way around the room, talking, drinking, and dancing. Despite being smaller in statue than most of the men and women, they commanded the room with their confidence and inclusion of all.

He also watched his sisters accept invitations to dance. They left the dais and moved off to the dance floor. They too talked with many, finding spaces at tables to sit and talk. The sons of Duke Tober often had their attention and the occasional dance.

Even Hovan got up to dance. His first dance was with Captain Laexa, who would not be mistaken for a warrior tonight. She seldom wore a gown; her beauty hidden under leather armor, potential suitors dissuaded by the sword and her look of command. Not so tonight. Ti'ek smiled.

Who would first have the courage to ask her to dance after the wizard?

Hovan also shared several dances with Cova.

After wishing a yawning Donnan good night, Shar sat next to her eldest son, who was still watching the celebration from the dais. "Why do you still sit here? This is not normal for you."

"The gathering fascinates me tonight. How the two of you move so effortlessly around the room. The interactions between families. Who is sitting with whom. That Hovan is wearing Shetteca turquoise tonight to show support for our family, instead of his normal auburn of the One he serves or the dark green of Forestton." Ti'ek turned and looked at his mother. "Have you noticed how much time Cova is spending with Hovan?"

"Maturity is sharpening your observations. People often speak without saying a word. For example, Cova has said she is interested in our friend, the wizard. Hovan has said neither yes nor no. But that was not first said tonight. You have not been paying enough attention to those two. You suggested she dressed as she did for Duke Tober's sons. I proposed another reason. The wizard and your sister have developed a special bond between teacher and student. It is not uncommon for them to take dinner together after her lessons. He visits Shetteca more often than Forestton. You have not seen him since the start of the cold season. We have several times. The frequency of his visits is better measured by the second moon than Equa, the third."

"Cova gets lessons that often?!"

"She is becoming quite accomplished in magic. I dare say she will catch you soon unless you pick up the pace, though she could never stand against you with a sword. Still, I do not know if these frequent visits are what is best."

"You do not approve?"

"It has not come to your father and me, so we have not had to decide." In a quieter voice, Shar added, "But a human marriage...even as young as Hovan seems."

In a brighter voice, she said, "Enough. Go." She gave Ti'ek a gentle push from the raised dais. "I will make sure no one takes your wine glass."

Prince Ti'ek made his way to the table of the Baron of Chelle, thanking the man for his tribute to the district leaders.

"Prince," asked the new Baroness of Chelle, "will you be journeying west with us against the cret'len?"

"Yes. 'Us'?" Ti'ek asked the young woman. "You are joining the expedition?"

"I have little battle experience, having been too young to fight during the war. While I hope I never need more, I see this as an opportunity to learn. Also, Chelle rides to support an elf my father respects. If the district leader sees fit to ride out, we will ride with him."

"The force grows stronger with your aid," said Ti'ek. "I look forward to traveling with you."

"I wish to fight by your side should it come to that. You ride with Forestton, I expect. Rumor says you are as skilled as your father."

"Rumors grow with the telling, Chelle," Ti'ek said, using her title as a sign of respect. "I am perhaps as skilled as my father was when he was my age, but I think not. Still, I thank you for the compliment."

"You are welcome, though the compliment is not flattery. Forestton provides mounted archers, I expect, as does Chelle. I simply wish to learn the most efficient way to use mounted archers; the profit of experience and a teacher. Plus, there is that sad bond tying Chelle and Forestton together."

Ti'ek looked at the young woman with raised eyebrows, nodding approval. He turned to the retiring baron. "I raise a toast to you, Baron. If your daughter's perceptions indicate the state of Chelle, the credit for its prosperity goes to you. While my father will miss your voice, the Barony should not suffer under the direction of your daughter."

"Thank you, Lord Prince."

Feeling excited and less contemplative, Ti'ek moved through the celebration, drinking and dancing with sporadic stops to refuel the stomach. Several times, he sought refuge at the table shared by Hovan and Tober. His sisters were often there talking with them and Tober's sons. The prince danced with the taller Laexa, teasing her about her gown. When she accepted offers to dance from others, he smiled. Hovan cited his illness as the need to limit his dancing, accepting dances with Cova or Laexa only.

With many of the younger celebrants, including his sisters, Ti'ek did not stop until it was time to toast the equinox, welcoming the first light of the new season.

CHAPTER 14

THE COMING COUNCIL

The morning dawned bright and cold. The quiet of the palace greeted Hovan's ears. His throat still hurt, and his body was tired, but that was all that remained of his sickness. He tried not to cough. Under the comfortable blankets, his stomach began an argument with the rest of his body for permission to leave the warmth and search for food. The debate did not end quickly, but eventually, the appetite prevailed.

Hovan stepped from the mass of blankets and quickly pulled his thick travel cloak around his shoulders. The morning air seeped through the clothes, but Hovan fought back, shivering, and strode through the palace to the kitchen. Only a handful of cooks tended to the needs of the early risers. Hovan ordered a hot breakfast and found a seat in the nearly empty eating hall.

Instead of breakfast, a message from Ke'en came saying that breakfast was in the conference room and the celebration was over.

Hovan descended to a lower level of the palace, past the guards stationed outside the door. A large fire snapped and blazed in the stone hearth at the far end of the rectangular hall. The light of the fire reflected off the stone walls. Occupying the center of the cavern like hall, a strong, thick, wooden table stood. Surrounded by chairs, the sturdy workhorse made no pretense of elegance. The firelight sank into the surface of the table, dulled and polished by years of use. An elf occupied the one large chair positioned at the head of the table. In front of him, spread out across the table, lay reports, recommendations, and maps. A large map of the district of Shetteca hung on the wall behind him. The remaining cut stone walls stood bare.

"How are you?" asked Ke'en.

"Better now that I have rested in warmth," answered Hovan.

"Have a seat, eat, and let us discuss the plans for the trip west."

As they ate, the district leader and the wizard discussed the western landscape. They considered the various roads and hazards in the hills leading to the Lordic's Wall, the defensive wall built along Feleine's western border. Which passages would be good for their troops? Which for scouts? Where in Feleine the cret'len may be or where they might run to? Interrupted by stories of adventures they had shared, remembrances of past trips served as references. One tale tied into another. And that into another as their talk eventually became centered on the telling of episodes linked by the thread of their friendship. Abandoning the reports, the two friends relaxed and related shared memories. They finished their Westgate tea. They fed the fire, satisfied their hunger, and replaced the morning tea with sips of past growing seasons' red wine, which loosened their tongues and warmed their souls.

"I look forward to riding with you again, my friend!"

"We have done quite a lot together, Ke'en."

Hovan and Ke'en relaxed for a moment more. Then Ke'en chuckled. "I think we have just failed the test of youth."

"Yes," agreed the wizard. "Yes, we are talking more about our past than about the future."

"Of all we have overcome, wizard, alone and together, let us not fall to the cret'len."

"To quote a wise, old man, knowledge is power, but only if used wisely."

"Wise, yes, but not so old ... anymore. Even an elf cannot avoid death forever."

"Pardon me if I try," said Hovan.

They smiled as they laughed at themselves. Gone was the time. Unproductive, but not wasted. They spread the maps and scouting reports across the table in front of them again.

———◆———

The Giver had set, and the district leader had been called to other duties. Hovan sought a change of venue and thought. The wizard walked past lines of bookshelves in an upstairs room of the Central Library. The end of his staff glowed, providing light that divided the darkness as he moved toward the proper row of bookshelves. He found the desired bookshelf, then the proper shelf, and then the book on healing. After verifying the title, Hovan returned through the array of bookshelves to a table. Other books lay open or stacked on the table.

Hovan sat down and pulled a blanket across his shoulders. He opened and began reading the book. Paper and a quill point pen lay to his right, ready to receive whatever notes and references the tome might reveal.

Thesian entered and sat at the far end of the table. His golden eyes reflected the soft light. He waited as Hovan read and turned pages in the flickering glow of a lantern.

When Hovan looked up, the high priest asked, "You are helping to plan the campaign, are you not?"

"Of course. I have for much of this visit of the Giver. She will rise twice more before Lord Ke'en holds the council. I am here running down a reference of personal interest."

"Any new insights?"

Waving at the books on the table, Hovan shook his head. "Another fruitless night."

"You will keep searching?"

"Endlessly."

"Or so you hope."

Tired, Hovan grinned and nodded. "I want to know what I did to myself after Suzhanee died; to understand the healing magic, the youth magic. I did not care when I tried it, but I care now."

"Why not just be happy that it worked?"

"How old am I?"

"Let me know what the council decides. Good night, Hovan." Thesian stood and disappeared into the shadows.

Hovan grew frustrated with all the meetings that occupied his time leading up to the council. There would be no need for it, he thought. Anyone who needed to know the details surely must know by now. Gradually, he let Ke'en and his elder son handle the administrative tasks. With Laexa, the wizard visited the Center for Protection to pay his respects for the support in western Forestton, to leave a donation, and to escape more meetings. Lessons with Cova also served as a pleasurable distraction. She always had a smile for him.

The time for the council finally arrived. Hovan arrived in the conference room before the others. He lit a fire to warm the room and hung the maps on the pegs in the wall. The wizard sat in the first seat on the long side of the table nearest the district leader's chair. He knew the chair to the right of Lord Ke'en's chair was for Prince Ti'ek. The chair for Lady Shar was to the left. She would come to show support for her husband and hear the beginnings. Hovan did not expect her to stay for the full telling of the plan. She knew and had approved it already, as he had, but she would have access to excuses to leave that he would not. Hovan wondered if Cova would accompany her mother.

He then directed his mind to review the plans yet again.

Knowledge is power, only if used wisely. Careful thought prevents misuse.

Lords Ke'en and Ti'ek entered the room. Lord Ke'en studied the room, checking the maps and counting chairs as the wizard had already done. "Ready?"

"Yes, Lord Ke'en," Hovan responded.

The chamber filled with captains and barons. First Captain Laexa arrived and took her seat. Men and women still commanded most of Shetteca's forces, despite having an elf as district leader. Hovan knew many of those seated before him as veterans of Shetteca's battles. Still, several younger faces occupied a few seats of command. The gathering seemed nervous to Hovan's eyes. Some because they did not know what to expect, and some because they did.

Wise of Ke'en. Mix the young with the veterans *and include only a few elves.*

Ke'en began the meeting with quick introductions. A clear and direct objective followed. "A force from the District of Shetteca is being compiled from her lands. The mission of this company is to locate the cret'len groups that are threatening the western lands of our district. Once located, the mission becomes very simple: convince them to move or reduce their numbers. We will cross the River Ke to defend Shetteca!"

The simple announcement sparked great enthusiasm, some stemming from relief. Before continuing, the smiling lord waited for the approving cheers to subside. Lord Ke'en swept his arms wide to include all those sitting before him. "The king himself will join us, for he wishes to see us in action!" Next, he outlined the strategy and responsibilities.

Hovan and Laexa joined the district leaders Ke'en and Shar and their children for dinner in their private quarters. After dinner, they retired into a large sitting room where a fire was blazing. Ke'en and Ti'ek compared notes on the council. Shar left to put the two younger children to bed.

Tired of plans, Hovan stood before the fire, watching the flames try to break free from the logs and fly. Cada and Cova joined him, each laying a hand gently on an arm.

"Ever reaching for the sky, but bound by life to the very wood from which it tries to leap," Hovan whispered his observation of the fire.

"Thoughtless and in service to others," added Cova.

The wizard nodded approval.

"Did you enjoy the conference?" Cova teased.

"I noticed you did not attend," the wizard responded.

"Thankfully, my father restricted it to those going to Feleine," said Cova.

"There was no need for you to chaperone us during the festival," Cada said.

"Speak for yourself, Cada," said Cova. "You had the attention of the charming son." Cova gave Hovan's arm a squeeze. "I was glad you were there, Hovan. For one thing, you saved me from the prince's boring younger son."

"I was sick and needed to sit often," said Hovan.

"Our father was watchful," said Cada.

"Need he be?"

"No more than you," Cada said.

"I am ever watchful. The unobservant may miss a vital piece of information."

"It is a wonder you ever sleep," joked Cova.

"The body has limitations, I am afraid to admit," said Hovan.

"You hope to eliminate them," noted Cova.

"Imagine the potential!"

The flames crackled, filling the silence as they sipped their wine.

"You spoke often with Duke Tober," said Cada.

"I knew him for a short time when I was younger," answered Hovan.

"Younger?" teased Cova.

"Did you learn much?" Cada asked.

"Not much, but some."

"District Leader Gerritt is upset, some said," noted Cova.

Looking at the fire, Hovan said, "A very remarkable year for wines, I am told."

"Yes, so my friends from the south tell me," continued Cova. "He is looking to the north for the cause of troubles, my friends also say."

"For him, everything is north. Including his strongest adversary and, perhaps, largest importer of wine."

"He has been speaking about our father and the troubles to our west in the same sentence and letting others draw their own conclusions," added Cova.

"Then he has drunk too much of his wine or hopes that others have," said Hovan. "The north will never turn on their charismatic leader and crown prince. Nor will the king without evidence as clear as a dragon flaming in the sky. Your father is an elf of integrity and power whose influence extends well beyond the borders of his district. Duke Tober brought his sons to meet you, hoping to ally his duchy with such an elf."

"I hope the adage about wine is not true," Cada said. "For the elves say: when the wine runs fine, it runs too well."

"Hovan, is it possible that Gerritt has stirred up the cret'len?" asked Cova.

Hovan took a sip of wine and continued to watch the fire struggle. "I think it so impossible that I had not thought of it before".

"Are you sure?" insisted Cova.

"No, but that is not his way. Beneath him. He attempts to weaken your father's influence. The troubles west are an occurrence he seeks to take advantage of."

The daughters returned their attention to the fire.

The wizard continued. "Though I am human and look no older than the king, I have known your father for many cycles of the Giver. I am away often now. However, I still count your father as a close friend and all his family as well. So, listen to me, you two. Gerritt is not behind the western troubles."

A sarcastic smile lurked under Cova's eyes. She said, "So, you are saying we have two problems to worry about."

"Oh, I think about Gerritt. But not often. Your father has the favor of the king and many others. As long as that is true, there is little Gerritt would risk doing. He speaks poorly of Lord Ke'en because he fears an elf on the throne. In my opinion, there is no better candidate."

"Shar has returned," said Cada. "Excuse me while I get her a glass of wine and see if Captain Laexa needs anything."

Cova's hand continued to rest on Hovan's arm.

Hovan said, "Perceptive of your sister to leave."

"Duke Tober's sons have no appeal to me." She gave Hovan's arm a gentle squeeze.

"I am pleased that you listen so closely to what you hear."

"Yes, I know. Knowledge is power."

Chapter 15

The Western Expedition

Hovan stood on the ridge next to Ke'en, looking into the mist. Nestled in the shallow valley below them, the River Ke ran full from snow melt and early growing season rain. The heavy breathing of the men and orvbacs seemed to give birth to this gray fog, which lay like a blanket over the soldiers of Shetteca. The hovering cloud, born from melting snow and warming weather, slowed their progress with its untimely arrival. Bivouacked at the north ford of the River Ke for two visits of the Giver, they organized supplies and waited for companies to arrive, including the king with Lady Velina and their guard. The cloud needed to clear. Fording the river, flowing strong, would be difficult enough without the fog.

"We aim for Teardrop Lake!" Lord Ke'en said as he stood on the small hill looking down. "Nature slows us. The Giver does not shine on our departure. Should we pick a different direction? Its name and its history cast a shadow over us."

Hovan felt the tension in his friend and tried to reassure him. He could not see the river below. Adversaries could approach with little warning. But sentries with longbows stationed along the river bank would see enough to know if someone had taken up position on the far bank. Anyone who might challenge the force from Shetteca would deal with the same problems.

"Our victory may change its name. People of Arre'ielle have not stood on the shores of that lake for ten cold seasons. I still advise we loop north toward Teardrop Lake, then turn south and west towards Lordic's Wall."

"Confident as ever, I see, Wizard."

The wizard pulled the hood of his cloak up over his blond hair. "We are only hunting cret'len."

"Only cret'len. Neither of us believes that. Is it wisdom or age that casts a doubt in our minds?"

"Experience, a mixture of both."

"Yes, an enemy and his friends... as the saying goes."

"If the cret'len are wise, they are already running," said Hovan.

"You know what Ti'ek would say to that."

Hovan chuckled, imagining Ti'ek's humorous protest of using cret'len and wise in the same sentence.

The fog stayed with them until the Giver set that night. However, when the Giver returned, the fog, like the snow, was mostly gone, leaving a gray, overcast sky. Hovan hoped to cross the river after one more night's wait.

Mounted on his orvbac, the wizard watched and waited on the hillside until it was time for the cavalry of Forestton to cross the ford. Laexa and Ti'ek were close by. Captain Vay would lead Forestton into the river. One by one, the companies descended to the ford and began the crossing. Forestton was next. Hovan had positioned Forestton well ahead of the king's crossing. He wanted Forestton and a wizard in position on the far side before King Dargladre entered the river, just in case. The scouts had found no evidence of cret'len, or anything else, nearby. Still, as Laexa would say, be cautious and prepared when circumstances allow. He expected a mental contact from both Lady Velina and Lord Ke'en, making a final safety check before the king forded the river.

Hovan rode clear of the cold water and climbed the river bank. Captain Vay sat on his orvbac in the field along the road, watching the line of soldiers moving into Feleine. His dark yellow eyes smoldering above his high cheekbones were the only emotion visible in his stoic military frame.

The wizard pulled his orvbac out of the line and stopped next to his captain. "Welcome home, Captain Vay."

"It has been too long since Arre'ielle was here, Lord." The husky tone of his voice betrayed his emotions. "This is not home if we do not live here and these creatures do. I am not sure if I want to ride any further into the district I grew up in. And see her suffering. I both fear and desire to see my house, if it still stands. We should reclaim her for Arre'ielle. We should, Lord Wizard."

"I look forward to the rebirth of Feleine. However, we travel with fewer numbers than we need for that. Do not underestimate the toll the war took on Arre'ielle. This is not the time. I share your pain, Captain. Though this was not home, I had friends here." Lord Hovan looked at his captain. "Remember why we are here. To protect Forestton and Shetteca."

Captain Vay nodded. "Yes, Lord Wizard."

The wizard lowered his voice. "Look. The king prepares to return to Feleine. Hope! The king hopes too."

The captain looked at the wizard, then at the river, and nodded again.

"Return to Forestton's banner, Captain," said Lord Hovan. "Stay alert. We must keep the king safe and have a successful return to Feleine. Let us feed his hope!"

Captain Vay walked his orvbac forward, heading toward the dark green banner of Forestton waving in the wind. His visage bore an uncomfortable contradiction of stoicism and tears.

Once across the River Ke, the orvbacaans and the soldiers from Shetteca spread out, searching the abandoned buildings and fields. The force moved only as fast as they could secure each area.

Plundered, damaged, burned, decaying.

"It is difficult to look at this," said Ti'ek.

Hovan shook his head in agreement. "The desolate, broken condition of the buildings and houses is heartbreaking. I knew some of the people who lived here."

"I hope Lordic's Wall is in better shape."

"It should be. Magic helped build the wall."

Scouts in pairs began returning from their assigned rides through Feleine. The Wizard Hovan rode under the Forestton banner so that the scouts could easily find him. Having planned their routes, he debriefed each upon their return. A map folded in an inner pocket collected notations.

Frustration grew in the wizard as the force left Teardrop Lake. The cret'len had to be found. The quick find Hovan had hoped for had not materialized.

"Something is not as you thought," teased Ti'ek. "Wizard, what has come of all your planning?"

"Something is not as I hoped," countered the wizard. "As loud and slow moving as we are, the cret'len could easily avoid us. It may take some time to search Feleine. I still wish to teach them to avoid the farms I protect. Better would be to convince them to move to the other side of the mountains. They may be south of the ford. There is excellent land there. Though I expect to find some sign before we reach Lordic's Wall."

Three visits of the Giver after fording the river, the tall, wide wall came into sight. In quiet dominance, Lordic's Wall stood in silence as if waiting for their arrival. Undamaged, looking much as it did when Arre'ielle's forces left, yet with small plants growing in places they should not be. Unlike the wall, the large metal gates, which allowed passage through the tunnel in the fortification, had not survived intact. Beaten and askew, they remained wedged in the open position.

King Dargladre, joined by Lord Ke'en and the wizards Velina and Hovan, climbed the stone stairs to the top of Lordic's Wall. King Dargladre looked not at the hills rising to become mountains, but at the lost district of Feleine gradually dropping away from the wall to the unseen River Ke valley beyond the rolling hills.

"When did a king last stand here?" King Dargladre said. "It must have been desperation and agony for my father to concede all this and withdraw."

"We had no hope of holding it. We barely held Shetteca."

"I know, Lord Ke'en. I have been taught." The king looked at his mentor and spoke as if reciting a lesson. "Called Lordic's Wall after the district leader who began the incredible project of a protective wall along the entire western edge of the Feleine."

King Dargladre looked along the wall, stretching away south. He then followed the line of wall running away north. "What foresight! A brilliant achievement by the people of Feleine and indeed all of Arre'ielle. To stand here upon this great wall, which had protected this district for generations, fills me with pride and immense sadness. We travel past these homes and villages left to cret'len and worse. To look out over this beautifully melancholy land...can we hope?"

"We can hope," said Hovan. "Many do. When Arre'ielle is prepared, I will be honored to help reclaim the district."

"A subtle way of saying that we are not yet ready, Lord Wizard," commented the king.

Ke'en answered for him. "Not yet. But we have hope!"

They moved toward the stairs, except for Hovan. He stood still as if listening.

"Something?" asked Ke'en.

"There is only a trace of magic left stored in the wall. I was not one of the wizards defending the wall, protecting the retreat. They must have exhausted it trying to fight off the attack. So much magic used. I can almost feel their desperation. I remember Shetteca. Imagine the effort it would take to restore it."

Ke'en put his hand on his taller friend's shoulder. "Shetteca survived. Feleine waits to be reborn."

They retreated down the stairs. In case something wandered through during the night, they set up camp well away from the gates.

When the Giver began sharing her light in the morning, the companies retraced their steps, intending to leave the gate village and search south. Two scouts came galloping down the road to the Forestton cavalry.

"My Lord Wizard, we have found them!" Mehannen, the older of the two scouts, brought her orvbac to a halt as she bowed to the wizard.

"Where?!"

Ti'ek and both captains of Forestton stopped with the wizard to hear the report.

"Moving through the foothills in the north triangle of Feleine. By now, I estimate they are near Talon Lake."

"They come from the north," muttered the wizard. Looking at Ti'ek, he added, "Just further north than I thought." Turning back to the scout, Hovan repeated, "Near Talon Lake?"

"Yes, Lord Wizard. They are a large group. We could not observe them for long."

The wizard pulled his creased map from the pocket of his hooded cloak. One finger slid down the map, connecting two unmarked points.

"They are nearly behind us!" Hovan met the eyes of the scouts. "They are not alone."

"No."

"What is their number? What else travels with them?"

"Besides several hundred cret'len, most on wolf back, we spotted Belingus and ogres. There is more we did not see."

"Well done." Grinning at Ti'ek, the wizard said, "Well, Prince, now what do you think of my plans?"

"Even a blind, furry tree climber finds a nut now and again."

Hovan shook his head in humorous disbelief. "Let us speak with your father. Please let him know we are coming. Captain Vay, you have command."

At a fast trot, the wizard moved up the line from Forestton's spot to the king's protected position in the middle. Ke'en stopped his orvbac off the road and waited. The king followed his lead, joined by the Wizard Velina.

"We found them," announced Hovan. "They are not alone. They are not where we look."

"Captains," bellowed the district leader. "Halt!"

While the companies came to a stop, Lord Ke'en, the wizards, and the king discussed the new information. Pointing to his map, Hovan showed the estimated position and course.

Ke'en asked, "What other scouts could confirm this report?"

"Teridan, but he and his partner have not yet returned," said Hovan. "That worries me. They should have finished their route before Mehannen. I fear now that they will not return."

"I do not think it is a coincidence that they are behind us," said Ke'en. "The question is: Are they heading for the river or for us?"

"I think us," offered Hovan.

"We will intercept them, so it does not matter," said Lady Velina.

Hovan noted the finality in her tone.

How like the captain of the Wizard's Corp to not ask for an opinion.

"Agreed," said King Dargladre. "If they are behind us by design, that would imply that we are being watched. They must know our number. And yet you think they come for us?"

Ke'en nodded. "Our surprise may be gone."

"They may not expect us to turn and close on them," said Hovan. "We may yet have surprise. Or at least, choice of location to attack."

"Then we need to move quick," said Velina.

Hovan added. "That far north, the forest may still be first growth: large trees with sparse undergrowth. Room for orvbacs to maneuver, but wolves may still be quicker. More thoughts, Majesty?"

The young king responded. "Yes. Stay quiet and let you work. I would think, though, that the forest will provide many blind spots."

"Well noted, Majesty," answered Ke'en. "We bring more force to bear. Our training should allow us to maintain proper structure. Surprise, if we can achieve it, and the hills will help us. We may have to hunt down scattering bands once we have turned back the initial thrust."

The district leader turned to his son. "Inform the captains of the new orders."

As Ti'ek rode off, Hovan watched Ke'en watching his son. A smile graced the district leader's lips. Hovan turned his orvbac to join Laexa, waiting at a respectful distance. As he passed Ke'en, he teased, "Careful he does not get your job".

The district leader laughed and smiled. "He may, in time. If all goes well."

Hovan rode toward the Forestton banner. "Laexa, tell me what you think of this. What do you suggest?"

"To quote a humorous young elf, we ride."

The forest canopy spread out high overhead, creating the shadows through which Hovan, Laexa, and Ti'ek crept. Hidden by the tree's eclipses, they navigated up the valley, progressing slower than expected, in and around a mix of wide, brown tree trunks and bright green saplings. Certainly, the Shettecan squads scouting the valley on either side were moving no faster. Cavalry could still move quicker in the spaces between the massive trees. However, the towering columns of tree trunks provided plenty of places an enemy could hide behind. The young trees and ferns trying to secure their place in the old forest provided cover where a cret'len or wolf could lie concealed.

Hovan led the way, using his short staff to move aside small branches. Laexa followed next with her curved sword in her right hand, ready. Ti'ek stepped over a fallen log and stayed close behind. They crept to the edge of a broad, gently rising clearing. Hesitant to move into the open, they squatted down.

The field of crumpled, tan grasses surrounded a few tall cember trees. Hovan knew these tall grasses would shimmer golden and stretch halfway up to his blond hair when fed by the long visits of the Giver in the growing season. Twisted and bent by this past cold season's wind and snow, the broken stalks did not reach the knees of his pants. Green shoots of the new growing season were not yet visible. The tall cember trees, blackened near their base by fires, towered above the slumbering grasses, waiting until twice a man's height to spread wide their branches, which swayed slowly in the breeze gliding down from the northwest. They stood apart from each other, forming islands of branches amidst the meadow. Reddish buds and small leaves of light green denoted that they woke up from the cold season sooner than the grasses. The meadow stretched away toward the peak of a ridge, where the evergreen trees regained dominance before dropping away down the other side.

The chilly breeze, almost unnoticed as they had moved up the leeward side of the ridge, played with their hair as they hid near the edge of the meadow. Straining to see between the trees across the clearing, Hovan flared his nostrils, trying to take in more air.

"What do your elf senses tell you?" asked Hovan.

"They cannot be far," Ti'ek whispered. "There is a faint stink mixed with the breeze. They may even be watching us now."

"No," answered the wizard. "The shadows hide us. The wind is with us, and we are expecting them, but not them us. Laexa and I will cross. Cover us should anything appear."

Hovan's hands weaved a flying spell, which he placed on Laexa. Then he crafted one for himself. He also formed an invisibility spell for Laexa before turning on his ring. Together, they sped across the meadow, not needing to touch the ground.

Hovan contacted Ti'ek and gave him the all clear.

Ti'ek then flew across the meadow. Pushing through saplings, he crouched down.

They crept over the ridge, through a stand of evergreens, and moved down the hill. The sounds of harsh voices rose from the bottom of the valley. The man, the woman, and the elf froze and exchanged looks, acknowledging that each had heard the sounds. Hovan held a hand up as he inspected the immediate surroundings.

Waiting while the wizard searched, Ti'ek checked his magic. Laexa's head turned from side to side, scanning, suspicious of the shadows.

Finding what he wanted, the wizard crept off to his left and downhill. Using the shadows and tree trunks as cover, the three meandered their way past the trees and fallen logs.

Sunlight flashed off a piece of the speckled, gray bedrock along a steeper section of the ridge. The exposed stone jumped down the ridge and quickly dove back under the blanket of soil and trees where it resumed a more gradual, hidden descent.

Concealed in the shade behind the bedrock, Hovan peered down into the valley. Beyond the descending curve of trees, the sparkling of a pond reflected the lighter blue of the sky off a softly rippled surface. Ti'ek and Laexa came up behind Hovan and kneeled next to him. Together, the three watched the sundry creatures moving under the trees near the pond below.

Many rider wolves, the fur on their backs matted down, had collected near a small cove. Resting or waiting, they used the opportunity to get a drink. Some of the cret'len kneeled and joined their steeds for a drink of water. The brown hair, which topped their heads, encircled their bodies and went down their short legs. Many wore leather vests. Belingus, as tall as an elf, collected water in skins. All carried swords and bows.

"Note the equipment," said Laexa.

"They seem well outfitted for this expedition," said Ti'ek. "Perhaps they too are faring better in this time of economic prosperity."

"Ogres with metal tipped spears, by the look of it," said Laexa.

"Ogres are not known for their smelting," noted Hovan. "Is the metal from the Belingus or someone else?"

Hovan touched minds with the Wizard Velina and Lord Ke'en, relaying the picture. Hovan stayed on one knee, his staff secured in the quiver diagonally across his back, watching those on the near side of the pond.

"What are you planning?" asked Ti'ek through a smile.

"Those on this side are tightly grouped. A few big spells will kill many and scatter the rest. The district leader will have time to bring his forces forward and hold this ridge." Hovan added, "They are not expecting a thing."

"I knew there was a reason you wanted to do this yourself," Ti'ek said. "I will check with my father to see if he has other plans."

Ti'ek was quiet for a moment. "He agrees and is organizing units to move forward." Ti'ek looked down at the creatures below. "Why not try to scare them off? Cause confusion? Violent by necessity, not by nature, as you say."

"A borrowed saying."

"I do not think they are here to be frightened," said Laexa.

"We can try if you wish," offered Hovan. "I respect the noble thought. I do not mind if they run away as long as they run far. Aim high."

Almost simultaneously, the hands of the wizard and the prince jumped into near identical sequences. Moving through revolutions in practiced motions, they molded orbs of fire in front of them. Hovan finished first. A sharp jab forward with his open palm launched the sphere. It raced around tree trunks, descending into the valley. The globe from Ti'ek followed close behind.

The booming tandem blasts destroyed the quiet of the forest. Tree trunks ignited and charred. Splashes came as branches blown off trees landed in the water, destroying the reflection of the sky. Cries of surprise carried up the ridge, rushing from the area as the rumbles spread out over the forest. The yells and howls continued after the booms decrescendo. Belingus and cret'len and wolves scattered in all directions.

Chapter 16

The Meadow

Ti'ek watched the confusion near the pond with a hunter's smile below his green eyes.

A singular roar, deep and loud, with a volume beyond that of any ogre, sprang up from the valley below, seeming to shake the leaves with its fierceness, wrapping the hills in its intensity.

The prince's smile vanished. "What was that!? Dragons do not live here!"

"No, they do not!" stated Hovan. "And a dragon would not be below us. Come, we must move!"

The wizard and the captain sprinted away.

Ti'ek lingered, wanting to spot whatever had produced that unintimidated challenge.

His father mentally contacted him. *"Be quick! Stay with the wizard! I will be there soon!"*

The young elf rose to follow Hovan. Ti'ek's defensive magic flashed red and deflected an arrow. The rush of motion from behind caused the elf to spin, reflexively drawing his curved sword. Three Belingus ran at him while a fourth launched another arrow which the elf's magic turned aside. Ti'ek deflected the first sword thrust, spinning past the attacker and slicing him in the side. The elf stepped into the second opponent, parrying his sword, and elbowed his face, dropping him. He exchanged parries with the third, keeping him between the archer, who had dropped his bow and joined the fight. A cry of pain burst from the elf's lips. He collapsed onto the ground.

Laexa appeared at his side and deflected the sword thrust aimed at the prince's neck. She dropped the Belingus with a slash to the abdomen. Spheres of fire sped past him. The fire darts collided with the two Belingus in front of Ti'ek and the one behind him, who had rolled onto one knee and sliced the prince's left leg from behind. More fire darts hit the four Belingus, ensuring that none of them would rise.

Hovan kneeled next to Ti'ek, who was clutching a gash in his hamstring. "Bad?"

"Bad enough," winced Ti'ek. "I cannot run."

Laexa stood guard, sword drawn, eyes searching. "We cannot stay here!"

Hovan encased the wound with both hands. "A quick healing spell. All we have time for, but it should stop the bleeding. Your flying spell should still be active. Use it! We must move!"

"What did you tell my father?" asked Ti'ek. "What scared him!?"

"Move!" commanded Laexa. "Talk later."

Voices and the snapping of a twig ended the whispered conversation. Hovan grabbed Ti'ek under an armpit, urging him off the ground and to fly up the ridge.

The thump, thump of arrows embedding in trees and the ground came from the forest behind them.

Ti'ek grimaced and fought to stay quiet. He was only partially successful. Grasping his leg with both hands, he hoped to stop the thin covering that the wizard had put over the wound from breaking open. Unfocused because of the pain, Ti'ek tried to speed up the ridge, but moved just above the ground, no faster than the wizard. Ti'ek noted the wizard ran up the ridge just behind him, but would not pass him. Laexa followed, her head in constant motion, scanning the trees, sword point following her eyes. Beads of perspiration rolled down the elf's forehead into his eyes. Sharp, tortured gasps of pain staggered from his throat as a small bough slapped his leg.

Thump, thump, thump.

Someone is coming with friends.

Before they reached the top of the ridge, the prince drifted to the ground. Pain overwhelmed his focus. He lost touch with the flying magic. Suppressed moans of pain escaped with heavy breaths.

Hovan examined the wound. Blood dripped and collected on the ground beneath the wound. He cut a piece of cloth and tied it around the blood stained pants and leg. The wizard gripped the gash with two hands to close the wound again.

"I can do no more now," said Hovan.

Please, no poison.

Thump, thump, thump. Urgency, which did not need to be voiced, demanded they move.

As Ti'ek struggled to his feet, Hovan threw an arm around the elf's back and one under his rump and lifted his smaller friend. He jumped off the ground, carrying the elf into the air. Laexa ran behind them.

A howl sprang up below. Yells joined the baying.

Once past the ridge's peak, Hovan lowered Ti'ek to one leg. They stood near the edge of the clearing. It was empty and seemed safe to enter.

"Go on across," said Ti'ek. "You cannot out run or out fly the wolves while carrying me."

"You return to your father," commanded the wizard. "Connect to the flying magic. Go now!"

"The wolves have found my blood. They will be here in moments. Leave me your ring. I will slow them down."

"Your trail is not one the wolves track by sight," said Laexa. "An invisibility ring is of no use! Fly now!"

"Your father is coming," said Hovan. "I cannot leave!"

"Why not?"

"Stop arguing!" demanded Laexa. "Go!"

Hovan scooped the elf into his arms again. He ran as fast as he could into the meadow. At an awkward run, Hovan headed for the largest cember tree near the middle.

Branches snapping, leaves crunching, and running footsteps chased them from behind.

Ti'ek saw drops of sweat seeping down the wizard's face. His eyes appeared unaffected by the strain, but only because the elf knew the wizard's thoughts were far away, reliving memories of his wife in danger and in need of help. One the wizard could not save. Ti'ek knew Hovan would save him or die trying.

And again, the prince felt the wave of guilt and loss that he had failed his friend and not helped protect Suzhanee.

The wizard carried him, though Ti'ek could feel the wizard's arms slowly sinking under his weight. Ti'ek looked back over Hovan's shoulder. Wolves carrying cret'len raced out of the forest. His eyes went wide as he tensed in fear. As his knee twitched, a wave of pain shot up his leg and spread throughout his body. He grasped the back of Hovan's cloak, fighting down the pain. A morbid thought shot through his mind.

This is not a bad place to die.

Laexa yelled, "Wolf riders!" She sheathed her sword and grabbed her bow off her back.

The wizard staggered to a halt. He placed Ti'ek next to the tree and turned to face the riders.

Ti'ek shot whistling flares of turquoise and green high into the air.

The Shettecan scouts must be nearby.

He released more flares.

<hr>

King Dargladre watched the bursts of green and turquoise sparkle above the trees farther up the valley.

"Stay next to me, please, Majesty," said the Wizard Velina.

King Dargladre did not ignore the urgency in Velina's voice. He directed a soldier to take the reins of his orvbac. "What do those sparks mean?"

"Turquoise is for Shetteca and Prince Ti'ek. Dark green is for Forestton, meaning the Wizard Hovan. They are calling for help. The sparks went up together. One is down or busy."

Velina's face went blank. "The fools. They attacked before Lord Ke'en had moved forward to support them."

"The Wizard Hovan?"

"Yes, Majesty. Prince Ti'ek has a deep gash in his leg and cannot run. Lord Hovan and Captain Laexa are protecting him."

"We move to help," said the king.

"The cavalry of Shetteca and Forestton are far closer and moving. I suggest we wait to see where we can best use our forces."

"Meaning, keep the king safe."

"Yes, that is the priority. Hovan has reported Belingus and ogres with the mounted cret'len. If the creature that made that roar appears, I will magic you to Avi'ot."

"Return to your father!" The wizard's right hand pointed, and five flashes leapt from his hand, one from each finger. His left hand mirrored the action. Another red cluster of five shot across the meadow toward the wolf riders. The wolves cut left or right, but not fast enough. Wolves came up short, tossing their riders, who met their own orbs of fire. Laexa's bow sang short, quick songs. After two more volleys from the wizard, the remaining riders sprinted back to the safety of the trees. The enemy, though, was not out of sight.

More cret'len on wolf back, joined by the larger Belingus, stood in the shadows of the forest. The Belingus raised their bows, smiling as they aimed.

Ti'ek hobbled behind the large cember tree, using the tree as both cover and support. The wizard, however, took two steps away from the tree and stood tall, the short staff stored in the quiver diagonally across his back. His chest rose and fell in long, measured breaths.

The Belingus hesitated. When nothing happened, they smiled again and drew back the strings of their bows. Arrows met the red defensive magic of Hovan and Laexa and deflected in all directions. The Belingus stopped smiling and fired again. Chaotically, the arrows bounced away from the protected wizard and captain. Frustrated, they did not draw arrows for a third attack.

Hovan raised his hands and stretched his magic into the shape of a thick rod. The rod wriggled to life. The wizard released first one, then two, then three flaming snakes, which hissed, slithering rapidly through the air toward the forest. Belingus and cret'len jumped behind trees. Before reaching the woods, the magical serpents stretched out to the full length of their bodies, turned sideways, and dove to the ground. The dried grasses along the edge of the meadow ignited with a flash of smoke.

"Captain, take the prince and run!" yelled Hovan.

"No!" Laexa said. "I leave when you leave!"

"I must stay. You know it!"

"I know. Prince, save yourself! Get to your father."

"And leave you?" asked Ti'ek. He did not move.

How could I abandon you to save myself? You are my friends. I failed to help protect Suzhanee, and she had died. I am supposed to leave you two to fight this threat without me? No!

Ti'ek saw the cret'len and Belingus through a haze of light smoke, low flames, and twisting hot air currents creeping out from behind the safety of the trees. Six Belingus approached the line of fire and were preparing to jump it when a deep voice from further back in the woods made them wait.

Ti'ek pressed himself against the back of the tree, making himself as small as possible. He knew the flames were nothing more than a stalling action. Hopefully, their calls for help would be answered soon.

"Come, Wizard, while we have a chance to escape," said the prince. "I can fly a short way."

"Leave!" yelled Hovan. "You are third to the throne!"

The stalks of grass crackled in the flames. Wind seethed through the branches overhead. Ti'ek heard the voices and movement of the enemy from across the meadow. Angered and scared by the wizard's stubbornness, Ti'ek vented his frustration and fright.

"You cannot hold them all off by yourself!"

"Go to your father!" insisted the wizard. "I must stay here! Go!"

A bass voice commanded something of the Belingus and cret'len in a language Ti'ek did not understand. He sensed the power in the voice and knew it expected to be obeyed. Someone of power had come.

"Suzhanee would not want you to die like this!" said Ti'ek. "Save yourself, Wizard."

"Yes, she would! What is the matter, Prince? Do you think a wizard cannot protect you?!"

Stunned by the vengeance thrown with the question, Ti'ek did not argue further. The anguish it revealed reminded him of a time, a few short growing seasons past, when Hovan would have welcomed a day like this. Fighting whatever was coming would silence for a time the doubt and pain festering in his mind until they dug their way back into his consciousness again. Or ended his life.

Ti'ek saw the wizard standing focused on the trees, hands ready for magic. Captain Laexa's bow had an arrow nocked, waiting.

"Prince Ti'ek, retreat," said Lord Ke'en. "That is an order!"

"The wizard is not leaving. Nor is his protector. Why are you ordering me to leave?"

Damn my leg!

"Withdraw!" Lord Ke'en repeated the command. "Now!"

The eldest child of Shetteca, in line for the throne of Arre'ielle itself, and injured. My rank should be an advantage! Not a disadvantage.

Ti'ek tested his wounded leg and collapsed against the tree in agony. The elf cried out in pain and frustration, for himself and for his friend, who suffered as much as he did, though in a different way. He slammed his fist against the tree trunk. Cheers and sadistic laughter reached his ears.

If I leave, maybe they will as well.

Ti'ek struggled into a standing position, no longer concerned whether his gasps of pain revealed his location. Strengthened by desperation, he controlled the flying spell and lifted himself off the ground. He flew toward the edge of the clearing.

The elf prince hesitated. It felt disloyal, cowardly. He hid among the trees, out of immediate danger, he hoped.

Hovan and Laexa stood tense, ready to respond to whatever entered the clearing.

Along the far edge of the meadow, the fire still burned, adding a blackened scent to the breeze. Smoke and flame danced in rising air currents, mixing with the light from the Giver. Belingus and cret'len gathered behind the narrow barrier of flames. Towering ogres joined. Something even larger further back came, which Ti'ek could not see clearly enough to identify.

A dark haired man, surely the source of the booming command, stood with the ogres. His dark coat, the color of his long hair, made him difficult to see in the shadows. A long sword hung from his belt. He held a round, metal shield in his left hand. Watching the clearing intently, this man swept his right hand forward. Two ogres jumped the flames and charged. He pointed to the Belingus. They launched a volley of arrows.

Hovan's hands sprang into motion and returned fire. Large darts flew toward the ogres. They exploded, one for each of the ogres' legs. The ogres tumbled forward with loud thuds and growls of pain. Enraged, they rose to their feet and charged again.

Laexa targeted the archers, firing in rapid succession.

More fire darts from Hovan slammed into the ogres. This time, they did not rise.

"I am safely in the forest," said Ti'ek. *"Leave, Hovan. The mind wills what the body cannot deliver. There are too many!"*

If Hovan heard any of Ti'ek's soliloquy, he made no response. Ti'ek, still hiding in the forest along the meadow's edge, saw the wizard tense. The young elf's eyes went wide with fear when he saw what stepped out from the trees.

May the One we serve protect us!

A bipedal creature covered in short fur, a brindle of green and brown, moved to the edge of the clearing. The gorzyne, towering above the height of a man standing on another man's shoulders, carried no weapon. It needed none. With its large, curved claws, the powerful jaws of its protruding muzzle, and its muscular tail, the large carnivore feared nothing less than a dragon. It towered over even the ogres. Green eyes, slit by a vertical, black pupil, looked at the wizard as if he were dinner.

"*Gorzyne!*" Ti'ek screamed in his mind to his father. "*A gorzyne!*"

"*I know. I heard the roar. May the One they serve protect Hovan and Laexa. Retreat!*"

A sonorous growl pulsated, vibrating the ground. The pounding of massive feet charging shook the field.

"Cover me!" yelled Hovan. The wizard took a half step back, turning his right foot ninety degrees. His hands began a pattern.

Ti'ek stopped watching the wizard. The prince's hands sprang into motion.

Help us now and ever after.

Ti'ek prayed as he launched handful after handful of fire darts toward the archers. He sent another quick image to his father and a brief message to Hovan.

"*I am sorry to see you fail to live forever. The Giver shines on your effort, though darkness approaches. Good bye, my friend.*"

As if in answer, a crisp, piercing detonation thundered across the meadow. A stroke of white lightning, sizzling through the air, met the gorzyne at the waist and continued into the forest. The thunderclap dulled all other sounds, casting a momentary silence over the meadow. Two young tree trunks, sliced off their bases, hung for a moment as if in shock before falling forward. They crashed into other trees, snapping and knocking limbs out of their path before landing with a crash.

The prince's jaw dropped open, and his eyes went wide in shock the instant after they had shrunk because of exposure to the blazing streak of light. It took several moments for his eyes to adjust.

"*You doubt a wizard?!*" Hovan mentally yelled at Ti'ek. "*Wizards have ways. Suzhanee would be proud of me!*"

Two clearly recognizable halves of the fur covered monster lay twitching and smoldering, bloodying the meadow several feet apart. The smell of charred meat drifted on the breeze, adding to the scent of burning grass.

The man stood at the edge of the clearing. He waved his arm. Wolf riders and Belingus and ogres hesitantly joined him. Pointing toward the wizard and captain, he uttered some harsh commands. The man let out a yell and ran forward. Wolves carrying their cret'len riders jumped the line of dying flames and accelerated to a sprint, followed by Belingus running, and the slower ogres.

The wizard released clusters of fire darts. Prince Ti'ek added more. The two friends fired as fast as they could! Laexa, out of arrows, waited, sword in hand, near Hovan. Wolves tumbled to a stop, but others came.

The elf sighed.

Too many.

More wolves fell, though their cret'len riders rose to continue the charge.

A blue glow appeared in front of the man, absorbing the two fire darts Ti'ek aimed at him.

Large balls of fire collided with two ogres.

"Target the ogres! We have a chance against everything else."

The final two ogres fell, thrown back by fiery blasts from both the wizard and the prince.

The man and Belingus continued their charge.

Ti'ek fired as fast as he could, though the elf could not match the speed of the wizard. The rapid pulses of fire darts hit the assault like waves striking the bow of a ship. Slowed, but not stopped. At least, targeting the cret'len on their quick wolves provided a few extra moments to fire more spells before the sprinting Belingus could cross the meadow.

Laexa moved in front of the wizard. She side stepped and sliced a Belingus, dropping him. She intercepted the man, preventing him from reaching Hovan. Ti'ek heard the clash of their swords as he noted three Belingus moving to surround his friends.

Ti'ek saw Hovan pull his short staff from his quiver, now reducing to staff fighting.

The safest way to attack a wizard. Hand to hand combat with the advantage of numbers.

Other Belingus moved to help the man outnumber Laexa.

Ti'ek targeted two of the Belingus heading toward the wizard.

I will not fail you again, my friend!

His next hand of fire darts dropped two Belingus moving toward Laexa. Ti'ek fired spells, trying to keep his friends from being overwhelmed.

Laexa was being driven back toward Hovan. Ti'ek noted she would not give up her position between the man and the wizard.

Hovan parried sword thrusts, circled off line, seeking an opening to drop his opponent.

More Belingus ran to the attack.

Ti'ek saw three of the Belingus fall, pierced by arrows in their chests. Two more arrows found their mark. The prince kept firing, hoping the miraculous source of the arrows was archers dressed in Shettecan turquoise.

We may get out of this yet!

Laexa gave more ground as the man used his strength advantage. His blue magic shield stopped the fire darts from Ti'ek.

A Belingus threw something at the wizard's feet. Hovan stumbled. The Belingus used the opening to slice his side.

Hovan cried out in pain and fell to one knee.

"Hovan!" screamed Ti'ek.

Ti'ek's spell dropped the Belingus who cut him. Hovan parried the strike from the other.

A yell answered from the woods behind.

"SHETTECA!"

The pounding of hooves grew closer. Orvbacs accelerated into the clearing, led by Lord Ke'en and Captain Vay. They charged across the clearing, the hooves of the orvbacs throwing pieces of frozen ground into the air behind them. Captain Vay's hand waved toward the wizard. The Forestton cavalry galloped, the riders in front standing in the stirrups to shoot arrows.

The Belingus near Hovan turned and sprinted toward the trees, trying to outrun the orvbacs. The wizard stayed on one knee, clutching his side.

Ti'ek focused his fire darts on the man still engaged with Laexa. He had not abandoned his attempt to reach the wizard. The man had forced Laexa back to the kneeling Wizard. The blue shield of the man was collapsing, but still protective.

Captain Vay yelled commands to the Forestton lieutenant. They slowed and directed their orvbacs to lower their heads. The spiral horns of the orvbacs passed close by the wizard and Laexa, one on each side.

Respecting the horns, the man backed away, his sword and shield held in fighting posture. Laexa signaled for him to drop his weapon. Frustrated, he growled defiance. He dodged right toward Captain Vay, then left, attempting to get around the orvbac's horns.

He failed. The orvbac threw the gored man to the ground.

More orvbacs galloped past Ti'ek, thundering into the field. Lord Ke'en directed a protective line of orvbacs form across the meadow. Archers took up positions behind.

Hovan, using his staff as a crutch, one arm wrapped around his abdomen, walked over to the bloodied man lying motionless. The wizard looked down.

Eyes noted his arrival, though no other part of the damaged body moved. Blood seeped out from around the man's arms that clinched his abdomen as if trying to hold squeeze the wounds closed.

"Why?" asked the wizard.

The only response he received was a weak grin as the man mumbled.

"No," said Hovan. "Magic will not heal that."

The man coughed once, interrupting his mumbling. His eyes slid closed just before his breathing stopped.

Ti'ek floated over to Hovan and Laexa. "We make a formidable trio."

The prince tried to sound upbeat, but could not force a smile. His leg throbbed. The magic had tired him. Ti'ek got no response from Hovan, who leaned on his staff with a faraway look smoldering in his blue eyes and breaths coming in long draws.

Reliving the loss of Suzhanee again.

The district leader rode to his son.

"As long as the wound is not poisoned," said Ti'ek in answer to his father's anxious look.

"Contact your mother once the healers have checked you."

Ke'en made eye contact with the wizard. "How bad?"

"I am not dead," Hovan said in an emotionless tone.

"Good. Keep it that way." Ke'en rode off, joining the cavalry preparing to advance into the forest and down the ridge.

Laexa checked Ti'ek's leg over. "Glad you are still in one piece. When a wizard says run, you run!"

"So noted," said Ti'ek.

Laexa turned to Hovan. "Let me see."

Hovan waved her off. "I stopped the bleeding with magic."

Soldiers and riders filled the meadow. Many pushed into the forest on the far side of the clearing.

Ti'ek heard screams, yells, and the sounds of fighting from over the ridge.

I cannot help you more today, Father. I am sorry.

Laexa looked at Ti'ek and then around the clearing at the many fallen bodies and the two halves of the gorzyne. "We are good."

"A gorzyne, Laexa!" stated Ti'ek. "Here! They controlled it."

Laexa nodded her head in agreement. "Good thing he was here." She tilted her head toward the wizard.

Hovan breathed out slowly. "That is why I said run."

Healers arrived to treat the wounds of Ti'ek and Hovan. Soldiers lifted them onto orvbacs for the trip back down the valley.

CHAPTER 17

PAIN

T he sweat on the wizard's face and back chilled him. The sounds of fighting faded behind him as he rode an orvbac, slumped sideways in the saddle because of the wound in his side. He rode at a slow walk down the valley, one arm clutching his side, following Laexa's orvbac without thinking. Healers had sealed the wound and stabilized the rib, which was broken. The bleeding had stopped. But not the pain; that was only lessened.

He did not care.

Reflections of the past glittered at him from every object he saw. In his mind's eye, screams erupted, fire was everywhere, and a lone woman cried for his help. The shrieks of a young woman, brown hair flying in the wind, echoed around the wizard's mind, closing his ears to all other sounds. The acute feelings of fear and doubt and longing and pain reverberated through his waking nightmare. He wanted to cry. Perhaps he did. Or sweat drops rolled down his cheek. The memories were triggered again.

* * *

Hovan lay in his hammock under a blanket. The healers had wrapped his side, supporting the broken rib. Using magic, they stopped the pain caused by the injuries they could see. The wizard's eyes focused on the white clouds drifting through a sea of blue overhead. Their shapes all perverted themselves into some portion of a tragic remembrance. The desperate figure cried in his mind, screamed. Round and round his head the woman's shrieks resonated. Fading low, screaming loud, crying for help. A runaway orvbac galloped on the shrieks, emptying him of all aspirations. Loneliness watched with lifeless eyes as the woman screamed again and again, out of reach.

⸻ ❖ ⸻

The wizard awoke in the dark, still in the hammock. Sleep offered only partial relief, for the visions invaded his dreams when he slept too long. The scene, in agonizing clarity, played itself out in his mind over and over and over again. It always ended with the same excruciating conclusion, the same horrifying failure.

CHAPTER 18

RECOVER

The bright Giver neared the end of her daily appearance. Ti'ek sat with his back propped up against a tree, cleaning and sharpening his weapons. A dark green cloak across his shoulders kept him warm. Laid out on a large cloth next to him were his sword, sheath, daggers with scabbards, quiver, and recurve bow. With a small, fine stone, he honed the points of his arrows. One by one, he picked up an arrow on his left, worked on the point, placed it down on his right, and picked up the next arrow. Thick bandages and splints immobilized his leg. The magic of the healers had silenced the pain, but the leg would not bear his weight.

The soothing smell of the cooking fire combined with the pleasant scent of the soup above it did not ease Ti'ek's yearning to help his father. He knew he would see no more action on this trip. The healer assured him he would walk again, but not after only one night's sleep.

Ti'ek looked over to the other side of the camp. Stretched between two trees, the hammock sagged under the weight of the resting wizard, covered by a thick blanket. Hovan's injuries were less serious. The broken rib would limit his motion. The cut from the sword was more serious.

Ti'ek thanked the One he served that he had dropped the Belingus, allowing Hovan to apply magic to the slice quickly.

Laexa walked out of one of the tents pitched in a semicircle around the central fire. She stirred the pot simmering over the small flames.

"Would you like some soup, Ti'ek?"

"Yes, thank you, Laexa. Get some for the wizard as well."

"I think he is asleep."

"Then wake him up. I am surprised you let him go so long between meals."

"I am his protector. Not his healer." Laexa ladled a thick soup and continued talking. "I play nurse while the battle passes me by."

She walked over to Ti'ek. "Here. Take your soup and spare me your remarks."

"Be careful what you wish for, Laexa. You may get the enemy you wish for, but one with a thousand friends."

"An enemy and his friends, I know. Why must all elves spend their lives collecting clichés?"

"Pieces of distilled wisdom," defended Ti'ek without a hint of acquiescence. "Wizard!"

"What?" came the grumbling response.

"Laexa has some warm soup for you."

"Later."

"No, my liege. You have eaten only two meals by my count since you played hero. Heroes certainly should eat better than that! I owe you my life for your stubbornness. I will not let you waste away. Eat the soup."

Laexa brought a bowl to Hovan. "Off the hammock."

"Let me sleep."

"Get up. If I must play your maid and nurse, you will not give me a hard time about it." She kicked the bottom of the hammock.

Hovan threw his feet over the edge, sat up, and took the bowl of soup. He fed a spoonful into his mouth and stirred before taking another spoonful.

Laexa filled a bowl with soup for herself.

Quiet settled over the camp as they ate.

Ti'ek noticed the lack of hot spices in the thick soup. Spices were the hallmark of Laexa's cooking. He took another swallow. "This is good! Who cooked it?"

Laexa looked over at the prince, but did not respond to the subtle insult.

"Tell me, nurse, when will your patient return to his duties?" asked Ti'ek.

"You? Keep up this bantering, Prince, and the only place you will go is to get your own food."

"I beg your pardon. I was referring to your other esteemed patient."

"You are in good spirits," said Laexa.

"Someone needs to brighten the spirits around here. My injury stops me from riding with my father. Your mood is gray because you are spoiling for a fight. He is intent on reliving past failures despite his brilliant victory!"

Through narrowing eyes, Laexa looked up from her bowl of soup at Ti'ek before glancing at the wizard.

The wizard stopped feeding himself and sat still, watching the ripples in the soup fade away and the cloud's reflection become clearer in the bowl. He hunched over the bowl.

"I should have let you die."

"But you did not, and I thank you for that!" stated Ti'ek. "In return, I will not let you destroy yourself now. Let go of the past, my friend, or it will haunt you to your death. You work ever to forestall death's arrival. Do not regret that you live. Celebrate your astonishing success over many foes, including a gorzyne! I grieve with you still and share your pain, as does Laexa. But we will not pity you. Instead, out of compassion, we demand that you move."

Hovan remained sitting on the hammock.

"My father's forces have broken the enemy and now hunt down scattered groups. Still, good men and elves may die as they root out the final weeds of opposition. Your power and guidance may save some mother from grieving. Do not be still when you can forge good by acting! I cannot go, so you must!"

Hovan lifted his head and looked straight up at the clouds drifting by.

"I will badger you, Wizard, until you move. Take Laexa and put her to use. Put yourself to good use."

Hovan put some soup into his mouth and swallowed. In silence, he finished what Laexa had brought him. He then placed the bowl on the ground and crawled back under the blanket.

When the prince finished eating, he hobbled to his feet. He strapped the sword to his left side and the daggers to his belt. He placed the bow inside his tent. When he came back out, he spoke. "I will inform the rear command that I need new guards for tomorrow. I give you one more night's sleep, Wizard, and another visit from a healer. Tomorrow after breakfast, you leave with your company of mounts and Captain Laexa. You will move forward to help as you can. I swear you will leave this camp if I must stumble after you, swatting your behind with my sword!"

Ti'ek left without waiting for a response. The wizard lay under the blanket with his eyes watching the clouds wander by above the trees.

Laexa collected the bowls. "Why should Captain Vay have all the fun?"

The Giver rose red through clouds. The prince woke early. He made sure that the Forestton guards would be ready to move at the end of the first meal. Laexa appeared soon after him, eager and ready to leave.

They sat through breakfast, which Hovan did not show for, discussing where the Forestton orvbacaan should head. Ti'ek passed along the latest news. The prince sat and waited a few moments after finishing breakfast before yelling, "Wizard!"

Ti'ek grabbed his crutches and staggered to his feet. He stared at the wizard's tent, ready to yell again, but saw Hovan standing just outside the tent in his Forestton green cloak, staff across his back.

The prince and the wizard met eyes.

"I will inform your father that you are ready to rule," stated the wizard.

"Do not curse me with responsibility," the young elf complained.

"I am cursed with your compassion. It is the least I can do."

"Leave," said Ti'ek, though he smiled.

"If for no other reason than to get away from you. I take Laexa to ride in your place."

"A woman to do a male's work?" teased Ti'ek.

Laexa spun and buried a dagger in the tree next to Ti'ek.

Ti'ek exchanged smiles with her. "Get him out of here."

Laexa walked over to Ti'ek and yanked the dagger from the tree. As she turned to leave, Ti'ek put a hand on her shoulder. "Put him to use," he said. "I do not want to repeat this."

"Thank you for sending me riding with him when he is in such good spirits." Laexa's sarcasm didn't escape the prince's notice.

"I would go myself if I could."

Laexa put her hand on top of Ti'ek's. "Yes. I know."

Leaving the prince standing and watching, the company rode out of camp. Ti'ek almost pitied the enemy found by this mournful wizard. The anger he would vent on them would be fierce. He hoped also cathartic.

CHAPTER 19

FIRESIDE

Red orange flames popped up in constant, though inconsistent, rotation and tried in vain to complete the escape into the night. A triangle pile of logs supported the flames' attempts to jump to the dark. Prince Ti'ek relaxed with his father, Hovan, and Laexa, savoring the remains of a large, hot meal and enjoying victory wine. With the main camp being broken tomorrow for the trip back to Shetteca, some of the extra supplies brought in case a prolonged stay was necessary were being joyfully consumed. Fires glowed in the surrounding areas, each lighting faces showing some happiness. Even the wounded were glad to be going home, though the trip might prove painful.

After draining his travel mug again, Ti'ek spoke. "Wizard, once again, we prove that power is knowledge. We met the force before it could clear the hills. Defeated it and kept the farmers safe."

"You mean knowledge is power," said Hovan.

"Yes, that is what I said."

"It seems I am forever pulling you or your father out of some mess," said Hovan.

Ke'en spoke up. "I was pulling your ass out of this fire."

"Now wait a moment. I only needed saving because I was saving him." Hovan pointed his finger toward Ti'ek.

"And he needed my help to do it, Ti'ek," added Laexa. "If you forget scouts exist, allow them to surprise you, and do not retreat when told to, then you are lucky to be alive. Knowledge is power and should be used wisely. Is that not correct, Prince Ti'ek?"

Ti'ek smiled. "Of course, Captain."

"How about this question, Wizard," said the district leader. "Why would a Preparer warrior lead an army against us?"

"Why?" asked Hovan. "Because they were here. Why us? Perhaps for the same reason."

"Gathering them, scouting us, learning the land, organizing supplies," said Laexa. "That is a lot of work just because things were here."

"I agree," said Ke'en.

"Overpopulation?" suggested Ti'ek.

"They have an abandoned district," said Ke'en. "Why march? And they brought a gorzyne?!"

"Yes, a gorzyne!" said Hovan, echoing the concern. "Not only bringing one, but controlling it! The soldiers of Arre'ielle hunted them out of this area long ago. Maybe one has found its way back."

"Returning under the control of a preparer," said Laexa.

"Are they building another stronghold?" said Ke'en. "Shetteca needs to know. The king wants an answer."

"Or have they already?" Hovan pulled his blankets tightly around him and lay down in his hammock. "Laexa, sing me to sleep."

"It would be more effective if I simply hit you over the head."

"Wizard, we have questions," said Ke'en.

"District Leader, I have no answers. Ask me again when we reach Forestton. I might think of one by then. May you find comfort in your dreams."

"Any other suggestions, Captain Laexa?" asked Ke'en.

"Another cup of wine." Laexa filled her mug from the wineskin.

"That is the second best suggestion I have heard tonight," said Ti'ek.

"Second best?" asked Laexa.

"Of course. Chasing away the chill of a cool night with victory wine and hot food while sitting around a crackling fire. My idea!"

"Laexa, is he always so modest these days?" asked Ke'en.

"He usually takes credit for every good idea. Tonight, he at least gave me credit for the second best idea."

Their laughter preceded a drink of wine. Soon after, the captain lay settled into her blankets, sleeping near the wizard.

Left to themselves, the elves continued their conversation in their minds, hoping not to disturb their human friends.

"I am sorry that I was not of more help to you, Father," said Ti'ek. *"Lord Gerritt will not think highly of me for being wounded in such a way. I apologize for the show of weakness, especially with the king here."*

"Being injured in battle is not a sign of weakness," instructed Ke'en. *"Strong elves die in every war. You, the captain, and the wizard killed many before we reached you! Learn from the experience, though. Laexa was right. Scouts should not have surprised you. Still, what you called a weakness may yet be a strength! King Dargladre and Lord Gerritt know the Lord Wizard Hovan will die to protect us. Our alliance is that strong!"*

The district leader sipped his wine before continuing.

"It may have worked out for the best. We were fortunate that the wizard found the gorzyne! Who else could have stopped it?!"

Ke'en met his son's eyes as he explained.

"Hovan knew the source of the roar. He chose the meadow to turn and fight because there he could see it coming. Ti'ek, he stayed in that meadow knowing a gorzyne approached and tried to get you to safety! He will get a big hug from Shar next time she sees him."

Ke'en's tone softened.

"Hovan has not often visited Shar and me during the last few circles of the Giver. Even when he comes to teach and dine with Cova. I am not sure why. We are a connection to better times, perhaps. Maybe he does not know what to say after losing Suzhanee."

"I do not see him often either," said Ti'ek. *"He stayed away the entire cold season. Maybe you should ask Cova. Still, I think he is better than he was, though he may never be his smiling, optimistic former self."*

"I fear that is too true! Losing a wife is tragic. And I grieve for the loss of my old friend. Now, his smile is rarely seen. I thank you for the friendship you show him. He finds comfort there. In spending time with Cova as well. He comes to Shetteca for dinner and training, and they talk. I do not know what to make of that, so I choose to make nothing of it."

"Laexa cares for him, too." Ti'ek adjusted the blankets around his bad leg. *"She is a skilled officer! She feared just such an attack, while I thought nothing of it. Hovan chose his first captain well."*

"Knowledge is power."

Ke'en sipped some wine and then tossed the skin to his son. *"Finish it or save it. I am going to sleep."*

The district leader rose and walked to his tent. When he reached the entrance, he turned and looked at his son.

"Do not fear what Gerritt thinks of you. He is a minor concern. I am proud of you, eldest son Ti'ek. He will hear it. We ride home victors!"

The flaps of the tent brushed closed behind him.

Ti'ek sat around the fire, thinking.

We did indeed kill many, including a gorzyne! Still, Laexa is correct. I can do better. I failed in Mohvradraan and nearly fell here. Yes, I can do better.

CHAPTER 20

THE RIDE HOME

After they forded the River Ke, the army from Shetteca split into two groups; one aimed toward Shetteca and the other toward Forestton. Captain Vay and the cavalry of Forestton took the forward position as they rode through Lord Wizard Hovan's region of Shetteca. King Dargladre and Lord Ke'en rode with the contingent riding to Forestton.

Before the Giver set on the first evening after crossing the river, the host of soldiers set up camp stretched along both sides of the road. Orvbacs attached to long lines grazed in fields with scattered trees. Hovan paid farmers for the use of their corrals and pastures for the Forestton orvbacs. The farmers were happy for the coins and the rare chance to see King Dargladre.

The king sent word requesting the Wizard Hovan and Captain Laexa to join him.

"Captain Laexa," Hovan said, using her title to gather her attention. "The king has requested us for a conference. You are requested by name. I am proud of your accomplishments, efforts, and insight, Captain. It is only right that others seek your counsel as well. Well done, Laexa. Welcome to the inner circle."

Escorted by a royal guard, Hovan and Laexa walked to a group of tents clustered together near the middle of many others. They filled the last two chairs positioned around a small fire. King Dargladre, Lady Velina, Prince Ke'en, and Prince Ti'ek sat waiting.

"We have safely returned to Shetteca," began the king. "I ask that you all speak what you think, including you, Captain Laexa, first to fear a problem.

Lord Wizard Hovan, as Foreston is your region, I start with you. What are your thoughts?"

"I am reluctant to speculate," said Lord Hovan. "Yet I think we can agree on three conclusions. First, the Preparers seek to send me to the One I serve. For what reason? Perhaps for fighting against them in the war and helping to save Shetteca. Perhaps because I did not die when they thought I would. Also, I helped destroy two of their strongholds. Second, a group of Preparers is organizing raids into Shetteca, specifically towards Forestton. This may be no more than a corollary of the first thought. Third, one man found a way to control a gorzyne."

"A controlled gorzyne," stated the king. "Wizards, how is that possible?"

"I do not know," admitted Lord Hovan. "We do not even use magic to direct orvbacs."

"You could," suggested Lord Ke'en, "if you used magic to move the reins."

"I suppose, with practice," said Lord Hovan. "But there were no reins on the gorzyne."

King Dargladre offered a suggestion. "None that we saw. Magical reins?"

"How would someone ever put reins on a gorzyne?" asked Lord Hovan.

"He must have started when it was young," said Lady Velina. "Used magic to beat it into submission."

"He would have had to kill its mother," said Lord Ke'en. "More likely, they secured the egg before it hatched."

Lord Hovan exhaled. "I do not think he could control an adult gorzyne. My experience with gorzynes is very limited, but they seem too aggressive. Too dominant. Too independent. Fearing nothing but a dragon or a larger gorzyne. He let this one loose on a field. Did he expect it to return?"

Captain Laexa reasoned for the group. "Then, our logic says that this was a young gorzyne and a valuable commodity, but one with a limited time for its use."

King Dargladre spoke. "To continue that thought, they may have others. And this Preparer warrior spent a precious resource in an attempt to kill Lord Hovan."

"If we think he targeted me," said Lord Hovan. "The heir to the throne was not far away."

"It was all I could do to keep between the Preparer warrior and Lord Hovan," said Captain Laexa. "He focused on Lord Hovan. Even trying to get around orvbacs to get to him. The Preparer did not keep the gorzyne in reserve waiting for Lord Ke'en."

"True," admitted Lord Hovan.

Lady Velina spoke. "There are reasons for them to focus on Lord Hovan, but the attention now, after so much time since the war, may indicate their growing strength. The group we defeated was too large for me to be comfortable with the idea that this was nothing more than an attempt to send Lord Hovan to the One he serves. Should my instinct be right, combined with their choice of Arre'ielle as a target again, we must be ready for more attacks. Where is their organizational center? Why is Lord Hovan so important to them?"

"Forestton is an easier target than Shetteca," offered Prince Ti'ek.

"The force we met did not have the strength to defeat and hold Forestton," said Lord Ke'en. "They could do no more than raid areas outside the walls."

"Even with a gorzyne?" asked Prince Ti'ek.

"Lord Hovan defeated it even without the magic stored in the walls of Forestton," said Lord Ke'en. "Though we are lucky that Lord Hovan found it before it reached our soldiers."

"Desperate for food?" offered Prince Ti'ek.

"They stole little food during the cold season," noted Captain Laexa.

"Feleine and the land west of the mountains provide sufficient resources to feed many more than we saw," said Lord Hovan.

"They did not avoid us," stated Lady Velina.

"Perhaps they are being Preparers and sending as many as they can to the next life," suggested Prince Ti'ek.

"The Lord Wizard's area is the closest to the hills," said Lord Ke'en, supporting his son's argument. "Lord Hovan's presence significantly strengthens the defense of the Forestton region. This may explain their focus on the wizard."

"That answer feels too simple," said Lady Velina. "This is too much effort to only claim farmers for the One they serve. They could simply cross the river and release the gorzyne. It would terrorize and kill many before someone with enough strength found it and stopped it."

"I would agree," said Lord Hovan, "but I have no better answer."

Everyone continues to use titles. A formal discussion that no one is comfortable with.

"What are your thoughts, King Dargladre?" asked Lord Ke'en.

"I wonder if we are not heading in the wrong direction. All indications suggest that they have re-established a presence in the area west of Shetteca, yet we march the other way."

Before the others could argue, he held up his hand to continue. "We are not prepared for that trip, I know. The journey might prove necessary, though. Have they gathered more than this force? I am concerned by the gorzyne. I agree with Lord Ke'en that we were fortunate that Hovan found it first. Was that a coincidence?"

"I do not think they knew we were there before we attacked," said Lord Hovan.

"Maybe what they wished for," suggested the king.

Lady Velina spoke. "I agree with King Dargladre and Captain Laexa. They intended that gorzyne for you, Lord Hovan. I suggest you be very careful where you go. The words from your contact in Avi'ot, the man watching your house, and this force that took a special interest in you. This is a lot of planning to only try once. Expect more attacks!"

The king spoke. "Any final thoughts?"

Captain Laexa nodded to King Dargladre, the sitting version of a bow. "Cret'len do not plan. Someone did. Controlling a gorzyne is unheard of. I cannot imagine anyone achieving that quickly. The weapons and dress were of a higher quality than these creatures normally craft themselves. Someone invested effort, time, and resources. I agree with Lady Wizard Velina. This feels unfinished and personal."

Hovan noticed the two women make eye contact, each acknowledging the other.

Well done, Captain. For nine cycles of the Giver, you have helped me. Lord Ke'en and Lady Shar accept you. Now, the king himself and Lady Velina! A tribute to your intelligence and experience.

But you conclude it is unfinished and personal?

Whatever this business with the Preparers is, it appears to be escalating and centered on me. Now, I wish it were just cret'len being annoying.

Perhaps not escalating. Perhaps, a plan that I do not know the entirety of.

There appears to be a plan. You are right about that. That alone worries me.

"Captain Laexa, your job as protector of Lord Wizard Hovan will become more challenging, it seems," said Lady Velina.

"You have done well these past cycles of the moons to protect your district," King Dargladre said to the group. "We need to do more. I suspect Lady Velina is right and that more attacks are coming. I hope this show of our strength will make them reconsider. We are on our guard now."

The king took a breath. Then he narrowed his view to the heir to the throne. "Was Shetteca properly prepared? I mean no disrespect, Prince Ke'en. Do you need help to hold your western border?"

"Do not fear saying such things, King," answered the district leader of Shetteca. "It is your right and responsibility to seek answers to difficult questions. It would be weakness not to ask. We will strengthen Shetteca's western border, though the River Ke is not the barrier for Shetteca that Lordic's Wall is for Feleine. With Forestton's aid, we will hold the River Ke."

"Yes, my leader and king," affirmed Lord Hovan.

"In time," said King Dargladre, "I hope to hold more than that."

"Now is not that time," responded Lord Ke'en.

"No, it is not. I feel it is time, though, that I show you more support than words. I will leave you men to help patrol the border, if you wish."

"Your support would be welcome. Thank you."

⸺⊙⸺

Lord Wizard Hovan rode his orvbac up to the open gates of Forestton. The garrison stood at attention with Captain Wod Dein directly above the gate, holding his sword thrust upward in salute. Hovan returned the salute with his staff. Captain Wod Dein and the guard assumed an at ease stance.

Well done, Captain. Extra ceremony with the king present.

The wizard dismounted and waited with Captain Laexa outside the gate. Captain Vay led the soldiers of Forestton home through the short tunnel under the wall. Soldiers escorting the king moved to the south practice field to set up camp. The portion heading to Shetteca turned their march north along the road.

After dismounting, Ke'en walked over to Hovan. "Thank you, Hovan, for your help. We could have managed without you, but not as well. Thank you for protecting my son."

Ke'en embraced Hovan.

"I feel as if he is my own son at times."

Ke'en waved his hand. A soldier walked a tall, black orvbac with thick fur forward and handed the reins to the wizard. "In appreciation for what you have done."

"An orvbac?" teased Hovan. "I saved your son, and you give me an orvbac. A whole orvbac?"

"Check the saddle bags, Wizard," groaned Ke'en.

The wizard opened two saddle bags. He raised his eyebrows. "Ke'en, my old friend, those saddle bags contain..."

"Your calling me an old friend belies your looks. You challenged death to protect my son. That is beyond price! You have my thanks, and Shar's. Also, you defeated the gorzyne, saving many! If you consider the gift unnecessary, then consider it compensation to the Forestton region. Your farmers bore the attacks this recent cold season."

Blue eyes acknowledged green with a bow of the head.

As Hovan handed the reins of the orvbac to a soldier of Forestton, Lord Ke'en produced a satchel. "In return for your help, Captain Laexa." He handed her the bag. The soft clinking of coins filtered through the walls of the bag.

"This is not necessary, Lord Ke'en."

"Perhaps not. However, unrewarded officers go elsewhere. You uncovered a problem in my district before anyone else thought to look. I am grateful."

Laexa opened the drawstring of the bag and looked inside. "Thank you for your gift."

Hovan then turned to Ti'ek, who sat on his orvbac. He took folded papers from inside his cloak and handed them to the young elf. "Please deliver this to Priest Thesian."

"Is there anything you do not tell him?" joked Ti'ek.

"Anything he does not specifically ask about, which I wish to keep secret. Take care of your leg."

Lord Ke'en climbed into his saddle. "My family looks forward to your arrival, King."

"I hear the food at the Forest Inn makes it worth a visit. I look forward to a bed. After a brief stay in Forestton, we will travel to Shetteca. I am excited to see your city."

Ke'en and his son fell in line with the column of soldiers moving north.

CHAPTER 21

THE NIGHTMARE

Hovan wore an auburn colored cloak. The hood cast a shadow, keeping the bright rays of the Giver out of the watchful blue eyes. He rode a brown orvbac at the head of a mounted patrol. Riding next to the cloaked figure, a lightly armored, young elf let his black hair play with the breeze, but held his energetic mount to a walk.

"It is a fine day for a dragon hunt," Ti'ek said in a tone that might lead one to believe that the prince was hunting small game for sport, rather than their present business.

Warm air drifted past from ahead.

The new leaves of the trees colored the forest light green, complementing by contrast the bright blue sky.

The wizard threw back his hood, revealing a head of gray streaked blond hair pulled back into a ponytail. He squinted in the bright light of the Giver, adding creases around the eyes to the ones born from age.

"It is not the weather that makes a dragon hunt bad, so how can it make it good?"

Before his face took on a stern demeanor, a smile briefly touched the corner of his mouth. With an austere look once again firmly planted on his face, Hovan turned in the saddle and mentally inventoried his small force. He then turned forward and resumed scanning the road on which the hired force was riding.

As they had on the previous visit of the Giver, the company rode down a grassy and abandoned forest road, which traversed a run of small hills heading toward the taller Vadraan Mountains. Hovan led, with Suzhanee riding close behind. The elf Ti'ek was to his right. Laexa rode behind Ti'ek, next to Suzhanee. Following in two straight lines rode the platoon of four hands of riders and one lieutenant.

Knowing the source of Hovan's tension, Ti'ek sought to reassure him in soft tones that would soon be buried in the arhythmic clomp of the orvbacs. "We have the right personnel: powerful and experienced. This little brown dragon will die. Do not doubt that, Hovan."

"Yes, but how many lives will it take before it is silenced?"

Ti'ek's lightweight mail, interwoven with strands of turquoise cloth, softly clattered as he settled back into his saddle. He followed Hovan's gaze forward. "I prefer when you attempt jokes, even if most of them are bad."

"As do I," said Suzhanee, nudging her orvbac closer to Hovan's. A dark green tie held her long dark hair behind her shoulders. Her golden eyes sparkled in her beautiful, tanned face, kissed by the Giver to be almost as dark as an elf's. "I love you, my husband, but you are becoming a gloomy bore. You have not tried a joke since we entered the dragon's territory. You are suffocating me with all this...protection. Captain Laexa, your bodyguard, mind you, hovers over me like a mother with a little girl. I am a magician and can protect myself better than most of the riders here! You spend more time looking for this cursed dragon than you do looking at me! I am getting jealous of this oversized varmint!" Suzhanee laughed.

Hovan smiled. He could not help it. Whenever Suzhanee laughed, he smiled.

"He smiled," Ti'ek deadpanned. "Look quick. It will be gone faster than the Giver on an elven picnic."

Hovan turned in his saddle and smiled at Suzhanee. With her hair perfectly framing her exquisite face, Suzhanee returned his smile.

"My love, I love you too," Hovan said. "A magician you are, with an excellent teacher, I might add, but I fear for your safety. I ride to steal a dragon's treasure and fear it will steal mine."

"The dragon will die. You said so. Prince Ti'ek said so. And so say I." Suzhanee's confident proclamation accompanied her beautiful smile beaming below captivating gold eyes.

"Yes, the sooner the better."

Hovan's back went straight as his eyes squinted to focus on something past Suzhanee, past the mounted orvbacs. The object of the search was in sight and closing fast.

A massive red dragon was gliding on quiet wings barely above the treetops.

"Not what we were told! How did it get behind us!?" Hovan vaulted from his orvbac. "Cover!"

He raised his dark wood staff. A sphere of orange fire shot up to meet the dragon.

The red dragon let out a roar of challenge, no longer needing to stay quiet. The orange ball struck the dragon, but it sparkled, deflecting the attack. It thundered over the group, sending a wind through the treetops and the orvbacs into a panic.

Orvbacs scattered, many bolting into the forest, seeking safety. Laexa, like many others, found herself on the ground, trying to avoid the hooves and horns in the chaos. The leather reins bit into Ti'ek's hands as his mount reared and shook its head and horns. He fought to stay on the terrified animal and battled it for control.

A crazed orvbac galloped past Hovan, slamming into his shoulder and throwing him to the ground.

On large, sweeping wings, the dragon circled.

Hovan stood and braced his feet. A blinding flash of white lightning leapt up and collided with the immense dragon, altering its flight. The accompanying clap of thunder seemed to add a jolting boom to the collision.

The red dragon sparkled again, though the sparkles were less intense.

After righting its flight, the massive dragon returned a stream of fire. The forest on one side of the road ignited in flames. Sickening screams erupted from the men and orvbacs caught in the inferno.

Amidst this confusion of fire, rearing orvbacs, and cries of pain, Hovan struggled to find space where he could fight the dragon. He tracked the path of the enormous dragon as he pushed away from a pair of orvbacs. His magic had protected him from the heat of the fire, but he no longer felt confident of the dragon's imminent death. He launched another bolt as it banked for a third pass. The bolt slammed into the dragon. It listed onto a straight path and focused on something smaller on the road.

Three hits?! And it still flies?

The wizard searched for his wife. Fear gripped his throat as he spotted her on the orvbac that had bolted past him and knocked him to the ground. Panic stricken, Suzhanee's runaway orvbac galloped down the road.

The once simple doubt in Hovan's mind now convulsed into almost inhibiting fear. Hovan's heart contracted into a tight, painful ball. He stopped breathing.

The dragon was not circling for a third pass. NO! It was not seeking to do more damage to the group that had hurt it. NO! It sensed weakness and was descending on Suzhanee and her out of control mount.

In desperation, Hovan took a deep breath and launched another bolt of lightning. Its thunder acting as his howl of anger. It slammed into the giant dragon, twisting it midair. The beast roared again, though not as a challenge, with almost no sparkle visible. It corrected its flight and flew on, gaining speed as it left.

Four spells?!

With the grace of a talon bird, the enormous red dragon snatched Suzhanee and her orvbac off the road and flew on.

A handful of fire darts from the young Ti'ek's hand failed to reach the escaping dragon.

Tears flowed unnoticed on the wizard's cheeks. Hovan caught the reins of an orvbac and ran it out of the chaos. He leapt onto its back. His staff slid quickly into the quiver on his back. The wizard grabbed the leather reins with both hands and exhorted his mount to gallop.

A somber and desperate Ti'ek followed.

How had he allowed himself to be so foolish and glib and fail his friend?

"Lieutenant," Captain Laexa ordered as she remounted her orvbac, "put five soldiers on those five orvbacs and have them follow me. Have the rest tend the wounded."

"Let me take the five and seek help," urged the lieutenant. "You now command the company!"

"You misunderstand, Lieutenant. I go to help the wizard! You command the company until one of us returns."

Amazed, the lieutenant yelled, "With five men!?" He added, "Captain, I know she was your charge, but if the Wizard Hovan cannot kill it, what can you and five archers hope to do?"

"You have not seen the last of the Wizard Hovan! That dragon will not live to see the Giver twice more. We go to help as we can."

Stunned, the lieutenant asked, "And his wife?"

Captain Laexa yelled over her shoulder, "Tend to the living!" She brought her large orvbac to a gallop and rode after Hovan and Ti'ek with five archers scrambling to follow her.

Ahead of all, with only the dragon ahead of him, but growing smaller in the distance as it headed toward the Vadraan Mountains, Hovan galloped with tears rolling down his cheeks, his cloak flying in the wind, hands gripping the reins trying to instill speed into the legs of his orvbac. In anguish, he could not think. He only felt pain, tightening his insides, sickening his stomach. As he watched, heartbroken, the swift dragon drew still further and further away toward the larger hills. Barely able to breathe, he rode and rode and rode.

CHAPTER 22

WELCOME HOME

Julian Orel recovered from his magic and confirmed that he was in the softly lit secret room below his detached garage. It had been some time since he had spent more than a few days at his house in Rockland County, New York. In addition to giving lessons to Ti'ek and Cova, hosting the wizard's Blessed Beginning gathering, and seeing to the management of Forestton, he had enjoyed fulfilling social calls and resting in the slowly lengthening and warming days of the growing season of Arre'ielle. Time spent returning messages of concern, support, or congratulations received once news of the successful, but troubling trip into the western hills made the rounds had helped battle bouts of loneliness.

Still, it was time to check in with his friends here. Also, a break from the memories of Suzhanee would help him. It had been a challenge to convince Laexa to stay behind, but he was safe here on this planet, which had little magic. Well, he had not really convinced her. More like told her he was safe here and Forestton needed her.

Drifting out of the cloak of responsibility would be welcome. A cloak, though, would help combat the chill of a New York spring night.

He pushed open the narrow door and moved into a small room with a wooden ladder secured to the wall. He stopped short and stiffened.

Visitors? It is not even dawn here. What is anyone doing here?

Stapled to an exposed stud, thin beige wires ran down the wall from above and ended in three small, illuminated lights. Julian looked at the top red light.

Motion in the living room.

He looked at the middle light.

Motion in the basement.

He then slid his eyes down to the bottom light.

Motion in the garage above me.

Using his cell phone, Julian connected to the app for his security cameras. The exterior cameras showed nothing unusual. Their history recorded no activity except for a brief period of blank screen over twenty six hours ago. The interior camera and motion detectors were not functioning. He closed the app and turned his cell phone off.

There was no magic on his house that he could connect to. Magic might draw attention if the right person were looking.

Someone has invaded my house. This is not the quiet welcome home I expected.

Could be nothing more than opportunists who noticed the house has been vacant recently.

But they had successfully evaded all the cameras. That suggests more than just random burglars.

There is little of value in the house. Hopefully, they searched it and moved on.

The lower level in which Julian stood seemed to have escaped detection. The upper end of the ladder ended at a wooden wall panel. This panel served as the small door into the garage and only pushed open. Julian hoped the door, nothing more than a wooden panel on hinges and identical to the other part of the wall, had been enough to hide the oddly placed, tiny addition below.

I could just leave. Laexa would prefer that. But what if they are more than simply thieves?

How did they avoid all the cameras?

No, I cannot leave. Things are happening at home. Did something happen here? If it is something more, my friends may need help.

Julian sighed.

Who broke into my house? Why would they do that? Are they still here?

More questions! Maybe I can answer some of these.

He reached behind his head and collected his loose, shoulder length, blond hair into an elastic band from his pocket. Then he chuckled.

Break into the house of a wizard. I will teach them how stupid that is. Maybe I will let them live to tell the tale.

With growing ire, he inventoried his assets. His 9mm semiautomatic pistol hung in a shoulder holster under his light jacket. His fully charged short staff hung ready in the quiver diagonally across his back. Suzhanee's engagement ring encircled his left pinky. His jacket covered the hawk pendant pinned to his shirt. He approached the ladder, rested and alert and armed. If they were hiding in his house, these transgressors would have their hands full!

Julian hesitated.

If someone is still here, they might know who I am. They avoided the cameras. That took some planning. Magic would help.

Move with caution and care until it is time not to.

The quote from his teacher repeated itself in his mind. He adjusted the keys in his jeans pocket so they would not rattle and pressed the button that reset the lights.

Julian climbed the ladder cautiously, alert for any noise from above. When he got to the top, he waited. Hearing nothing, Julian pushed open the wall panel just a little and listened again. He then stepped out and pushed the door closed. It clicked behind him.

His parked SUV filled most of the small garage. Nothing appeared to be missing or out of place, though it was too dark to be sure.

Stepping to the window in the side door, he peeked past the curtain. A nearly full moon cast the empty backyard in dim shades of charcoal. No lights shone from his house.

He activated the ring on his finger and faded from sight. It was perhaps unnecessary since the waning moon would provide little light, and anyone looking for him should know to watch for someone invisible. The hawk pendent provided defense magic. He slipped into the backyard through the side door.

The house was quiet, dark, and appeared undisturbed. The wooden steps leading up to the back porch would only stay quiet with magic, so Julian avoided them. Moving among the shield of pine trees along the property border, he crept down to the street. The only cars parked on the street were further down near his neighbors' houses. A small light illuminating his mailbox and house number glowed as it did every night. His house appeared as he had left it, except for a few small piles of leaves blown up against the front porch.

He crept among the trees until he was perpendicular to the side of the house. Julian approached a basement window. Kneeling, he looked in. Julian saw two people sitting in chairs facing the open door to his small, sparsely decorated basement office. A submachine gun rested across one lap. A pump action shotgun leaned against the chair of the second person. Both wore blue jeans, sneakers, and casual long sleeve shirts. Dress typical of this world.

The light from the LED ceiling lamps in the office shone through the door. This room in the basement, with the lights always turned on, had the look and placement of a secret room, if someone were looking for one. Everyone else would assume that the lights had been left on by mistake. On his home world, most secret rooms were in protected locations. Behind guarded walls and below ground, where neither magic nor nature could easily alter them. Julian was less confident in his old farmhouse to provide that level of protection. Thus, he had created the appearance of a second one, though it did not have the typical one way door.

Do not be where they are looking.

Another lesson from his teacher. He had succeeded in this instance, it seemed.

Armed individuals sat outside his basement office, watching his fake secret room.

A very odd place for someone born in this world to be waiting. Off worlders waiting in my house? They have probably thrown chairs into the office, hoping the alteration would ruin the magic. That might have killed me if I magiced into the altered secret room.

How did they even know where to find me? Trouble from home has followed me here?

Laexa will be furious when she finds out. Unless I return and bring her.

Focus. Two watching the room in the basement. Only two invaders to come after me? Not if they know who I am.

They could not be sure that I would not return by a more conventional method. Others in the house must be watching the driveway.

How about replacements to relieve the ones on duty? There must be more. Where would the others be? Sleeping, if they had spent more than a few hours on alert.

Unless there was a wizard with them.

No. There are only seven wizards in all Arre'ielle, and one of those is retired. I could not conceive of another here. However, they may have magic. That may be how they got past the cameras without being seen. Actually, if they got to this planet, then a high level magician is involved. But is the magician hiding in the house?

And more guns? Probably. I have one.

Attack now or wait until light? Darkness would aid surprise. But I am already invisible. Darkness would make it harder for me to see them.

Besides, the longer I delay, the more relaxed they might get. They may give away their positions and number.

So I wait. But for how long?

Out of sight of the windows, Julian sat, leaning against his house, listening for any movement inside. Dawn was still a few hours off. He could be patient. In his mind, he pictured the layout of the house and planned.

Should I bring Laexa? If I face this threat without her and again do not *allow her to do her job, she may leave me. I do not want that. She is my protector.*

Julian stood and put his left hand in the vertical position. But his right hand did not move. He pictured Laexa with her sword and daggers against the intruders with shotguns and submachine guns.

Laexa will not understand the threat. She will not know what to do. Not be able to fight them. Sword against shotguns! They will kill her unless I protect her. She is most protected if she is not here. I cannot bring her into this unprepared and have her die. No! I will not do that.

She will not understand, but Suzhanee will.

Julian sat back down. He hugged his knees for warmth. He waited. To save their energy, he turned off the ring and pendent. He sat alone in the dark, growing cold, with only the songs of the crickets to keep him company. As dawn approached, lone birds added their calls to those of the crickets and the distant frogs.

A click, barely audible in the post dawn quiet, signaled the back door being opened. Julian leaned over to check the basement. Two figures, armed as before, sat in the chairs. From further inside, the floor creaked.

At least four of them. Time for action. I simply will not tell Laexa how long I waited to attack.

Julian contacted the engagement ring and hawk pendent while stretching to warm up and loosen his legs. He stepped back and looked at the house through his outstretched hands. As if molding a shell around his house, he cast a spell. Julian did not want the coming fight disturbed by the local police department. This was for their safety and his privacy. When he was done, he stepped inside the invisible field around the house. The intermittent singing of the birds and frogs faded away. He hoped the quiet would go unnoticed for a moment.

Julian cast another spell followed by a third.

He then knelt and looked through the basement window again. He released the first piece of magic he had prepared. An image of himself walked out of the office doorway from inside the office. Julian moved his head back and forth. Julian's image mirrored his movements, glancing between the two armed men. Both men sat upright. One shouldered his submachine gun, releasing a burst of bullets at the image. The image of Julian darted back into the office. The men moved toward the office, weapons shouldered and ready to fire again.

Not here to welcome me home.

Julian sprinted to the side of the porch and launched himself over the rail. He floated down the porch to keep the old floor boards quiet. He reached the kitchen window halfway down the back wall and risked a look inside.

A woman stood near the left side of the kitchen by an open door, looking down into the basement. Another figure waited by the open back door, watching the woman. This pair carried weapons similar to the pair below: the woman near the stairs with a Colt SMG and the man by the back door held a pump action shotgun.

Julian's hands danced. Two flaming spheres shot in tandem from his hands, sped along the porch, and darted inside. The first one bypassed the man near the back door and slammed into the woman. A blue glow sprang into existence, protecting her from the blast, but the force of the blow sent her tumbling down the stairs. The second sphere struck the man by the back door, knocking him off his feet. A blue glow appeared and protected him from the fire as well. Stunned by the blast, the man shook his head and rolled to his knees.

A staff knocked his gun aside. A kick to the face sent him sprawling onto his back.

Julian stepped on his wrist, trapping his gun hand, and leaned on the staff, pinning the man's chest.

"Why are you here?"

The man stared back. Blood from his nose trickled down his cheek. Jerking his knee to his chest, he grabbed for a knife in his boot.

Julian sent a pulse of magic through the staff, shocking the man. The knife fell from his hand. Julian stepped harder on the trapped hand. "Why are you here?"

"Send you on your way."

The man yelled to warn the others and reached for the knife.

Another pulse of magic surged through the staff. The yelling stopped as the man went limp.

With practiced precision, Julian slid his staff back into its quiver. A fast coil of hand motions sent a spray of fire darts flying down the basement stairs before dissipating. The shuffling of people scattering to evade the small spheres of fire was the commotion Julian wanted to hear.

The sound of footsteps charging down the stairs from the second floor alerted him to other attackers incoming. He slid the kitchen table against the basement door. He held the doorknob for a moment and focused.

Divide and conquer. Good luck with the door.

He moved toward the rectangular entryway leading to the dining room. Gunfire splintered holes in the basement door behind him. A grin turned his lips.

Julian peered into the dining room. A woman moved from the living room across the room, taking slow, measured steps, which limited the floorboards' creaking and kept her head steady. Her eyes stared down the barrel of her Colt SMG. A man with a 20-gauge shotgun, held tight against his shoulder, followed her. The woman dropped to one knee. She said a command in a language Julian did not understand. She opened fire. The red glow around Julian deflected the bullets that came too close as he pulled his head back. He heard the soft thud of the bullets punching holes in the plaster wall across the kitchen.

Julian's hands began a quick dance. He drew an invisible line in the air, shoulder high, while he stared at the entryway to the dining room. A rapid sequence of footsteps signaled someone accelerating through the dining room, as he expected.

Julian's hands started again, then paused.

The woman hit an invisible line, stopping her head and shoulders. Her white sneakers continued forward, then up and nearly over her head. She landed hard on her shoulders and neck on the kitchen floor.

Julian's hands completed the paused spell. A pulse of three orange fireballs turned the corner, pummeling the man.

Julian grabbed the stunned woman's arm and flipped her onto her stomach. He knelt on her back with her arm twisted behind her. He looked at her companion in the dining room, who lay groaning. Julian launched a handful of fire darts at him. The man groaned more, but did not rise, his blue shield no longer visible.

Pressing hard with his knee between the woman's shoulder blades, Julian pulled his 9mm. "Why are you in my house?"

The woman stayed quiet. Bullets chewed up the doorknob.

"Why are you here?" Julian repeated. His knee dug into her back.

"I think it obvious," said the woman, her speech accented, more so than Julian's.

A shotgun blast punched a hole in the door, leaving a jagged semicircle where the doorknob had been a moment before.

"My soldiers come. I am protected by my shield. Time to prepare you and send you to the glory of the next life."

Julian pressed the nozzle of his handgun against the back of her neck. "My gun is inside your shield. Prepare me? Send me to the One I serve? Your soldiers do not come fast enough!"

The basement door began to slide open, the damaged kitchen table still providing resistance. The woman struggled to free herself. Julian doubled up his hands on the handgun and fired two bullets into her neck.

A shoulder and tilted head sighting down the barrel of a pump action shotgun appeared in the partially open doorway. A blast threw Julian up against the cabinet door of the wood pantry, though his red shield glowed and prevented the pellets from reaching him. The double click of the shotgun reloading preceded another blast, which slammed Julian into the plaster wall as he scrambled through the entryway into the dining room.

Julian crawled to the man laid out in the dining room. One arm snaked under the fallen man's back and was not trying to be freed. The tips of his light brown hair were singed black. Julian could find no pulse.

The scrape of the kitchen table across the floor signaled the release of those in the basement.

Enough of this! Attack me, do you?

Julian holstered his handgun and began hand motions. An orange sphere, larger than the previous ones, flew into the kitchen and darted right toward the basement door. The loud explosion shook the house and only partially masked the screams of pain and the bouncing of a body down the stairs.

Apologies, farmhouse.

Julian launched another sphere, which followed the same path.

He cautiously entered the kitchen. Fire ate at the exposed studs of the wall near the basement door, which had caved in. The kitchen table lay at an angle, burning, with two legs splintered off. A man lay motionless on the floor next to a shotgun, flames sprouting from his clothes.

Julian waved his hand back and forth, extinguishing the fires. He walked to the basement stairs.

At the base of the stairs, another man lay still, a shotgun nearby. Next to the man, the woman whom Julian had first seen in the kitchen stood, swaying on her feet, blood dripping down the side of her face, one arm clutched protectively near her body. Her other hand held the Colt SMG. She fired, unable to aim properly with one hand and her stance unsteady. Julian's shield glowed red as he stared back at the woman. She slowly turned the weapon toward her abdomen and pulled the trigger.

Julian stood and listened. He heard silence. He removed the magic quieting the house and listened again. Julian heard only crickets, frogs, and the morning birds.

He pulled out his cell phone. He pressed the green icon next to the name Tom. Cutting off Tom's sleepy hello, Julian asked, "Have you left yet?"

"Left? I'm not even awake." Tom, more awake, asked, "What's wrong?"

"Six people just tried to kill me in my house. Are you armed?"

"I'm in bed! Which house?"

"Rockland! Keep your gun close. I will call you again soon."

Speaking with his mind, Julian reached out to Racine. *"Racine, can you hear me?"*

"Hello, Julian," came a cheerful response. *"You are up early. Did you just get back?"*

"Racine, is everyone safe?" Adrenaline gave speed to his question.

"Yes. Why?" The cheerful tone faded.

"I returned home to find people waiting for me," said Julian.

"In Forestton? Did they try to hurt you?"

"At my house in Rockland!"

"Here!?" exclaimed Racine. *"Where are you now?"*

"At my house. Trying to hide the damage and the bodies."

"Are you hurt?"

"Nothing serious, bruises. Can I move into the lodge?"

"Of course. How can we help?"

"Not sure yet. Still figuring things out."

"Magic to the lodge," said Racine. *"Bring Sanlar and me back. We will help you figure things out. And help keep you safe!"*

"Good plan. I need to secure the house first. Be there soon."

Pulling his semiautomatic handgun, he searched the rest of his house, but found nothing more than wrappers and food containers in the bedrooms and living room.

They must have waited for some time.

Grabbing the arms of the dead man in the dining room, he pulled him into the kitchen. He dragged or carried the other bodies, making a pile of six corpses. A quick search of the bodies revealed wallets and car keys with an Avis sticker, which he shoved into his jeans pocket. He took knives, semiautomatic pistols, and smaller revolvers from the bodies.

He snatched a small garbage bag from under the sink and dumped the wallets inside.

Next, he made a pile of the guns.

I need to go to Forestton before going to the lodge. Laexa will be furious if I do not go get her.

What to do with the bodies? Where to hide them so they will not attract attention? Forestton.

I should bring the guns too. Dangerous to leave those. But that is too much for one trip. I will be back soon.

Julian sat on the floor and pulled three dead bodies into his lap. He placed the garbage bag of wallets on top. His hands danced through the long spell, right hand moving around his left, held like a vertical blade. He disappeared along with the three corpses.

⚬

The wizard appeared in the Forestton secret room. He climbed the two flights of stairs to the main floor and searched out Captain Laexa, Forestton's first. He found her seated in the kitchen, eating a late lunch.

Laexa's eyes narrowed as she scanned his blood stained clothes. "What happened? Are you hurt? Decided it is better to take me with you?"

"I was attacked at my other house. No injuries. Join me downstairs, please."

They descended to the secret room. Hovan showed her the three bodies while giving her the short story of the early morning events.

"What better place to hide them?" he asked rhetorically. They dragged the bodies out of the secret room and into the hallway.

"Look them over. See what you can find. I will take this one."

They searched the bodies. Hovan began pulling clothes off one woman while Laexa checked another, going through pockets and looking for tattoos or marks which might provide a clue.

"May the One you serve defend you!" exclaimed Laexa. "Preparers!"

Laexa pointed to the brand on the woman's upper thigh.

"She said they came to prepare me. I did not believe her! I thought it was bad English."

"On that world!? In your house?! You cannot go there again!"

The wizard did not respond.

How did they follow me there?

How did they find me?

Why do they even want to find me?

Why bother with me?

Leave me alone!

Laexa interrupted his thoughts. "We have to figure out what is happening!" Concern and apprehension gave a rushed beat to her exclamation.

They found brands on the other two bodies as well.

Hovan contacted Princes Ke'en and Ti'ek, who were both in Shetteca, relaying the report.

"I will put magic on them to preserve the bodies," said Hovan. "We may need them. I need to go back to the house, at least once more."

"I am going with you!" Laexa grabbed his arm so he could not leave without her. "We thought that planet was a sanctuary. That you were untouchable there. Now we know that is not so. Preparers are there looking for you!"

There is no winning the argument this time. She is responsible for protecting me. I would be a fool to leave now that someone has attacked me.

"Accepted. We need to reset the secret room. There are more bodies to bring here. An empty house is one thing. An empty house with dead bodies in it will start a search."

Hovan and Laexa took towels, got on their hands and knees, and washed the floor clean of blood. The room must look the same for the magic to work. It must look as Hovan had memorized it.

Laexa put the dirty towels into a canvas bag and brought them upstairs.

Hovan thought of leaving while she was gone, but decided against it. She would be furious and would be within her rights to leave her position as his protector. He had too much respect for her to mislead her.

He heard her descending the stairs and met her in the hallway. She stood before him with her sword belted to her waist, daggers within easy reach, and dressed in a leather jerkin. Her gear was in stark contrast to his jeans and collared shirt, sporting patches of blood, with the sleeves rolled up.

"You did not leave," she stated. "Good. That would have caused issues between us. I instructed Captain Wod Dein to keep Forestton on low alert."

"I agreed to your coming with me. But dressed like that will be a problem."

Her dark brown eyes and lighter brown hair with tinges of red would at least not attract much attention beyond that of an athletic, attractive woman.

"Come. There are some elves I wish to introduce you to. Perhaps they can help. Put your hand on my shoulder."

Hovan began the spell.

⸺◆⸺

Julian reached consciousness sooner than Laexa. Slowly, he turned his head, verifying that they were in his room in the lodge. He took two deep breaths, which fully restored his alertness.

"Racine, we are here in my room."

"Sanlar and I are in the lobby, ready to travel. We?"

"My protector is with me."

"Excellent. She should be. We will come up."

Julian guided Laexa to the bed. He sat her on the edge before opening the door to the hallway. A few moments later, Racine, Sanlar, and Lily walked in.

"Any problems here?" asked Julian in Dahican.

"Nothing," answered Racine, responding in his native language. "Introductions?" He gestured toward Laexa.

"Give her a moment more."

"Any injuries?" asked Lily, stepping past Sanlar.

"Only bruises and a sore shoulder. I will be fine."

"Of course you will," said Lily. She put her hand on his shoulder, assessing it for damage, despite agreeing with him. "Your shoulder will be fine. I will see to it later."

"Thank you, Healer," responded Julian.

Laexa rose to her feet next to him. A little shorter than Julian's six foot two frame, she looked down on the elves, who were each about five foot seven.

"Captain Laexa, I introduce you to Lord Racine of Liscam, his protector Sanlar, and healer Lily."

She bowed. "It is my honor to meet you," responded Captain Laexa in Dahican.

Julian continued. "I present Captain Laexa, First Captain of Forestton, and my protector."

The three elves bowed to her in formal greeting.

"I took three of the six bodies to Forestton. They have the brand on the upper thigh. Preparers."

"May the Ones we serve protect us!" exploded Sanlar. His hands moved in front of his body, perhaps to emphasize his words, thought Julian, but more likely an instinctive move into the ready position. "Preparers here? On this planet? And they know about you?"

"Yes to all three."

"You are in grave danger. It is good that your protector is here." He nodded, emphasizing his approval. "We are all in danger. They will want to prepare the people of this planet. People with no magic to protect them! That will be too much for them to resist. But you...you are strong in magic." He pointed to Julian in cadence with his words. "You they must kill to secure this planet. They will take great pleasure in killing you!"

Racine nodded, agreeing with Sanlar. "We are not wizards, and they may not know of us. You, Julian, they will hunt. Let us get back to your Rockland house to learn what we can before we abandon it."

"We need clothes for Laexa," said Julian.

"We have nothing that will fit her," said Lily, shaking her head and looking at the tall woman. "She will have to deal with whatever you can give her."

Julian shook his head in half-hearted agreement. "The baggy look is in."

He pulled a pair of jeans from his dresser, a tee shirt, and a hoodie. He tossed them to Laexa, saying, "This is all I have here." Opening the closet door, he chose a belt and a coat. "There is a better selection at my house."

They moved into the hallway as Laexa changed. When she opened the door, she held her hands out, asking for approval.

"Good enough," said Lily. The elf knelt and rolled up the cuffs of the jeans. "The boots can stay for now."

"Leave the sword," Julian said. "Hide some daggers under the coat. I do not expect trouble. We have magic and weapons more suitable to this place. Do you have your green brooch?"

She nodded yes.

Julian went back into the room and hid Laexa's things behind the closet door. He studied the room, checking that everything was in its place.

"We will arrive in a small room under my garage," Hovan said.

"You can move all of us?" asked Lily.

"I am a wizard. Do you have a defensive spell?"

"Yes," she said. "Racine put one on me."

The five people barely fit in the dimly lit room. Julian went up the ladder first and moved into the garage. He looked out the window and checked the security cameras using his phone.

"Nothing," Julian said.

Laexa looked at his SUV. "What is this?"

"Later. Activate your brooch, please." Julian turned on his defensive magic as well.

The three elves turned on their disguise magic: Racine as a Caucasian man, Sanlar as a Hispanic man, and Lily as a beautiful, light brown, Indian woman, not changing her natural skin color.

Julian led them across the yard to the porch. Laexa took the rear point. Racine and Sanlar walked on either side of Lily, keeping her in the middle of the diamond. No guns were visible in case some kid from one of the nearby houses was playing among the trees, though it was probably too early. Handguns were within easy reach if needed.

Julian advanced up the porch steps and looked in the kitchen window. Three dead bodies lay piled off to the side. Reddish brown pools of blood, blood stains, spatter, and smears discolored the gray tile floor. Radiating cracks in the dull white plaster walls stretched out from large holes. The holes revealed charred wooden wall studs. The broken wooden kitchen table, pushed up against the stove, remained where he had left it.

He waved everyone inside.

The competing scents of gunpowder residue, charred wood, and blood confused their sense of smell with a sickening array of aromas.

Julian pointed at the stack of shotguns, handguns, and semiautomatic machine guns. "Those are loaded. Be careful. Laexa, do not touch those for now." Looking around at his damaged, invaded house, he took a deep breath. "What do we do first?"

Racine spoke. "Sanlar, secure the weapons. Captain Laexa, if you would help me search the bodies. Lily, stand watch by the windows. Julian, pack what you need."

Julian headed upstairs to the bedrooms. He pulled out two suitcases and began stuffing clothes in. Ten minutes later, he walked into the kitchen, dragging the suitcases. Lifting them over the blood and debris in the kitchen, he placed them on the back porch.

"Anything on the bodies?" asked Julian.

"More brands on the upper thighs," said Laexa. "Knives and something they called bullets." She gestured toward Racine.

Julian listed the tasks that needed to be completed before leaving. "I need to move the bodies to Forestton. We need to find their rental car. Remove the guns. Clean the blood in view from the windows. I expect someone will eventually look in once the house has been vacant for a time. Then, pack up and leave."

"You, with your protector," stressed Sanlar, "take the bodies to Forestton."

Laexa nodded in agreement.

"I will pack the weapons for transport," continued Sanlar.

"Lily and I will clean up the kitchen," said Racine. "Fire should burn the blood, but not the tiles."

Julian brought a dark wood rocking chair into the kitchen. He sat. They piled the three dead bodies onto his lap. Laexa stood behind him, hand on his shoulder. After a moment, they disappeared.

When Julian and Laexa returned, the kitchen looked to be in far better shape than when they had left. The blood was gone. A dust pan and broom, resting in the corner next to a partially filled garbage bag, explained the missing pieces of wall that had dirtied the floor. The kitchen table lay propped up against the wall in the dining room, out of sight. The back door and window were open, airing out the smell.

"We can do nothing about the holes in the wall," said Racine.

"We will pull the blinds and hope for the best," offered Julian.

"I organized the basement as well," Sanlar said.

"Let me shower and change into clean clothes. Then we can search for their rental car."

After putting on a clean set of clothes, Julian led Laexa out the back door. They walked the neighborhood in the morning sunlight, searching for a car that beeped when he pressed the button on the key fob with the Avis sticker. Laexa had insisted that she come. Her inability to speak English worried him should they meet a neighbor out for an early morning stroll with their dog, but her presence helped present the image of a couple enjoying a chilly walk. It also helped that she had found some better fitting clothes.

Four streets over, a car beeped. Julian climbed into the driver's seat and motioned for Laexa to sit in the front passenger seat. Laexa looked around in wonder as Julian drove the minivan to the local mall.

"They call it a car. A machine. No animals needed. Please do not touch anything."

After searching it and finding nothing useful, he wiped their fingerprints from the key and the car's interior. He left the minivan unlocked with the keys inside, parked in the lot. Racine picked them up, driving Julian's SUV, and drove back to Julian's house.

Julian loaded his suitcases and his laptop computer into the SUV. Sanlar and Racine handed him garbage bags with the guns wrapped up. He placed these on the floor of the back seat and hid them under a few bags of food from the refrigerator.

Everyone walked back into the house to make one last inspection.

"I will magic Sanlar and Lily to the Lodge," said Racine. "We will see you and Captain Laexa later this morning. Stick to smaller roads. Avoid tolls and license plate readers."

Julian watched them until they vanished. He then locked up the house and walked to his car with Laexa.

Leaning on the open driver's side door, Julian looked at his house, locked and empty, mentally saying goodbye. He settled into the driver's seat. After showing Laexa how to use a seat belt and the radio, he took them through a drive thru Dunkin' Donuts and bought Laexa her first black coffee.

With a coffee cup cooling in the cup holder, Julian drove two and a half hours to the rolling hills of western Massachusetts, known as the Berkshires. He spent most of the time answering questions from Laexa about Earth. Explaining the airplane that flew over was difficult.

⸻⟡⸻

Julian drove up the long driveway up the hill to the lodge. They saw Racine standing on the front porch, waiting for them. Sanlar appeared a few moments later. The group unloaded the car. They moved Laexa into a room on the second floor next to Julian's room.

"Lily has made us lunch," said Racine. "Let us all sit together, eat, think, and talk."

"Thank you, Racine," said Julian, "for letting us move in on such short notice."

"You are welcome," answered the elf. With a smile, Racine laughed. "You make seeking refuge and sanctuary from violence seem like a man kicked out of his house by an irrational roommate. Your room is yours, as always. We are happy to have Captain Laexa with us."

The five sat around the kitchen table. Lily had prepared sandwiches and served them with water and cold beer.

Julian motioned to Laexa to help herself. "Eat while I think." Ignoring the conversation, which was centered on explaining the new items to Laexa and her relaying news from home, he ate and thought.

Laexa will need proper clothes and weapons training. Lily for the first. Sanlar for the second.

We must find the Preparers before they find us again. That would require the services of Racine's and Tom's private investigator company.

How many of them are we looking for? We would need to kill them. Kill them all. They will certainly come for me again when they realize I am not dead. How much time do we have until they realize that?

Where are their secret rooms? We must destroy them or kill any magician who memorized them.

The rest of the group sat in conversation. All three elves had dropped their human disguises. Easier than English for the elves, they spoke in Dahican, the language of the elven kingdom of Dahica, the country of their birth. This was one of the two languages they shared with Laexa. The other was Rel'ellon, the human tongue of Arre'ielle. The elves preferred their native language.

Racine gently broke into Julian's thought. "Care to share your thoughts?"

"They must be located and removed," Julian both stated and questioned his host.

"I know," responded Racine. "I wonder how long they have been on Earth. If they have assimilated into this society, we may never remove them all. They may understand this world better than we do."

"First action is to find them," stated Sanlar. "Find them. Kill them. Keep them out!"

"Without them finding us," added Racine. "We will start with the rental car and the dead bodies, the names, faces, wallets, guns."

"We must warn other off worlders that Preparers are here!" insisted Lily.

Not sure if that is a good idea. Telling others may expose us. She is a healer, though. Her views are quite different. She may see the need for violence while simultaneously detesting it. I see no way of solving this without it.

"Who can we trust?" asked Sanlar.

"Yes," agreed Racine, "we must move carefully to not reveal ourselves while still locating our prey and protecting as many as possible."

"We have work ahead of us," concluded Julian. "We will need the investigating skills of your group, but also the skills of those like Sanlar, Laexa, and me."

"I fear you are right," said Racine. "Hopefully, we will not need the skills of Lily too often."

Sanlar stared at Julian. The elf leaned forward on his elbows. "This world will be impossible for them to resist. You must die for them to succeed. They will want to find you again, for you are too strong. You are in danger. Your protector must stay by your side. I know you are a wizard, but you are just one man."

"We are all in danger," said Racine. "But I agree with Sanlar. You, Julian, most of all. May the One you serve protect you."

After sipping his coffee, Julian spoke. "I am the hunted and the hunter."

Laexa added. "I do not know this society, but I assume it is like any other. Filled with mostly good people worthy of protection. With your exceptional ability, you are required to respond to their great need."

"So, we should stay and fight, as few as we are?" asked Julian.

"Rhetorical, I assume," stated Laexa.

"Yes, my protector."

Laexa nodded.

"It is time I called Tom again." Julian dialed.

"Tom, good morning. It is Julian. The ones that attacked me are members of a group called Preparers, when translated into English."

"Preparers?" asked Tom. "What are 'Preparers'? Where are you? Will we still see you tomorrow?"

"The One they serve promotes leaving this worthless life and taking as many with them as possible. At the lodge. Yes." Julian took a breath. "We need to talk. They should not be able to trace me back to you. However, I do not know how long they have been watching me. Be careful, Tom!"

"Cathy and I need to work on some cases today in Boston. After, we will come to the lodge."

"I suggest you go to your parents' house as planned. They may need to be protected. I need to gather my thoughts and sleep."

"You think my parents are in danger!?"

"I do not know. How did they find me?"

"Julian, finding you is easy; you have a driver's license, a bank account, and a credit card. Anyone could do it. I advise you not to use your credit card. Why do they want to find you? What do they know about the rest of us?"

"How did they know to look for me here?"

"Yes," agreed a worried Tom, acknowledging the importance of the unanswered question. "All right, I'll see you on Long Island tomorrow. Keep in touch."

Julian touched End on his phone.

CHAPTER 23

FRIENDS AND STRANGERS

Julian Orel's eyes snapped open as his body shook. Breaths came in short gasps. His abdomen clenched emptiness. The sheen of warm sweat covering his face masked any tears he might have shed. Upset and confused, he tried to figure out where he was. The nightmare of his wife's death had battled its way into his sleep again.

He had fallen asleep soon after his phone call with Tom. His body was still adjusting to the Eastern time zone, and he had not slept last night. The soft yellow light from the afternoon Sun seeping through the closed blinds backlit his room at the lodge. Julian freed himself from the twisted sheets and worked his way to the bathroom. In the dark, he took a cold shower. He stood, shivering under the cold spray, trying to wash away sleep's memories. Unable to.

Finally, he pulled himself from the cold water and, still shivering, dried himself off. Turning the bathroom light on, he shaved and combed his blond hair. He walked into the bedroom and checked the time.

Damn.

Quickly, he dressed.

When he was ready to leave, Julian looked himself over in the dresser mirror. The reflection revealed a tall, young man dressed in a neat pair of jeans and a slim leather jacket covering a banded collar dress shirt closed at the neck. The jeans concealed an ankle holstered compact semiautomatic handgun. Not his pistol of choice, but easier to conceal than his preferred shoulder holstered 9 mm. The spring evening may develop a chill later, but he could not plan on keeping his jacket on all night. The youthful face was handsome, well defined, and emblazoned with a set of deep blue eyes. Those catching eyes had often shown forth with confidence, perhaps arrogance. This was not one of those times. Now, they were the slowly flickering eyes of a tired man who felt decades older than he looked.

Cleaned, shaved, and dressed, Julian picked up the gift bag with 'Happy Graduation' in bold, rainbow print and left his room. Laexa was not in her room next door. He headed down the stairs. She would argue again that she must go with him. But he did not know how that could work. He was not in the mood to debate, but slipping out quickly would only infuriate her.

Julian walked into the kitchen. Lily looked over from the counter where she was cutting the florets from a head of broccoli. Her eyes scanned his outfit.

"Very nice," she said. "She is out back getting a handgun lesson from Sanlar. Good luck."

Julian mumbled, "Thank you."

When he turned the corner to the portion of the backyard that served as a range for both handguns and archery, he found Sanlar and Laexa sitting at a table reloading magazines.

Choosing not to sit, Julian spoke to his first captain in Dahican. "You do not speak English. You cannot come."

"I do not need to speak."

"You speak no language native to this planet. It is a family party. Your presence will require explanations and introductions."

"I can wait in that machine you call a car. I will be close and watching the entrance."

"That would attract attention. You would not be close enough to protect my back."

"If I cannot go, then you should not go either!" Laexa said.

"I respect your opinion, Captain. You cannot come to the party. I feel I should go. These are my friends, and they may be in danger. As a protector, you can understand that. I will be back late tonight. I am rested and carry weapons."

Laexa stood. Julian could see her anger in the squint of her eyes and the set of her jaw. "Preparers hunt you. You go to a place where you may be expected. And you choose to go without me?"

"I do not choose this, but I see no other way. If I am expected, then this family needs me. Most of the family do not know who I am. I cannot explain you. You are not a cousin visiting from overseas." Julian chuckled. "You do not blend."

"You are in danger! This is my job."

"Then let us return to Forestton and never come here again. Leave this world to fend for itself. Is that what you advise, protector?"

Sanlar straightened on the bench and broke his silence. "No, you cannot."

Laexa exhaled in frustration. "Then take protector Sanlar. He speaks."

Sanlar looked up at Laexa. "I will not leave Racine."

"Even better. Take them all. I will use my formidable skills to guard the dogs."

Julian chose not to respond to her sarcasm. He took a few moments to consider this new plan and let some of the tension drift away. Hoping Sanlar would reject the proposal, Julian asked, "Sanlar?"

"Possible. Melissa did not invite us, though we at least know Tom and Cathy and have met his parents."

"Safety in numbers," challenged Laexa.

Julian took several deep breaths to continue thinking and find his resolve. He sat down and gestured for Laexa to sit.

"Option A: the Preparers do not know of Tom and his family," said Julian. "There is no threat. Option B: they suspect and are watching. If so, arriving with a non-English speaking warrior and two or three elves using disguise magic would confirm their suspicions. Option C: they know. If so, the family is probably dead already or taken. Or they wait for my arrival to attack."

"I favor A, fear B, and do not want to even think about C. What is the priority? Protect me, the Rosses, or this planet. You are both protectors. I know your answer. If I am to fight for this planet, then I become a protector as well. Secrecy matters. I do not need magic or language lessons to attend the party. What would you have me do? Do not ask what I want. I want Suzhanee."

"Being noble?" asked Laexa.

Julian noted the resignation in his protector's tone.

It only took questioning the safety of a planet to convince her to step back. Nice to know my safety is so important to her.

Sanlar said, "We need you to win the war."

"The Rosses may be in danger," said Julian. "If not, your presence may bring them danger. It is a long drive. I need to go."

Julian rose.

Laexa walked in silence with him to his SUV. When they reached the car, Laexa spoke. "I feel I should be with you. By your side. Protecting you. Or at least have your back. I respect your decision, but I fear your fatalism."

"Go with noble. Fatalism simply makes it easier to enter the battle."

"May the One you serve protect you."

The four hour drive passed without incident. Julian paid little attention to the rolling hills of western Massachusetts and eastern New York, or the trees which lined the Taconic Parkway he followed toward Westchester, or the larger buildings which sprang up as he passed into New York City. He had studied all these during other trips. He seemed to not notice the passing sights he usually found so intriguing. All he hoped for was little traffic on the Throgs Neck Bridge and the Long Island Expressway.

Julian struggled to burn off the mental fog that veiled his usually disciplined mind. He tried reviewing what he knew about this dangerous and expanding danger.

Preparers in Feleine are *bad enough. Preparers here could be disastrous. The two together suggested a well conceived plan. Is this a new crisis or a continuation of an old one? Well, that does not really matter. Where are they, these people who wanted me dead?*

An image of a long haired brunette screaming burst into his mind.

Focus, damn it!

Gorzyne killed. One for our side.

Surprise attack repelled. Two for our side.

But six attackers, none of whom seemed to know enough magic to transport them to this planet. So, the magician is here somewhere and probably not alone.

Someone has been teaching these bad guys higher level magic. Magic that allows them to move planets and control a gorzyne.

I hope the IDs of the attackers provide us with a direction before they strike again.

Julian ended his mental soliloquy as he turned his car onto the lawn lined neighborhood roads of western Suffolk County. He cruised the suburban streets, now careful to notice what he saw.

Business is business, whether you find it, or it finds you.

He turned onto the Rosses' block and drove up the street. Even if he had not known which house was the Rosses', he would have had no trouble locating it. The car filled driveway and the loud music from the backyard identified which residence was celebrating a college graduation. Julian locked his car and checked his surroundings. He would have preferred to carry his staff with him. But this persona required that it stay hidden in his car.

Tom Ross met him at the front door. His close cut, dark brown hair and glasses would have made him look like a typical white male college professor, complete with a clarity of speech and wide vocabulary, except for his height and muscular arms. The slight gaunt appearance of his face completed the look of someone who exercised regularly.

"It is good to see you, Julian," Tom said with a weak smile. "You're late. You had me worried."

"Good to be seen," answered Julian in a subdued but sincere voice.

The two friends exchanged a look of concern. Tom ushered Julian inside.

Together, they walked into the living room. Melissa was there, adding another present to her growing stack of graduation gifts.

Julian looked at Melissa and, as always, her beauty touched him as if she were a beloved memory. A surge of adrenaline and nervousness surged through him as he again took in her features. Her hair glistened over her shoulders like a dark, moonlit river flowing smoothly, engulfing a stone in its path. Her eyes, as she turned toward him, sparkled with intelligence and humor. Like sunlight off polished wood, her eyes sparkled a shade lighter than her hair. She was Melissa. He felt conflicted and young again.

"Here is another gift for your collection, Melissa." Julian hid his unsavory emotional state in his soft accent. "Congratulations on your graduation from college. A noble pursuit, well accomplished!"

"Thank you," said a smiling Melissa. She gave him a warm kiss on the cheek.

Sometimes he wished she would not do that. It was a taste of something he hungered for, but could not have.

"The party's in the back." Putting her arm around Julian, Melissa announced energetically, "Now that you're here, my party proper can begin!"

Reluctant to do so, but not cheerful enough to let Melissa sweep him away from other concerns, Julian gently unwrapped Melissa's arm. He shook his head no. "I need to talk to Tom first. We will join you soon."

Melissa slowly lowered her head, letting her hair seductively hide part of her angular face. After framing her face, the hair dropped to the curve of her breast. From behind the shadow of her soft, dark hair, she flashed Julian a smoky, alluring scowl. She enticed. "Come, enjoy the party. Come with me."

With the speed of a shooting star, Julian's heart quickened and his hands unconsciously flexed, almost reaching for her. His gaze burned through the hair obscuring Melissa's eyes and saw all that was important in her smoldering, brown eyes. His blue eyes deepened in response to a shade of yes.

Images of another young, long haired brunette, this one riding a galloping orvbac, flashed through his mind, followed immediately by the stabs of pain. Melissa's nubile figure filled his lonely eyes. Her tempting words echoed through his receptive mind. "Come with me."

Half unbelieving what he was saying and half flinging the words at her, Julian said, "No, I cannot." He softened and added, "Not yet."

Melissa swung her hair back and faded.

Switching from temptress to employer, Melissa said, "All right, but make it damn quick. This is my party. Tonight is for celebration, not business, as some serious types seemed to have forgotten." She looked at her brother as she said the last part.

Behind her solemn, almost hurt tone, the warmth in her eyes again stirred an emotion in Julian. He could not help but smile and then cursed himself for weakness. Mimicking her serious tone, but exchanging the hurt for scared, he responded as one would to an employer. "Yes, Miss Ross."

Melissa walked past Tom, complaining under her breath. "Doing business at my graduation party!"

Tom returned, "You didn't think I drove all this way just to see you, did you?" The older brother and younger sister exchanged sarcastic grins.

Julian noticed Tom staring at him. Tom said in a voice that was two parts humorous and one part concerned, "I have never seen any male withstand Melissa's siren's gaze!" When Julian neglected a response, Tom asked, "Are you alright?"

"Conflicting dreams. New troubles."

Tom nodded understanding. "Let's talk in the office."

Julian followed Tom upstairs and into the kitchen. Mr. and Mrs. Ross sat around the kitchen table, seeking refuge from the festivities. Tom's father was a Marine, retired, who kept a close watch on his only daughter. Mrs. Ross was obviously the source of Melissa's beauty. She was tall, like her children, but could wear heels when dancing with her six foot four husband. Cathy, Tom's wife, chatted with them while waiting for Tom. After exchanging hellos and a quick joke, Julian, Tom, and Cathy headed to Tom's old bedroom, which his parents had converted into a home office.

Tom settled onto a loveseat with Cathy. Julian sat in the desk chair. When Julian did not start, Tom asked, "Have they found anything yet?"

Julian answered. "Not much. Elves and computers." Julian gave a hand gesture, signifying futility. "I was not at the lodge and awake for long. The credit card number and Washington driver's licenses should bring up information." Julian looked at his two friends as if gauging them. "This is going to get violent. Think whether you want in before acting. Once in, your family is in as well."

"We don't have a choice, Julian," said Tom. "So, dispense with the theatrics. Tell us what you know. Who are Preparers? Why do they want you? What are we up against?"

Julian began. "Preparers advocate ending this life. Death is a necessary step to the great afterlife. This temporary existence is near meaningless for them beyond a brief waiting period to prove their worth. This life must end so the next life can begin. While alive, they seek to teach or 'prepare' as many as possible to understand the necessity of death and the futility of living. Despair and torture are used to make you want, even beg, to be sent to the One you serve. Do not get taken alive! Do not let someone you care about get taken alive." Julian emphasized these last points with his finger.

Tom sank further into the cushions. "I hadn't heard of Preparers before. When I heard the fear in yours and Racine's voices, I was afraid it was something like this."

"Because we know you, we become targets too," stated Cathy. Like Julian, Cathy was a blue eyed blonde, though she was considerably shorter than her husband. Shorter in stature, but not in intelligence, she would joke.

"And them," said Julian with a wave of his hand, indicating the rest of the Ross family. "I will do my best to stop them. I do not know if I can on my own. You are my friends! I feel responsible since they followed me here. People on this planet simply do not have the magic to protect themselves!" Julian's voice faltered for a moment after stumbling through his unorganized explanation. "It will not be easy! Preparers play by a different set of rules."

Cathy tightly gripped her husband's arm and pulled herself close. Tom's brow furrowed as his lips pressed into a thin line.

"Julian, your needing help to get information is one thing," said Tom. "However, you asking us to help to deal with someone on this planet full of technology but magically inept is cause for alarm."

"Tell us about the 'last time'?" asked Cathy.

Very good. She has enough composure to continue following rule number three: when you have an information source, keep collecting until it runs dry.

"A few years before the wars in Arre'ielle, I accepted a job to remove a group that was preying on the local people. Ke'en was busy in Shetteca and unavailable. We did not complete the mission the way I would have liked. Yes, we chased off the group and damaged the stronghold enough to make it unusable. However, we only secured part of their stronghold and never searched the entire complex. They neglected to tell us that the Preparers for the Afterlife controlled the hidden stronghold until it was too late to make changes. I would have organized differently and brought a stronger force. This opponent is the last one I want to find me." A moment later, he added in a quieter voice, "They nearly got Suzhanee...alive."

Julian closed his eyes and took a slow breath. After another deep breath, he opened his eyes. "It was before we married and strengthened our relationship. That trip showed Suzhanee what I did for a living and the dangers in my life. It did not scare her off! It scared her, but she did not leave me!"

He took a breath. "I miss her."

"I wish I could have met her," said Tom.

More calmly, Julian finished his reasoning. "I figure they traced me to this world, though how and why I matter, I do not know. There seems to be a lot going on here and at home."

Concerned, Cathy continued. "If they know you are here, they must know about Forestton. If these people are as dangerous as you say, is Forestton..." Cathy paused.

"Standing," offered Julian. "I left only yesterday."

"Why wouldn't they simply wait for your return to Forestton and attack you there? Why go through all this?"

"I go to Forestton sporadically and have not been staying long. Attacking me in my town or in Shetteca would be dangerous for them. A troop of Preparers would have difficulty waiting for me while going unnoticed. Few individuals can defeat me. Also, I think this unprotected world must be very enticing to them. Imagine what they could do here! Who could stand against them with magic supporting their violence? They need me off Earth if they want it for themselves. I will not give it to them."

"Why do you want to hire us to do the background checking?" Tom asked. "Why don't you do it yourself?"

"First, your group could do the searches better than I could. All that private investigation computer stuff, internet searches, recognition software... Second, if a religion such as this establishes itself on this planet, it will be dangerous for everyone, but especially for the off worlders living here. They may find your association before locating me again. Your use of magic to get in and out of places and move things, limited and concealed as it is, might attract their attention. The right person will see the disguise magic of the elves if they look for it. Third, when I find them or they find me again, I will need all your help. We may need even more help than that."

Tom and Cathy grew quiet. Tom stood up and absentmindedly walked the length of the small room. After a few moments, Tom said, "It seems we have no choice but to help. How could we not help a friend? Plus, we will need you to get them off the planet."

Tom spoke with his emotions in control and subsiding. "Our chance to save the world!" he said with a sly smile.

"God damn it, how like you," started Cathy. "If you're not out battling death by making yourself young, you're out battling death directly. I've always been told that wizards are arrogant."

Relieved that the interview was over, Julian responded to Cathy's taunt, saying, "You are simply envious, my little friend, because when you are my age, you will look it."

"I am not short!" yelled Cathy.

"Really," Julian countered, approaching a teasing quality, but with his emotions adding a darkness to his voice. "What matter of creature are you, then? If you were human and five foot four, you would be short." Softening his tone to take the edge off, he asked, "Besides, how many wizards do you know?"

Cathy smiled.

To change the subject without appearing to do so, Julian asked, "Has your family noticed anyone unusual about lately?"

"No. Not that they have said."

"Let us join Melissa's party," said Cathy. Motioning Tom and Julian toward the door, Cathy added, "Before she comes looking for us."

CHAPTER 24

STRANGERS IN THE NIGHT

When Julian reached the backyard, he stopped and looked around, impressed. Strings of colored lights, blue, red, green, and yellow, hung from the trees, softly lighting the festive gathering. Two large speakers connected to someone's playlist filled the crowded yard with unending music.

She must have understanding neighbors.

Various snacks and finger foods covered one table. A second table held the makings for all types of assorted drinks. Two kegs kept the cold beer flowing, leaving no one waiting. Even nature seemed in accord with Melissa. The evening was a comfortably cool Long Island evening with bright stars overhead and a carpet of green grass below.

Eat, drink, and be merry. A concept put into action. There are a lot of people here doing just that. Melissa is popular, as beautiful women often are.

So many people are here.

Just as Tom, Cathy, and Julian walked out the back door, Melissa strode up to them.

"It's about time you got down here!" Melissa said. "I was just about to come up and drag you down. Really, Tom, let him play. If he's got writer's block, maybe some fun will loosen him up."

She wrapped her arm around Julian's arm, holding it tight, positioning herself between Julian and the other two. "No more business tonight, okay, Tom?"

"Fine by me," exclaimed Tom. "I'd rather drink beer than deal with his problems."

"Good. Food and drinks are on the tables. Please help yourself."

Taking the less than subtle hint, Tom took Cathy's hand and, together, they headed for the keg.

Smiling at Julian, Melissa said, "I'm glad you came. I haven't seen you since Boston. Tom said you were busy, feverishly writing, but that's not it, is it?" Without waiting for a response, she added, "I got worried you'd stay away tonight, too."

Julian looked into her brown eyes looking up at him and said, "I am glad I came." He paused. "I have been away. Issues at home have kept me busy. You know writing is not all I do."

"I know, but I don't know what else there is. You don't let people in easily, Mr. Orel."

"There always seems to be a distance between us we do not close," Julian agreed. "Perhaps someday I will tell you my story, but I am not sure you will like what you hear."

"Tom says you're a conflicted man with an angry past."

"How like the writer."

"I want to know you, Julian," said Melissa. "But I won't wait."

"Be careful what you wish for, Miss Ross. I am terrified of hurting you."

"Hey, Melissa," someone yelled. "We need a picture."

"Sounds like someone is jealous," joked Julian.

"He is not my type," stated Melissa. "But he is funny."

"Go. Be the good hostess. I should say hi to Mike."

Melissa kissed his cheek. "Later."

Julian took a long, slow breath as he walked toward Tom's seventeen year old brother. Mike had the athletic height, over six feet, that both brothers had inherited from their parents. He also had the same dark brown hair and brown eyes that the whole family shared.

"Mike." Julian nodded hello.

"Julian," Mike stated formally, with a matching nod. Mike's eyes never left a beautiful, clearly older woman. "What are the odds?"

Julian looked at the woman, then back at Mike. "Slim to none. She is your sister's age."

"Pessimist."

"Realist."

"Not every pretty girl has a boyfriend. Melissa doesn't." Mike looked at Julian. "Though I think she wants one." Noticing Julian's empty hand, he said, "You get a beer and I'll get a date."

"Good luck."

Beer in hand, Julian stood with his back to the house, watching the ebb and flow of the crowd. Tom and Cathy were slow dancing, her head on his shoulder, despite the fast paced music. Mike had delivered a full plastic cup to his prospective date and started a conversation. Melissa flashed in and out of groups. A few of Melissa's friends he had met, but most of the crowd were strangers.

Eventually, Mike wandered over to him.

"No luck, Mike?" asked Julian.

"She's got a boyfriend."

Together, they refilled their beers and grabbed a snack.

"Have you finished another book?" Mike asked.

"Not yet, but almost. You will like this one too. A pretty, redhead woman helps the main character. Her best feature is her intelligence. She is really, really smart. Lots of one liners. Reminds me of a teacher I had."

"Make her beautiful and put her on the cover. It's about time you put some good sex in your books."

"I thought you would appreciate it." Julian glanced around and said, "There are a lot of people here."

"I love it when Melissa throws a party. One of the few times my parents let me drink beer."

"There are too many people here."

"Since when are you nervous?"

Julian shrugged his shoulders and sipped his beer.

Tom and Cathy emerged from the crowd and joined them. "Drinking with my younger brother?" joked Tom.

"He's all yours," said Mike. "He's no fun tonight." Mike walked off.

"Are you okay?" asked Cathy, turning toward Julian.

"I do not feel comfortable around all these strangers."

"These are Melissa's friends," argued Tom. "She's an excellent judge of character."

"Who is a friend of a friend?" asked Julian. "I would prefer to head inside. I would leave, but that would upset her."

"She won't be happy with you inside, either." Pointing up, Tom said, "We can sit up on the deck."

"Can we bring more of these?" Julian held up the finger sandwich.

"Of course," said Cathy. "You two head up. I'll get the food and refills."

Julian looked around the party for Melissa. She stood across the yard with her back to him. They slipped inside and past Mr. and Mrs. Ross, who were still hiding in the kitchen. Tom explained they were seeking sanctuary on the deck.

Cathy returned, balancing a plate of small sandwiches on a triangle of beer cups. "Sandwiches and a refill for each of us."

"Thank you for the food," said Julian. "I have not eaten much."

Tom looked at Julian. "We could tell Melissa that you're not feeling well so you could leave. However, I'm scared that you're scared and feel more comfortable with you here."

"I understand," said Julian. "I feel so exposed here, though. I will stay for a while."

Tom spoke. "You could stay here tonight. Tell my parents you had too much beer. They won't mind."

"You may be safer if I leave," Julian said. "The bad guys may not know about you."

"They wouldn't be looking here if they did not already suspect," returned Tom.

"Tom, there are many people here who we do not know."

"If my family may be in danger, I would rather have you here. If someone has already spotted you, then nothing more is at risk."

Before Julian could respond, Cathy interrupted. "Gentlemen. Tom's parents are just inside the door. And people below can see us. Sip your beer and quiet down, please."

Both men did as they were told.

"The door is closed and the music is on," defended Tom.

"I did not think we were that loud," continued Julian.

"Sure, sure," said Cathy. "Gang up on the one being rational."

Julian looked at Cathy. "I do not think I was being irrational."

"Me neither," said her husband. Looking at Julian, Tom said, "You want our help. I want yours. Stay one night."

"An attack on me here would be dangerous for everyone. If I leave, people might only see us as passing acquaintances."

"You're sitting here having a beer with my wife and me in my parents' house. There is nothing 'passing' about it. My family is safer if you are here to protect them."

Cathy again interrupted. "Keep your voices down. If you two insist on arguing, take it into the office."

Julian was quiet for a moment. He stood and walked inside. Tom followed.

CHAPTER 25

WHAT NEXT?

Cathy remained sitting on the deck, looking out over the party.

I don't know who is right. Geez, a wizard is scared! I'm scared too. Perhaps if I told Julian that, it would sway the argument in Tom's favor. It does not sound like the people looking for him care who they hurt along the way.

She picked up the plate of finger sandwiches and entered the kitchen.

"Is everything okay?" asked Mrs. Ross. "The boys look upset."

"They…" was all she could say before Melissa cut her off.

"Where did Tom take Julian?" demanded Melissa, speaking from the hallway by the kitchen entrance.

"I think…" Cathy stopped when Melissa turned and marched down the hall.

"Why is she upset?" asked Mrs. Ross. "It's her graduation party!"

Mr. Ross turned and looked at Cathy, his eyebrows raised, seeking an explanation.

Cathy put the sandwiches down, stalling as she thought of an answer. In a speech more rapid than she wished, she tried to explain. "Tom and Julian disagree about what they should do next. Melissa is unhappy that they're talking business at her party. I'll go talk to them."

"You do that," said Mr. Ross, dismissing her to carry out his order.

Mike passed the kitchen before Cathy exited. "Melissa, some of your friends are wondering where you are."

Cathy moved down the short hall, trying to pass Mike, hoping to catch up to Melissa before she reached the office. She saw Melissa put her hand on the doorknob. The door opened just a little before Cathy caught up with Melissa. They could hear voices from inside. Cathy tried to close the door, but Melissa pushed her hand away.

"My being here puts many at risk," Julian said. "I should not have come."

"If you are not safe here, neither are we," argued Tom. "Stay the night."

"No one is hunting you. It is safer if I leave."

Melissa pushed the door fully open. "Who is hunting you?"

Mike stood next to her, looking lame and confused. "I tried to keep her downstairs."

The red in Tom's cheeks slowly faded as shock replaced his ire. He sat in the desk chair, looking at Melissa and Mike. Cathy ushered in her husband's younger siblings and closed the office door. She saw Julian's fingers twitching and then curl into a ball. Uncertainty silenced the room as eyes darted from one face to another.

CHAPTER 26

REVEAL

Finally, someone moved. Julian walked over to Melissa and Mike. "Sit, please." He checked the hallway and then closed the door again.

"What is going on?" Melissa insisted.

Tom and Cathy looked at Julian.

Julian looked at Tom. Tom said nothing. Julian started speaking in barely more than a whisper. "I am in trouble. Some people are looking for me. They want to kill me." Before Melissa could voice her disbelief, Julian stopped her. "There is a lot you do not know about me."

"Such as?" Melissa asked.

At that, Julian chuckled. "Oh, Melissa, you would not believe me if I told you!"

"Try me," challenged Melissa.

Julian's laugh sounded almost evil. "It is not that easy."

"Why not?" asked Melissa.

"Because you would call me a liar to my face."

"Try me anyway."

Julian turned to her brother again. "Tom?"

Tom opened his mouth to speak, but stopped short of words. Finally, he said. "Your call."

"What should I do?" asked Julian to no one in particular. "That is something I have been saying a lot lately."

Focusing on Melissa, Julian admitted, "Melissa, I do not know what the right move is."

He directed Melissa and Mike to sit on the loveseat. "If you do not know where the river flows, consider well before getting into

the boat. The proverb is more rhythmic in my native language. We all have moments when we must decide to get into the boat or not, without knowing the path of the river."

Julian paused before asking. "Do you really want to know? Is it not enough to know that I am in danger? Once you see behind the curtain, there is no going back."

"Behind the curtain? What? Are you the Wizard of Oz?"

"No," said Julian. "The Wizard of Forestton."

Melissa and Mike sat next to each other, looking at Julian, waiting for the joke.

Melissa finally asked, "Is that supposed to be funny?"

"No. Do you want me to explain? Do you want to take the boat ride?"

"You are late twenties and a writer. How much trouble could you be in?"

"I am older than that and a non-credited writer partner of a pen name, for a reason," explained Julian.

Pointing to her older brother with a nod of her head, Melissa asked, "Is my brother in danger also?"

Julian looked over at Tom.

Tom answered. "I think so."

"And us?"

"Possibly," said Julian.

Melissa reached an unhurried conclusion. "Then, I think you owe us an explanation. I will not forget or ignore what I heard. If my father finds out that you brought trouble to this house..."

"This is awkward," said Julian. "You will not believe me, but I trust you, so I will try. However, only on two conditions. You tell absolutely no one! That condition is for your safety and mine. No one, not even your parents. In addition, we will make use of your eyes. You must tell us if you see anything unusual, like people around the neighborhood that you do not know."

Melissa and Mike nodded.

Julian focused on Melissa. "You said in Boston that you wanted me to talk for a change. To hear about me. Do you still want that? You may not like what you hear."

Melissa nodded again. "Yes."

"I was not born on this planet. I travel here using magic. I am what you would call a wizard."

Mike tilted his head. "How much beer have you had?"

"Not enough." Annoyed but understanding, Julian told them, "Watch carefully."

His hands blurred through a quick, precise, choreographed pattern. Suddenly, hanging in the air in front of them were four flames: red, blue, green, and yellow. Julian directed them around the room, playing follow the leader, dodging between Tom and Cathy, skimming over Mike, swirling around Melissa's head. Eventually, they lined up and melted together into a white flame, which Julian held in his hand. He closed his hand on the flame. It vanished.

"It is a simple spell."

Mike was smiling, wide eyed. "How did you do that?"

"Magic," Julian responded.

"I'm serious," said Mike, looking around the room. "Tell me how you did that. Lights, lasers, holographs, how?"

"Directed application of mental energy."

"What?" said Mike and Melissa together.

"Magic," asserted Julian.

"Bullshit," said Mike. "Magic doesn't exist. This practical joke is taking a long time to become funny!"

Julian's face froze in anger, then ever so slowly melted. "Okay. Mike, explain this."

Again, his hands weaved a pattern. When he finished, nothing happened immediately, but he was staring at Mike.

Mike let out a startled mumble. Something was lifting him off the loveseat. He reached out and grabbed Melissa's arm.

"Let go!"

Mike did as Julian demanded and floated up. He twisted in the air and hovered upside down. He moved again. Julian was only inches from his face.

"What holds you up if not magic?"

Mike had no answer.

Melissa stood up. "You're in on this, Mike?"

"No, I swear."

With his mind, Julian reached out for Melissa.

"Oh my God."

She floated up next to Mike. Frightened, she looked at Julian.

Julian lowered both of Tom's siblings to their feet. Melissa and Mike did not move from where they had landed. They looked at each other, felt around them, and stomped on the floor.

"Magic does not exist!" Melissa stated. "Stop playing tricks on me!"

No one responded.

"Stop it!" she yelled.

Julian took her by the arm and sat her on the loveseat again. "You too."

Mike sat next to Melissa.

"I told you that you would call me a liar."

"This is not funny!" said Melissa.

Stiffly, Julian explained. "You asked to know what was up. I tried you, like you said. Magic, wizards, and soldiers with swords exist. Only not on this world. I was born on another planet and travel by magic. It is nothing to be afraid of."

He took Melissa's hand and rubbed the back of it with his thumb.

"I am a wizard and human, like you and Mike."

She pulled her hand from Julian and, standing up, moved away.

"Melissa," Julian cooed to Melissa as she hovered in fear by the door. "I told you that you would not believe me, and you said try me. You are in the boat now. Show me I was right to trust and that you have the strength to open your mind. There are a few of us off worlders who are aware of each other here. We occasionally get together to discuss things: how to adjust, news from home. You may wish to meet them. It may help you unravel your confusion. You can ask any question you like. We will answer them."

Melissa reached for the doorknob. Before she could leave, Julian rushed over with his two hands held in front of him, pleading for her to wait. He put one hand on the door and held up one finger, asking for one minute.

Starting with a hesitant explanation and ending in an emphatic cadence, Julian spoke. "Yesterday morning, people waited for me at my house and tried to kill me. For your safety, for my safety, for the safety of your family, do not mention this conversation to anyone!"

"I...I have to get back to my party," stuttered Melissa. "I've been away too long."

"Yes," suggested Cathy, "perhaps we should all head downstairs."

Cathy hurried to catch up with Melissa. Mike followed them out of the room without saying a word. Tom lagged behind. Julian never moved.

"Can you arrange a meeting at the lodge for next weekend?" asked Julian.

"Yes," said Tom. "I'm sorry."

Julian stopped him. "Whatever happens, happens. I was careless as well. Maybe it is for the best. I dislike deceiving her." He paused, then added, "Now, at least, she will not mind if I leave."

"I still want you to stay," said Tom. "But, with Melissa and Mike upset with you, I don't think I could justify that without more explanations to them... and my parents."

They left the office. Mr. Ross stopped them in the hallway. "Is everything alright?"

"Yes, Dad."

Sensing that this was not enough for Tom's retired military father, Julian spoke. "Melissa was not happy with Tom and me discussing business instead of celebrating her graduation. Tom and I are having a bit of a business disagreement. I tried a poor joke that was not received well."

"She is upset."

"I apologize," said Julian. "That was not my intent."

Mr. Ross nodded and backed into the kitchen, allowing Tom and Julian to walk down to the front door.

"Call me if anything comes up," said Julian. "Otherwise, I will see you at the lodge in a few days."

"Okay."

CHAPTER 27

THE BERKSHIRES

It was late when Julian crossed over the short bridge and opened the gate leading to the long, curving entrance to the former rod and gun club. As he closed the gate behind his car, he could hear the swift, narrow stream running below the bridge, though he could not see it in the dark. He drove slowly up the driveway. As he crossed to the porch, he looked up at the bright white dots of the stars shining in the clear sky above. He stopped to watch.

Which star was the Giver? Can I even see it from here?

Stars are so massive, but seem so small. I am even smaller.

Julian locked the main door behind him. Hungry, he turned into the dining room, heading toward the kitchen, and stopped.

Laexa sat at the dining room table. The pommel of her sword was visible, leaning on the table near her. A semiautomatic pistol was within reach.

"I think someone should be on watch," explained the captain in her native language of Rel'ellon. "I volunteered since I was going to wait up for you anyway. Any trouble?"

"Nothing violent. Melissa and Mike overhead Tom and me talking. I told her about the Preparers and the danger, but she does not believe me."

"I wish she were right."

"Me too. Who will relieve you on watch?"

"Sanlar told me to knock on his door."

"I will take the next shift. I slept in the afternoon, and I am hungry. See you in the morning."

"No, I am not tired. I know it is dark here, but the Giver must be shining in Forestton." Laexa held up a book. "They gave me this book of maps to look at. Can you translate for me?"

As dawn approached, Laexa decided she had seen enough of maps and went upstairs to bed. Just after sunrise, the two black Labs wandered into the dining room with their tails wagging, foretelling the arrival of Sanlar.

Too many thoughts were racing around Julian's head to even consider sleep. After gathering his fishing equipment and his handgun, he walked down to the pond. He fished his favorite spot, where the noisy stream quieted and dispersed into the small lake.

Racine joined him an hour later.

"I thought I might find you here," Racine said. "Sanlar thinks you are an idiot. Keeping watch all night and then sitting outside fishing by yourself."

Julian nodded understanding. "Sometimes, fishing is better for thinking. Fishing also provides breakfast."

"Success?"

"No, but I have not really tried. Throw your line in."

Racine settled himself on the bank near Julian and cast his line. Julian sat staring at the water, occasionally adjusting his line.

"No words this morning?" asked Racine.

"I have too much to think about. Last night, Tom's sister and brother overheard us. I tried to convince them by showing them some spells, but they do not yet believe in magic and elves."

The stunned look on Racine's face spoke more than his muttered expression. He broke into a soft laugh. "I understand their disbelief."

"Melissa overheard us. Then we had to explain. I invited Melissa and Mike here next weekend. I assumed you would agree. Please, tell me if I overstepped my bounds."

"Not at all, my friend. Tom's family is welcome."

The two fell silent for a time before Julian continued. "What have I gotten us all into? On our world is one thing, but not here."

"Fighting Preparers is a noble task whether it is to defend a region or protect a planet, despite what profit it might reap you. You came here to remove yourself from the memories of Suzhanee and the responsibilities of rank. A new world to occupy your mind. A fresh start. I cannot comment on the rest of your life's work, but there is no dishonor in these chapters."

Julian adjusted his line again. "I knew there is a reason I like you."

Racine chuckled. "Do you think they will try to establish a following on this planet?"

"Yes. We must throw them off the planet! Let the emptiness of space have them. Such a religion should not exist anywhere, but especially not here on a world with no magic to protect itself."

"Of the Ones that are served on our world, no following has moved here. I wonder why."

"I am curious about that, too," agreed Julian. "At first, I thought it was because these people were too skeptical of new religions to leave already established ones. However, many people search for power, or a purpose, or for someone to explain everything to them. All any of the Ones we serve need to do is to exert a little magic and people would flock to them. Even you or I could establish a respectable following that way."

"Why has the One we serve never established a fledgling comunity here?"

"I never asked," said Julian.

"Maybe none of them consider a world full of nothing but humans worth-while."

Julian smirked, but said nothing in response.

Racine continued. "Maybe it has already been done, and you and I simply do not know enough about the religions here to recognize that they are the same. Or at least follow the same messages. Perhaps the teachings are here. Are our values different from those preached here?"

"I think they are the same," said Julian. "The names are different, but the ideals are not. What about Lily?"

"She said she did not come here as a missionary for the One she serves, thus has no authority to establish a temple here."

"In other words, she is not high enough in rank to act on her own."

"Something like that," said Racine.

"The Preparers have opened the door to this world," said Julian. "I wonder if that will start a greater exchange of ideas."

"The servants of the One they serve will not hold that door open for others. If they are using it, then it must be closed."

"Yes," said Julian, nodding in agreement. "That may be as dangerous to me as the Preparers. The known portal listed in the central libraries must be the one they used to come here originally. If they are smart, however, they no longer use that secret room as you and I no longer use it. They would establish other secret rooms. If we are to keep them off this world, we must find and destroy these rooms, or the magicians who use them, as well as the one on record."

"Your high priest will not like that," warned Racine.

"Worse, the One I follow might not approve," said Julian. "The One I follow may consider it a breach of my contract."

"I do not know those details. It is not my place to ask you."

Julian slowly began. "I was outside the walls of Shetteca during the siege. I thought I could take advantage of the chaos caused by the influx of soldiers forced north by the king's offensive. But no."

Julian took a slow breath. "I was desperate. About to be killed. My emergency ring activated. Not sure how, as I was kept busy fending off attacks. No time to trigger it. Healed, I was sent to protect Shetteca. Suzhanee was in the city. I would have accepted any conditions to get back to her."

Julian paused again, then continued. "The way I figure it, if I am to protect this planet, I need to close all the portals available to the Preparers. What difference does it make if I make the One I follow mad at me? Preparers are worse."

"You are a gambler," Racine said.

"I do not like to fight the odds," Julian said. "I prefer to arrange them in my favor. Hence, my fascination with knowledge. This time, however, the two most probable outcomes end with my death. One, the Preparers find me and do what they will. Two, I find them first, remove them from this world, and close all the portals. By removing the knowledge from the central libraries or destroying the portal on record, I would break my agreement."

Julian sighed. "I retired to get away from all the fighting, only to have it follow me. It took Suzhanee. What more does it want?!"

"The One we serve has compassion. We are with you, weak as we may be. You are not fighting alone, my friend. I could not sit by and watch them consume this world. Sanlar is already restless to be at them!"

They continued to fish under the rising sun. The camaraderie of sharing an unsuccessful task eased Julian's growing tension.

Julian stirred. "Have you ever wondered how someone on our planet of Ra'viinen wrote a description of a location on Earth in sufficient detail to serve as a portal?"

"Yes, I have, and I do not know," answered Racine. "Before we came, Sanlar and I researched as much as we could. All reports suggested it was safe. I had heard of Carrie and her trips here while researching at the central library in eastern Dahica. We even met her there on one of her visits home. She vouched for the validity and safety of the secret room in Scotland. Have you asked?"

"I asked while preparing for my trip here. My preparation was less thorough than yours. In despair over Suzhanee, I was not tenacious in pursuing an answer. I was told it was not my concern. Perhaps now it is."

"The story of how a portal description on Earth got into the central libraries on Ra'viinen would be interesting to hear," suggested Racine.

Julian nodded, but changed the topic. "I can no longer use the name Julian Orel. I will have to change my name."

"Which one now seems good to you?"

Julian thought. "I think I will use Micah Falco. An uncommon first name that reminds me of stones; strength! Yes, I will become Micah Falco."

Racine shrugged his shoulders in partial agreement. "Is mica not a soft rock?"

"Picky! It is still a rock. Granite does not sound like a great first name. I am Micah Falco."

"What about Falco Granite?" teased Racine.

"Sounds like a quarry company or a kitchen design store. No, my new name is Micah Falco."

"Micah. Not bad, I guess. Short, like an elf's name."

When hunger told Micah that it was time for breakfast, they had not caught a single fish. He stood up, put his fishing rod down, and cast some magic. Quickly, he had two small brook trout.

"There is no sport in that," said Racine.

"No, but there is breakfast. Do you want me to throw yours back?"

"Yes, we have food in the kitchen."

Micah returned both fish to the stream. They swam away.

After breakfast, Micah could no longer ignore the need for sleep. He went upstairs to his room. His nightmare forced itself into his dreams again. A lonely pain woke him. He dealt with it quietly with help from a glass of bourbon and slowly fell back asleep.

CHAPTER 28

EXPLANATION?

Melissa woke up early the morning after the party and began the mindless task of cleaning up. As she collected the used paper plates and loaded the dishwasher with serving bowls and utensils, she thought about nothing, too tired and busy to devote much effort to thinking. She wanted to forget the events of last night, but it proved impossible once Tom and Cathy started to help. She said very little to them beyond good morning.

If they want to explain, then they can start with I'm sorry!

With her parents lending a hand with the cleanup, there was little opportunity to talk. Unless Tom wanted to try this joke on them.

Melissa stole glances at her older brother when he was not looking.

Why?

Mike walked into the kitchen, looking like he had not slept. Melissa exchanged a quiet, confused look with him. All the events of last night that she was trying to deny overran her refusals like an ocean wave washing over a sand castle. Mike said nothing, just looked at her, asking with his eyes if she had an explanation. She looked away, past confusion and into resentment.

Melissa saw Mike jump on his bike and ride away.

I wish I could get away too.

Melissa heard Cathy saying goodbye to her parents upstairs in the kitchen. Footsteps coming down to the living room could only be Tom.

"I'm sorry that you're upset, Melissa. That was not our goal. I know it sounds unbelievable. Come to the lodge in the Berkshires. We will prove it all."

"Not your goal? Scaring me with that ridiculous story!"

Tom pulled his right pant leg up. A small pistol was on his ankle. "I'm worried."

"That's supposed to impress me? You want to impress me? Tell Dad this story. I'm not stupid, Tom!"

"We know you are not stupid. That is the only reason Julian took the risk of telling you. I may have to tell Dad, but not yet." Tom held up his hand. "One at a time. Come to the lodge so we can show you. I can't show you here."

"Why? Magic doesn't work on Long Island? Oh, I forgot. You are not the wizard; the alien Julian is. You're just playing as his pawn in this game. And to think I thought Julian was special."

"Spare me the insults. He is more special than you realize. That he trusted you is a tremendous compliment."

Tom twisted his right hand around and pointed at the fireplace. A small ball of fire shot from his pointed finger and shattered into sparks on the back of the hearth.

"Magic does work in Long Island. I'm just a novice."

In silence, Melissa watched Tom walk upstairs to join his wife.

Tom and Cathy put their bags in the backseat. They waved goodbye. Tom settled into the driver's seat for the drive back to Boston.

Melissa watched from the front steps. No words came to mind.

"Are you okay?" asked Mrs. Ross.

"Older brothers can be so annoying," Melissa said.

⋯⋯⋯◆◇◆⋯⋯⋯

Melissa lay on her bed reading a page in a novel for the third time. Her mind kept wandering. A knock on her bedroom door barely preceded Mike opening the door.

His "I have an idea" trumped her "Leave me alone", stopping her protest.

"Maybe we felt nothing lifting us or saw anything moving the lights around the room because nothing moved. We only thought things did. Could Julian have hypnotized us?"

"Hypnotized?" questioned Melissa, head tilted in doubt.

"Magic?" Mike countered.

Melissa looked skeptical, but considering the alternatives, she let Mike continue.

"Think about what happened. We interrupted an obviously staged argument. It prepared us to hear a story. Julian immediately took charge. Hardly anyone else talked! When he 'moved' us, we ended up right back where we started. All that time they spent in the office before must have been setting up some light show. They used our imaginations against us. That is what we think a wizard can do. He hypnotized us, Melissa. With help from Tom and Cathy."

Melissa stayed quiet.

"I can't think of anything else. Want to see the websites I've been reading?"

"I don't think it's that easy," said Melissa.

"Strong personality. Focusing on his hands to do his tricks. Saying what we want to hear. Telling us to relax."

"I don't think so. Tom did something before he left. Made fire from his fingers. Hypnotism? Magic? Evil men hunting him? None of this makes any sense. I am so pissed at them! Confusing me. Scaring me. I want the truth, or revenge!"

"How do we find out?" asked Mike. "Go to the lodge?"

Melissa did not answer right away. Instead, she sat and thought the affair through again. Her eyes narrowed above lips pressed thin.

"We start with Julian. If he knows we're coming, he'll cook something up. We can surprise him at home. Let's go to his house tomorrow after you get home from school. We'll just show up. He won't be ready for anything."

Mike rubbed his hands together. "Expose the lie. This could be fun."

CHAPTER 29

PHONE CALLS

Micah's cell phone began playing a Mozart symphony. He had again chosen the midnight to five watch and was grabbing a few hours of sleep in the late Monday afternoon. The cell phone finished several measures before he reached for it on his bedside table.

"Hello."

"Julian, it's Mike. It sounds like we woke you up. Gee, I'm sorry."

In the background, Melissa mumbled, "I'm not."

"Melissa and I are at your house," continued Mike. "We want to talk to you."

"What?" asked Micah, slow to recognize what Mike was saying.

"Where are you?" asked Mike. "Sorry for waking you up."

"You are at my house?" Micah's voice was rising in alarm.

"Yes."

"I am not there. You cannot stay there! Go! Get in your car right now. GO! GO!"

Micah heard Melissa saying, "I heard him."

"GO! NOW! And do not use the name Julian anymore. It is not safe. GO!"

"Okay, okay," said Mike. "Why?"

"Do not hang up. Talk to me as you leave. MOVE!"

A loud knock on the door preceded Sanlar pushing it open. "What is wrong?" said Sanlar in his accented voice.

"They went to my house! Here, talk to them while I get dressed. I may have to magic there."

Micah pressed speaker and tossed the cell phone to Sanlar. He gabbed a pair of jeans and pulled them on.

"Hello," said Sanlar.

"Hello," returned Mike.

"You should not be there," stated Sanlar.

"We are getting in the car now," explained Mike. "Is Julian all right?"

"No, he is scared for you. Call him Micah. Do you see anyone there?"

"Only Melissa and me are here. Call him what?"

"Drive away," instructed Sanlar.

"Tell them not to talk to anybody!" yelled Micah.

"Do not…"

"I heard him," cut in Mike.

"Give me the phone back," said Micah. "Why did you go there?"

"We wanted to talk to you."

"Are you driving?"

"Yes, well, Melissa is. We're pulling out now."

"Do you see anyone around? Any cars pulling out after you?"

"No. Julian, what's the big deal?"

"I told you. People tried to kill me there Friday morning. Others might watch the house. My name now is Micah." He hesitated. "I understand you do not believe me, but do as I tell you! It may not be safe there."

"Julian, you're a ghost writer. Why would someone want to kill you?"

"Get away from my house! Do not use Julian!"

"We're leaving the neighborhood," said a subdued Mike.

"Check for cars following you again."

"No cars anywhere."

Micah sat on his bed with his pants on, but his shirt still unbuttoned. "Keep talking to me until you are a few exits down the highway."

"Okay. Melissa says to say she's pissed at you."

"Tell her I am glad she is alive to curse me."

"Good thing you feel that way because she just did again," explained Mike.

"I am sorry, Mike. I should have told you to stay away from my house."

"We're near the highway."

"Good. Good. Mike, tell Melissa to calm down and drive carefully."

"We're heading south."

"Does she want to come to the lodge early?"

Micah heard Melissa cursing in the background.

"Aahh," said Mike. "I'll take what she just said as an 'I'm thinking about it.'"

"When you get home, call me again."

"Okay."

<hr>

Tom pushed the green answer button on his cell phone.

"Hi, Tom," said Mr. Ross. "It's Dad."

"Hey, Dad, how are you?"

"I'm good. I'm worried about Melissa. What happened at her party? She won't talk about it, but she's obviously still upset."

"We didn't mean to upset her. We're sorry. She overheard a conversation between Julian and me that she wasn't supposed to hear." To head off any more questions, Tom added, "We've invited her up to the Berkshires this weekend to set things right."

"What did she hear that upset her so?"

"I was hoping you would not ask that." Tom hesitated before continuing. "Julian is very private about some things. For one, his previous career. He used to be a mercenary. Then he was military. Then, a mercenary again. Now he's mostly out of that line of work. I know your opinion of mercenaries, Dad, but Julian was always careful who he worked for."

"So he says. He appears too young to have done that."

"He's older than he looks."

"Mike knows as well, doesn't he?" asked Mr. Ross.

"Yes."

"Does Julian still take jobs?"

"No, but his experience helps us with the private eye stuff on occasion."

"There's more, isn't there?"

"Dad," stammered Tom, "I...I don't feel right about saying too much about Julian."

"Is he okay?"

"No," was Tom's curt answer. "We're working on it. If you don't mind, Dad, I'm going to leave it at that."

"Can I be of help?"

"Perhaps," Tom said optimistically. "But not yet."

CHAPTER 30

STUDENTS

When Micah came downstairs, the Sun had almost reached noon. Laexa sat at the kitchen table eating a sandwich.

"Lily made a bunch of these," she said, and held up a sandwich. "She put them in the...cold machine. There may be some eggs and bacon left from breakfast."

"Refrigerator in English," said Micah, sounding out the word for her.

"That does not translate to Dahican or Rel'ellon."

Micah shook his head. "No."

"Lord Racine and Sanlar are working on the security system. They said you would know what that means. Lily is washing clothes. You and I are in charge of watch duty and the dogs, and cleaning the kitchen."

Micah nodded understanding. He pulled a wrapped plate of eggs and bacon from the refrigerator and heated it in the microwave. With his breakfast in hand, he sat next to Laexa.

"And we will train," stated Laexa. "Sanlar suggests your practice has lapsed. He did not seem impressed with me."

"Take no offense, Laexa. You are dealing with a stubborn wizard. We should add practicing English to the list."

"They are driving to Boston after dinner. Racine left this note for you. Too many new words for me."

Micah took the handwritten note and read the two lines.

A company called Historical Art, Inc. employed all six assailants.

That company has offices in three cities: Seattle, New York, and Edinburgh.

Micah put the note down and began eating.

Laexa asked, "What does that mean?"

"Those that attacked me worked for the same company. That business has three offices, meaning at least three more secret rooms to find and destroy. Probably an equal number of magicians. All three offices are in English speaking cities. More incentive for you to learn English. This also suggests a larger and more dispersed organization than I expected. They may have been on this planet for some time. We can start learning about these cities: maps and pictures. But we will need more information before developing a plan of action."

Micah sat back and stretched his arms over his head. He took a slow breath in and out.

"More than you expected?" asked Laexa.

"And more than I feared."

"And Tom's sister, Melissa?"

"She is a good person. But now she is confused and scared. Once I can show her more magic and elves, she will understand. She is smart."

"And pretty?"

Micah locked eyes with his protector. "I do not think you will like her when you first meet her."

"Why is that?" asked Laexa.

"Perhaps I am wrong. I will leave that for you to discover."

He finished eating. "I will take care of the kitchen since I know where things go. You can play with Berk and Shire."

"Then training," said Laexa. "We do not want to disappoint Protector Sanlar."

⸺◆⸺

Micah watched the minivan roll down the driveway, leaving behind growing frustration and two energetic dogs. The Sun was heading west. Racine hoped to be in Boston before dark, but after rush hour.

The wait for the computer searches to produce actionable results would continue until they had resolved most of the cases in Boston and New York. The other members of the private investigation company could not yet devote much time to the research.

Between bouts of writing and exploring with basic internet searches, Micah spent a good deal of time exercising with Laexa. They retreated into exercise, at least twice a day, to keep busy. It also made him so tired that he could sleep, except for the flashes of memories, undisturbed. His mind used the time of rest his body demanded for bursts of irritating thought.

Danger to himself and others moved like wind blown ripples on a lake. He was the hunted! But also needed to hunt, but for now could not. People whose only offense was that they had met him were in danger. The danger threatened to include them even if they did not believe him or did not want to be a part of it.

At times, he sat with Laexa in front of a wide screen monitor, comparing maps with pictures and videos online. He also taught her basic English words.

By Thursday evening, Micah felt his frustration growing. Melissa had not returned his texts. No new information reached him regarding the Preparers or Historical Art, Inc. He could only wait.

He decided he did not want to stay in the lodge anymore and would check on his other students. After feeding the dogs and telling them they would be back in a few hours, Micah changed clothes, organized the room, and contacted Ke'en and Ti'ek. With Laexa's hand on his shoulder, he began the hand motions that focused his mind.

⸎

Once the Wizard Hovan made himself known, the guards unlocked the gate separating the Shetteca Secret Room from the rest of the district leader's stronghold.

"We received word of your pending arrival, Lord Wizard," said a guard. "I was instructed to direct you to Princess Shar in the practice arena."

"Thank you."

As Hovan and Laexa walked toward the stairs, Hovan said, "I am quite safe here, Laexa. I will be with the princess and do not plan to pass the inner walls."

Laexa understood. "I would like some food I am used to. I will also talk with other followers of the One I serve. Check for any updates on the cret'len or Preparer activity."

Hovan found Cova with her mother, watching Donnan at sword practice. Hovan motioned for Cova to stay seated. He joined them.

"Any news from your other home?" asked Shar.

Hovan responded. "Still being collected. I find it frustrating to be so ineffective at something I was once so good at."

"It is difficult to master two worlds."

"Well said."

"I was not expecting you so soon," said Cova. "You have dressed for practice."

"I must keep my students on their toes."

"I shall change and meet you in the courtyard."

"Is now a good time?" asked the wizard.

"Your visits are always a good time," said Cova. Smiling, she rose to leave.

Hovan sat next to Lady Shar, watching Donnan and his instructor go through some moves.

"Donnan loves this," said the proud mother. "He has his father's agility and my competitiveness. He is young, though, and I am not sure if I can trust him with a sharp blade yet."

"Will I have a third child of yours as a student?"

"Elves travel many paths. However, I think he will stay with the physical arts for some time. He wants a full size bow and to compete in the archery tournaments, but lacks the height and strength. Donnan wants to be the best in the family!"

"I shall warn Ti'ek when I return to Forestton."

Shar laughed. "Donnan will have the match put to song should the day come when he defeats his older brother."

Her tone changed when she turned to look at the wizard. "We instructed Ti'ek not to ride patrols. He would be too easy a target with only a patrol to protect him."

"Wise," agreed Hovan. "We are uncertain what their aim is. Beyond me, that is."

"Your death could have significant ramifications both here and on the other world."

"I see the ramifications there. But here on Ra'viinen, I think it would take more painting to render my demise into a mural."

"We agree," said Shar. "Thus, Ti'ek does not ride patrols."

Noting the finality in her tone, Hovan said, "I do not object, Shar."

Taking Hovan's arm, Shar apologized. "I am sorry, Hovan. I am a mother worried about her children. And about a friend."

"Let us be as prepared as possible. You see to your student. I will see to mine."

Hovan stood, bowed, and left for the courtyard. He arrived in the walled courtyard before Cova. He scanned the walls and doors out of habit, not genuine concern.

Cova arrived a short time later. Her cyan shirt, which stretched across her chest, buttoned up the back of her neck, forming a tight collar. The loose sleeves flowed to her wrists before being collected into a cuff, allowing freedom of motion. Her black pants did not hide her figure and allowed motion a dress would obstruct. A dark red tie kept her straight, black hair away from her bright green eyes.

I wondered if she would have dressed like this if her mother were not busy with her little brother. They trust me.

I wish I did not have to be trusted.

His hands wove a quick spell. Hovan turned and faced the smaller elf.

"Today, defensive spells."

"They are boring."

"Necessary, though. Since you are the target of these spells, cast them before entering a dangerous situation. This allows you to respond to danger with immediate offense. Thus, even if you are not the quickest, you may still be the victor." Hovan extended his finger at Cova. "Never underestimate surprise! The surprise may simply be that you are prepared and defended. You already know how to defend against non-magical projectiles. Prepare yourself."

Hovan pulled three small stones from his pocket. He watched her hand motions. When she finished, he threw one stone low. It hit her red shield and deflected aside. The wizard threw another. The red glow held.

"Excellent." Hovan held the third stone for an extra moment before throwing it low at Cova's feet. This stone skipped through the shield past her feet, which she did not move.

"Not fair," complained Cova.

"What is the lesson?" asked the wizard.

"Do not trust your magic more than you have to."

"Excellent. Why cast a defense against non-magic arrows and such? Always cast the defense spell against all projectiles: magical and non-magical. If you had, you would have stopped the fourth stone."

"I did what you said to do," countered Cova.

Hovan loved her spirit. "I said, prepare. You chose the minimum spell. Lesson two: choose the maximum defensive spell. Since you have time, be as prepared as possible."

"I know the counter to fire darts. That is not the maximum."

"No, it is not," agreed Hovan. "Today we move on to lightning defense. Mirror my hand motions."

Cova copied his sequence.

"That you recognize as fire dart defense. When you master that, it can be done with one hand. Greater defensives require two hands. Fire darts have little momentum. Lightning and blasts have momentum in addition to their heat and energy. The defense must be further away from you, denser, and layered to absorb some of the momentum. Even with a proper shield, a direct hit will move you." Hovan demonstrated the hand motions as he spoke. "You need two hands. One hand holds the layer you just built while the other braces it to the next layer. Work inside out. Envision a series of four fire dart layers with cross braces in between."

Hovan modeled the new hand motions twice. The finished product shimmered pale red. "Note the distance and internal supports."

He stood behind Cova to help move her hands and arms in the correct manner. Twice more, he performed the motions with his hands over hers. "Remember," he whispered into her ear, "hands only focus the mind; envision what you want to build."

He released her arms and moved back, watching Cova. He could see her layers as she built them, but each faded after she braced it to the next layer. She finished with two layers braced to each other.

"Well done."

She began again.

Her next attempt was better. Hovan gave her the hand signal to try again. Her third attempt improved.

Hovan moved behind her again to guide her hands. He placed his hands over hers to reinforce the motion. Cova laced her fingers of one hand through Hovan's and pulled the hand close to her body. The scent of her hair combined with the warmth radiating from her and the touch of interlaced fingers tempted him. He closed his eyes, enjoying the moment, and breathed in. Only for a moment.

"No, Cova," said Hovan. He slowly pulled his hand free and stepped back.

Cova turned and looked up at Hovan. Her green eyes, beautifully framed by her elven brown skin, conveyed regret and frustration with a glint of hope.

"If I distract you, perhaps we need to find you another teacher," said the wizard.

"Hovan, I do not want someone else," stated Cova. "I worry about you: spies here, Preparers there, cret'len doing who knows what or why. You fear for the future me after the Giver has passed round a hundred times. We do not know what will happen in ten circles, much less ten times ten. Why must we deny now for later?"

Hovan spoke softly. "I will not be selfish and leave you with the loneliness and pain I feel now for the many years that you will outlive me. You are right. The future has yet to reveal herself, but that is the best outcome we could hope for. I am a human. I will not do that to you."

"You force me to face painful emotions now that perhaps I would never have to face."

"You are young and can hope to find one better suited to you than I am."

Cova paused. Then she slowly asked a question. "If you had known you would lose Suzhanee so early, would you still have married her?"

Hovan had no immediate answer. Instead, he walked to a bench along the wall and sat down. Using the wall as a backrest, he watched the beautiful elf watching him. "I care for you too much to put you where I am now."

"I have no say in it?" asked Cova.

"You will not change my mind. Do not try."

"Because I might?"

"It would be weakness in me if you did, Princess."

"If I were not my father's daughter," said Cova.

"If I had not lost Suzhanee, I would not know to what I would be condemning you."

"You are young by magic. You will master that magic!"

"I have not yet and did not know how it worked when I used it," said Hovan. "Foolish of me. I will not base your happiness on such a slim hope. And I warn you, elf princess, that we are in the middle of a crisis that grows more serious. You must focus on your studies! Not on a human trying to accomplish the unlikely task of deciphering youth magic. Even healers will not investigate it."

"I fear for you."

"And I for you." With humor, Hovan added, "And I for me, too."

"Do not say that. You only need time to work out the youth magic." Smiling, she turned to work on her spells.

He stood and watched her go through the spell once more.

"Well done," he said as she constructed three layers. "You continue to practice. I am going to Forestton to give your brother a lesson."

"You are leaving so soon?" asked a surprised Cova.

"While my resolve holds, Cova." He held her eyes with his. "Before you intoxicate me further. Give my regards to your parents and sisters. Tell Donnan his sword work looks excellent."

"Where is your protector?" teased Cova.

"Do not worry. I will not leave without her. I do not wish to face the wrath of Captain Lacxa."

"Allow me to walk in and wait with you until she returns."

⸺◆⸺

Hovan and Laexa arrived in Forestton and looked for Cova's older brother. Once he had collected them, he led them to the south practice field. His emotions were still running strong. He needed another outlet and a distraction.

Cret'len. Melissa. Preparers. Cova. A world to protect without being found. And all I can do is wait.

Practice, then.

The Giver had moved noticeably across the sky when Hovan realized that his two partners were only continuing the spar with him to ease his mind. Hovan looked at his two friends and lowered his staff. "The Giver says it is time for dinner. I do not want to eat alone tonight. Dinner is on me at the Forest Inn. Wine included, Ti'ek. We will ask Captains Wod Dein and Vay to join us."

"If we must," joked Ti'ek. "I grow restless being forced to stay in Forestton. Reading reports from patrols is no substitute for riding them. Even your staff practice was a welcome change from walking the walls. Dinner and wine at the inn are even better!"

"Please collect the equipment. I will go find the captains." Hovan slipped his staff into its quiver on his back and walked toward the town gates.

Laexa and Ti'ek watched the wizard walk toward the gate.

"I am glad he ended the staff practice," said Laexa. "He has much on his mind."

"There are many themes woven together composing the music that comprises our friend. Kismet still composes the arrangement, but there are more sad themes than pleasant ones."

Laexa glared at Ti'ek, annoyed. "Yes, elf. That is what I said." She grabbed the bag and began putting the equipment inside.

CHAPTER 31

PARADIGM SHIFT

Melissa and Mike surprised everyone by arriving Friday evening. Micah was training outside with Laexa and Sanlar when they pulled up the driveway. Micah and Sanlar hurried to the front of the lodge.

Sanlar bowed. "Welcome to our home. I will show you your rooms."

"Welcome," added Micah. "We will wash up and meet you inside."

Tom and Cathy pulled in before Micah returned downstairs.

Micah and Laexa entered the Fireplace Room. Melissa was about to speak, but stopped when she saw the tall woman with chestnut brown eyes and reddish brown hair follow Micah into the room.

"Before we talk, I would like to make an introduction," said Micah. "It is my honor to introduce Captain Laexa, First Captain of Forestton and my personal protector." With a gesture of his hand, he presented Captain Laexa.

Laexa bowed.

"It is a pleasure to meet you," said Melissa.

"Captain Laexa does not speak English. I will extend your greetings to her and introduce you."

Speaking in Rel'ellon, Hovan introduced Melissa and Mike.

Laexa said, "Please tell them I am honored to meet them."

Micah translated.

Laexa turned to Micah and spoke in a low voice. "I will leave you to talk. She looks too much like Suzhanee. I do not like her. The constant memories will not help you find your smile. Why do you visit her?"

Laexa left as Tom walked in. They exchanged short greetings in Dahican.

"Please sit," offered Micah. He chose his rocking chair.

"I want to apologize," Melissa began. "You trusted me, and I called you a liar. I'm sorry, Julian."

"Apology accepted. Call me Micah. Julian Orel is no longer a safe name."

"I'm sorry too," said Mike. "But it is difficult to accept. Are you really in trouble?"

"Yes." Micah began slowly rocking. He slid his hand over the polished, curved arm of the dark wood chair. "This is my favorite chair. It is the only piece of furniture I brought with me when I moved to this world. Hand crafted by the king's artisans in Avi'ot! One of the rewards I received for serving the king regent. It reminds me of better days. I could not leave it behind."

"Is it magical?" asked Melissa.

Micah chuckled. "No, simply well made. I brought it here when I abandoned my house in Rockland."

Melissa and Mike exchanged glances. Melissa spoke. "We believe you now, but we have so many questions. I don't know where to begin."

Mike said, "Begin with some more magic."

Micah sat up in his chair and sent two fire darts slamming into the back of the fireplace. "My favorite offensive spell. Quick and effective."

"How do you do that!?" Mike said. "Could you teach us?"

"If you wish, I will teach you. I teach Tom and Cathy, and others here."

"Show me how to do that light trick."

"To learn magic takes more than a few brief lessons. Like a piano, it requires practice and practice to master the hands and the mind."

"Then how can you be a wizard?" asked Melissa. "If it takes so long to control magic, then it must take decades to be a wizard. You are not old enough."

"I thought you said you believe me."

"Julian, it's difficult to understand," Melissa said. "You are Tom's age, and a wizard?"

"I am a wizard. I am older than I appear. Call me Micah."

"Show me what you really look like," she said, then slowly added, "Micah."

Micah continued to rock back and forth in his chair. "This is how I look. A few years ago, I risked playing with," Micah paused, searching for the proper description before settling on what felt incomplete, "youth magic. Very dangerous. I did not understand the magic, but I did not care. Fate, it seems, has other plans for me. The magic worked as I hoped. Upon reflection, I may have had help. My body appears to be late twenties."

Melissa sat with a neutral look on her face.

"You do not believe me," Micah continued. "I thought it would take time. Want to experience more magic?"

"Yes," erupted Mike.

Micah removed a ring from his pinky. He walked over to Melissa and held out his hand. Sparkling in the middle of his palm lay a lustrous, silver ring with a red stone inlaid around the middle of the band. She picked it up and studied it.

"My favorite chair is not magical. This ring is."

"What does it do?" asked Mike.

Micah slipped it onto the pinky of his left hand. He vanished from their sight. Melissa stood, surprised. She gently reached out to where Micah had been standing. Her hand met Micah's. He was there, but she could not see him.

"It can make the wearer invisible," he said from an unseen mouth.

He came into view. He took the ring off and held it out to Melissa. "Put it on."

Melissa and Micah stared at one another.

"The moment of truth," she said. She took the ring and, without examining it further, slipped it on her ring finger.

She looked at her hand and the ring. The ring was attractive in its simplicity: silver with a thin red stone embedded in the metal. "It fits my finger." Melissa paused. "I can see my hand."

"The wearer can see oneself, of course," explained Tom. "Besides, you are still visible. You must imagine yourself invisible. Activate the ring using your thoughts."

Melissa imagined herself not being seen. At first, nothing happened.

"Mental focus, Melissa," said Micah. "Imagine looking into a mirror and not seeing yourself." Melissa imagined looking in the standing dressing mirror in her bedroom.

"I can't see you!" exclaimed Mike.

Shaken and still skeptical, Melissa, visible again, took it off. She handed it to Mike. "You put it on!"

Mike reached for it with a broad smile on his face. He shoved it onto a finger.

Melissa saw Mike, then she didn't. "If you are in on this, Mike, I will kill you!"

"You can't see me!" shouted Mike.

"No!" Melissa said.

"Ohh, the fun I could have with this!" Mike reappeared. He took the ring off and inspected it.

Melissa sank into the couch. "I don't understand any of this," she mumbled. "I want to believe you, but none of this makes any sense to me."

Tom moved next to his sister and put an arm across her shoulders to comfort her.

"I would not lie to you, Melissa," said Micah, sitting in his rocking chair. "To Mike, yes, for a good cause, but not to you."

"Hey," complained Mike.

"What are you?" asked Melissa.

"A retired wizard being searched for by some old enemies." Micah chuckled. "Sounds ridiculous, I know."

"Or a plot line for a book," said Tom.

"Are we really in danger?" Melissa asked with a slight tremor in her voice. She looked from Micah to her brother.

"I think so," answered Micah. "Do not go back to my house."

"Micah?" Mike interrupted, fascinated by the ring.

"Yes, Mike," answered Micah, taking his eyes from Melissa and looking at Mike.

"What stone is this?"

"Ara ekcar, in my native language. The name means blood stone or heart stone," answered Micah. "The elves have another name for it. Here, I guess it is a ruby."

"Elves?" questioned Mike. "Are these markings on the inside written by elves?"

"No."

Mike paused after Micah's one word answer. Then he continued to ask questions. "What language is it?"

"The language of my country," said Micah. "We call the language Rel'ellon."

"What does it say?"

"I hoped the inscription would escape attention, at least for now. To your credit, it did not."

"Where did you get the ring?" asked Melissa. "It looks like a woman's ring."

"Knowledge is power," said Micah. "Roughly translated, the inscription reads, 'Suzhanee, to remind you of me when I am not in sight'. That language is more economical than English."

"Who is Suzhanee?" asked Melissa.

"She was my wife. I gave her this as her engagement ring."

Melissa rose to her feet. "You're married? And you never told me?!"

Tom still held Melissa's hand. She resisted his attempts to urge her back onto the couch.

"I was until her death."

"Why didn't you tell me before?"

Tom answered, trying to intervene and prevent either his friend or his sister from getting hurt. "Melissa, how could he, without explaining everything?"

"Julian, you never told me you had a wife! And children?"

"No, and use Micah," answered Micah, his frustration growing again.

"Damn you, Micah."

"Don't do this, Melissa," pleaded Tom.

"Other worlds, magic, wizards, and wives. How many? You're not twenty six. Let me guess, you're three hundred and Merlin's cousin, or is that another of your names? We might be killed because of you?"

"Stop it!" yelled Micah. "I did not get you involved in this. You did! You insisted on an explanation. I gave it to you. Do with it what you like. But do not stand here, accuse me of lying, and take out your frustration on me. Not where Suzhanee is concerned. I loved her!"

"You got my whole family involved!" Melissa ran to the door and left.

"Don't yell at my sister, Micah!" Tom ran after her. "She's scared and confused!"

Micah rose and walked over to the fireplace just to have something to punch. He slammed his fist on the stone mantel. "Anything else you want to ask, Mike?"

"I'm sorry I asked about the words."

"Do not be. I would have if I were in your place." Micah added, "I am very touchy where my wife is concerned."

"Was she killed by the people who tried to kill you last week?"

"No. But she died a violent death that I could not keep her from."

"I'm sorry."

Micah nodded. "Thank you. Play with the ring. I will get it back from you later."

Leaving Mike in the Fireplace Room, rolling the ring in his fingers, Micah walked through the lodge, out onto the front porch, and down the steps to the gravel path. He crossed the small wooden bridge over the stream and strode up the slope of the large hill. Disappearing into the trees, he followed a familiar old logging road. His heart was beating quickly. His mind was jumping from image to image.

To get control of himself, he focused on the forest surrounding him, trying to identify as many forest noises as he could. The soft, arhythmic shifting of the leaves was soothing. It reminded him of his rustic world and of his parents' home.

The Sun was setting as he climbed the hill. Only the top of the tall hill where Micah stood was lit. As he watched the star kiss the world good night, the evening breeze softly tugged at his loose hair. The peace and innocence of the hills calmed him. There was no danger native to these hills that could harm him.

Breathe in–1, 2, 3. Hold. Breathe out–1, 2, 3. Hold.

Micah surveyed the serene hills, watching them slip into the shadows. In the valley, the lights of the houses greeted the night. Points of white from the buildings below took up positions in the dark like stars in a constellation. Everything seemed as it should. The unending cycle of day to night progressed without a single moment's hesitation. As the Sun sank, it paid no heed to Micah's worries. The world would not pause for any of Micah's problems. The laws of nature considered them too small to even notice.

He cataloged the events of the last week.

Six Preparers have tried to kill me and failed.

We have leads on where to look for those who may still be here, with more info to come.

I remained concealed, I think. The Rosses have not been attacked. Nor the lodge.

Mike believes. Melissa will by the end of the weekend, if not sooner.

Micah took a deep breath of the woodland air.

Preparers are out there somewhere. I need to decide on my next move.

Make it a good one.

His frustrations lowered notch by notch. Micah stood tall and silent with the evening breeze softly shifting his hair. Doubt, with some of his anxiety, floated from Micah like a leaf leaving a tree, slipping away with the night breeze. He did not doubt that he would do all he could, though the outcome was dangerously uncertain.

He would not abandon these people to fend for themselves. When the time came, he would do his best, no matter the cost. However, that time had not yet come.

Control yourself and prepare.

Let Melissa and Mike grow.

Do not be so damn sensitive!

Easier said than done.

I miss you, Suzhanee. I will do better this time.

The sky darkened. The Sun let go of the high clouds it had turned orange, then gray. Micah descended into the darkness on the far side of the hill. He walked in the dark woods for over an hour, recovering some confidence in the peace, lowering his restlessness by running plans through his head, and thinking about the demonstration set for Melissa and Mike tomorrow. When he returned to the lodge, he spoke with no one and went to his room. The solitude was therapeutic. He felt his presence would be disruptive. If someone wanted to talk with him, he was not hard to find. No one came. He stayed in his room, reading, until he served the midnight watch.

———— ◆ ————

It was almost noon on Saturday when Micah came down from his room. He had slept later than he had expected. He learned that the other members of the private investigation company had arrived and had held a meeting that morning to discuss the situation. They formally voted on accepting Micah's job offer, developed an initial plan, and assigned tasks.

Darkening clouds and increasing wind foretold that the rain would come sooner than forecast. Racine, Cathy, and Lily, with help from Melissa, scurried to cook a meal in place of the planned barbecue. The coming storm put the outdoor demonstration on hold as well.

Micah talked Tom into joining him for a jog along the logging roads before the storm hit.

Tom went to his room to change into running clothes.

Micah detoured into the kitchen. "Melissa?" asked Micah. "May I talk to you?"

Melissa turned from her conversation with Cathy and the vegetables she was slicing. She wiped her hands on a kitchen towel before walking over with a smile on her face.

"Good morning, Micah, or I should say, afternoon." Her tone was teasing, but gentle.

"I apologize for yelling at you last night. It was five years this spring, but I am still sensitive about the death of my wife. With all that is happening, my emotions are closer to the surface than I prefer. I am sorry."

"Julian, I mean Micah, please! You don't need to apologize. I'm so embarrassed that I acted that way when you told me about her death. It's just … I'm…"

"I know," said Micah.

Melissa gave him a hug. In a formal, compassionate voice, she spoke as if hearing of the death for the first time. "Micah, I am very sorry to hear about the death of your wife, Suzhanee."

"Thank you." Micah nodded to her.

"I don't think Captain Laexa likes me."

"Perhaps not. Partly because you yelled at me. She is my protector."

"Partly?"

Micah shrugged his shoulders. "Tom and I are going for a run. I will see you later."

"Okay," said Melissa. "Micah?"

"Yes, Melissa."

"I am still frightened."

Micah nodded understanding. "They must get past me first. That is not an easy thing to do."

An image of a brunette on an orvbac flashed through his mind. "I know my failure to protect my wife does not give you hope. I swear I will do all that I can!"

"The others think you can do quite a lot. Somehow, I find that comforting." Melissa smiled. "Go get your run in. It's going to rain soon."

As Tom and Micah headed out, they passed Sanlar giving Mike a martial arts lesson.

Micah said, "Teach him how to use a staff."

Tom suggested, "A pistol."

The two jogged for a few minutes in silence as they found their stride. It would be a slow jog up and around the hill. Micah noticed that Tom's fanny pack seemed weighted down. He assumed Tom had a handgun stored there.

"Your brother and sister came around quick."

"Quick? Quick?!" repeated Tom in amazement. "It took a week, meeting elves and a wizard, seeing magic, and playing with an invisibility ring! Plus, Cathy and I vouching for everything!" Tom laughed. "I think what put them over the top was the conversation with Racine, Sanlar, and Lily last night. Seeing the elves without magic."

"Did Sanlar talk much?" Micah asked, questioning the quantity of words from the usually succinct elf.

"Yes!" said Tom. "He is very passionate about fighting the Preparers."

"Talkative, really? Well, he is a protector."

"He is less concerned with whether they believe us and more concerned with their understanding of the coming danger, the need to fight."

"It will come to that," agreed Micah.

"That's what led to Mike's lessons. Though I think more handgun training would be better."

"Hope he learns quick."

"He kept asking about you. You're getting another student."

It was Micah's turn to laugh. "Michael Ross, the James Bond of the magic world."

The two friends jogged on, exchanging jokes at Mike's expense.

"We should not make too much fun of him," said Micah. "We are going to need all the help we can get."

"Yeah," agreed Tom. "There is someone else we might want to recruit."

"Who?"

"My dad."

When Micah stayed quiet, Tom began listing the arguments. "Retired Marine officer, weapons training, small group tactics, combat experience."

Micah added another argument. "His family is in danger. It is respectful to warn him of the threat."

"I wouldn't have to keep avoiding his questions about you."

Micah chuckled. "James Bond would not keep the secret anyway. How do you want to do it?"

"I think you and I should tell my parents together."

Micah nodded agreement.

———◆———

By the time the early dinner was served, the ruffled, charcoal clouds were dropping their load of rain, falling diagonally through the wind. The day had become a chilly, wet spring evening. Everyone except Sanlar gathered in the dining room.

Racine moved to the seat at the head of the table.

"We elves have a saying," began Racine. "Translated, it goes, 'All friends are good friends worthy of trust. If not, then they are not a friend.' You are friends. As friends, we welcome you. In this house, there are many secrets, and thus only friends are welcome. This weekend, we invite you to share some of our secrets. This is an honor that carries the responsibility of trust."

"It is time to eat and acquaint ourselves with one another. Our group comprises myself, Sanlar and Lily, Anton, Tom and Cathy, David, Paul and Carrie." Racine pointed out each person as he introduced them. "Carrie, who was the first of us here from Ra'viinen."

"Sanlar keeps watch. Our guests this weekend are Tom's sister Melissa, his brother Michael, and the one now known as Micah with his protector, Captain Laexa. It is our custom that we tell no more of ourselves than we wish. I extend this privilege to our guests. I will remove my disguise and leave it for others to decide if they wish to do likewise."

Following Racine's lead, Carrie and Lily morphed into brown skinned, black haired elves.

The meal was an intriguing mixture of Dahican cuisine and traditional American cooking. Micah had supplied a few bottles of Sojourn Mountain red wine and some supplies with a quick trip to Forestton. Everyone found something they enjoyed, even if they did not enjoy everything.

Coffee and tea, along with an elven after meal drink, phonetically translated as kobine, tasting similar to tart citrus, transitioned between dinner and dessert. Dessert was fruit from both worlds.

"We had planned an afternoon demonstration of magic and physical arts," began Tom, "but the weather is not cooperating."

A disappointed Mike asked, "Can't you do it inside?"

"There isn't enough room for what we planned."

"Can we go somewhere larger?" asked Mike.

"With this weather, there is no place near," said Micah. "The only place I can think of is the south practice range at Forestton."

"Where's that?" Mike's question spawned some laughs from around the table.

"My town," responded Micah. "I am its lord. However, I could only take four at a time."

"Why?" joked Melissa. "Your space ship out back only fits five?"

"Great!" said Mike. "Take Melissa and me."

"How long does it take?" asked Melissa.

"Wait a minute," protested Tom, with the suggestion being spoken into reality.

"Only a couple of minutes," answered Micah, ignoring Tom's protest.

Mike stood up. "A few minutes! Let's go!"

"It's safe, isn't it, Tom?" asked Melissa.

"Yes," Tom admitted. "But…"

"We will be with a wizard!" exclaimed Mike, his hands emphasizing his words. "A wizard! What's the worry? It's his town!"

"We will be safe, Tom. We will stay in Forestton and keep the visit short. Just a few hours. I will only take Melissa."

"Why is that?" demanded Mike. "I want to go!"

"Mike, you are not an adult on this planet. You need to ask your parents. Melissa can choose for herself."

"What?!" exclaimed Mike. "I'll be eighteen in two months!"

"I will not disrespect your parents by giving you privileges you do not have." Before Mike could argue again, Micah continued. "Perhaps sooner. Tom and I think we should tell your parents."

"Are you sure, Tom?" asked Melissa.

Before Tom could answer, Micah explained his thoughts. "There is a threat to his family. It would be respectful to tell him. Same reason you wanted to know."

"Also," offered Tom, "he can help us."

"First, do you want to visit Forestton, Melissa?" asked Micah.

"Yes," said Melissa, smiling. "Show me your home."

"When can we expect you back?" asked Tom.

"I want to go!" challenged Mike.

Micah checked his watch. "Before morning. No, Mike. I want my ring back."

CHAPTER 32

A VISIT TO FORESTTON

Hovan waited for Melissa and Laexa to become aware of the Forestton Secret Room. When Melissa's eyes noted her surroundings, he held her by her shoulders and directed her toward the exit, pushing open the secret room door with his hip. She walked with an uneven stagger and would have fallen if not for Hovan. The wizard sat her down in a cushioned armchair just outside the door. Hovan then retrieved Laexa. He sat her in a chair next to Melissa, keeping a hand on each shoulder to steady them.

"We are in Forestton, Melissa." He motioned for her to stay seated.

"Last time I felt like this, I had a really good time the night before."

Hovan chuckled. "It passes quickly. Take slow, deep breaths."

"I feel warm."

"It is summer here."

"Ohhh," said Melissa, still unsteady. She took some breaths and straightened her back.

"Feeling better?"

Melissa's nod was unconvincing.

Switching to Rel'ellon, Hovan asked, "Laexa, how are you?"

"Better. I will take myself up the stairs and change. See to her."

"Walk, Melissa. I will help. Let us get your blood moving."

Together, they climbed the two flights of stairs to the main floor. By the time they reached the kitchen, Hovan noticed Melissa moved with more ease. He sat her at the kitchen table and gave a mug of water.

"Stay hydrated. We are in my house in Forestton. We arrived in the Forestton Secret Room below us. By memorizing that room, I can magic there from anywhere. You are on another planet!"

"Does traveling by magic always make you feel like that?"

"Yes. You get used to it. We need to change into more appropriate clothes before I escort you through my town. If you are ready, I will show you more of the house as we make our way upstairs."

Melissa stood. "Lead the way."

Hovan led her down the hall and into the main receiving room. Polished light wood furniture and comfortable couches, adorned with throw pillows, spread across the large gathering room. The room swept around a generous fireplace, opened on two sides, leaving the fireplace as a rectangular island in the middle. Its chimney rose to the ceiling as a sturdy stone column.

A portrait hung on the side of the chimney facing the door. The painting depicted a woman and a man, both dressed in expensive looking clothes. Their smiles exuded joy. The attractive young woman wore an elegant red dress trimmed with yellow and green. Colorful spring flowers adorned her long, brown hair. A man in a formal robe, also trimmed in yellow and green but a deeper red than her dress, stood next to the woman with his right arm wrapped around her waist. A short staff was prominent in his left hand. The creases around his eyes as he smiled spoke of complete happiness and a passing youth. Gray strands scattered among the blond hair gave him a dignified appearance. His eyes seemed no older than those of the younger woman next to him, who shared his exuberant smile. Their blissful expressions radiated into the room, filling the study with rapture as the burning wood did when the fire was lit, enriching the room with its pleasant scent.

Melissa's eyes swept around the room before coming to rest on the portrait. She studied the painting for a few moments. Her lips stretched into a smile. She looked at Hovan and then turned back to the picture. "Is this your wedding portrait?"

"Yes. I was forty three years old, by our calendar."

"That would make you... more than twice my age! Still younger than my dad." Melissa studied the picture a moment more before continuing. "Wow, she could be my sister!"

"Yes," said Hovan in a hushed tone.

"Micah, I'm sorry for all the times I flirted with you. You must have thought of Suzhanee every time."

"Melissa, everything reminds me of Suzhanee. I knew the teasing was you being you. There was no harm meant. Sometimes I liked the flirting. It helped battle the loneliness." After a pause, he added, "Some of the time."

Melissa smiled, touching his shoulder to comfort him.

Hovan looked at the portrait of his wife. "Suzhanee changed my life twice: the day I met her and the day she died. There are days when I cannot come in here. Some days, all I do is stare at that painting. I love it and hate it."

Quietly, Melissa asked, "How did she die?"

Hovan slowly breathed in, then out.

"If you don't want to talk about it, I understand."

As if he did not hear her, Hovan began. "A few years after our wedding, I accepted a job to kill a young brown dragon. I had been told it had been preying on the local herds." Hovan took a breath. "A massive red dragon, rearing young, surprised us and attacked. The dragon killed her. I failed to protect my wife."

"I'm sorry."

Hovan nodded thank you. "I never figured out how the red dragon knew we were there, or how it got behind us." Hovan took a deep breath and exhaled, counting to three. "Come. We should change clothes. I am the Lord Wizard Hovan here. You are my honored guest."

Hovan led her into the main hallway and up the front staircase. They visited the library and then the Hovan's laboratory and workroom. The wizard pointed out the door to Prince Ti'ek's rooms before taking her to one of the large rooms on the other side of the mansion.

"In these closets are clothes that may fit you. Suzhanee was taller than you, but otherwise... Wear the yellow cloak."

"This closet is bigger than my bedroom!"

"Welcome to the Lord's Manor." He helped her pick out an outfit. "I am going to my room to change. I will meet you in the hall."

Hovan changed and returned to the hallway. Dressed in his favorite auburn cloak and carrying his dark staff, he waited. Melissa walked out of the suite a few moments later wearing a light cloak woven of soft yellow material. The cloak clung to her shoulders, held in place by a tie. A light green gown hugged her breasts and waist before sweeping to the floor.

"Do I look the part?" Melissa did a spin for Hovan.

"You look regal!"

"I feel like a fairy tale princess."

"Stay here long enough, and your beauty may entice someone to make you a real one."

Hovan held out his arm, which Melissa took. "Let me introduce Forestton to you."

The wizard led her upstairs and through a door onto the roof of his house. A table surrounded by chairs and loungers provided seating. Tall potted plants and trees gave decoration and shade. Melissa's eyes looked around the terrace. She stepped to the railing to view Forestton. She then expanded her gaze to include the protective walls of the town and the green fields and trees beyond.

A turquoise spark flew into the air near the gates. Hovan responded by sending a spray of red flares above his house.

"Prince Ti'ek comes to meet us. Turquoise for Shetteca, the city governed by his parents."

"How do you know?" Melissa asked, surprised.

"I can move you across great distances by magic. Are you surprised that I can send my thoughts across town? I am not sure how best to describe it to you. In my mind, I spoke with Prince Ti'ek. I said hello and asked if he was in Forestton. He said yes. I informed him I have a guest from the other planet. The turquoise flare was showy... and unnecessary."

"Telepathic?" asked Melissa excitedly. "Say something to me."

"I cannot. Elves learn to do it naturally and usually only among family members. Humans need magic."

"Okay," a disappointed Melissa said. "Why were your sparks red?"

"Red is the color of the One I serve. My religion, so to speak. Turquoise is for Shetteca. A reference to the river running through the city. Forest green for Forestton."

"Is that why you wore red to your wedding?"

"Yes, Suzhanee and I served the same One."

Spreading the cloak as she spun, Melissa asked, "Who's yellow?"

"The king's court. King Dargladre of Arre'ielle."

She pulled the cloak tight to her body as if to hide it. Concerned, Melissa asked, "Should I be wearing this?"

"I thought it was a good idea. I was the Royal Wizard to King Regent Ke'en. Suzhanee and I had yellow cloaks for royal functions, red for the One we serve, plus Shetteca turquoise and Forestton green. The townspeople will assume you are here under the king's protection. Come to visit one of the king's favored wizards." Hovan made a small bow. "Your beauty adds to the image."

"Thank you, Micah." A smile graced her lips.

"You are welcome, Lady Melissa. Let us go down and meet the prince."

Captain Laexa was waiting for them in the hallway by the front door. She wore a leather jerkin over a dark green shirt with an insignia on the shoulders. A sword hung at her waist. Two daggers in scabbards at her waist were within easy reach.

"First Captain Laexa will be our escort."

"We need a chaperon?" joked Melissa.

"Poor translation. Bodyguard is better."

"Do we need one?"

"Not in my town. Still, it is part of her duties."

"She looks impressive, formidable, wearing those weapons. Like a heroine in your books. I would feel safer if she liked me."

Hovan did not respond.

You are a constant reminder of Suzhanee. She does not like that I do this to myself.

He led Melissa into the small courtyard in front of his house. He turned and explained the significance of the mountain talon bird over the entranceway.

They strolled, her arm wrapped around his, toward the gates. Hovan kept a running soliloquy of descriptions. His words seemed to go almost unnoticed by Melissa. Her head turned left and right, but she said little.

He was sure she noted the salutes and respectful nods that the wizard and the captain received.

"They greet you with such respect," said Melissa. "Quite a contrast to my teasing."

"Laexa is the first captain. I am the Lord Wizard Hovan. Approaching is Prince Ti'ek. Son of Crown Prince Ke'en and Princess Shar, the lord and lady of this district."

The prince's straight dark hair, skin the color of a dark tan, and jade eyes marked him as an elf. He appeared taller than he was due to his lean, athletic frame and long legs. The rapscallion smile on his lips added to, rather than detracted from, his confident look.

When Hovan spoke, introducing her. Hovan then turned to Melissa. "Prince Ti'ek, eldest son of Crowned Prince Ke'en and Princess Shar."

Prince Ti'ek's bow was deeper and more formal than needed. Clearly, he wanted to impress.

Equally trying to impress, Melissa bowed and returned, "Pien'na."

Ti'ek straightened to his full height. His smile broke into a wide grin.

Hovan looked from the prince to Melissa with raised eyebrows.

Melissa's smile slipped into a grin of concern. "Did I say that correctly?"

"Well enough," said Hovan. "Where did you learn that?"

"Lily taught me last night."

"It is an informal greeting among friends or between a couple romantically involved. Lily presented herself as a friend and not as a girlfriend. It was an inappropriate greeting for a lady to use with a prince she has never met. Used in this context, you are flirting with Prince Ti'ek."

"Oh, I meant no disrespect!"

Hovan saw the smile leave Ti'ek's lips. "Disrespect is not the emotion that Prince Ti'ek is feeling."

Hovan, Ti'ek, and Laexa spoke for a moment. Ti'ek turned to Melissa. He dropped his head, tilted to one side, with his lips in a frown.

Hovan and Melissa renewed their walk toward the main gates. Laexa followed at a respectful distance behind. "Prince Ti'ek will join us for an early dinner at the Forest Inn."

"What time is it here?"

"Early afternoon."

"Are the days the same here?"

"The days are shorter, but the years are longer: twenty of your hours in our day and four hundred thirty one and a half days in our year. We must stay late enough to watch the moons rise!"

"Moons?"

"Yes. We have three: Equa the Bright, Mito, and Ette. You can see Equa in the sky in the west. Mito and Ette will rise later."

Melissa turned to look. "It's not as big as the Moon. Our Moon, I mean...my Moon. You know what I mean."

They laughed at her confusion.

"What planet am I on?" asked Melissa.

"The elves call it Ra'viinen. There are other names, but since the elves outlive everyone else, their names usually stick. They derive it from the Dahican word for mother."

They walked toward the three flags waving in the breeze above the gates.

"I take comfort in seeing those flags," stated the wizard. "To me, it means everything is as it should be. Ten or so years ago, as a war swept through this region, that was not the case." Counting down the flags, he explained, "Arre'ielle, then Shetteca, then Forestton."

The lustrous metal gates of Forestton, folded against the inner walls of the tunnel, allowed passage under the protective wall of the town. The darker shadows under the wall and the metal gates framed the light from the Giver and green grass visible through the tunnel. Hovan led Melissa not to the gates but turned aside and up the wide stairs to the top of the wall.

The Wizard Hovan pointed out more features of his small town. With a sweep of his hand, Hovan showed the empty field bisected by a wide road, which lay before the gates.

"This area is where the summer caravans rest and set up stands selling their goods to the townspeople. We are fortunate that one is not in town today. Otherwise, it would be difficult to get a table at the inn."

A smaller road ran out from the gates to join the larger one after crossing a stone bridge. "That stream is the reason travelers first stopped here. The town of Forestton was built out of the surrounding forest, hence the name."

Turning Melissa to the north, he said, "Ride that way for two or three days and you will enter Shetteca, the city of Prince Ti'ek's parents." The road crossed a short, wide bridge over the small river and disappeared north.

Turning her 180 degrees, he instructed, "Caravans traveling that way reach Avi'ot, the city of the king whose color you wear, in about two to three weeks."

Arm in arm, Hovan and Melissa strolled along the wall. The base of his staff tapped out a slow beat. "All the land within a day's ride in any direction is under the jurisdiction of Forestton. My region. It is mostly farms and ranches. Forestton belongs to the district of Shetteca. Shetteca to the country of Arre'ielle."

"I feel like I'm in one of your stories."

"In a way, you are. This world provides the backdrop for our stories, as it does for others."

Melissa gave Hovan a questioning look.

"Yes," said Hovan before she asked the question. "I am not the only writer of fantasy from this world to publish in yours. It seems much of your fantasy landscape comes from this landscape: elves, wizards, dragons. Even the word orc could be a variation of an elven word meaning small evil creature. The word is uaqua. The elves use it to refer to any of the smaller, less cultured creatures found on this planet, not one particular species. It is also an insult."

"Are any of the novels true stories?"

"No, but a few borrow ideas, at least, within artistic license."

"Yours?"

"No."

"How long have you lived on Earth?"

"Four years."

"You speak English well."

"I have learned much from Tom and Cathy. That is how Tom and I met, if you remember. He taught that English as a second language class. I lived in Boston for a time after Scotland before moving to my house in Rockland County."

"That was true?"

"Yes." With an overly dramatic, sad undertone, he breathed, "Now, I need to find a new home." Pointing his staff, he brightly added, "Besides this one."

They continued walking along the wall. "Tom and I make a good team. Though I have a knack for languages, my grasp of English is not firm enough to write novels. I am the ideas, Tom the words. At least, that is how we began. The separation is becoming less now."

The wizard's staff tapped out a few more beats, with Laexa's quiet footsteps following. "My English is far better than Tom's Dahican. How people relate fascinates me. Language is the means. I speak three languages: English, Dahican including the western dialect, and the language of Arre'ielle called Rel'ellon. I am passable in a fourth language."

"If Tom lived in Dahica, his elvish would be very good," said Melissa, defending her older brother.

"Elven describes the people and their culture," corrected Hovan gently. "The language is called Dahican, derived from the country of Dahica. Other elves speak other languages."

When Hovan and Melissa were midway across the south wall, Hovan stopped and looked out over the south practice field. Archery targets and lines marking distances defined the limits of the large practice field. A bow shot beyond that, a semicircle of trees bordered a large, grassy meadow populated by cylindrical stone and wood markers set in the ground. Some were in groups while others stood alone. They stood in silence for a few moments, with Melissa watching the sky and Hovan eyeing a marker set apart from the others. At this distance, he could not read the inscription.

"The sky seems different," said Melissa.

"Yes," agreed Hovan, returning his mind to the conversation. "I think there is more oxygen. I have more endurance here."

After another moment, Melissa laughed. "Can I take photos? Mike will want to see pictures. They might also help to convince my parents."

"Okay. Be discreet. Things like cell phones are not here. Do not upload them to the internet when you get home. It would be evidence of what you know."

Melissa hid the cell phone close to her chest as she took some photos.

"I think Mike will be here soon enough," said the wizard. "Come, let us finish our tour."

"Yes, my lord," joked Melissa.

They walked back to the town gates and then through the market square.

"The market is fascinating," said Melissa quietly. "But the eye colors more so! Yellow eyes and red eyes, the many shades of brown. Green, gold, and dark gray."

"My blue eyes are rare. Few blonds."

"I feel short here."

"You are," joked Hovan.

Melissa stopped at a stand displaying metal jewelry.

"If I promise to pay you back, will you lend me some money?" whispered Melissa.

"I am the lord of the town," said Hovan. "No one would dare ask money from me! What would you like?"

"These earrings. Does this pattern have meaning?"

"It is a human rendering of a traditional elven symbol for contentment, peace of mind."

Noting her interest, the woman who owned the stand offered them to her. While Melissa did not understand the woman's words, her outstretched hands offered the earrings as a gift. Unsure what to do, Melissa looked at the wizard.

Lord Hovan leaned in so only Melissa could hear. "It would be rude to refuse the gift that you so clearly want. Take them, smile, and nod your head in thanks."

Hovan spoke with the woman in what Melissa now recognized as the language of Rel'ellon. After a brief exchange, the woman smiled and nodded eagerly. Hovan escorted Melissa away.

When they were a safe distance away, Hovan laughed quietly. "You almost blew your cover."

"How?"

"Your English, for one. Also, a lady of the King's Court shopping in a town market for second quality earrings? I explained they are a gift for a friend's young daughter and that you were hoping to find true elven earrings. She assured me she could get you a pair. I requested two pairs to make it worth her effort. When they come in, I will hold them for you."

"I think these are beautiful."

"They are. Not the best example of human workmanship. The finer human and elven pieces are stunning! We are heading back to my house now. I will show you some elven jewelry before we go to dinner. They were Suzhanee's."

Melissa looked at Micah, her expression a question.

"It's okay. I want to show them to you. You cannot take any jewelry home, though."

"Why not?" teased Melissa. "She gave these to me. They are mine!" She clutched the earrings in her hands, protecting them.

"Wearing elven earrings while Preparers are looking for me would be dangerous for you. The observant person would notice them."

"Ohh."

"When she delivers your elven ones, and the danger has passed, you will have them," said Hovan.

"Do you think we'll be okay?" Her tone held both hope and fear.

"I think you will be."

"Me or us?"

"You. I am not sure about others."

"Are you sure about you?"

"Me least of all," said the wizard. Hovan turned to Melissa and smiled. "The Sun shines; enjoy. A translation of a saying we have here."

"You're a complex man, Micah."

Hovan nodded, but said nothing in return.

Once inside the wizard's house, Hovan brought Melissa back up to the second floor suite. He handed her a carved stone jewelry box.

"Suzhanee rarely wore earrings. Too easily grabbed in a fight. She was more fond of rings, bracelets, and pendants. I had added magic to many of her favorites."

Melissa sat with the box at a dressing table. Enthralled, she explored the jewelry box, pulling out various samples. Holding each to her ear, she looked at her reflection in the mirror.

"I see what you mean about the quality. Some of these look almost too wonderful to wear!" Melissa looked up at Hovan, smiling. "Almost."

Turning her head from side to side, she compared the earrings from the market with the ones of the same pattern from the jewelry box.

"I think I like mine better."

Hovan's brow wrinkled. "You do?"

"Yes. I discovered them."

Reaching across, Hovan pulled out a set of silver earrings. Three slender, twisted silver strands hung from each earring. "These were my favorite."

"I don't think they would look good on you," teased Melissa.

"On Suzhanee."

Melissa held them to her ears and looked at her reflection. "The silver stands out under my dark hair. I like the way they move. They attract attention. May I wear them to dinner?"

"Yes."

They headed downstairs and found Ti'ek putting away dishes in the kitchen. Standing in front of a cupboard, dressed in a light green tunic and leggings to match, with a sword and dagger belted to his waist, he did not look the part of a butler.

"No servants?"

"I never felt comfortable with too many people having access to my house."

Melissa made no answer besides moving to help Ti'ek. The elf slapped her hand and shooed her away. Melissa smiled and nodded understanding. She sat next to Hovan at the kitchen table.

"Isn't Laexa a servant? Your bodyguard? I assumed she lives here when she went to change."

"Laexa is my protector and the first captain of Forestton." Hovan hesitated while counting in his head. "She has been with me for nine years now. First, as protector, then became my first captain. Now she is a close friend and advisor. She works for me, but that does not define our relationship."

"Romantic?"

"No, that does not describe it either." Hovan teased, "Why? Jealous?"

"Maybe," said Melissa.

Taking care to spoil the exchange, Ti'ek chose that moment to join them at the table, wearing a broad smile.

Hovan returned the tease. "Your timing is as good as ever."

"Always looking out for you," said Ti'ek. "Are we taking her out drinking?"

Hovan laughed. Loud.

"What?" said Melissa.

Hovan laughed again, hesitating to answer her question.

"Come on, come on," continued Ti'ek, gesturing toward Melissa. "Tell the flirt we are going drinking."

"What?" demanded Melissa.

"The prince wishes to share a bottle of wine with you," said Hovan.

Turning and meeting Ti'ek's eyes, Melissa said, "Oh, does he?" She glanced at Hovan before returning her stare to the prince. "You tell the prince that I have gone drinking with larger men than he and still come home with my virtue."

Hovan relayed the message.

Ti'ek sat back in his chair. With a wave of his hand, he asked, "Is that a challenge?"

In response to Hovan's translation, Melissa shook her head. "No, Prince, a warning."

Ti'ek smiled. "I think it is a challenge."

"How did I become the middle man here?" asked Hovan of Ti'ek.

"As usual with women, you wait for the moment instead of creating it. To the Forest Inn!" Ti'ek rose and offered his arm to Melissa. She accepted.

Laexa joined them in the main hallway.

Once past the open double doors of the Forest Inn, its proprietor, Taz'niet, threw her arms wide and called, "Welcome, lords and ladies!" She was a tall woman whose hands accentuated all that she said.

"I had heard, Lord Wizard, that a visitor from the king's court was in town. I am honored that you dine with us!"

"Where else, my friend, but the Forest Inn when in Forestton? The king delighted in his visit to your inn and has spread the word of the excellent cuisine! Nothing but the best for my friends. And for Prince Ti'ek too."

Ti'ek chuckled at the jest and patted Melissa's hand to return the tease, noting whose arm she was on.

Hovan smiled. "Please, a table for four and a bottle of my favorite red."

Melissa sat and accepted a menu from a waitress with yellow eyes. Hovan gently took it from her hand as Ti'ek replaced it with a glass of wine.

Melissa listened as Hovan interpreted the menu. After a few descriptions, she simply asked Hovan to order for her. Besides, she was not hungry, having eaten a short time ago. "Is this the same red wine we had with dinner?" Melissa asked.

"Yes, though this is an older vintage. Taz'niet, the owner, knows it is one of my favorites. She tries to keep some on hand. On quieter days, I will come in and share a bottle with her over a meal. She is an excellent source of local information and a friend of sorts."

The server took the dinner order. She returned Melissa's look with a polite nod. Melissa observed her eyes. "Yellow eyes look exceptional! Exotic, exciting, and yet soothing."

"The king's eyes," explained Hovan. "They run in his family. That is why yellow is the king's color. In elves, green eyes often go with royalty. My blue eyes are simply nice and uncommon."

"So much seems different, yet so much is similar. Even our fine prince, here." She leaned over and flirted with Ti'ek as she spoke to Hovan. "So different with those elven green eyes and bronze skin, yet the same when faced with a pretty girl. Ahh, drink your wine, Prince." Melissa smiled. "At least you can have wine tonight. I am not on the menu."

Hovan translated, doing his best to convey the tone and not to laugh.

Ti'ek spoke and kissed Melissa's hand. "Ti'ek is wondering. Since the menu often determines the wine to be served, will the wine being served help influence the menu?" His tone needed no translation.

"No, Prince."

Laexa chimed in. "Ti'ek, should I tell her there is no reward for out drinking an elf?"

"The evening is young, and the bottle is full." He toasted and drank.

"And you are too, as usual, with yourself," joked Laexa.

Hovan raised his glass to toast. "To friends and better days." He repeated in English.

"Tch, tch, tch." Ti'ek shook his head. "The Giver gives; savor her gift! The moment is now. Breathe it in!"

Hovan translated. Melissa raised her glass in salute. She moved to clink glasses, but Hovan stopped with a touch of his hand. "That is not part of the custom. That means something else here."

They raised their glasses and drank.

A flute, a hand drum, and a string instrument played lively music as they ate dinner and enjoyed the second bottle of wine. The crowd grew, filling most tables, and a few couples danced.

Melissa and Ti'ek enjoyed refilling each other's wine glasses. The third bottle came after dessert. Hovan and Laexa drink little of this bottle. Hovan had magic to do tonight. Laexa was his protector. When Ti'ek suggested a fourth, Hovan recommended retiring to his house and sitting in the chairs on the roof to view the moons. Ti'ek thought that was a wonderful idea!

Hovan took Melissa's arm as they rose to leave. "The moment?" asked the wizard of Ti'ek, who was slow to rise. Ti'ek frowned in return.

"Protecting me?" asked Melissa.

"Yes, from a falling elf. Prince Ti'ek has had more than his share of wine tonight." Melissa adjusted her feet as she stood. "I suggest you have as well."

Hovan secured her arm as Taz'niet came to wish them a good night. "My guests enjoyed themselves as always at the Forest Inn. May your inn continue for an elven generation!"

"I am honored to have such guests! Our wizard, the prince, the first, and a lady from the king's court! Your pleasure is my pleasure!" Taz'niet put her hand on her chest and bowed. She rushed away to serve other guests.

"Micah," whispered Melissa. "You didn't pay for the meal."

"Taz'niet forgets to bill me for the meal," said Hovan with a wave of his hand. "I forget to collect the taxes on the inn."

They exited the inn and felt the evening breeze caress their faces. They began a slow walk back toward the wizard's house through the long, late afternoon shadows. The soft breeze played with their hair and brought them rural scents. Ti'ek, taking measured steps, walked a few paces in front of Hovan and Melissa.

"I don't think I need to worry about Prince Ti'ek anymore tonight," said Melissa.

"No," agreed Hovan. "Not that you ever needed to."

Melissa settled against Hovan's muscular arm as they walked. "And you?" asked Melissa, smiling at the wizard.

"Friday, I was a liar. Today, I am a friend. That is good enough for one weekend."

Melissa protested. "Micah, I didn't mean that. I just..."

"I know. No offense meant. None taken. Now you know all my secrets. I need to get you home. The Moon has long since set over the Berkshires."

"I am sleepy."

"I think seeing the moons here will have to wait for another visit."

"Yes, my lord."

Melissa nestled on his arm, vulnerable and seductive and so close. He tried to stop his mind from wandering to hopes or memories. They walked on, each in his or her own thoughts. The wizard held the door to his house open for Melissa, holding her elbow so she would not trip.

"May I see your wedding portrait once more before we leave?" Melissa asked.

"Here, we call a wedding portrait the 'Lasting Smile'. Some who are less optimistic about marriage shorten the name to just the 'Last Smile'."

The others gathered by the entrance as Melissa looked at the painting again. She took a photograph.

Ti'ek remarked, "More than a passing resemblance."

"Time to go, Melissa," said Hovan.

With Hovan as translator, they exchanged goodbyes. Ti'ek bowed and kissed Melissa's hand. "I hope you took no offense from my jests tonight, Lady Melissa. You must come again and allow me to show you Shetteca!"

"Thank you for making me feel welcome, Prince. I look forward to returning!"

Ti'ek excused himself and climbed up the stairs without incident.

Melissa changed back into her own clothes and put the earrings away. She found Hovan and Laexa waiting for her again in the hallway, dressed for the lodge.

Hovan motioned for the women to lay a hand on his shoulder. "Click your heels together three times and say, 'There is no place like home'."

"Shut up," said Melissa. "I'm not looking forward to this. At least now, I'll have an excuse for not feeling well when I get back."

Hovan began the spell.

CHAPTER 33

SHAPE OF THINGS TO COME

T om woke up early and peeked into Melissa's room. Opening the door a crack, he saw, by the dim light of the morning sun filtering through the closed blinds, his sister sound asleep, wrapped in a blanket.

To Forestton and back. I guess she's a believer now.

He located Racine in the new security room, formerly the attic, on morning watch duty. The top room of the lodge offered a view of the front, including the long driveway winding down the hill. Shafts of yellow light filtering through the trees made the morning mist visible. To Tom, the view through the new security cameras made the beautifully serene and rural image seem mechanical and uninspired. Monitors for the cameras further down the driveway were off, unconnected wires hanging across the top, as were the ones for the bridge and gate which crossed the stream to the main road. The sensor on the gate blocking the entrance to the short bridge crossing the stream at the base of the driveway was active and shone green. A short slide on the rolling chair reached a window overlooking the rear of the lodge, still shrouded in shadow, and another set of monitors for the rear cameras.

"Morning, Racine. Is everything okay?"

"All is quiet."

"Why are you still on watch? No one relieved you?"

"I only came up a short time ago. Micah relieved me after they returned. I slept for a few hours."

"I'll send Anton up so you can get started on breakfast. Anyone but Anton cooking. I'll get started on the computers. Sanlar is right. We must put more effort into finding them!"

"There are other cases to wrap up," said Racine. "We have work to finish. The business cannot just fold up and go away. We need the money to finance our operations, if nothing else."

"I understand, but nothing takes precedence over finding the Preparers. We need to delegate more to the staff and shift some to subcontractors. Do you think the Preparers have done nothing? Do you realize how frightening it is to me that they scare you, Sanlar, and Micah?"

"Rally the forces," said Racine.

Tom took his coffee and walked into the computer room, pushing the power button on the smartboard as he passed. He sat at the first computer in a line of three on the long table running down the middle of the room. The opposite side of the table was the mirror image, with three more flat screen monitors. Tom posted a list of assignments on the smart board: driver's licenses, gun serial numbers, corporate holding, building plans, employees, private residences.

Cathy joined her husband soon after Tom sat down. David wandered in with a yawn and a steaming mug of coffee and asked where they were.

Tom pointed to the board. "Get to work."

Paul and Carrie came in together. "You humans get to work on these machines of yours," joked Carrie. She kissed her husband goodbye. "We elves will see to the food."

The last to arrive were Berk and Shire, who barked and then quickly wandered back out, tails still wagging, finding no one to play with.

Racine called breakfast at 8:30 am. Those filing in from the computer room found Sanlar, Mike, and Laexa seated in the dining room, filling their plates with eggs, toast, hash browns, and fruit. They sat and joined in.

"Are Melissa and Micah back?" Mike asked his brother.

"Yeah," answered Tom. "I checked on Melissa this morning. Micah left a note in the kitchen. They went to the Forest Inn. Seems Melissa and Prince Ti'ek had a wine drinking contest." A few chuckles came from around the table.

"She better have won," joked David.

"Maybe not," argued Sanlar. "She is not a big human."

"What's wrong with shorter humans?" asked Cathy. Her complaint brought more laughter.

"Nothing, love, nothing," appeased Tom.

"Who is Ti'ek?" asked Mike. "What's so funny?"

"An elf prince who lives in Forestton," answered Tom.

"What time do you plan on leaving, Tom?" asked Racine.

"As soon as Micah and Melissa are awake and ready to go. My dad will not be easy to convince."

Sanlar lowered his fork to his plate. His brow furrowed in thought over his dark brown eyes. Looking at Tom, Sanlar asked, "Do you think your father can help us?"

"Yes. With his military experience and weapons training, I think he could be a lot of help!"

Sanlar's question surprised Tom. The normally taciturn warrior was becoming a surprise advocate for the defense of his adopted world.

"Then it is important that we have his help! We must stop the Preparers! There is nothing more vital. His family, his country, and indeed, his world is in danger. Your father was a warrior, yes?"

"He served in combat to defend our country," said a proud Tom.

"I will convince him!" Sanlar's heavily accented assertion tensed with conviction.

"You're coming?" asked Mike hopefully.

"Your father is a warrior and a protector. Deceiving men like us is difficult, as we have experienced danger and uphold honor. We bear the burden of protection. He will see a fellow warrior in me. I will convince him. Racine and I are going." Sanlar filled his fork and began eating again.

Racine raised one eyebrow and looked at Sanlar. Racine leaned closer to Laexa and whispered.

"I think it would help for my parents to meet an elf." Tom's voice reflected his surprise and relief.

"Yes, but you stay here," said Sanlar.

"What?" said Tom.

"You must work on the computers," said Sanlar, as if stating the obvious. "Micah, Racine, and I will convince your warrior father. Melissa and Laexa will help."

"Yeah, brother, you have responsibilities," teased Mike, pointing a fork at him.

"No, no, no!" insisted Tom. "I will be there when my parents learn of all this!"

"We will do what we can," stated Sanlar. "You must do what we cannot."

"Tom," interrupted Racine, "what if we bring them here?"

"That is a lot of driving. How can we convince them to come here?"

"With Micah's help, we will only need to travel one way. If I show them an elf, that should make them curious."

"You can move by magic the way Micah does?" asked an excited Mike. "Are you a wizard, too?"

"I am not a wizard, but I can perform some advanced magic," said Racine.

"So, you, Micah, Sanlar, and Melissa will drive down and bring my parents back?" reasoned Tom. "Take Melissa's car and leave it there?"

"No," said Racine. "I will drive one of the minivans. Laexa is, of course, coming as well. Then we will bring your parents here and explain everything to them."

"Hey, why am I left out again?" demanded Mike.

"No need for you to come," replied Sanlar between bites. "Stay here and help."

Tom held up his hand, stopping his brother from arguing further. "It's a long drive just to end up back here. If they're going by minivan, then there is room for you. But I think there are things here you could do to help. And here you can hang out with elves and practice shooting. Your choice."

By 9:00, the humans were back in front of the computers. Racine and Carrie tackled the dishes. Sanlar invited Laexa and Mike to practice hand to hand fighting with him.

Micah poked his head into the computer room just before 10:00, hoping to find a running partner.

"Not now," said Tom. "We must focus. How was Forestton?"

"It went well. Melissa may have a headache when she wakes up."

"Okay. No stories now. Take the dogs on your run. Laexa is out back."

Melissa finally made an appearance an hour later. "Is Mike here?"

"How do you feel?" Tom asked his sister. "Want food?"

"Yeah. Whole wheat toast with aspirin and a glass of water."

Tom chuckled and stood. "I'll help you."

He led the way to the kitchen. Mike was there, making a sandwich.

"The aspirin should be over here," said Tom.

Melissa sat at the kitchen table. "Mike, we should get going if we're going to beat the traffic."

"I'm not going," answered Mike.

Tom explained. "Micah, Laexa, Racine, and Sanlar will go with you and break the news to Mom and Dad. You will convince them to come here. Micah and Racine will use magic to bring you all back."

"I have to travel that way again?!" Melissa groaned, putting a hand to her head.

"Check," said Tom. "Are you good to go? Racine will drive."

"I'll be fine," answered Melissa, waving her hand and dismissing his concern. "I prefer the car to that other thing they do. Can they bring us all back?"

"I'm afraid so."

Melissa moaned in defeat.

"You score no points with this crowd for out drinking an elf," Tom said, and laughed.

After she took the aspirin, she mumbled, "He seemed able to handle his wine to me."

CHAPTER 34

STRANGE FRIENDS

Racine and Sanlar settled into the front seats of the blue minivan. Micah and Laexa claimed the middle row, leaving the back row for Melissa. Micah placed a long cardboard tube next to him. The minivan rolled past the trees and down the hill from the lodge.

Micah asked Melissa, "How do you suggest we approach your parents?"

"Be straightforward. Show them magic and elves. That worked for me. My father will respect the direct approach. He will not believe a word you say. Show them."

Thanks to New York traffic, it took close to four hours to reach the Rosses' house.

Melissa walked into the house and yelled. "Hi Mom. Hi Dad."

"In the kitchen, Melissa," came her mother's response.

Melissa led them through the living room toward the staircase at the back of the house. Micah carried the long tube. The sliding glass doors before them opened onto a patio under the deck. Melissa turned left up the stairs to the second floor.

Mrs. Ross closed the refrigerator door as they entered the room. A smile spread across her face as the unexpected guests walked into her kitchen. "This is a pleasant surprise! Racine, Sanlar, how are you?"

Mrs. Ross noticed that cheerful look on her daughter's face. With a wave of her hand toward Micah, she said, "And it's good to see you, too. Now that she's happy again."

Mrs. Ross looked up at the tall woman with reddish brown hair standing next to Micah. "I don't believe we've met before. Welcome to my home." Mrs. Ross held out her hand.

Micah spoke to Laexa in his native tongue. Laexa nodded. She stepped forward and completed the handshake. With a slight bow, she stepped back.

Micah addressed Mrs. Ross. "This is Laexa. A visitor from my country. She does not speak English. She is pleased to meet you."

"Where's Dad?" asked Melissa.

"On the deck starting the barbeque," said Mrs. Ross, pointing through sliding glass doors. "I hope I have enough hamburgers."

Melissa started for the door. "Don't worry about dinner, Mom. We have a suggestion."

"Where's Mike?" interrupted Mrs. Ross.

"Still at the lodge," Melissa said over her shoulder as she walked onto the deck.

"He has school tomorrow!"

"We'll explain!" came the answer from outside.

Mrs. Ross turned and leveled her motherly gaze at those standing in front of her. "Is Mike alright?"

"Yes," said Micah. "He is fine. Well, a little annoyed." Micah's lips slipped into a grin.

Mrs. Ross looked at Micah and drummed her fingers on the counter. "That devilish look on your face must have driven your mother mad."

"We thought it would be easier if we explained just once," Micah said, and then looked out onto the deck.

"Don't worry about the barbeque, Dad." Melissa's voice pleaded with her father. "Just come inside." Melissa verbally pulled her father into the kitchen.

Once he was inside, but before he could offer a hello to the others standing there, Mrs. Ross insisted, "Well?"

"You know that I've been mad at Micah since my party. He, they, explained some things to me. We want to explain them to you."

"Why isn't Michael here?" demanded Mrs. Ross. "He has school tomorrow. Finals are coming up!"

"I think this is more important than one day of school."

Mrs. Ross's only response was to raise her eyebrows.

Mr. Ross's gaze left his daughter and moved from one face to another. His stare stayed longest on the one face he did not know. All four returned his look with poise.

Micah felt sure that Mr. Ross noticed the at ease military stance of Laexa and Sanlar.

"It looks like we are ganging up on you," began Micah. "I had not intended that. Tom told me you have been asking about me, Mr. Ross, and even offered help. We are here to reintroduce ourselves and ask if the offer of help still stands."

"We need all the help we can get," added Sanlar.

"May I use your dining room table?" asked Micah.

They moved into the dining room and stood around the table. Melissa moved the centerpiece. Micah pulled a long, rolled woven cloth out of the tube and placed it on the table.

"I know you will find what I am going to tell you difficult to believe. I promise it is the truth. As you know, I was not born in this country. What you may not know is that I have a military and mercenary past."

"Tom told me," said Mr. Ross.

"Did he also tell you that five years ago, my young wife died?"

"Ohh, Julian, I'm very sorry!" offered Mrs. Ross. "You must have married young."

"Thank you. I do not talk about it often. I come here because I need a change. An escape from the memories. Though I go back often."

Micah held onto one end of the cloth and rolled the bolt away from him down the dining room table. It opened to reveal a map. "This is the country of my birth."

Both Mrs. and Mr. Ross leaned in to look at the map.

"I can't read this," said Mr. Ross.

"What country is this?" asked Mrs. Ross.

"The name of the country is Arre'ielle," said Micah.

"I've never heard of it," said the two Ross parents together.

"That is our name for it. I was born in this area." Micah pointed out a south eastern section. "I now live in this town when I return. It translates to Forestton, meaning town from the forest. The reason you have not heard of Arre'ielle and the reason you cannot read the language is that," Micah hesitated, then completed his sentence, "I was not born on this planet."

"Julian, I'm not in the mood for games!" shouted Mr. Ross.

Holding Mr. Ross's eyes, Micah said, "This is no game!"

Reaching inside his jacket, Micah carefully pulled his 9 mm pistol and placed it in the center of the map.

"You dare bring a gun into my house?" demanded Mr. Ross.

"A week ago Friday, six people from my planet, armed with guns, waited for me at my house, intent on killing me."

Micah heard Mrs. Ross's sharp intake of air, but did not look away from the retired Marine staring him down.

"I killed all six. I have not returned to my house since. My name is now Micah Falco. The name Julian Orel is not safe. Melissa and Mike overheard me and Tom discussing it during her party. They did not believe me any more than you now do. We will provide proof."

Mr. Ross turned to walk away. "Don't waste my time!"

"Your help is no longer offered?" asked Sanlar. He took the silver chain hanging around his neck and lifted it over his head. Sanlar morphed from a Hispanic man into a muscular elf with black hair and dark brown eyes.

Racine's change was equally startling, except his piercing green eyes shone forth from his light brown face.

Mr. Ross looked back and forth between Racine and Sanlar.

"What are you?" demanded Mr. Ross.

"Elves from the same planet as Micah."

"Elves?"

"Aliens?" uttered Mrs. Ross.

"Alien elves?" asked Mr. Ross.

Mrs. Ross turned her head to look at Laexa.

Micah said, "She is human like me."

Mr. and Mrs. Ross looked at Melissa.

"I'm your daughter."

Racine addressed Mr. Ross. "We are taking a risk by exposing ourselves. But you are Tom's family. Those who attacked Micah are a danger to all of us. Not just because we know him. But because of what they can do and will try to do to the people of this planet. We ask for your help to prevent them from doing what we know they will try. We hope our resources and strength are enough to stop this threat. Please allow Micah to show you what he can do. Then you may better understand the danger we face."

Mr. and Mrs. Ross stood speechless, with eyes darting from face to face. Before their confusion could contract into resentment and anger, Micah spoke again.

"I have carried a handgun every day for a week now. It is not my preferred weapon, though. I find them limited, loud, and inaccurate."

"Your military training wasn't very good, then, was it?" countered Mr. Ross.

"I am an expert at what I do! My training did not include any handguns or rifles. They do not exist on my planet."

"No, of course not, you have ray guns!" said Mrs. Ross.

Micah picked up his handgun and returned it to its shoulder holster. He rolled up the map. "Better! Join me downstairs in the living room. I will show you my preferred form of attack."

Micah moved toward the stairs, but Melissa's parents stood firmly in place.

"Mom, Dad, when Micah was Julian and told me this garbage with Tom swearing it was all true, I wanted to beat them both up. This is why I've been upset all week. I have no other explanation for what I've seen this past week. None other than they are telling the truth. Come downstairs and just watch. If you can offer me any other explanation, please tell me."

Mr. and Mrs. Ross slowly followed Micah to the stairs as if being pulled on an invisible leash by Melissa.

Once in the living room, Micah took off his jacket. He noted a faint smile on Melissa's lips, suggesting amusement at her parents' coming reaction.

"A martial arts expert?" asked Mr. Ross.

"I am not bad at hand to hand fighting. I try to avoid it. It is not my strength. Sanlar and Laexa are better at that than me... except perhaps with a staff." Micah bowed to Sanlar and then to Laexa. "This is what I prefer."

Micah turned and thrust his left hand toward the fireplace. Two fire darts shot from his fingers and slammed into the cinder blocks.

"I can vary the strength and guide each independently."

He brought his right hand waist high and shot four more sequentially into the fireplace. "Racine," he said.

Racine faced the fireplace. A pair of fire darts streaked from one hand, followed by a pair from his other hand.

Mr. Ross stared at them, eyes wide, mouth closed. Mrs. Ross stood close to her husband, grabbing his hand as she stared at these strange friends before her.

Micah directed their attention back to the map. Reaching out with his mind, he held one end and let it roll open toward the floor, and then rotated it. He stood before the floating map as if he were making a presentation.

"This is the capital city of Avi'ot. I was born in a town that is too small to be noted. It is in this area. Where I call home now is in this north district of Shetteca." He circled Shetteca with his finger. "In this town called Forestton. It is my town. I am its lord. My name given me by my mother is Hovan. Thus, I am called the Lord Wizard Hovan of Forestton, when translated. I can take you there if you wish. Melissa was there yesterday. I think the visit was the final piece of the puzzle convincing her that this world is not all that there is."

Mr. Ross's eyes were shifting from the floating map to Micah to Melissa. His eyes narrowed, and his lips grew taut.

The map hanging in midair rolled up.

His mouth opened to speak, but closed again. It seemed as if his mind was spinning, stuck between evidence and denial, too confused to form words.

"Mom, Dad, one reason Mike isn't here is because we plan on taking you to him. To the Berkshires. Now. By magic."

Sanlar faced Mr. Ross. Their brown eyes met and held each other's gaze. "Racine and I will go first. I will see you soon, Mr. Ross. You and I share a common purpose: protect others! Many are in danger! We need your help. It will be my honor to train with you and fight by your side." He bowed and put his hand on Racine's shoulder.

Racine held his left hand vertical like a blade. His right hand shaped magic around it as he whispered foreign words.

"What are you doing?" asked Mr. Ross. "I don't understand what you are saying."

Racine continued with is hand motions and whispering, not responding to the question from Mr. Ross. Everyone else stayed quiet, waiting.

Racine and Sanlar vanished.

Mrs. Ross gasped and took a step back.

Mr. Ross stood for a moment before rushing forward, waving his hands through the air where Racine and Sanlar had stood.

"Where did they go?" demanded Mr. Ross, his face red with irritation.

"To the lodge in the Berkshires, Dad," explained Melissa. "Come, let Micah also take us there."

"Magic? You're saying that you can do magic?!"

"That is how it would translate into English," answered Micah.

Micah held out his palm. Four colored flames appeared, floating above his hand. "Your science is as foreign to me as this magic is to you. I was frightened to near panic the first time I saw an airplane fly over... a roaring metal dragon!"

Mr. Ross's mouth hung open. He recovered and pulled his cell phone from his pants pocket. He punched icons and then held the phone to his ear. His eyes intense with increasing anger.

"Mike, where are you?" After a pause, he demanded, "Put Racine on the phone!" It seemed as if the tall man might crush the phone in his grip. He held his fierce pose. "Hurry up!" he barked into the phone. Then suddenly his eyes grew wide. His mouth opened into an expression of disbelief. He lowered his hand to his side and looked at Melissa and Micah.

They heard Racine speaking.

"Dad, I don't know how they do it," pleaded Melissa. She took her mother's hand and held it in both of her hands. "Somehow, they do it. Let Micah take us to the lodge."

Mr. Ross ended the phone call. He turned to his wife. His shoulders sagged as he exhaled. He put his arm around his wife, who nodded in unspoken agreement.

Mrs. Ross took her husband's hand in her hand. She said to Melissa, "You and your brothers have no idea what the punishment will be if this is a joke."

"I value your safety," Micah said. "This is not a joke."

Micah arranged them around him. Each placed a hand on him. He began the hand motions around the vertical left hand. They disappeared from the Ross's house on Long Island and reappeared in Micah's room at the lodge.

When the Rosses had recovered, Micah led them down the flight of creaking stairs to the main level. The rest of the crowd met them in the main lobby of the lodge. The large wooden door stood open with the afternoon sun lighting the porch beyond in shades of yellow and orange. Only the closed screen door kept the bugs at bay.

"Now my parents have traveled by magic! Why am I always the last?" Mike's whine elicited a laugh from almost everyone except his parents.

Mr. Ross walked out onto the porch, followed by Tom. The gravel parking area spread before him until it merged into the long driveway, which wound its way down the hill. His eyes shifted to the valley that lay below him. Hills hidden beneath trees rose in uneven ascents to his left and right. Turning, he inspected the porch.

"Yes, Dad," said Tom. "You're in the Berkshires."

Mr. Ross opened his cell phone and checked his location.

"How?"

"It translates as magic," said Tom.

Together, the father and son walked back inside.

Once back in the lobby, he faced Mr. and Mrs. Ross. "I am the Lord Wizard Hovan of Forestton. This is my protector and First Captain Laexa of Forestton. Racine is Lord Racine of Liscam, though he no longer uses the title. Sanlar is his protector."

Sanlar strode forward and offered his hand to Mr. Ross. "Welcome. It is difficult, I know. We have much to do. Much to protect."

Mr. Ross shook his hand.

"So, Mom, can Mike miss one day of school for this?" asked Melissa.

"You won't find any of this taught in school," added Mike.

"That is the truth!" agreed Mrs. Ross. "But Julian brought us..."

"Micah," corrected Micah.

"Micah," continued Mrs. Ross, sounding irritated, "brought us here quick enough. He can bring us back just as quick." Before Mike could argue, Mrs. Ross added, "You will get your chance to travel by magic... though you may not like how it makes you feel."

"I am sorry, Mrs. Ross. I cannot. A magician must have perfect memory of a place to successfully arrive there using magic. I cannot picture your house well enough."

"Stay tonight, Mom, Dad," said Tom. "We had a demonstration for Melissa and Mike planned for yesterday, but the storm washed it out. We can do it for you tomorrow. Let Mike stay to make up for missing the chance to travel by magic and see Forestton. He'll be home tomorrow night in time for school on Tuesday."

"We'll see, we'll see," said Mrs. Ross, waving her hand as a white flag at her eldest son. "I'm too confused to argue right now."

"Come, have a seat," offered Cathy. She led them out of the lobby to the Fireplace Room. "Would you like some food or something to drink?"

The group left standing in the lobby watched them pass through the door into the Fireplace Room.

"That went well," said a smiling Tom.

"I will go on watch," said Sanlar. Eyeing the humans with his intense brown eyes, Sanlar insisted, "You must get back to work."

Paul, joking, said, "Yes, sir." He saluted Sanlar, winked at his wife Carrie, and left with David.

"I will relieve you after dark," said Micah. "I want to stay with the Rosses."

Sanlar nodded approval and headed for the stairs.

"We will take care of dinner," Racine said as he pointed to Carrie for help. The group parted in opposite directions: Racine and Carrie to the kitchen; Micah, Laexa, and Tom to the Fireplace Room.

Tom found a seat near his parents. Cathy handed them each a glass of water.

Melissa asked, "Would a beer help?"

Mr. Ross shook his head no.

"Are you sure? It helped me."

"No," Mr. Ross whispered.

Tom spoke. "I'm glad you are here, Mom and Dad. For one thing, it makes it easier for me. Less I need to hide. I know this is difficult. The circumstances are less than pleasant. However, all that we say is true."

Micah began. "We will tell all we know. If you wish, I will take you to my world. Information first. Then the demonstration will help you understand what our challenges are. What questions do you have?"

"Can I see your ring again?" jumped in Mike.

"I was not talking to you," said Micah with a sigh. "Yes, you can. Show your parents how it works."

Mike put the ring on and vanished. His parents stared, but said nothing. He reappeared with a smile.

Mr. and Mrs. Ross spoke at the same time. "How did you do that?" "Are you all right?"

"I can show you pictures!" offered Melissa.

"Pictures?" asked Mike. "You didn't tell me you have pictures?"

Melissa opened her cell phone. She sat next to her parents. "Here are a few pictures of Forestton I took yesterday!" She swiped through some photos. "Here we are on the wall. That's the road. The practice field."

"Enough," her mother interrupted. "This is too much, too fast."

"Do you want to try the ring?" asked Micah.

Mrs. Ross shook her head no. She looked at her husband, who nodded his head in agreement.

"Give us a chance to absorb all this. We're going to drive home tonight and think. Mike will go to school. We'll go to work."

"I want to learn more about this," stated Mike.

"I know, Mike," said Mrs. Ross. She held up her hand, signaling him to stop. "So do I. I'm sure your father is as curious as you are. But you've had a week to adjust. Give us a few days. Besides, we brought no change of clothes, no toothbrushes, nothing. We have work tomorrow. You have school."

Mike looked at his parents and moaned in defeat.

"Will you come back next weekend?" asked Tom. "We need your help."

"Enough," the retired Marine stated, calling his children to order. "Enough. We'll let you know. I think we will. Melissa, your car is here? Come, Mike."

CHAPTER 35

THE COMPETITION

After Anton relieved Micah in the security room, Micah detoured through the silent kitchen for a snack and a beer to quiet his mind. He watched the Saturday morning sunrise for a few minutes from the back deck. The Sun arrived in dramatic style, producing a beautiful theater of pinks and oranges accenting streaks of high, white clouds. Impressed by the majestic scale of nature, he sipped his beer in silence, watching the star creep higher. Finally, his body pressed him for sleep. He went upstairs to his room.

By the time he woke just after noon, the lodge was busy with activity. Groceries from a morning trip into town were being carried into the kitchen and pantry. He grabbed a bag and helped. Keyboards clicked in the computer room. A vacuum hummed somewhere on the second floor.

With so much activity, Micah expected little success in recruiting a running partner. Paul overheard and volunteered to keep Micah company. He recruited his wife to join. Micah had seen little of the Ross family since they had arrived from Long Island the night before. Tom, though, jumped at the idea, saying it was a chance to see something other than a flashing screen. Tom convinced his dad to join them. Together, they challenged Mike, who had no excuse when his older brother offered him a pair of shorts. Sanlar said the idea of group training was brilliant! Laexa, of course, would join without question since Micah was going.

Sanlar and Micah were the first two to gather on the front porch. Each looked over the other and nodded approval. Tied to Sanlar's lower right leg was a large knife in a sheath. A leather shoulder holster stretched across his back and chest with a black handgun tightly strapped in. Micah held his shoulder holster, with his 9 mm semiautomatic in it, in his hand.

"For Mr. Ross," he said.

Laexa arrived wearing shorts that were too big and a shirt that was too small. She held out her hands in apparent exasperation, complaining to Micah. "Elves are too short. And you are too tall. Someone, please take me shopping."

Paul and Tom arrived next with weighted fanny packs.

Carrie had a small handgun holstered on each ankle. As she stretched her legs, she smiled at Paul. "Ankle weights."

Carrie looked over at Laexa. She chuckled. "Nice outfit, Captain. Need some help shopping for athletic wear?"

Laexa's shoulders sagged in frustration. "Please."

"Amazon to the rescue."

When Mr. Ross arrived, Micah held out his shoulder holster. "For you, Mr. Ross. It has a full clip. The chamber is empty."

"Do you think it is necessary?" Mr. Ross asked.

"Yes," Sanlar stated.

Mr. Ross hesitated and then accepted the holstered weapon. "What about you?"

"Guns are not my preferred weapon. I have my magic."

The group of seven started from the gravel driveway and headed over the wooden bridge into the woods. Forty minutes later, the sweaty group returned with Mike bringing up the rear with Mr. Ross. Mr. Ross was bent over with his hands on his knees, catching his breath.

"Seems like we have some work to do," Mr. Ross said to his younger son, who was leaning on the porch railing, breathing deeply, sweat dripping off his face. "Those hills are tough." Turning to his older son, he added, "You seem alright."

Tom stretched his arms high over his head as he breathed in long breaths. "I'm no match for these two," he said, nodding toward Sanlar and Micah. "Captain Laexa is in their class, it seems. Anyone who wants a shower before lunch and the show, grab it now."

The weather appeared perfect for the afternoon barbeque and demonstration. Micah grew excited as the gathering neared.

I can show off a little. Have some fun. Be myself. Nothing more to hide.

He arrived in the yard behind the lodge wearing his favorite cloak, dark leather boots, and a tan cloth shirt. His short staff was in its quiver diagonally across his back. Out of character and out of sight was the occupied shoulder holster.

As the eldest, Racine began the presentation, speaking in his soft accent. The elf stood in front of the others, who sat at picnic tables. A charcoal barbeque stood off to the side. He wore comfortable blue jeans and a loose polo shirt. Despite the normal attire, his high cheekbones and brilliant green eyes, combined with his straight black hair and bronze skin, presented an attractive, exotic look.

"I was born in the Dahica Kingdom. Dahica is a kingdom predominantly of elves. I am the eldest child of the Duke and Duchess of Liscam. The story that brings me here with Sanlar is in parts very sad and may be told some other time. Sanlar and me have traveled together for many decades now. We came to this world fourteen years ago. A short time by elven standards. We elves live long, averaging twice the lifespan of the humans of our home world. Our planets are different in some ways, but not in others. The most obvious difference is the absence of technology. Instead, we have a highly developed field of, for lack of a better word, magic. Our goal today is to convince and entertain, as well as warn. The demonstration will not be long, so I ask Tom to start the coals first. Tom, if you would."

Tom stood and launched a single fire dart into the fluid soaked charcoal. A large flame sprang to life.

"You can do that?" asked his mother, eyes wide, eyebrows raised.

"It isn't too difficult. It makes my fingers tingle. Micah has been teaching myself and Cathy."

Racine, still standing before the group, spoke again. "We are showing you all this because we expect to need your help after what happened at Micah's house in Rockland."

Micah stood and addressed those gathered. "Those that attacked me are part of a group whose name translates to Preparers. They are very dangerous. I did not know they were here on Earth until the attack at my house. They underestimated me. I expect they will continue searching for me and other off worlders that are here. They are a threat to everyone. They want to prepare those they can for the next life by killing them and doing it in a way that makes you want to die. This means torture, anguish at watching a child die crying, despair at one's own helplessness. They will use any means to show you the worthlessness of staying alive, the meaningless of this life."

Micah took a breath. "We need to remove them from this planet and stop them from returning. We cannot ignore them. Your authorities would never believe us. However, removing them and keeping them off this planet will not be easy. I commit myself to this task. One I regretfully invite you to join."

"Have you all accepted this mission?" asked Mr. Ross.

"We have," answered Tom.

"My children will not be involved in this!" insisted Mrs. Ross.

"I have made my choice, Mom," responded Tom in a calm voice. "I had never seen or heard of a Preparer before last week. Yet, I look and see the fear they inspire in powerful men and elves that I respect. They cannot have me, my family, or my world without a fight."

"Well said, Tom, but perhaps too easily said for one who has never seen combat," Mr. Ross responded.

"No, I haven't. But if what I've been told is true, I will, at least on a small scale. Knowing what I know, Dad, what would you have me do?"

"I will not answer that until I know more."

"Fair enough, Mr. Ross," said Micah. "Let us continue with the demonstration planned to help you understand."

Racine continued. "We have the honor of having two masters among us: Sanlar, a master of the physical arts; and Micah, a master of the magical arts. A competition between the two arts might add some excitement to the afternoon. Sanlar will start with an archery display."

Two archery targets stood on the grassy field, one halfway across the yard and one near the far end. Beyond the second target rose the hill up to the forest. Small deciduous trees faded into larger pines near the top.

Like Racine, Sanlar wore clothes of this world with his handgun holstered under his arm. His hair, though, was longer than Racine's. He replaced Racine before the group and stood in line with the targets. He carried a compound bow and a quiver of arrows.

"This is not a bow typical of my home," he began in an accent stronger than Racine's. With passion and a joyful smile, he added, "I like these compound bows!"

He drew an arrow and fitted it to the string. Soon after sighting the target, the bow sang. The arrow found the center of the close target. He repeated the process for the farther target, taking only a moment longer to sight the target. This time, the arrow pierced the second ring.

"What do you think of guns?" asked Mr. Ross.

"Very effective and quick, though loud," admitted Sanlar. "The silence of an arrow can keep surprise for longer."

"Both have their limits," said Micah as he walked to the lawn. "Ready, my friend?"

Sanlar nodded and pulled a third arrow from his quiver.

Once Micah was a short distance across the lawn, he faced Sanlar and pronounced, "Ready."

Sanlar eyed Micah down the arrow and released it.

Mrs. Ross gasped in surprise. A red glow enveloped Micah and deflected the arrow. Sanlar dropped his bow and quickly pulled his handgun.

This time, Mr. Ross reacted. "What?!"

Sanlar fired. Again, the red glow protected Micah. Sanlar fired once more, but still Micah smiled behind the red shield.

"You have got to be kidding me?!" exclaimed Mike.

Sanlar offered the gun. "Mr. Ross?"

Mr. Ross stepped forward and accepted the gun. He snapped out the clip and examined the bullets. Satisfied, he reinserted the clip, aimed at Micah's chest, and squeezed off one round. The bullet deflected away harmlessly.

"How much can the glow stop?" asked Mr. Ross as he handed Sanlar's pistol back to him.

Micah walked back toward the tables. "Fire darts, shotgun blasts, lightning bolts. It all depends on how I make the shield. How much energy I put into it. What shape it is. How many layers I build."

"Lightning bolts?" questioned Mike.

"Yes. I need a stronger spell for that."

"Don't tell me you can fire lightning bolts?"

"Of course. I am a wizard. The Lord Wizard Hovan. Member of the court of First Prince Ke'en, member of the Wizard's Corp, and a past King Regent's Wizard." Hovan bowed to Mike. "When my wife, Suzhanee, died, I traveled here. Something different to see. No memories attached. A chance to heal, or at least dull the pain. It is my honor and pleasure to introduce you to my passion, magic."

He fired two fire darts from his left hand. They hit the center of the close archery target, igniting it. Two more spheres shot from his right hand, igniting the far target.

"No reason to waste targets." He waved his hand. Both fires went out.

"Magic is as useful as your technology. We use it for everything from defense and attack, to preserving food, to building and reinforcing structures, to communication, and moving from place to place. My specialty is offensive and defensive magic, the arts of battle. Lily is a healer. She uses magic to fix the body. She can do things that would astound you!"

"Does everyone on your planet do magic?" asked Mike.

Micah looked at Mike between his outstretched hands as if he were holding Mike's head. Micah smiled. Everyone turned to look at Mike. His lips were moving, but no words reached their ears.

"Ohh, you have got to teach me that one!" exclaimed Melissa.

Micah waved his hand to dispel the magic.

"Sorry, Mike, I could not resist. To answer your question, most people could do magic to some extent if they had the opportunity and motivation. Some people cannot find someone willing to teach them. Others cannot afford it or do not have the time. A highly trained magician is uncommon. Wizards are rare! Only seven in my country. I was lucky."

Micah laughed as an image of his childhood flashed into his mind. "My parents realized the trouble I would get into if not for the challenge and discipline of magic. And the opportunity it would provide me. They arranged for me to...practice with, learn from, study under...Tom, what is the word?"

"Apprentice."

"Yes, yes. I became apprentice of a local magician that my father knew through his merchant business. My dad was a good man. He never took offense that his only son did not continue the family business. What I accomplished would have made him proud. He died before he was an old man. He never saw the full success I achieved."

Micah waved Sanlar and Tom forward. "Enough stories for now. Let us get on with the demonstrations. Next, we have a contest between Sanlar's bow and Tom's magic. The rules are simple. Both stand with their backs to a target. On the word, both turn and fire. The first to hit wins that round. I set a new target. They go again. We will play to three points. Prepare, please."

Tom and Sanlar moved to the front and got ready.

"Good luck, honey," yelled Cathy.

"He is going to need it," joked Racine.

"Hey, that's my brother," Melissa said.

"That will not help him beat Sanlar."

Micah reached out with magic. He moved the near target off to the side and positioned the far one halfway down the field.

"Ready?" Both nodded yes. "Go!"

Both turned. An arrow found the target before a fire dart hit.

"One, Sanlar," said Racine.

"Come on, Tom," encouraged Melissa and Cathy.

"Prepare." Both turned their backs to the range. Micah moved the target further back to Tom's side of the yard. "Go."

Again, an arrow hit first. "Two, Sanlar."

"Prepare." Directing with his hand, Micah guided the target closer, but kept it on Tom's side to give him an advantage. "Go."

"Three, Sanlar," announced Racine.

"Wow, shut out," said Mike, disappointed.

"Not a fair match," admitted Racine. "We want to show you magic, but also show you it has limits. I am sure that Mr. Ross with a handgun would beat all." Racine rolled his head to look at the wizard. "... except perhaps Micah. Do we have a contest, gentlemen?"

Micah looked at Mr. Ross and said, "I am in."

"Go for it, Dad," exclaimed Mike.

"Careful, Dad," Tom warned. "He's good. Very, very good."

"If he is faster than a handgun, I have to see," said Mr. Ross. "Count me in."

A cheer went up from the rest.

Mr. Ross walked over to Sanlar. They exchanged a few words as Sanlar prepared his pistol for Mr. Ross.

Micah put his staff and cloak aside and swung his arms around.

"Five on the wizard," said Paul. "Any takers?"

"Done," said Mike. "Show them that Marine training, Dad."

Both men took their starting positions.

"Ready?" asked Racine. Both men nodded. "Game is three points."

Racine prepared a spell and then moved the target to the middle and at twenty paces distance.

"Go."

Micah and Mr. Ross spun and both fired at the target.

Mr. Ross looked over at the wizard in surprise. Micah grinned.

"One for Micah," announced Racine. "Prepare."

The next target was ten paces and to Mr. Ross's side. "Go."

Again, Micah won.

"Two for Micah," said Racine. "Prepare."

Racine moved the next target far down range, still on Mr. Ross's side. "Go."

"Three for Micah."

Mr. Ross stood and stared at the wizard.

In return, Micah said, "It is not fair. You have never played this game before."

"I have a handgun!" exclaimed Mr. Ross.

"I have magic!"

"I would not have believed it if I hadn't seen it," said Mr. Ross as he shook his head and handed the gun back to Sanlar.

Sanlar did not take the gun. "Wizard," challenged Sanlar. "My bow and his pistol versus your magic."

"Sanlar," said Micah, "we do not want Mr. Ross to lose twice on his first day playing."

"We'll take that as a yes," declared Mr. Ross. "How is this played with teams?"

As Racine explained, Sanlar ran inside for more bullets. "Multiple targets. The first team to hit all targets scores the point. You have the advantage with two shooters."

While Sanlar refilled the clip, he and Mr. Ross quietly discussed strategy. Once the three contestants stood ready with Micah in the middle, Racine placed the first two targets midway down the field opposite Mr. Ross and Sanlar.

"Go." All three spun and fired, but fire darts reached the targets first.

"Ready." Racine moved the target opposite Sanlar closer and the one opposite Mr. Ross further away. "Go."

Again, fire darts won.

"How are you so fast?" asked Mr. Ross.

"Years of practice. I can guide the fire after it leaves my hand. I do not need to aim before firing. Just fire and look."

"Ready," called Racine. He kept the targets as they were and pulled a third one onto the field, placing it near the far one. "Go."

The second report of the handgun followed the first one immediately and beat the third delayed fire dart to the new target.

Micah shot Racine an irritated glance.

A cheer went up from the Rosses.

"Go, Dad, go," encouraged Mike. "I want my five bucks back."

"I never said how many targets were in use," said Racine. "Ready."

Racine placed the three targets ten paces away.

"Go." Again, an arrow sped to its target. The handgun sounded twice.

No fire darts flashed down the field.

Everyone looked at Micah, surprised that he had not turned.

He stood staring with unfocused eyes as if he were listening to a distant sound. His inaction captured everyone's attention. He raised his left hand and flashed the elven military signal for caution, followed by the one for cover.

Sanlar immediately nocked another arrow and began scanning the woods. Racine's hands took a ready position in front of his body. Laexa suddenly had a large dagger in each hand. They began backing toward the picnic tables, studying the hills.

No one spoke.

The silence added to the apprehension now spreading through the group. Eyes jumped sporadically from the stationary wizard to the two elves to the tall woman brandishing daggers. The three on alert watched the trees, which suddenly seemed to sway with an evil foreboding. As if waiting for a sign, everyone else hesitated.

Micah came out of his trance and held out his left hand. His staff flew into it. His voice was a growl somewhere between indignation and disbelief. "Forestton calls for help!"

Racine barked out orders. "Anton, get up to the security room. David, Carrie, open the gun vault. Tom, you have a gun? Good. Get to the front door and block it. Paul, go with him. Everyone else, grab as much food as you can and get inside!"

As if released from a spell, the group sprang into action. Hands grabbed bowls and plates and rushed them toward the door.

Racine waved his hand over the coals. They went cold. As he moved toward the porch, he waved his hands, closing the shutters of the windows along the first and second floors.

Micah moved near Laexa and handed her his handgun. They continued to search from tree to tree, ready should something jump out. They backed up, moving around tables and benches toward the lodge as the rest of the group moved inside behind them. Sanlar was the final one through the door, locking it behind him. Calling Mike to help, they pulled furniture across the floor, barricading the door.

Racine and Micah spoke quickly in the hallway. Micah spoke in Dahican so Laexa could understand. "Forestton is under attack! Prince Ti'ek is calling for help. We must go!"

Turning to Captain Laexa, Micah said, "We need to change and leave!"

"Who is attacking?" asked Racine.

"He did not say. If it is who we fear, they may attack here as well. I will return as quick as I can."

"We may not hold them off for long," said Racine.

"There *might* be danger here. I do not know. But Forestton *is* in danger!"

"You must go, I know," Racine agreed. "I only meant that it might not be safe for you to return tonight."

"I will come back as soon as Forestton is safe."

"Perhaps that is their plan. Force you to defend two worlds in one night."

"Maybe. Or perhaps they do not know I am still alive."

"I prefer that thought. There are too many here for me to magic out. We look for your return."

The two banged forearms. "Secure the lodge. I must find Mike."

Confused, Racine asked, "Why?"

"He has my ring. Then I must change clothes." Micah took the pistol back from Laexa and holstered it.

Micah, followed by Laexa, ran to the kitchen. "Mike?"

"What is going on?" demanded Mr. Ross.

"My town is under attack and calling for help. I must hurry! Mike, I need my ring back."

Mike grabbed it from his jeans pocket and handed it to him.

"Listen to Racine. I hope for no trouble here. I will return as soon as I can."

"Micah, you can't leave us!" exclaimed Melissa.

The fear in her voice was a physical sensation to Micah, reminding him of another desperate woman's call.

She grabbed his arm. "You must stay!"

"I will come back if I can. Forestton needs help! You are safe for now." Micah pushed her hand off. "Listen to Racine and Sanlar."

Laexa put her hands on Melissa's shoulder when she tried to grab Micah again. With a firm grip, she guided Melissa a few steps back away from Micah. Laexa moved between them.

To Micah, Laexa said, "She is not Suzhanee."

"You can't leave!" Melissa yelled again.

Mrs. Ross moved to her daughter's side and hugged her.

"Micah, please. You must stay! I'm scared! You can't leave me!"

"I have no time!" Micah insisted.

He ran to the stairs leading up to his room, followed by Laexa. Moments later, he came back into the hallway dressed in his auburn cloak over clothes from Forestton, staff in its quiver across his back. Laexa met him wearing her captain's dark green cloak over her leather armor. A sword hung at her waist. He nodded to her. She returned the nod and placed her hand on his shoulder. His words and right hand weaved the travel magic around the vertical left hand held in front of him. They vanished.

CHAPTER 36

THE BATTLE FOR FORESTTON

Hovan contacted Prince Ti'ek. *"Are you in Forestton?"*

"Yes, near the front door. Where are you?"

"Just arrived with Laexa. Coming."

Hovan sprinted down the hall. Ti'ek began reporting before Hovan slid to a stop on the polished stone floor.

"There is a fight underway for the town gates. We closed the gates, but they fought their way in through the walkway. Captain Wod Dein and the garrison fight to regain control. I am embarrassed to say that four magicians, each with a swordsman protector, have trapped me in here. There are other groups within the town. A force is preparing to assault the walls from wagons on the caravan field."

As if to emphasize his point, a blast shook the doors.

"It will take more than a magician to break through my door! Prepare your defensive magic."

Hovan spread his hands, pulling a protective, shimmering ball into existence. He put his hands into the ball and pushed the sides of the sphere, expanding and shaping it until it encased his body. He then built additional layers of protection before letting the soft red glow fade.

The wizard tapped a square tile on the wall with the top of his staff. "Ti'ek, have you contacted your father?"

"He is asking for help and will come now that you have cleared the Secret Room."

A three-dimensional vision of the front courtyard appeared in the stone. Two figures stood near the door. A large stone from the walkway, too heavy for them to lift, floated between them. Guiding it with hand motions, they swung it into the front door like a battering ram. A loud boom resonated through the house. Four men armed with swords and bows stood guard.

An explosion reverberated from above. "The roof," Captain Laexa noted. "We must hurry!"

Hovan tapped another tile. A view of the rooftop terrace materialized in the stone. A decorative railing ran along the edge of the roof. Two men stood near the end of the veranda, alternating blasts at the penthouse door.

"Magicians," noted Ti'ek. "Must have flown up."

The wizard put his hand on the wall and stood motionless. "I have activated the house defenses. Upstairs first."

From the decorative tops of the corner posts, small spheres of white energy shot out in pulses of three. Blue glows instantly surrounded the two assailants. They spun to confront their attacker, but found none. The two men's rapid hand motions attempted to weave spells to brace their weakening shields. Their blue glows shrank until they vanished under the persistent attack. Their mouths opened to scream, but the magic did not transmit the yells inside the house.

Hovan studied the view of the courtyard. From the corners of the house, spheres of red fire rained down on the two magicians. As the sphere of blue around the magicians withered, their guards ran. A spray of fire darts brought down three before the courtyard stood empty.

"Know your enemy," quoted Ti'ek in ridicule of the dead that had attacked a wizard's house.

"Knowledge is power." Hovan opened the door and stepped into the courtyard. Cries for help and clashes of combat came at them from multiple directions.

"We must get to the gates!" urged Laexa.

The wizard nodded and spoke to Ti'ek. "Defend the house until your father arrives! Laexa and I will activate the wall defenses and secure the gates."

Ti'ek stepped back inside and closed the front door.

The wizard and the first captain ran north to the nearest point of the town's protective wall. He placed his hand against the wall and leaned on it with his eyes closed. Sword in hand, Laexa stood guard, eyes scanning, guarding her wizard. A green shield rose out of the wall above them. Racing in both directions, the shields spread across the crenelated wall, protecting the walkway behind the parapet. A cheer filtered down from the wall's defenders.

———◄O►———

Captain Wod Dein stood at the apex of a semicircle of soldiers, restraining the enemy's entry by fighting sword to sword. The pressure of bodies was all that limited the influx into the town and prevented the gates from being fully opened.

Thank the Ones that Prince Ti'ek had ordered the gates closed. That has saved the town to this point. And that these attackers are not skilled with swords.

Above the gates, men climbed over the walls from ladders or ropes. Arrows flew up to meet those climbing over the wall.

If the enemy force secures the wall above the gates and begins firing down on this position, we will lose the gates. If the gates fall, Forestton may as well. The enemy has won the position inside the gates. They are creeping open and inward!

"Fight!" he yelled. "Fight. Your lives depend on it. And Forestton depends on us!"

Where is the prince now? Captain Laexa? Why is the wizard not here? Has not Ti'ek contacted the district leader?

Magic may save the town! If help is indeed coming, it had best come with the speed of a hunting talon bird! We need help!

Captain Wod Dein did not notice the green shield that sprang to life on the walls. However, the flash of red light that burst from the metal gates instilled him with hope! He noted the swing of the gates change direction.

The red glow shoved any person within an arm's length of the gates off their feet, clearing a space for the gates to close. The magic threw the attackers just inside the gates inward, causing them to fall onto those trying to fight their way in.

Captain Wod Dein and his men took advantage, striking down the swordsmen knocked off balance and stumbling.

The two halves of the moving gate slowly swung closed and pushed the attackers trying to enter Forestton backwards into the tunnel. The men regained their feet and struggled against the slow, methodical motion of the heavy, glowing gates. They set their boots onto the smooth stone road and pushed with their hands or backs or lowered their shoulders against the red light. Unabated, the gate's progress continued until the rectangular tooth like edges interlocked. A loud thud marked the end of their journey. The clanging of metal on metal signified the locking mechanism settling into place.

The wizard and the first ran west through Forestton.

"I need to get up on the wall where I can see!" said the wizard.

"Ti'ek said their wagons are on the caravan field," said Laexa. "That would put the west and south walls in the most danger. Head to the bastion south of the gates."

Laexa led the way through town as they sprinted for the gates. With a spell from Hovan or swordplay from Laexa, they ended any skirmishes they encountered.

The market area was a maze of hastily abandoned tents, turned over tables, and scurrying people. A few merchants stood defending their wares. Many were collecting their merchandise and preparing to run for cover. The wizard and the first weaved their way through the market. The clash of combat grew louder.

Prince Ti'ek did not like being told to stay behind to guard the Secret Room, but knew that this conduit must remain open for aid to flow into Forestton. Captain Laexa's instincts as a Follower of Protection to rush to the town's defense added to her responsibility of being the wizard's protector. Captain Laexa would not leave her charge, the Wizard Hovan, as he prepared to enter the battle! That was not open for debate.

Ti'ek could not yet control the advanced magic needed to unlock the town's defenses. Nor could he draw energy from the wall or house defenses. Hovan could do both. And he was a wizard. And this was his town.

I must train more. I failed him in Mohvradraan. Now I am left behind.

Ti'ek closed the front door of the wizard's house and waited. He did not wait long.

"Where are you?" asked Lord Ke'en.

"Near the front door. Hovan and Laexa have gone to the gates."

Ke'en sprinted down the hall. "The Wizards Velina and Kazmerin come. Velina brings a magician and Kazmerin a healer. What do you estimate their strength to be?"

"Difficult to say. They hid in the forest and under the guise of a caravan. My estimate is only two or three hundred. Not enough to take Forestton. Why?"

"A noteworthy question, but one for later. Are your shield spells active?"

⁓◦⁓

Hovan and Laexa found the approach to the gates blocked by soldiers helping Captain Wod Dein defend the gates. The wizard rotated his right hand, forming a flaming sphere. He pushed it forward. It shot away. He made the same motion with his left hand. The two balls of fire sped in tandem, above the soldiers, over the wall, and dove left and right of the gate tunnel. Flashes of fire from the explosions flickered over the top of the wall.

The ardent cheer rising from the defenders celebrating the arrival of their wizard blended with the screams of the injured.

Hovan vanished and rose into the air. Fire darts pulsed in threes, targeting those fighting soldiers dressed in deep Forestton green. Hovan cleared the battlements above the gates of opponents and, with help from those fighting on the ground, the area inside the gates.

The fervent salute spread and grew! The attackers trapped inside the closed gates threw down their swords and pleaded for mercy.

Floating above the wall, Hovan paused and looked out beyond the town. Men were rushing across the field toward the west wall, carrying ropes and some ladders. Smaller groups headed for the south wall.

There are not enough attackers to subdue Forestton. What am I missing?

He flew on to the south bastion. From there, he could defend west and south.

⁓◦⁓

Laexa left those who surrendered to the soldiers of the garrison so she could follow Hovan, who was flying to the south bastion as agreed. She pushed her way past the soldiers toward the stairs.

"Move," she yelled.

Armed men and women crowded the bailey, some fighting each other. Others dressed in Forestton green uniforms pressed forward to support the gates or reinforce the walls. Laexa forced her way up the stairs, yelling to clear space, sliding between bodies.

He is safe enough in the air. Arrows could not harm him.

Keeping herself calm, she continued moving. The walkway filled, impeding Laexa's progress. She looked in the air to the south, but could not see the wizard. The area immediately around her was safe, but weapons clashed between her and the south bastion.

I do not have time for this! If enough of them attack him when he lands, he might have to fight hand to hand. Protecting him is my job!

Her sword went to work. She glanced up often, trying to find Hovan as she wound her way south in and around skirmishes. She hoped she would not see him. He was supposed to be invisible.

I cannot let him get too far away from me.

◄O►

Ke'en stepped out of the front door of the wizard's house. He looked west.

"Hovan defends the gates."

He stood without speaking for a moment more, and then reported. "Velina is here. Kazmerin departs."

The father held out his arm toward his son. "Will you fight by my side, eldest son?"

The younger Ti'ek clasped his father's arm in a show of support. "With honor! And by your side, I will drink victory wine tonight!"

"You and I will take the south wall. Velina and her magician will defend the north wall. The east wall falls to Kazmerin."

Ti'ek nodded approval of his father's plans. "Velina agrees as well," said Ke'en.

The two elves sprinted away from the wizard's house. They encountered a few fights in the streets. They helped the residents or soldiers engaged with attackers that had walked into the town before the threat was clear. A handful of people gathered around the district leader and his son as they ran through the streets to the south wall's defense.

◄O►

Lady Wizard Velina had scrambled her most advanced student into action once she received the king's permission to defend Forestton. Other magicians and the retired wizard Mucenrion were called to protect the king in her absence.

Together, Velina and Perrotia stood in the courtyard of Hovan's house, preparing their defensive spells. The Wizard Protector Kazmerin joined them in the courtyard, leading an unsteady healer.

"Deep breaths!" said Kazmerin to the healer. "It will pass soon."

A bolt of lightning thundered across the sky. The bolt struck something above town and split into two cracks that zigzagged through the air like fracturing glass. A deafening clap of thunder stunned them into momentary silence. The body of a man arched over the rooftops of the town, twisting and rolling. The man slammed into a building in the eastern part of town.

Lady Velina's sharp intake converted into a plea. "May the One he serves protect him!"

"The lightning broke. Hovan was whole!" said Kazmerin.

"Still, I hope we do not need a burial marker!" Velina responded.

"Healer, get that wizard on his feet!" Kazmerin pointed east. "Lady Velina, may she go with him as protection?"

"Be quick, Perrotia!" said the royal wizard. The healer and the magician ran off. "Ke'en is changing paths to the gates. His son continues south."

"Velina, you go to the north wall as planned. I will go south and help Prince Ti'ek. Be careful! They came ready for a wizard!"

"But three?" She grinned. "Fight well!"

They tapped forearms and raced away in opposite directions.

Laexa flinched when the stroke of lightning shot through the air, flashing above her. The immediate detonation of thunder was deafening. She spun, tracking the path of the cloaked man, who twisted through the air toward the eastern side of Forestton.

"By the Ones, I just got here!" she yelled. Groaning, she ran for the stairs which climbed down from the south wall, hoping there would be less crowded than the ones near the gate.

Ke'en ran through the streets toward the gates. There was fighting taking place within the town, but he no longer had time to stop and assist.

"Shetteca is here! Shetteca is here! To me, Forestton!" The district leader raced to the steps leading to the bastion south of the gates as he called. He saw Laexa springing away.

I hope she finds him with breath still in him!

He dispatched fire darts left and right to clear a space, freeing defenders to form up around him.

Ke'en paused and connected to the wall's stored reserve of magic.

"Come now, if you dare!" he yelled in challenge. "The energy of the wall runs through me!"

Grappling hooks, tight against the top of the wall, secured climbing ropes. The tops of ladders appeared between other crenels. Hand to hand combat continued along parts of the west wall facing the caravan field.

Ke'en sent small explosions of fire shooting one by one along the edge of the wall, pushing down ladders, cutting ropes, and aiding soldiers dressed in dark Forestton green. The attackers backed away from the wall.

You hesitate. As well you should now that a magician is on the walls.

Laexa slowed her run to a jog. She estimated that Hovan would have landed in the east section of town on this lane or the next. The cries of battle and clashes of metal were behind her to the west and south. A quick look up at the walls showed a few soldiers watching outward with swords in scabbards or arrows nocked but not drawn. The sounds pulled at her like a blunt reminder that Forestton needed her.

The faster I find him, the sooner we can return to battle.

The short lane was empty. She jogged to the next with her sword still in her hand. Hovan sat slumped with his back against the narrow two story building. The left side of his face was red and bleeding from scratches and short gashes. He seemed to hold himself together by wrapping his left arm around his chest. His cloak lay open, its ends charred. Blotches of blood stained his white cloth shirt. His left leg bent at an unnatural angle. Hovan's eyes were open but did not register the captain coming to a stop two houses away.

A man whom Laexa did not know was kneeling next to Hovan, moving his hand across the wizard's leg.

A tall woman locked eyes with Laexa. She stood between Laexa and Hovan. A tie loosely held her wavy reddish hair, pulling it back out of her face. Her light blue tunic, secured at the waist by a belt, gave way to summer weight leggings of a darker blue. The woman rolled her hand palm up in front of her, and a ball of fire materialized in it.

Laexa shifted her focus back to the man next to the wizard. He seemed to be tending to the broken leg.

"Captain Laexa of Forestton," said Laexa to the woman with the burning sphere of fire in her hand.

"Easy enough to claim," the woman responded. "Lord Wizard?"

Hovan did not respond.

"Lord Wizard?" she repeated. "Do you know this soldier?"

"Give him a moment," said the man kneeling next to Hovan. "He is still dazed."

The man leaned in and whispered something to the wizard.

Hovan rolled his head and looked at Laexa. "Perrotia, that is Captain Laexa, my protector."

Perrotia closed her hand, extinguishing the fire ball.

Laexa sheathed her sword as she stepped forward. "How bad is he?"

— ◆ —

Ke'en walked north along the west walkway behind the parapet, launching small, fiery red spheres. Drawing on the magic stored in the walls, he could keep this spell pace until the moons joined the Giver in the sky! He was not the source of the magic, only the force that shaped it, choosing form, energy, and distance.

The force is smaller than Ti'ek thought. Their skill and tactics are poor. We are winning most of the hand to hand battles.

A smile crept onto his face.

This attack is perhaps not the threat that Ti'ek made it out to be.

Ti'ek! His magic is not advanced enough to tap into the magic stored in the walls. Yet he defends the south wall.

Even I can only fire one spell at a time. I am no wizard.

Someone beyond the wall has blasted Hovan, an invisible, protected wizard, from the air!

No wall has a wizard on it.

Winning this battle may not be so easy.

Ke'en heard two explosions, one after another, from the south wall. The wall's green shield would protect his son from those blasts if it had not been Ti'ek who cast the attacks. The explosions reminded the district leader that there were other magicians to subdue.

"Help!" came a weak mental cry from Ti'ek. *"I need a shield!"*

Ke'en spun and searched the south wall for his son. He saw Prince Ti'ek trying to rise to one knee, having trouble staying balanced.

"A shield," Ti'ek said again. He knelt, unable to stand, leaning against the wall.

"Son, the shield is in place."

"Those blasts came from inside the town," said Kazmerin.

"From inside?"

Racing before another blast killed his son, Ke'en raised a green shield behind Ti'ek. *"Ti'ek, injuries? Report!"*

Ti'ek hesitated. Then he said, *"I will not miss out on my share of victory wine."*

"On your feet then, Prince, and earn that wine! You must defend the south wall until you are relieved!"

"Yes, sir." Ti'ek braced himself against the wall, shaking his head to clear it. He pushed off and rose to his feet.

From the top corner room of the Forest Inn, a large sphere of blue fire sped toward Prince Ti'ek. The green shield glowed brightly as the blue fire shattered on it. A second attack rose at an angle from the ground in the south part of town. It too broke on the green shield behind Ti'ek.

Ke'en could not see the magician among the buildings below, but the one in the Forest Inn he might have to engage.

Four small spheres of fire shot up and headed toward the top of the south wall, but these targeted the opponents fighting members of the Forestton garrison. More fire darts found targets left and right of Prince Ti'ek.

"The prince now has some space," said Kazmerin. *"I will hunt for the magician down here."*

A challenging roar of cries rose from the group outside the walls. The district leader spun to look west and saw another wave of attackers charging the gate. Ke'en glanced back at the Forest Inn, deciding which to deal with first: the magician hiding there or the force charging the west wall.

A ball of blue fire shot out of the corner room toward him. Decision made. A rapid hand motion raised a shield to defend himself. Another sphere of fire sped toward the defenders on the walkway above the gate. Ke'en provided a green shield along the inside wall, matching the shield facing the field. His hands stayed busy bringing up shields to protect the backs of the Forestton defenders in chaotic fashion, defeating spells fired from the inn and from inside the town. Connected to the magic placed in the wall, he could provide protection faster than the hidden magicians could launch attacks. Forced to defend against the spheres of fire, he could not slow the group rushing the wall or support his son.

A thoughtful plan.

A volley of fire darts shot up from among the buildings in the southern portion of town and found Forestton green clad targets.

"*Kazmerin,*" called the district leader. "*Can you eliminate the magician on the ground? I am busy catching spells.*"

"*I am hunting for him.*"

Spells flew from Ti'ek's hands. Though he could not fire as fast as his father or use the power stored in the wall, his hands stayed in constant motion, selecting targets beyond the wall and some men that climbed over the crenels.

More fire darts rose from inside the town, but now green shields encased most of the walkway on top of the south wall.

"*I found him,*" said Kazmerin.

The soldiers on the west wall shouted for the district leader's help. A swarm of men, shields raised hoping to deflect the arrows fired from above, had already reached the base of the bastion. They braced ladders against the wall. A handful of men, though, did not wait for the ladders. They jumped into the air, flying at Ke'en and the Forestton defenders.

A thick gray mist enveloped Lord Ke'en, reducing his visibility to the length of two men.

"Close in and move south!" he commanded the soldiers with him.

He pulled his sword and ran south along the walkway, keeping one hand on the wall, trying to escape the cloud or, at least, not be where he was last seen. He heard explosions within the town and vented his frustrations in words he would not want to hear coming from the mouths of his children!

"*District Leader, I will take that help now!*" called Ti'ek.

"*Lord Ke'en, engage the magician in the inn!*" called Kazmerin. "*I am under attack from both magicians!*"

Vexed, Ke'en called, *"Velina!"*

Ke'en heard fire darts whizzing near him. Someone nearby cried out in pain. He gripped his sword with both hands, waiting for an opponent to appear in the cloud. Instead, the breeze strengthened and tore into the cloud.

"Dad!" called Ti'ek.

"Lord Ke'en?" asked Kazmerin.

The stiff breeze ripped the cloud to nothing.

Ke'en heard the Wizard Velina's call. *"A wizard is on the wall! The wind turns!"*

Ke'en yelled the elven saying, "The light of hope shines bright through the clouds of doubt."

He looked north. Velina, her arms directing magic, launched spells from various points on the north and west walls.

Ke'en sheathed his sword and spun to the south. He released small orange spheres, which dove over the wall into the south practice field. *"Kazmerin?"*

"Defenses holding," came the response. *"Rebuilding shields as fast as the two can attack, but I cannot counter. Attack one, please!"*

Ke'en walked south along the west wall. He continued to spell to support his son. *"Ti'ek?"*

"I have few spells remaining."

Ke'en glanced east between spells. He saw a ball of dark orange angling down from the Forest Inn to a target on the ground, presumably Kazmerin. It disappeared behind the buildings. The yellow and orange light of its explosion reflected off the walls of buildings.

"Kazmerin?"

"Holding! Engage one so I can deal with the other!"

The Forest Inn will have to be repaired, thought Ke'en.

He launched two spheres of fire set to explode inside the room. They sped along parallel paths and slammed into a blue shield outside the window, shaking the inn. The explosions did not reach the magician. Flames ignited on the outside of the inn. The district leader waved his hand, extinguishing the fire.

"A shield protects the corner room! Ti'ek, can you see the magician on the ground?"

"No time to look! I am using my bow."

"Kazmerin, I must support the south wall and my son. Any suggestions?"

"Go to the south wall," responded Kazmerin.

"Hold strong, Kazmerin!" came a familiar voice. *"Laexa and I will deal with the inn."*

"Welcome back to the fight, my friend!" cried Ke'en with relief. *"How are you?"*

"Unbelievably mad!" came the terse response.

"Velina, you have the west wall," informed Ke'en.

"Understood," came the response. *"There is no strength left in the forces north and west. Perrotia reports that the east is quiet. The only danger is south and the magicians!"*

Ke'en used fire darts to clear a path for himself as he moved along the curtain wall. Groups of attackers surrendered, throwing down their weapons. Forestton would withstand this assault. Still, more Forestton defenders might die before they subdued the remaining attackers. Ke'en positioned himself on the bastion formed from the junction of the south and west walls, launching spells to prevent his son from becoming one piece of the remaining damage.

•◦•

Hovan flew with Laexa up the north side of the Forest Inn. They opened a window on the third floor. Whoever had rented the room had decided that it was safer to be somewhere else. Hovan floated down the hallway, unable to put any weight on his broken left leg. Once outside the corner room, he nodded "ready" to Laexa.

The wizard opened the door, silenced by magic, and hovered into the room. A light skinned woman with wavy brown hair stood facing the south window with her hands gesturing as she formed a spell. Hovan fired a large fire dart followed by another. A blue defensive glow surrounded the woman when the first fire dart hit. She stopped her hand gestures and spun to face her attacker. Her eyes went wide with surprise when she saw a warrior with a drawn sword charging her and a floating figure with a bruised and bloodied face firing pulses of fire darts. Desperate to flee, she threw herself out the window.

Laexa dove through the open window and followed! Hovan flew forward.

Though able to slow herself, the magician pounded into the ground hard. Hovan saw her roll over, her lips wearing a smile. Her smile vanished. Her eyes widened in astonishment and fear. Laexa was diving at her, sword held ready to attack!

Fire darts slammed into the blue defensive shield. The magician had time only to stand before another fire dart hit her. The magician drew a long dagger to defend herself, but Laexa's sword quickly ended it.

Hovan landed next to Laexa and gave her a congratulatory slap on the shoulder. *"Kazmerin?"*

"Done with the magician on the ground," answered Kazmerin.

"Ke'en?" Hovan questioned.

"Many have surrendered!" said the district leader.

"We have one more magician to find," said Hovan.

"Once Kazmerin is on the south wall, I will be free to pair up with you."

"I am free to triple," said Velina. *"Your plan?"*

———— ◄O► ————

Hovan flew just above the rooftops from the Forest Inn toward the south wall. Somewhere outside the town was the magician who had blasted him with the bolt of lightning. Hovan hoped the magician's aggressive nature, the nature of a Preparer seeking to harm, would cause him to strike again. If the magician turned and fled, they might never find him. A Preparer magician roaming through Shetteca would be dangerous. That was reason enough to kill him or her. In addition, Hovan wanted revenge. For himself and Forestton!

Hovan shots fire darts toward the ground, hitting nothing. He wanted to be seen, but not be obvious about it. He stayed low, just above the wall's green shields. It was nothing short of arrogance to show himself again.

The arrogance of a wizard, I hope the magician thinks.

Come on. Where are you?

A second bolt of lightning thundered through the air over Forestton on this cloudless afternoon. It blasted through the image of Hovan moving over Forestton and dissipated over the forest northeast of town. The image of Hovan vanished as the immense power ripped through it.

Ke'en sent a rapid fire of spells at a man seated on an orvbac near the end of the line of wagons. The Wizard Velina's eyes traced the district leader's stream of fire darts and launched another set of fiery spheres. The man's blue shield glowed under the steady barrage.

"We have him lit!" announced Velina.

Unsettled by fire darts whizzing just over its head, the orvbac shook its head and stomped. The magician tried to turn the animal and move behind a wagon while his free hand attempted to rebuild defensive shields. He was successful at neither of his tasks. Hit by the rapid sequence of spells, the blue glow contracted and then vanished. Killed by the fire darts and thrown by the orvbac, the man twisted and fell, meeting the ground with an awkward thud. The orvbac sprinted away.

Forestton's wizard shot a spread of red and Forestton green victory sparks into the air. The district leader added Shettecan turquoise. Lady Wizard Velina fired sparks the color of the king's yellow. Lord Wizard Kazmerin's fireworks were protector brown. A tired cheer rose with the sparks. Hovan placed his hand on the wall. The green defensive shields sank into the parapet.

CHAPTER 37

QUESTIONS

Along the wall and in the bailey, the victors helped the wounded and guarded those who had surrendered. There were fewer of the former and more of the latter. Hovan held a meeting of the wizards, Lord Ke'en, Prince Ti'ek, and two captains of Forestton on the bastion south of the gate.

"Captain Wod Dein and Prince Ti'ek, well done!" Hovan said. "You identified the threat and defended the town! Forestton is in your debt! Thus am I." He made eye contact with each and nodded respectfully. "Thank you! Work remains to be done, though, before we pour the victory wine. Captain Wod Dein, organize parties to tend to the wounded and secure the prisoners. Keep a minimal guard on all the walls. I will watch from here. Bring the bodies of the magicians to my house. Where is Captain Vay?"

"On patrol near the river," reported Captain Wod Dein.

"Send out a second patrol," ordered the Wizard Hovan. "Have them join up with Captain Vay and inspect the western ranches."

Captain Wod Dein nodded and left.

Lord Ke'en spoke. "Shetteca will send two orvbacaans south to help patrol. Shar has organized healers. Lord Kazmerin, will you help with the transport?"

"Yes, of course."

"King Dargladre has ordered that healers stand ready in Avi'ot," said Velina. "I will bring them here."

"Extend Forestton's gratitude to King Dargladre," said Hovan. "Thank you, Lady Wizard Velina, for fighting on Forestton's behalf."

The Wizard Hovan next turned to Kazmerin. "Thank you for your timely arrival, Lord Wizard Kazmerin. Please express my thanks to Lord Kor'tinne for allowing Forestton to make use of his district's wizard."

Finally, he turned toward Ke'en. "Thank you, Lord District Leader."

Ke'en smiled at Hovan following the formal use of his title. He then turned to speak with Lady Velina. "Contact me when you are ready to magic into Forestton with the healers. I will coordinate with Prince Ti'ek the sequence of arrival into the Forestton Secret Room."

Lord Ke'en and Lady Velina, with Perrotia holding her shoulder, each began spells. They vanished.

Lord Wizard Kazmerin waited to hear the *"Shetteca, clear"* call from Lord Ke'en. When the call came, he wove his spell around his vertical left hand and disappeared.

With only Captain Laexa and Prince Ti'ek remaining, Hovan's tone became more casual. "Laexa, thank you for fighting in Forestton's defense and for finding me. Take some of the garrison. Secure and search the caravan. Then search the fields."

Laexa shook her head no. "It took me long enough to locate you after the lightning strike. I will stay by your side. Ti'ek can lead the search."

The wizard asked Ti'ek, "Can you?"

Ti'ek shook his head no. "I have no magic left."

"Laexa?" Hovan tried again.

"No. You need a healer."

Hovan sighed. "Ti'ek, stay behind the walls. I cannot send the third to the throne out there with so little protection. Head back to the house. Extend encouragement and thanks as you walk through town. Send word to the Forest Inn to prepare food. Have the injured brought to the market square. Help with the arrival of the healers. Direct them there when they arrive. Rest after you choose an excellent vintage."

"Yes. I will send a healer to you."

"No. I will go to one later. Let them do the triage. Save those who can be saved. My life is no longer in danger."

Ti'ek nodded. "As you wish." The prince turned and began a slow descent of the stairs.

"No healer?" asked Laexa. "What is your plan?"

"Stay here on the wall. Rest and keep watch. I may need to magic to the other world."

Laexa held his arm, lowering the wizard into a sitting position.

Hovan was quiet. The after battle sounds drifted through the air around Forestton: moans of the wounded, cries of victory and relief, tears of reunion, mournful wails of losses discovered, clicking of boot heels on stone and stairs, and the shuffling of objects and bodies being moved.

"Racine says safe and secure," the wizard told his first, but she made no sign that she heard. Laexa's silence captured Hovan's attention. She stood watching over the walls to the fields west of town. Alarmed, the wizard asked, "What is wrong?"

She motioned for him to stay seated. "Rest. I am asking myself why? Why do all of this? Even if they had won today, they would never hold the town against the forces Lord Ke'en would bring."

Hovan floated up next to Laexa. He balanced on his right leg and his dark brown short staff. "I agree. We can conclude, then, that holding the town was not their goal. Laexa, I am deeply concerned." The hushed tone of the wizard was more gripping than a scream. "I am not worth all of this. This is two well planned attacks on me in ten visits from the Giver. There must be more that they want. But what?"

"Two attacks on you?" Laexa shook her head in disagreement. "I think different. You were not supposed to be here! If they had killed you on the other world, then you would not have responded to Ti'ek's call. This force was moving from wherever they came from prior to that attack off world."

"True." After a moment, Hovan urged his first captain. "Where did they come from? Another question. Laexa, please secure the wagons. It may give us clues. You will see me sitting here on the wall. My leg will not allow me to move without help or magic. I am as safe with you here by my side or out there searching the wagons. I am letting the magic from the wall trickle into me to restore some energy. What you find may protect me in the future."

Laexa looked over at the wizard. "Persuasive. Besides, all those orvbacs are valuable."

"I did not think adding that would help me win the argument."

"It would not."

"Be careful. I know you are not an heir to a throne. Your safety is important to me."

Laexa nodded and left to collect a small group of soldiers to accompany her.

Hovan scanned the fields before turning to consider the buildings. Some bore damage that would need attention. The black scar on the near corner of the Forest Inn stood out like a beacon. Hovan thought about leaving that as a reminder of this day.

No. There are too many battles in the memories of these people. They do not need a remembrance of another.

Hovan hoped the healers were at work, saving as many as they could. His life was not in jeopardy, and he could tolerate the pain for now. Hovan cleaned the blood off his face and arms.

As he watched the chaotic activity crisscrossing his field of view, the wizard felt a sense of pride in his small territory. Forestton had performed well! However, guilt and doubt also made their presence known.

How could I have allowed a simple deception such as a fake caravan to threaten the existence of the town?

Simple, I was not here. Laexa was away with me. Ti'ek was administering to the demands of Forestton.

Ti'ek and Captain Wod Dein recognized the danger and acted in time. Still, they are not the Wizard Hovan. They do not have my abilities.

If I had been here defending the town, then fewer residents of Forestton would need a healer, fewer homes would hang gray cords to honor the dead, fewer buildings would need repair.

I should have been here.

The responsibility for Forestton is mine. I have left it to others for too long; since Suzhanee's death. It is time I took responsibility again.

With all that is happening, I have little choice.

It seems the time granted me by the universe to mourn Suzhanee has ended. Events are being arranged to thrust me back into the role I built for myself.

Suzhanee, I miss you. What is going on?

The strike of boot heels on stone grew louder and brought Hovan out of his thoughts.

Captain Wod Dein strode toward him. Two soldiers followed, guarding a third man. A length of rope tied the prisoner's hands behind his back and wrapped around his arms, securing them to his sides. The captain put up his hand, stopping them. He continued to the wizard alone. "This man says he is a farmer from

Mohvradraan. He says the Preparers will kill his family if he does not fight for them. He asks that you spare their lives and let them tend to their wounded.”

“What is your assessment?” asked Hovan.

“They do not sound like the words of a Preparer, but I am not ready to release him.”

“Keep him at a distance from me,” Hovan said to his captain. Addressing the prisoner, the wizard asked, “What is your name?”

“Samaaren, Lord Wizard.”

“Why are you here?”

“Preparers have control of Mohvradraan. They say they will prepare my wife and two boys if I do not do as they say. I do not want to! But my family is captive.”

“You are a farmer?”

“Yes, most of us forced to serve are.”

“Where is your farm?” asked Hovan.

“Along the road, north of Marvgrette.”

Hovan thought for a moment. “What is the woman’s name that runs the Le’geanni Orvbac Ranch west of South Bell Hill?”

“The Le’geanni Ranch is north of Marvgrette and my farm, not west. An older man, Ankotah, with help from his daughter Jivatta and her husband Baydenen, manages the orvbac ranch. I sell them feed for their orvbacs at the end of each growing season.”

Hovan took a long breath in, then out, as he considered his options. “Do what the captain tells you,” commanded the wizard. Lowering his voice, he spoke to Captain Wod Dein. “Instruct him to tell you who the farmers are and who the Preparers are. Separate the groups based on that. Collect the names of anyone claiming to be a farmer and the location of their farm. Send that list to me. Put the Preparers in the prisons. Set up a camp on the south practice field for the farmers and let them tend to their wounded there. Give them medical supplies. Guard them!”

“Send them healers?”

“Only,” stressed the wizard, “after the healers have tended to all from Forestton who need attention.”

Captain Wod Dein bowed and left.

Hovan ate the small meal that was delivered to him. He remained on watch on the south bastion. The pain in Hovan’s left side and leg was increasing. The adrenal surge from battle and the effects of the healer had faded and was fading.

He would need to seek more attention from a healer soon, but for now, he sat on the wall.

Ke'en, Kazmerin, and Velina returned and joined Hovan at his post.

"We need answers," said Ke'en. The district leader stood watching Laexa and the soldiers searching through the wagons and the bodies on the field.

"The king will insist," Lady Velina confirmed. "Or at least credible theories. Expect to be called to Avi'ot in a few visits of the Giver." Her dark hair twisted in the breeze. "We thought they would try again. And they have. Will they attack another time?"

"The walls need to be recharged," stated Hovan.

"We can discuss that when you are in Avi'ot," replied Velina. "I must return to the king's side. Well fought, wizards and lord! See you in the king's Hall." Her hands danced, and then she vanished.

Hovan looked at Ke'en and Kazmerin. "Any thoughts?"

Kazmerin asked, "Are these Preparers?"

"The reports say that some of the dead have the brand on the upper thigh," answered Hovan. "Many who surrendered are claiming to be farmers from Mohvradraan, forced into service with their families held as hostages by Preparers in Mohvradraan."

"If that is true, they will be desperate to get back," said Kazmerin.

"If any of the magicians contacted someone in Mohvradraan, they would not get there in time to save their families," said Ke'en.

"We cannot release them," said Hovan. "We do not know who we can trust yet. Also, those in Mohvradraan would learn what happened here. Who is alive and who is not."

Lord Ke'en asked, "Why us?"

"I hope that a study of the bodies and wagons will give us more clues," began Hovan. "We met them in the western hills, and they had a gorzyne. I still do not know how they controlled it. Now, they attack Forestton with seven magicians! Is it an attack on us or on me?"

"I hope this is not a blow to your ego, Lord Wizard," said Ke'en. "However, they must have built this small army before trying to assassinate you to have it here so soon after that attempt. This attack on Forestton served some other purpose. You were supposed to be dead!"

"Perhaps," offered Kazmerin, "they want the same as last time: fields for crops and people to prepare."

"They should expect no more success than before," answered Ke'en.

"Thus, what has changed?" asked Hovan. The two men and the elf exchanged looks. Their eyes darted from one face to another.

Hovan asked again. "What has changed?" After a pause, he asked, "Can they challenge the Wizard's Corp?"

"I saw nothing here to suggest that," said Kazmerin. "This may be nothing more than Preparers preying on the weak. Forcing the farmers to do their destructive bidding and then kill their families."

"They had seven magicians here," noted Ke'en. "That shows a greater magical presence among them than before. One at least is advanced enough to travel by magic! And controlling gorzynes? To train these magicians requires time."

"A gorzyne was not here," remarked Kazmerin. "Perhaps they only had the one."

"All good thoughts, but no answers," said Ke'en. "We need more information. Knowledge is power."

"I will put more thought into it once we have the reports," said Hovan. "My leg hurts."

"Shall I send for a healer?" asked Ke'en.

"No," answered Hovan. "I have something else in mind." Hovan shot red sparks into the air. When Laexa turned to look, Hovan signaled her to join him.

When she returned, Hovan asked, "Did you find anything interesting?"

"There are some expensive orvbacs!" answered Laexa. "They stole some from local farms, but they also raided someone's high priced stable."

"Some prisoners are claiming to be farmers from Mohvradraan, north of Marvgrette," explained Hovan.

"Le'geanni Ranch?" suggested Laexa.

"The famed Le'geanni Ranch," crooned Ke'en. "At least those two puzzle pieces fit together."

"Yes," said Hovan. "I hope Ankotah and his family are safe. If the prisoner's words are true, we fought farmers forced into service to protect their families."

"We were fighting farmers?" Captain Laexa looked at the wizards and the district leader. Her shoulders sagged with the realization.

"So it seems," answered Lord Ke'en.

"Preparers on the other world. Preparers here. Preparers in Mohvradraan? Gorzynes, magicians, hostages..." Hovan's list trailed to an end.

"Add in the cret'len, Belingus, and ogres that we fought in Feleine," said Ke'en. "I fear they are coming again. We responded well to protect Forestton. We need more information if we are to protect all of Shetteca! Knowledge is power."

Hovan and Ke'en looked at each other.

I know what he is thinking. Someone needs to go to Mohvradraan. I do not want it to be me.

Lord Ke'en broke eye contact and turned to look at the caravan field. "I want to talk to the farmers and see what those wagons can tell us." He turned back to Hovan. "You need a healer. Thank you for your aid, Lord Kazmerin. Well done, Captain Laexa." The district leader headed for the stairs.

"My leg hurts," admitted Hovan. "Laexa, I am going back to the other world to check in and request help from Lily. I will return in the early morning. Join me if you wish, but I think there is more work for you to do here. You are Forestton's first captain as well as my protector."

"I am your protector first."

"Ready to travel, then?" asked Hovan.

"Never and always," responded Laexa, frowning.

Chapter 38

The Victor Returns

Racine's mental call penetrated Micah's consciousness a moment after the pain in Micah's body re-announced itself. Disoriented, Micah feared his magic had gone wrong. He could not feel the floor beneath his feet, but felt pressure on his side. Micah blinked his eyes open, confused and alarmed that his room appeared sideways. A sharp pain on the right side of his head trumped the older pain on the left side. As the mental fog of the travel magic cleared, he realized he had fallen when he arrived, producing the pressure along his right side, the new pain in his head, and the strange view of his room.

The dome light overhead lit the room as it continually did when Micah was away so that the room always looked the same. Closed blinds hid the two double hung windows for the same reason. These windows offered no light to brighten the light blue walls and pine bedroom furniture at this time of the Massachusetts night.

He touched minds with Racine. *"Laexa and I are here. Come, and please bring Lily."* Belatedly, he added, *"Is all still safe here?"*

The door opened. Sanlar hurried in with Racine close behind. Micah lay on the floor, struggling but unable to rise. The visible left side of his face appeared bruised, swollen, and bore red cuts and small blisters. Black burns on his clothes mixed with the brown blood stains that darkened his torn shirt and damaged cloak.

"Lily," bellowed Sanlar.

"See to Laexa," said Racine.

He knelt next to Micah. "Rest easy, my friend. All is quiet here. How bad?"

"Lightning," said Micah. "Burns. Broken leg. Bruised and battered." With pride, he added, "Forestton stands!"

"Of course it does," said Racine as he gave him a reassuring smile.

Sanlar helped Laexa to sit on the bed.

Footsteps heard running down the hall preceded Lily's appearance in the doorway. She hesitated for only a moment, comparing Laexa sitting on the bed and Micah lying on the floor. She dropped to one knee next to the more injured of the two.

Micah repeated his description succinctly. Lily listened while sliding her hands along his body. She slowed her evaluating when she reached his left leg and the left side of his chest. The elf healer ended by holding Micah's head.

"Concussion also," she added to his list. "These injuries are several hours old. A healer treated these?"

Laexa, recovered now, explained in Dahican. "Yes, a scared healer working fast to appease an enraged wizard."

"He should have been the first one tended to after the battle," reprimanded Sanlar. "That is his duty and yours!"

Laexa stood and looked down at the shorter elf protector through narrowing eyes. "He accepted only enough healing to return to battle. His quick return saved lives! With the battle won, he sent the healers to treat those they could save while maintaining a watch on the wall, freeing men to see to the needs of the town. I know my duty! He performed his!"

Sanlar stepped back and bowed. "The actions of a protector. Forgive me. I meant no disrespect."

"Help me get him on the bed," said Lily. "I will hold his left leg."

Working together, they lifted the wizard. Micah winced until they had him positioned on the bed. He lay still and exhaled.

"Yes," said Lily. "The pain first."

Micah closed his eyes and let his head sink into the pillow. Lily cut his trouser leg to examine the broken left leg. She placed her hands on his shin. He felt the pain slowly recede.

Micah heard Tom arrive at the door, slowing his footsteps down from his sprint up the stairs.

Racine, who had backed off to allow the protectors room to position Micah, gave Tom the report after Tom's rapid, "How is he?"

"Broken leg, concussion, bruised ribs, and burns. His injuries are treatable."

Mike's comment of "My God, he looks bad!" was almost humorous enough to bring a smile to Micah's face.

Lily barked out orders. "Warm water for washing, cool water for drinking, towels, medical supplies, and room to move. Everyone out except his protector."

"I will get the supplies and towels," added Sanlar, offering contrition.

Racine directed Tom. "Warm some water, not too hot. Send Mike up with cold water in a pitcher with ice and glasses."

Tom called his brother. "Let's go, Mike."

Once the pain in his leg had reached the level of only aching, Micah told Lily, "Thank you."

With Laexa's help, Lily removed his cloak and shirt. The elf healer began examining the damaged ribs.

Micah lay still, eyes closed, propped up on the bed with pillows behind his back and head. A towel lay across his chest. His stained, burnt, and torn auburn cloak, once his favorite, now lay crumpled on the floor. A frayed shirt with blackened, charred edges and brown blood stains lay on top. The left pant leg, sliced open to the thigh, revealed a swollen leg bruised purple and yellow.

He heard the door click. Micah opened his eyes and looked toward the door. Sanlar entered carrying a large first aid kit. Mr. Ross followed with a pile of towels. Laexa walked over and took the towels from Mr. Ross, nodding thank you. She placed the towels next to the bed.

Melissa appeared and tapped her dad on the arm.

"Why are you awake?" Mr. Ross asked his daughter.

"You could sleep?"

"No," admitted Mr. Ross, "but Mom finally fell asleep. Still upset?"

"Yes. But Mike said he was hurt bad. I wanted to see." Melissa nodded her head toward the tall woman with the sword. "Not something you normally see around here."

Micah put his finger to his lips, asking for quiet. He waved for them to come closer.

When he turned his head, he revealed the cuts and blisters on the left side of his face in varying shades of red, yellow, and mauve that far outnumbered the few cuts along his right cheekbone.

"But you can stop bullets! How did they hurt you?"

"The healer needs to stay focused," Micah whispered. "She is numbing the pain in my ribs. A magician waited for me to show myself. I was defending the gates of the town. A lightning bolt hit me. My magic protected me from most of the energy, but the force slammed me into a building. I do not know if the leg broke when I hit the building or the ground. My ribs are at least bruised, if not broken as well."

"You should go to the hospital," said Mr. Ross.

Micah shook his head. "Lily is far better than any doctor. She can sense and move the body in ways that they cannot."

"Is the battle over?" Mr. Ross asked.

"I would not leave if it were not." Micah caught Sanlar's eyes, but continued speaking to Melissa and her dad. "They attack a small town. Three wizards, a district leader, and a magician magic in to defend it!" Micah and Sanlar shared a soft, guttural laugh.

"Was Prince Ti'ek hurt?" asked Melissa.

"Not bad. He is probably drinking wine as we speak. He will be happy to know you asked about his health."

"Don't tell him. He'll get the wrong idea. Forestton seemed so peaceful last week."

Micah nodded. "Unfortunately, violence exists. So do skilled, good people struggling to tip the balance in favor of peace. I think your father would agree."

Melissa looked at her father, who stood stoic and silent. Turning back to the battered man lying in the bed, she said, "It seems a contradiction that we have to fight for peace."

Mike entered the room carrying a pitcher of water, an ice bucket, and three glasses on a tray. He placed them on the desk and stood looking at Micah. Laexa said something to Sanlar, who nodded.

With a hand motion, Sanlar directed the Ross family out the door. "Lily needs to work. Micah needs to rest."

"Feel better," said Melissa.

<hr>

Micah woke up later the next morning than he had intended. He suspected Lily had something to do with that. Laexa sat at the desk eating breakfast.

"How are you feeling?" she asked.

"Better than I expected, though I hope Lily can do more."

"She stopped in earlier and checked you over. She said you heal faster than an elf."

Laexa carried breakfast over to her patient. Laexa handed him the plate and fork. "Eat. I will get more." She then pointed to a pair of crutches leaning against the wall near the headboard. "Lily cautioned against trying to walk today."

Micah sighed an embarrassed acknowledgment.

Micah accepted the food with more joy than the prospect of hobbling on crutches. He cleared the plate and was waiting for more. Laexa returned with Lily and a second plate of food.

While Micah ate, Lily held her hands on his head, then his splinted leg, and then his wrapped left side. She nodded approvingly. "You are doing well. Rest, eat, and stay off the leg."

"When can I walk on it?" asked Micah.

"With consistent treatment, seven days." Before Micah could complain, Lily held up her hand and emphasized, "Use the crutches and magic to keep the weight off your leg. You want it to heal properly! Rest the leg as much as possible. Your ribs will not be happy with you moving about either. Mind your concussion! Eat. I will be back to give your next session of treatment later."

"Thank you for the touch of your magic! I promise to rest as much as duty allows."

"As much as duty allows?" repeated Lily, a questioning tilt of her head. "I suggest more. You are welcome. Rest now. Duty allows." To Laexa, she said, "If he is in pain, do not hesitate to call me."

"Thank you, healer," responded Laexa. She bowed in thanks to Lily before the elf left.

Rest sounded like an excellent idea to Micah, but he was troubled. Questions ran through his mind.

What information has the caravan revealed? What damage has the town sustained? How many casualties? How can I divide my time between the two worlds?

Micah contacted Lord Ke'en. Ke'en's response cut his queries short.

"I will fill you in when you return. How are your injuries?"

"I am being treated by an elf healer."

"An elf! Excellent! I will see you soon?"

"Yes. It is still morning here."

Micah tried to touch minds with Ti'ek, but he was asleep.

"Ke'en wants us to return," he said to Laexa. "Says he will answer my questions then."

"Effective strategy, knowing you. When do we go?"

"I need answers here, too."

Tom knocked on the door. "Do you want to telling the story of yesterday's fight? We would like hear very much."

"Your Dahican is getting better," commented Laexa.

"Thank you," said Tom.

"Storytelling is what you and me do," said Micah in English. "We must also discuss what to do next. We did not finish yesterday."

"Seems longer than a day ago. When you finish eating, can we meet downstairs? Your injuries have done much to convince my dad that the danger is real."

"Glad to see that getting blasted by lightning had some positive outcome," said Micah. "I will be down soon."

Micah wanted more food. Instead of sending Laexa, he decided he would go down himself. With Laexa's help, he changed clothes.

"Where did you sleep last night?" asked Micah.

"Here on the floor. I chose to stay. I have slept in worse places."

"Yes, we have," agreed Micah. "So, I know the comfort of a bed. Stay in your room and sleep on a bed." He pointed left. "I will be downstairs. You fought yesterday too and need to rest."

"I am tired," admitted Laexa. "If you leave the building, wake me up!"

"Understood. I will return for my next healing session. After that, we return to Forestton."

Micah looked at the crutches and then resigned himself to the indignity. He hobbled out of the room, ignoring the chuckles coming from Laexa, trying to navigate his staff and the crutches without tripping or taking out a lamp. His ribs quickly objected to moving with crutches. He wove a spell and began to float.

He hovered down the flight of stairs to the main floor. Mrs. Ross was passing through the lobby. She stopped and watched him float down.

"Julian!" Mrs. Ross said. She stared at his battered face and crutches.

"Micah, please," he reminded. "Call me Micah."

"Are you in much pain?" asked Mrs. Ross.

"Enough to tell me what I should not do," he said. "Not the mighty wizard today, huh?"

"Why not go to a hospital?"

"Lily is better, Mrs. Ross. Besides, I would have to explain how this happened. We need to stay hidden."

"Did Lily say it was okay for you to be out of bed?"

"No, she did not, but I will be fine in time," responded Micah. "Thank you for your concern."

"You're welcome," she said. "I was told your injuries were bad. You don't look good. It just doesn't seem right that you are out of bed so fast."

"I heal fast. Faster than I used to. Plus, Lily is treating me with magic."

"Faster than you used to? Most people heal slower with age. I am told that you are older than you seem. How old are you?"

"Fifty, give or take. The years are not the same on both planets."

"Fifty?" asked Mrs. Ross in surprise.

Micah nodded. "Part of my foolishness after my wife died," he answered. "My body seems to be late twenties."

"I don't understand."

"Me neither, to be honest. I would like to sit. I am getting food from the kitchen and then going to eat in the Fireplace Room. If you like, I will try to explain more."

"I'm not sure I want to know more. You upset my daughter again! And I am not happy that you brought danger to my family."

"I am scared that they followed me here. And troubled that your family is in danger. But I did not bring them."

Micah turned his back on Mrs. Ross. He floated through the dining room into the kitchen, in no mood to be reprimanded by someone he was trying to protect.

CHAPTER 39

THE TELLING

Tom opened the front door and scanned the porch, looking for his mother. Mrs. Ross sat in a wicker chair, watching the trees waving in the breeze in the valley below. Tom walked over and knelt beside her.

"Mom, Micah is about to tell us what happened at Forestton yesterday. Do you want to hear?"

Mrs. Ross stayed quiet for a few moments before speaking. "I never wanted to hear about the missions that my husband carried out. He was in danger. I knew. But I did not want the facts, the concrete knowledge. Fewer visuals to invade my sleep. I'm not sure if I want to hear about Micah's battle."

"I understand, Mom," said Tom.

"Do you?"

"I think so. I carry a gun for a reason. I worry nonstop when Cathy goes out on a job. Not that what we do is as dangerous as what Dad did. But when I can't be with her, I can't rest until I hear the front door close behind her."

"It was weeks sometimes before I heard that screen door close," whispered Mrs. Ross.

Tom held his mother's hand and said, "I think you should come and listen. It will educate you about what we're dealing with."

"I don't want my children in danger."

"You already know enough to have nightmares. Come hear about the strength of the good guys."

"Because of Micah, my family is threatened! How does that make him good?"

"Come and hear."

Mrs. Ross hesitated, then rose and followed her son inside.

When they entered the Fireplace Room, Tom walked his mother over to where her husband sat. Mr. Ross had adapted Micah's rocking chair as his own since Micah sat with his leg propped up on pillows on the sofa.

Tom noticed that many of the faces were radiating excitement, but not his father's. The stoic Marine expression on his face said the pending story was business.

Mrs. Ross placed her hand on his shoulder. Mr. Ross covered her hand with one of his own before rising and offering her the chair. Tom sat down next to his wife, Cathy.

Micah began with his disappearance yesterday. His story soon had the full attention of his audience. Even Mike stopped asking questions.

Mr. Ross was the first to ask a question when Micah finished. "What do you propose to do now?"

Racine answered. "Three stages, as of now. Complete the computer searches to build a framework of the organization opposing us. Then, begin monitoring each location in person. Last, remove the Preparers and the portals."

"How does one remove a portal?" asked Mr. Ross.

"Change the memorized location or eliminate the magicians who know it. Destroy all descriptions of the portal."

"Why do you use words like remove and eliminate when you mean kill?" Mrs. Ross's question brought sudden silence to the room. "Kill. Murder."

"They will kill. This is protection of you, of us, of others," answered Racine in his accented English.

"I do not want my children involved in this. You speak of this as if it were a covert government operation, but you're nothing more than vigilantes. This is murder!"

"It is a covert operation," responded Tom, looking at his mother. He glanced at his father for support, but Mr. Ross stayed mute. Tom continued in a calm, measured voice. "Against an enemy that has targeted us specifically. Your children are in danger. The only way to get *us* out of danger is to *kill* these people and close the portals."

"This is murder! You cannot kill people who haven't done anything. You cannot *remove* someone because of what they *might* do."

"They invaded my house and attempted to kill me," said Micah. "They have attacked me both here and on my home world," said Micah. "They killed people of Forestton who only fought to defend their homes."

"Those who committed these acts are dead or captured, you say. The others here have not yet done anything."

"They plotted the attack. That is a crime."

"You have no proof of that. Innocent until proven guilty. Otherwise, it is homicide. That is the way it works in this country. I taught my children to know better!"

"They are not citizens of this country or even born of this world," answered Tom. "I know that doesn't mean that they have no rights. Nevertheless, this is self-defense."

"Not until they do something. I want you to stay out of this!"

"They have done something," said Micah.

"They will do more," added Racine.

"You are not the government fighting some terrorist group. You can't do this!"

"I am!" was Micah's firm answer.

"You are what?" Mrs. Ross snapped back.

"I am the government fighting a terrorist group, as you put it. I am the Lord Wizard Hovan of Forestton, member of the Court of Shetteca, member of the Wizard's Corp." With growing righteousness, he continued. "In defense of my home and person, I am pursuing this threat that has followed me into a foreign land to kill them before they strike again. This *is* a covert operation authorized by my government. I have hired this group to help carry out the mission."

Mrs. Ross paused. "You have an answer to everything, don't you?"

"Certainly not."

Not yet ready to give up the argument, Mrs. Ross persisted. "My son will not commit murder. How will you know who are the ones to be killed and who are unknowingly working for them?"

"Yes, Mrs. Ross," said a composed Racine. "That is the hardest part! We must carry out our surveillance with great care, both online and on the ground. Time consuming, but of utmost importance. We have two protectors, Sanlar and Captain Laexa, to act as our conscience. Those who are innocent must be protected!"

Mrs. Ross surveyed the room but made no more arguments. Her trembling hand squeezed her husband's. His steady hand squeezed hers in return.

Micah spoke in a composed voice. "Mr. and Mrs. Ross, may I offer you what I offered your daughter? Visit Forestton for a short time. See what they have done to my town. I can take you there and bring you back."

"Yes," said an eager Mike. "And take me this time!"

Mr. Ross said, "Allow me to speak with my wife." Together, they left the Fireplace Room.

A few minutes later, the door opened, and Mr. and Mrs. Ross returned.

"Is Forestton safe?" asked Mr. Ross.

"Give me a moment," said Micah. He closed his eyes for a minute. "Yes."

"I accept."

"Yes," Mike said, jumping to his feet and clenching both fists.

"My wife prefers to stay here," said Mr. Ross. "Tom will go in her place to assist me in understanding what I see. Sorry, Michael. Your mother insists that you stay."

Micah turned to Lily. "May I ask for a treatment to limit the pain? I will have to use the crutches."

CHAPTER 40

THE TALLY

Hovan led his visitors up the stairs from the Forestton Secret Room. The wizard came first, followed by Tom and Mr. Ross. Captain Laexa came last, carrying Hovan's staff. The wizard's journey up the staircase progressed slowly, hopping one step at a time. His dislike of the crutches, forged by the embarrassment and the perception of weakness they portrayed, was further fueled by the frustration elicited by moving with them.

They will be an excellent addition to a fire!

"Can I help you?" offered Tom.

"No."

"Why not use magic?"

Hovan grumbled and continued hopping.

Using magic would be disrespectful.

As he climbed the flight of stairs, he contacted Ke'en and Ti'ek, notifying them of his return and asking their location.

"Where are we?" asked Mr. Ross.

"In my house in Forestton. The room below, where we arrived, is the Forestton Secret Room. By memorizing that room, I can magic here from anywhere. Forestton is in the District of Shetteca. The map I showed you was of the country of Arre'ielle. We are in that country now. On the planet Ra'viinen. The crops are growing taller, but it is not yet time for the Harvest Festival. My first thought was to show you the town and countryside from the roof of my house. After climbing those flights of stairs, I do not wish to climb more right now. Besides, two elves that I wish you to meet are near the town gates. Let me sit and rest for a moment. This way, please."

Hovan entered the kitchen and lowered himself into a chair. He motioned for Mr. Ross and Tom to join him at the table. Tom accepted. Mr. Ross moved away from the door, but remained standing in a relaxed but ready stance.

"May I offer you something to eat or drink?"

"No, thank you," said Mr. Ross. "I do not feel comfortable here. I don't want to stay long. Show me what you wish me to see."

Laexa spoke to Hovan and then left the kitchen. "Laexa is going to her rooms to put on clean clothes," Hovan explained. "She asks that we wait for her before leaving the house."

"You said it was safe," said Mr. Ross.

"I believe it is, but you still asked for a gun. My protector wishes to stay by my side. She is expected there. The expected can be calming; the unexpected can raise anxiety. I want to show you a part of my world. You are on another planet! Also, I will introduce you to the leader of this district, an elf named Lord Ke'en, prince and heir to the throne of Arre'ielle. His son is Ti'ek. Prince Ti'ek is the elf that your daughter drank wine with when she came. Both elves are near the town gate. I told them we would meet them there. Together, we can see Forestton from the walls!"

"You told them?"

"Yes, I contacted them using my mind as we were climbing the stairs. Elves can speak to their children with their minds. With practice, that ability can extend to other elves. With practice and magic, human magicians can learn the skill as well. I am a close friend of their family and can mentally contact Lord Ke'en, a longtime friend, and his son, who often lives here in Forestton."

"A few minutes ago, before we came here, when I asked you if the town was safe, you contacted someone here," stated Mr. Ross.

"Yes, I contacted Prince Ti'ek."

"Yesterday, someone contacted you telling you about the attack on Forestton," Mr. Ross continued.

"Yes, Prince Ti'ek."

"This Lord Ke'en is an old friend of yours, you say," said Mr. Ross. "Melissa told me you're older than you seem. How is that possible?"

Hovan paused for a few moments as he tried to choose the correct English words. He settled on the short and unsatisfactory, "I do not know."

The hesitation in Mr. Ross's response Hovan recognized as a sign of the internal debate Mr. Ross was having with himself on the topic, 'Is he a liar?'

Hovan pushed into the silence before Mr. Ross could reach a conclusion. "I am not trying to be evasive. I do not understand what I did to cause my body to change as it did. My wife had died. I was in despair. I tried for a do over, if you will. Get younger and try again. Arrogant and fatalistic, I experimented with healing magic that is not well understood. During the Battle of Shetteca, I received some extraordinary healing when many thought me dead. I hoped for a similar result."

Hovan considered adding more, but thought better of it. Mr. Ross was still adjusting to his new view of the universe.

To change the subject without seeming to change it, he asked, "Would you care to see a portrait of my wife?"

"Yes, I would," answered Mr. Ross.

"Come, let me show you a painting." Hovan pushed himself into a standing one leg stance and grabbed the hated crutches. "Would you mind carrying this? It hits the crutches if it is in the quiver." He handed his staff to Tom.

Hovan escorted Mr. Ross into the large receiving room toward the front of the house. He let the painting of him and his wife, Suzhanee, capture his attention. The wedding day portrait, with its joyous smiles, brought a bittersweet upturn to the wizard's lips.

"My wife, Suzhanee," Hovan stated.

"She was an attractive woman," said Mr. Ross.

"Yes," came the response.

"She reminds me of my daughter."

"Melissa thinks so as well."

"She saw this?" asked Mr. Ross.

Hovan nodded. "When she was here. She received the full tour. We should get started on yours. I will bring you upstairs where you can change into clothes appropriate for this world. I need to change as well."

When they came back downstairs, the three men found Laexa waiting in the hallway, dressed in clean clothes and with wet hair. She deftly accepted Hovan's staff from Tom, who had not offered it.

Hovan led them slowly toward the western end of town. The afternoon Giver, which shone bright in the blue sky, was well above the walls.

"How do you feel?" asked Laexa in Rel'ellon.

"Using the crutches is painful, even after Lily's magic."

Hovan directed the Ross's attention to the Forest Inn. "That large building ahead of us is the inn for this town. As we get closer, note the burns on the upper floor, south side. From there, the magician was firing spells."

"How did she get inside?" asked Mr. Ross.

"She walked in. They approached the town under the disguise of a caravan. Caravans are common from the start of the growing season until early in the cold season. They are always welcome. The money they spend in town forms a significant portion of the local economy. However, Forestton had received no advance notice of this caravan. When they did not immediately send in a representative, Prince Ti'ek grew suspicious and had the gates closed. That simple act saved the town. But several Preparers had entered the town already. They simply walked in."

As they made their way along the stone streets of the wizard's town, they heard short bursts of clapping from many of the residents whose paths they crossed. The staccato burst was short; only three or four strikes. Laexa returned the claps as they passed those bearing injuries from the battle or when memorializing a person on whose door frame hung an arm's length, gray cord.

Hovan wanted to share in the exchange of claps, greetings to honor the injured and dead, but the crutches kept his hands occupied.

Yet another reason to dislike them.

Hovan noted more points of interest to his guests. Places where fights occurred the day before. Damages resulting from the battle. Features of his world, such as the two visible moons of the three in orbit around the planet. They walked through the marketplace.

It is good to see the merchants setting up their tables again.

As they crossed the open space near the gates, they saw Ke'en and Ti'ek, father and son, waiting for them in the bright light of the Giver. Above them and above the gates, the three flags floated in the air and bore witness to who still controlled this town. Hovan felt pride and relief seeing them play with the wind.

The beauty of the flags! It took quite an effort to keep them flying.

Hovan noticed that Prince Ke'en wore clothing more in keeping with his position as district leader than the quickly assembled attire he had worn during yesterday's battle. Dark brown, leather boots bore a shine and stretched up his calf. A Shetteca turquoise, lightweight cloak with red piping and the Shetteca silhouette embroidered on both arms, swept off his shoulders. The cloak reached under his arms to his waist, where buttons held it across his middle in elven fashion. A dark tan shirt, with sleeves ending just below the elbow, covered his arms. The closed cloak and expensive attire suggested that he would not need the sword stretching the cloak at his left hip. A green leather tie gathered his black hair at his neck, keeping it out of his eyes. District Leader Ke'en presented the perfect image of a person of authority here to get things done!

Ti'ek dressed more like a soldier. His sword was accessible if needed. A light-weight metal and leather overshirt protected a green cloth shirt. The left side of his face still bore the marks of yesterday's fighting.

Hovan nodded greetings to the two elves and began the introductions in their native language of Dahica. "Lord Ke'en, the Giver graces the meeting of you with Tom Ross and his father, Mr. Ross. Prince Ti'ek, you have met Tom before. Now, join your father in meeting Mr. Ross."

Turning to his other guests, Hovan repeated the introductions in English. "Tom and Mr. Ross, allow me to introduce you to Crown Prince Ke'en of Shetteca and his son, Prince Ti'ek. The appropriate greeting would be to make a small bow from the waist, hands held palms up. Then, clasp forearms as warriors."

The wizard turned to Lord Ke'en and showed the exchange.

Prince Ke'en took the initiative, as was his place. He offered his hands to Mr. Ross, the senior, as he bowed. Mr. Ross repeated the gesture. Then they each grasped the other's right arm just above the wrist.

Hovan translated the greeting from Lord Ke'en. "Welcome to the District of Shetteca. You arrive on a day of both celebration and sorrow. May your visit have time only for the former."

Speaking through Hovan, Mr. Ross responded, "My son and I are honored to meet you. While Tom learned of this world some time ago, I first heard of this planet only a few days ago. So, I fear, I shall have time neither for celebration nor sorrow. Only curiosity and confusion."

Ke'en smiled in appreciation of Mr. Ross's word play. "Perhaps your curiosity will take you as far as Shetteca?"

"Not on this trip, though I know my daughter wishes to see your city. Today's visit is brief, with a return this evening."

Ke'en looked at Hovan. "Will you be returning to Forestton tonight? Your captains have questions, repairs need to be made, soldiers to be honored, plans made."

Ti'ek jumped into the conversation during the moment that Hovan hesitated. "Knowing that you and the first were returning today, I was reluctant to speak for you."

"You can speak for me," said Hovan, feeling some frustration at Ti'ek's formality.

"Yes," said Ke'en, cutting off his son's response, "but Forestton needs its leader. Forestton needs you!"

"Yes," said Hovan in a serious tone to match Ke'en's. "I had not planned to stay away."

"Good. In addition, the king requests your presence at the King's Assembly in two visits of the Giver to bear witness to the attack."

Slightly surprised, Hovan asked, "I will not be going as your counsel?"

"No, Shar will sit by my side. King Dargladre has also requested Captain Laexa and Lord Kazmerin. Lady Velina will be there, of course. I want you to come to Shetteca tomorrow evening so we can discuss. We need to think this through. Find answers and make plans. The king deserves no less from us. The southern lords will attempt to undermine us. We must prepare."

"I am sure that they would love to offer their theories."

"Yes. The king is young and they think weak. More important, we must anticipate what will come next. We must determine what the Preparers' next move is so we can plan others. Knowledge is power. Finish showing Forestton to Mr. Ross and then bring them home. Ti'ek, now that he is awake, and I will continue to work. When can you join us?"

"We should not be too long, Ke'en."

"Good. How do you feel?"

"Better than last night."

"Better still tomorrow!" said Ke'en, his optimism returning to his voice.

"One can hope," said Hovan as he bowed to the elves.

Turning to Tom and Mr. Ross, the wizard gestured toward the wide stairs near the gates that climbed up to the battlement. He re-gripped his crutches and hopped toward them. Switching to English, he said, "The best views will be from the top of the walls."

When Hovan reached the foot of the staircase, he stopped and looked up the length of the stairs. The wizard then grumbled, having to ascend another flight of stairs on crutches.

Tom asked, "Why not use magic and float up?"

"It seems wasteful...inappropriate...dishonorable," said the wizard, sorting through his English vocabulary for the correct word, "to those that died here yesterday defending Forestton to avoid this discomfort here in the town where the battle occurred."

He headed up the stairs. When he reached the top, he balanced on one foot and waved his hand to the panorama.

"Now that we have reached a position of height," exclaimed the proud Lord Wizard, "look at Forestton and the lands surrounding her!"

Mr. Ross obliged, slowly turning to see the town laid out before him, the practice fields to the south, the stream weaving its way past the front of Forestton, and the abandoned wagons sitting on the grassy caravan field. Tom, though he had seen these sights before, turned and looked, as his father did, at the alien yet not so strange lands.

North of the vacated caravan was a chaotic heap of bodies. The south practice field bore the opposite. Here, bodies lay side by side, sky blue clothes over them, near the wall. The Forestton soldiers were guarding the farmers from Mohvradraan camped further out.

"Our strategy was to have wizards on the three walls facing the attack. With the town defenses activated and a wizard on the walls, Foreston would be impenetrable by such a force as this!" As he spoke, Hovan pointed to the various positions he referenced. Mr. Ross and Tom followed his directions, surveying the town. "Neither of the elves, Prince Ke'en nor Prince Ti'ek, are wizards. When the lightning bolt put me out of action, the magical defense of the town fell to the two elves until the other wizards could arrive."

"Ke'en divided his attention, defending the west wall and protecting his son, who defended the south. It seemed as if they knew Ke'en could not defend both walls."

Hovan began moving south along the top of the western wall, recreating the path that Ke'en had followed. Mr. Ross walked, eyes scanning this new world. Tom walked alongside Laexa.

"Soon, two wizards reached the walls and connected to the town's magic. I was finally back in action. Forestton was safe."

"You store magic within these walls?" asked Mr. Ross.

"Yes, but not everyone can use it. It is dangerous if you do not have the skill to control its power. I have trouble expressing the concept in English. There is not a phrase for it. The magic must recognize you."

"Similar to having the password for a defense system?" asked the former Marine.

"Good analogy!" said Hovan.

"What type of magic do wizards use to stop an army?"

"The small fire darts I showed you are excellent for individual targets. However, to combat groups, larger explosions work well: blasts of fire or lightning. Other possibilities exist for other needs."

"You can vary the distance and strength of the magical explosions?" asked Mr. Ross.

"Yes, and guide them and even have the fire explode in shapes."

"Mobile, guidable artillery with situational power," noted Mr. Ross.

Hovan nodded in agreement, though he was not sure if he understood all that Mr. Ross had just said.

When they walked to the corner bastion joining the western and southern walls, Hovan pointed to the south practice field. "These are the men and women who died defending Forestton. Honored they are!"

Mr. Ross looked over the twenty three bodies laying on the green grass, one next to the other. "Where will they be buried?"

"We will not bury them. Those wishing to honor them will stand for them in ceremony. We place their bodies on a pyre, releasing their spirits. Those assembled urge the One they served to claim their spirits and bring them safely to the next life. We will honor them by presenting ourselves as witnesses to their merit."

"Stand for them?"

"Yes. Part of the custom among us. If you respect the person, you go to the Burning Ceremony, a poor translation, to honor the person. Family members will place wooden or stone markers in their memories in the, I suppose, Forestton Memorial Field. Our words convey a meaning between graveyard and commemorate. You can make out the area there beyond the South Practice Field."

Hovan pointed to the semicircular clearing cut into the forest. Hovan did not desire to mention Suzhanee's marker. If Mr. Ross wanted to know, he could ask.

As the story ended, the three men grew quiet.

Mr. Ross looked around, reaffirming what he saw before him: a town on another planet. He fixed in his mind the more prominent features of Forestton. "I have walked on the walls of castles in Europe. They are pieces of history. Remnants of an earlier time on Earth, made obsolete by the advancement of artillery."

"Magic reenforces these walls. Anyone with enough power to threaten these walls must deal with me. If they can reach my walls, I can reach them. I will have the power of the walls supporting me!"

Tom looked around. "This does not feel like history."

CHAPTER 41

A CONVERSATION IN SHETTECA

Hovan walked slowly with a limp down the hall toward the private meeting room of Ke'en and Shar. Laexa matched his pace. Despite Lily's warning, he walked without crutches, instead using his short staff as a walking stick. He needed to work strength back into his left leg. In the morning, he would take Laexa to Avi'ot to attend the King's Assembly. It would be too humiliating to shuffle into the Hall of Arre'ielle for the King's Assembly on crutches. Some would see it as weakness; others, as failure.

He would not serve as Lord Ke'en's first advisor, though he had done so many times. Shar would serve instead. Some would see this as a demotion even though Shar governed the district with Ke'en and was equal to her husband in rank.

Hovan and Laexa would attend by special request of the king. A request that was not a request. They were called before the king to report on the events unfolding around Forestton. Questions would be asked. Explanations expected.

Prince Ti'ek would not be present, though. Instead, King Dargladre ordered the prince to stay in Shetteca until his parents returned. The king did not wish for himself and his first three heirs to be in one place at the same time.

Cautious, but perhaps not uncalled for.

Hovan knew Ke'en hoped tonight's discussion would provide water to germinate ideas. Their own safety required accurate predictions. King Dargladre rightfully wanted answers.

To have thought of it before is to be ready for it again.

Without credible theories, the southern lords would have excuses to belittle Shetteca. Lord Gerritt would waste no opportunity to foster doubt in the king's mind of Ke'en's ability to rule or to weaken the faith that others had in Shetteca.

Shetteca needed to be strong. And for the other districts to trust in Ke'en's and Shar's leadership.

If the Preparers are again coming in force to the north, Shetteca will need the full support of the king and every district leader.

The wizard and the first of Forestton walked into the small gathering hall of the leaders of Shetteca. Cova and her younger sister Cada were helping servants set out wine and water and a light fare of food.

"Welcome," said Cova with a smile for the wizard. Passing by in playful annoyance, Cova greeted Laexa, first formally as the first captain of Forestton, and then informally as a family friend. Turning her back on Hovan, she politely ushered Laexa toward the food and drink still being arranged.

Hovan smiled at her teasing disrespect.

"My mother is putting Givette and Donnan to bed. Father and my elder brother are still in conversation with other leaders of the district. We expect them soon. What can I serve you, Captain?"

"Water, for now. Perhaps wine later."

Cada poured Laexa a glass of cool water. "A clear head runs through cool water. Am I right, Protector?"

"Yes, and thank you." Laexa accepted the offered water. "The wizard, though, would prefer wine. Red."

"Yes, I know," responded Cova with a smile as she reached for a wine glass.

Hovan did not rise to Cova's unspoken teasing. As Cova poured the wine, he limped over to the open balcony doors. He knew that if he walked out onto the balcony and looked east, he would see the domed Central Library rising above its neighbors. He avoided that sight and looked out from the shadows south toward the large main gates of the city. Cova found him there and offered him one of the two glasses of wine she carried.

Hovan accepted the glass. "How adroit of you," said Hovan, "to tease me while also clearing space for us to catch a moment alone."

"Is a moment alone with me something you look forward to?" asked Cova.

Hovan repaid her teasing by smiling before he tasted the wine. "Thank you for the glass of red."

The wizard looked out at the city.

"I am glad to see you off the crutches," Cova said. "The bruising is much reduced. You do heal quick."

"More quickly than I remember doing so in the past. Then again, time often obscures the past. I have not been this young for many circles of the Giver."

"What a paradoxical answer!"

In acknowledgment of her observation, he saluted her with his wine glass.

"Are you convinced that the Preparers are coming?" asked Cova.

A few heartbeats passed before the wizard answered. "I think so, but I am not convinced."

"Yet you will plan as if you are."

"Yes."

"Prudent. My parents and I agree."

Hovan faced the elf seeking his affection. "Your opinion is worthy of note. I enjoy the teasing and the time we spend talking over dinner and at practice. Thank you for thinking of me what you do. Please do not push for more now, though. I know what you want."

Cova looked toward the city. "My mother has become my advocate and my counselor. She advises me to be as involved as my elder brother is, perhaps more, since he spends much of his time in Forestton. But with you, she preaches caution."

"I did not know that you and Shar spoke about us."

"She fears for the elf in a human elf relationship, as do you." Cova sipped her wine and then asked, "How old are you?"

Hovan nodded in acknowledgment of the argument behind her question. "Well done." Changing topics, he asked, "Why did you not follow your mother's advice and go to the meeting with your father and brother?"

"And miss a chance to serve you wine?" joked Cova.

A door closed behind them.

"Hovan!" called Shar. "The leg could not have healed this fast! You should be sitting. No crutches! You look good. Not too badly bruised. I thought your face would look worse. That is not what I meant! Come. Sit."

Wrapping her arm in his, she steered him toward the couch along the wall. "Should we elevate your leg? Walk slowly. Where are the crutches?"

"Shar, I will be fine," protested Hovan.

Shar continued walking him slowly toward the couch. "I know. I hope so. I know. We are all worried."

"Our wizard friend is too intelligent to not be afraid, but also too proud to be mothered," said Cova to her mother.

"Ti'ek did not like my fussing over him either," admitted Shar.

"I will make sure our guest is comfortable," said Cova.

"Yes. I think I would like a glass of wine before this conversation in Shetteca begins." Shar excused herself.

Cova settled Hovan on the couch with a pillow under his leg. She fetched him a plate of sharp Shettecan cheese to go with his refilled wine glass. Hovan heard Shar dismissing the servants.

This is to be a private conversation.

As his wife had done, Ke'en called out, "Hovan!" when he strode into the room, excitement giving volume to his voice. "On time, as always! Ti'ek, a chair for your mother and one for yourself. Laexa, Cova, Cada, come. Bring a chair. Let us keep the wizard company."

They arranged a semicircle of chairs around the couch.

With everyone seated, Ke'en began. "We have questions to answer tonight and expectations to fulfill tomorrow at the King's Assembly. The goal tonight is to turn from reactive to proactive. We must decide what their next course of action is so we can decide ours and advise the king on his. Captain Laexa, tonight you are here as my counsel. With the wizard's permission, I ask that you speak freely."

"Laexa, you know I have no secrets from the district leaders or their family," said the wizard, granting his permission.

"Thank you, Hovan," said Ke'en. Turning to Laexa, Ke'en asked, "How bad is his leg?"

"Ke'en!" complained Hovan, realizing the district leader had just circumvented him.

Laexa laughed at the district leader's maneuvering before answering. "His healer told him to stay off it for five more visits of the Giver, which he has not done. He is healing faster than she expected, though she fears that putting weight on the leg may prevent it from healing properly."

"I will not go to Avi'ot on crutches!" insisted Hovan.

"I agree," stated Ke'en. "When is his next healing session?"

"He should be there now," said Laexa.

Ke'en looked at Hovan, waiting for his response.

Hovan explained, "I will receive treatment when we return to Forestton tonight and before we leave for Avi'ot in the morning."

"Agreed," said Ke'en.

"I do not need you to agree."

"I do anyway," responded Ke'en. "Now to business. First question: Do we all agree that the Preparers are responsible for the attacks in Shetteca?"

There were no dissenting voices.

"Next: What do they hope to gain? If they do control Mohvradraan, as the prisoners say, why attack us for Shettecan farmlands? Or is our wizard friend all they want?"

"Who would challenge their control of Ovada?" asked Hovan, using the disrespectful Dahican name for the Mohvradraan region to emphasize his next sentence. "Dahica will not march north. Could Veon'ocha? The city-state has influence, but lacks numbers. Veon'ocha is a long ride past Mohvradraan. The snow elves are between Dahica and Mohvradraan but are only loosely unified. King Dargladre may be the only one to challenge them for control of Mohvradraan."

"Attack us before we attack them?" offered Ke'en. "If Arre'ielle truly were in danger of falling, Dahica would aid us as they did during the war."

"Maybe they just want Shetteca," said Shar. "Farmlands, a buffer for Ovada, a piece of the pie called Arre'ielle instead of the whole pie."

"A bite of pie now and perhaps another bite later," added Cova, supporting her mother. "Last time they tried for the whole pie. Maybe they have learned."

"The mountains are a better natural buffer than the open fields of Shetteca," said Ke'en.

"I would agree," said Hovan.

"That may be your opinions, but not theirs," responded Shar. "If their attack on Forestton had gone as planned, I would lead Shetteca now, not you, my love."

Ke'en nodded in approval.

"I do not think they could have predicted the fall of Forestton with certainty," argued Hovan.

Shar challenged the wizard's conclusion. "If their plan had worked, they would have assassinated you before the attack. You were not supposed to answer Ti'ek's call for help! However, they knew Ke'en would! That lightning bolt was meant for Ke'en! Without you, without Ke'en, they expected to overwhelm the walls and kill Ti'ek. Without your being there, they did not fear a quick response from other wizards. Thankfully, three wizards responded quickly and saved Forestton."

Speaking his thoughts, Hovan worked through the logic. "So, I would have been dead. Ke'en and Ti'ek killed defending Forestton. That would leave Shar as district leader of Shetteca. And heir to the throne of Arre'ielle as Ke'en's wife. In fact, the first three heirs to the throne would be female elves! Oh, Lord Gerritt would not like that!"

"And I do not have Ke'en's experience," said Shar, "and could not plan and lead the defense of Shetteca as well as my husband can."

"Which would give Lord Gerritt the leverage to pressure the king to name a new heir," said Hovan.

"And perhaps even name a new district leader for Shetteca," added Shar. "One with military training, perhaps."

"The king would not abandon Shetteca!" insisted Hovan. "Gerritt does not hate Shetteca. He simply hates the idea of an elf on the throne. Arre'ielle would march to her defense!"

"Yes, Hovan," countered Ke'en. "It is one thing to defend a region. Yet another to conquer it. If they control this city, how does the king dislodge them? The force needed would weaken Arre'ielle. Could they put a second army in the foothills of Feleine, threatening to drive south if the king marched north?"

"We saw nothing in Feleine to suggest they had that type of army," argued Hovan. "The mission of the small force was to hit Forestton and withdraw, not hold. We have little evidence beyond the words of enemy soldiers to suggest that they have more."

Ke'en tilted his head as if in appreciation. "Wise on their part to show only what they need, if indeed they have more. We marched into the hills at the end of the cold season and found what we expected. We returned satisfied and proud of ourselves! Perhaps that force searched us out so we would not suspect more."

"I did not expect a gorzyne," added Ti'ek. "A nice touch, if that was their goal."

"Yes," said Ke'en, picking up on his son's thought. "A gorzyne, Hovan! You, me, and my son were all in the same forest as a gorzyne, a dragon's cousin! If that blade had cut your leg instead of Ti'ek's, could you have stopped the beast? Did we meet just enough force so that we did not look for more? A force with a real chance of killing some of us?"

"How *did* they control a gorzyne?" asked the wizard rhetorically.

How could they learn to do something that I cannot? How did they do that?

Ke'en nodded, acknowledging the question but offering no answer.

"Hovan," challenged Ke'en. "Should an army appear from Feleine, how would Shar call for help if we were not here? An army with gorzynes?! With you or me here, the Wizard Velina is a mere mental touch away. The king's orvbacaans gallop to our aid. The other wizards arrive within heartbeats of the call for help. With the wall defense activated and wizards on the wall, Shetteca is safe. Even from gorzynes. Unable to contact for help, Shar's message would not get through fast enough to stop Shetteca from falling."

"Interesting hypothesis," said Hovan. "However, the events did not unfold that way. We are all here. Do you still think they will attack?"

"If they believe they can take Shetteca, I think they will come," answered Ke'en.

"They attacked Forestton with a force designed to withdraw with supplies. They want me dead. That we know. Why does there need to be more to it?"

"I answer your question with a question," said Ke'en. "If they have Ovada, why antagonize us? Another question is, why you?"

Shar answered. "Because Arre'ielle will not let them have Mohvradraan without a fight." Continuing, Shar returned to the original question. "The fields of Shetteca are a significant addition to those in Ovada. It would give them a wider base to breed a larger force and land to reward the loyal and bribe the mercenary while weakening Arre'ielle."

Hovan shook his head in disagreement. "I am not convinced that they will attack now that their plans for Forestton have failed."

"The only way to be sure would be to send someone to Mohvradraan to find out," said Ke'en.

No one spoke.

As if a thunderclap had silenced the room.

Not me!

Cova snapped her head around to stare at her father. She traced the path of his gaze to the face of the wizard.

Hovan sat with a blank look on his face.

Not me.

A memory of Suzhanee flashed through his mind. She rode her orvbac, smile on her face, hair tossing about in the wind like a flag, watching mountain talon birds circle above. They crossed Isla Pass and began the descent toward Mohvradraan. "Look, talon birds. I declare them harbingers of our coming success in killing the dragon." She laughed and smiled.

Hovan nearly cried.

He had returned through that pass without his wife. Successful in his mission, far richer from the sale of rare red dragon fur, but emotionally destroyed.

Not me.

Creases slowly formed around the wizard's eyes as he squinted to stare back at the district leader. Slowly, he turned his head to look down the length of the couch, looking at no one, looking past his elevated injured leg. His eyes stared at the wall.

"Who now living in Arre'ielle has more experience in Mohvradraan than I do?" Hovan asked the rhetorical question as if it were a guilty verdict.

"I do," answered Lord Ke'en.

"Yes. The king would never let you go," said Hovan in quiet admission. "Nor Ti'ek. Three moons that orbit the throne." Hovan took two deep breaths and made a simple statement. "I do not want to go to Mohvradraan."

"I know, my friend. Mohvradraan or Ovada, whatever the name, its memories are fierce for you! *We* do not ask that you go."

Ke'en's phrase, with the slight emphasis on 'we', conveyed to Hovan who the 'we' were.

The king needs someone to go. The king needs answers.

Hovan lowered his head, catching his forehead in his left hand. A slow inhale preceded a slow exhale.

Cova glanced at her father and then at the wizard. Unable to offer more than a comforting hand on his shoulder, Cova rose from her chair. Shar held up her hand, stopping her daughter, who reluctantly...slowly...sat back down.

"Hovan, nothing is decided," said Ke'en. "There are more questions we need to answer."

Hovan nodded and looked back at his friend. "If what you suggest is true, they would have to move quick. They must expect Arre'ielle to prepare for the possibility of an attack. The king should move his forces now."

"We agree," said Ke'en. "Shar and I reached the same conclusion. We expect an attack before the cold season sets in."

"The Harvest Festival would be perfect," stated the wizard. "Let us harvest the crops and then take them from us as we celebrate."

"You have a cruel mind," said Shar.

Hovan looked at her. "These are cruel people."

"Attacking near the end of the growing season makes sense," reasoned Ke'en. "They can live off the land and do not need supply lines."

Laexa interrupted. "That still gives us several passes of Ette to prepare. The Wizard's Corp could be ready at a moment's notice to challenge them. Perhaps if Forestton and Shetteca had fallen, no secret room would have been available. But with Forestton standing, the Wizard's Corp can gather and arrive at the north ford of the River Ke before one visit of the Giver passes!"

"She is right, Ke'en," said Hovan, with hope returning to his voice.

"Yes," agreed Lord Ke'en. "The River Ke would be a good place for the Wizard's Corp to engage them. The river would slow their ground forces. The hills would provide clear sight and height to launch spells. But only if we know they are coming. We will not meet them in that valley because we have patrols no further west than the river. They can get that far undetected."

"Unless someone goes to Mohvradraan," said Shar.

Ke'en continued. "Where would the wizards attack them? Open field battle? If one is to fight wizards, then that is the way to do it. No stored magic in walls to use. One could flank, surround, and overwhelm the wizards. There are only six wizards! Lady Mucenrion, as great as she was, is too old to ride to battle. Retreat to Forestton or Shetteca? Let them ravage the lands, killing and burning. Neither answer is acceptable to us."

"The wizards would have to leave the safety of the walls and join with the force sent from Shetteca and Forestton," said Ti'ek. "Hopefully, other districts will send help."

Hovan stated, "The Wizard's Corp is formidable and cannot be dismissed so easily."

"That brings us to the next question," said Ke'en. "What do they have that can overcome the Wizards?"

"We are assuming much!" emphasized Hovan. "That they have a sizable army, that they are planning to attack Shetteca, and that they can defeat the Wizard's Corps! Maybe their defeat at Forestton was critical. They did not kill me or you. The Forestton Secret Room sits ready for use."

"That is a plausible explanation," said Ke'en. "We could tell the king that it is done and that they have no second moon following their first. Still, they have shown us a lot! A large force in the abandoned district of Feleine. A controlled gorzyne! A separate attack on Forestton with seven magicians! An attack on you off world supported by magic! There is at least one advanced magician capable of travel by magic! Combine all these with the words of your prisoner. We may not believe him, but we must consider it. I am not comfortable with the conclusion that there is not more."

"Even if we do not think there is more, it is our duty to find out," said the wizard, completing the thought. "And someone must go to Mohvradraan."

"Yes," agreed the district leader. "I know of nothing on this planet that can stand against the Wizard's Corp. I am humbled to admit that I do not know everything. Knowledge is power, my friend. What can they have?! More gorzynes?"

Hovan shook his head, unable to offer an answer. "I do not have an answer. Gorzynes, I think we could handle. Still, I have no idea how they control it. How many could they bring?"

Ke'en scanned the semicircle. "Anyone?"

"If they are indeed coming again, they must have some plan for the Wizard's Corp," reasoned Laexa. "Or they will do no more than send out raiding parties from Feleine." Laexa turned to look at the wizard. "Now that I have been to the other world, Hovan, I have a question. Could you transport guns by magic?"

Hovan's eyes went wide. "I have never thought of that! What a fool I am to not recognize the knowledge I have! May the Ones we serve protect us! I have been worried about what they could do on that world with magic! I have not thought of the reverse!"

Hovan sat up on the couch with his back as straight as a board. "Guns, Ke'en! Guns and artillery! Mr. Ross said it! Castles are obsolete on his world because of artillery. They could arm their forces with guns! That force would not need to be large, and it could challenge the Wizard's Corp! And with gorzynes?!"

"I do not know what you are speaking of."

"I will send you an image." Hovan touched minds and showed him the submachine guns he had taken from the men who had attacked him. He then sent an image of a cannon sitting on the walls of a castle in Scotland. Ke'en passed it on to his wife and children.

A somber silence settled over the room. Hovan drank wine as he thought.

Finally, Ke'en spoke. "Now perhaps we have all the pieces of the puzzle."

"Who is teaching them magic?" Laexa asked a rhetorical question. "Seven magicians were at Forestton. At least one is on the other planet. There must be more. This points to a plan long in the making. A plan with creativity. They learned to control a gorzyne. Eight magicians and counting. How many gorzynes? Guns too? A match indeed for the Wizard's Corp!"

Cova asked, "Can the Wizard's Corp prepare for this?"

"Prepare?" Hovan asked. "Yes, we can prepare for anything. But what do we prepare for? And preparing does not guarantee victory. This will require thought and practice. I know how to use a gun. I own some. One is in Forestton, but I do not know enough about them to know what is possible on a larger scale."

"I will inform King Dargladre," said Ke'en.

The district leader was quiet for a few moments. "Lady Velina is speaking with King Dargladre."

Everyone waited quietly.

"The king, with Lady Velina's approval, suggests that this is not an appropriate conversation for open council until he knows more. Hovan, the king would like you to bring your gun with you tomorrow and meet with us at the King's First Meeting before the assembly."

Hovan nodded acceptance. "As King Dargladre requests."

Ke'en relayed Hovan's answer to Velina. To the group, Ke'en said, "The king sends us his thanks."

"Ke'en," said Hovan, "the man I introduced you to yesterday was a protector on his world. He could provide us with the knowledge we need, if he is willing."

"Do you think he would teach us?"

"Laexa, does a protector ever stop being a protector?"

Laexa shook her head no. "However, we are not his to protect."

"The last question of the evening: What should we do now?" asked Ke'en. "Some parts are obvious. We have already added patrols along our western border and moved forces closer to the river. The food stockpile in the city is being increased. Hovan, we need you to teach us about guns or convince this Protector Ross to help us. What else?"

Captain Laexa spoke. "We must protect the farmers west of Forestton. Too many raids from the hills have threatened them. Before the war, Feleine was the protection. For Feleine, there was Lordic's Wall. But not so now. The River Ke is not enough!"

Lord Ke'en nodded in agreement and looked at his wife, who spoke. "We had designed a stone fort for the north ford. After the apparent success in Feleine, we did not continue with the project. Now we should renew our efforts to fortify the river crossing."

"Shetteca will restart the construction of the fortification of the ford," agreed Ke'en. "We will ask the king for assistance. What else?"

"The walls of Forestton need to be recharged," said Hovan. "Repairs continue. I must hire replacements to bring the garrison to full strength. Laexa has sent word to the leaders of Protection to enquire if any protectors are seeking a full time position. I have also sent a message to the mercenary guide."

"I think the king should position several orvbacaan in the hills north of Forestton," said Ke'en. "From there, they can reach the ford, Forestton, or Shetteca. Do you agree, Hovan?"

"Yes, maybe even closer to the river," said Hovan. "The king should send a formal request to Dahica asking for aid. They will most likely refuse for the present. Perhaps they can contact Veon'ocha and collect information for us."

"I have already contacted my brother," said Ke'en. "He does not expect Dahica to do more than prepare. Still, that is a start. The forces of Westgate are being readied should they need to drive north over the mountains into Mohvradraan. He has friends among the snow elves and would be allowed through. Perhaps some might join him. As the Duke of Westgate, he has influence. My brother will ask them what they know of Mohvradraan. He will also send word to Veon'ocha to learn what he can."

"Other plans will have to wait until after the king's meeting tomorrow," said Hovan. "The Wizard's Corp will have to train for this new threat. Before that can happen, the king must inform the lords about guns."

Shar spoke. "We have covered a lot of ground tonight. I think we should leave it here and prepare for tomorrow."

"I have one more question," said Cova.

Ke'en nodded approval.

"Why Hovan?" she asked. "Much of this seems centered on him. Is it because he is a power they must eliminate to defeat Shetteca, or is there more?"

Hovan answered. "The reason you mention is reason enough. I helped attack two Preparer strongholds, one before the war and one after. I fought for Arre'ielle against them during the war. They believe they killed me once or should have. They will detest that I am here opposing them again. If Ke'en's hypothesis is accurate, someone must deal with me to subdue Shetteca. They also need to remove me if they are to secure the other world. I oppose them in both places. Killing me would be a motivating bonus."

"Hovan, you need to meet with the healer," said Shar.

Her three children smiled at the thought of their mother treating the wizard as she would treat one of them.

"Yes," said Ti'ek, shaking his finger at the wizard, "and go straight to bed afterwards." Everyone laughed, but Hovan and Shar.

Hovan struggled to his feet. Cova rose to help him, but Laexa, his protector, was closer. When Hovan was steady on his feet, he said to Ke'en, "We still have little more than theories."

Ke'en nodded in agreement. "Yes, but we have much to do to be ready in case we are right. Prepare for the worst, hope for the best."

"Talk with an elf, hear a proverb," quipped Hovan. In a quiet tone, almost a whisper, Hovan said, "I do not want to go to Mohvradraan."

Not me. But then who?

"Hovan to Mohvradraan?" There was a tremor in Cova's voice. "Can you refuse?"

Hovan and Ke'en exchanged looks. Hovan turned and looked into the pretty jade eyes of Cova. "Reputations produce expectations."

"The king will request that you go," concluded Cova.

Hovan nodded, exhaling.

Shar stood next to her husband. "This mixing of knowledge of the two worlds is dangerous."

"Dangerous knowledge," agreed Hovan. "Magic there. Guns here."

"Plan on saying that to Priest Thesian?" asked Ke'en.

"I know better," responded Hovan.

Ke'en put his hand on the wizard's shoulder. "Go see your healer. We need you at your best." He took a deep breath. "We did well to protect Forestton. Now, we must focus on defending Shetteca. We will all need to be at our best!"

Acknowledgements

While writing is often a singular activity, publishing is not. Many people have helped me along the way. Some through their critiques and teaching. Others by helping me to get it presentable and published and noticed. Thank you to all of you!

I gratefully acknowledge the following for their help!

Developmental Editor
Claire Ashgrove

Copy Editor
Steven Moore

Cover Design
Toulla Corti

Proof Reader
Lisa Gilliam

My Beta Readers
You know who you are!

About the Author

Thank you for choosing to read my first novel. My name is Christopher Iolaire.

By day, I am a high school science teacher. Teaching has been my passion for more years than I care to admit. I consider myself fortunate to have discovered such a gratifying career. The daily interactions with the students are very rewarding, especially those amazing "Now I get it!" moments. Helping someone succeed is success.

Crafting this narrative has been another passion of mine. I am thrilled to have finished my first novel. Completing this book has been both a challenge and a joy. Taking my writing from a hobby to a finished manuscript to a published author involved a steep learning curve.

I hope you enjoy 'Forestton'. Keep an eye out for my second book, 'Shetteca'. If you wish to stay updated on what is new and upcoming in my writing world, you can subscribe to "The Hovan Narratives" at Christopheriolaire.com.

Amidst the busy schedule of teaching, grading, and running to my son's hockey games and practices, I will continue to pursue this magical passion of writing.